NO LONGER PROPERTY OF
SEATTLE PUBLIC LIBRARY

# What's Not to Love

ALSO BY EMILY WIBBERLEY AND AUSTIN SIEGEMUND-BROKA

*Always Never Yours*
*If I'm Being Honest*
*Time of Our Lives*

# What's Not to Love

## EMILY WIBBERLEY
## AUSTIN SIEGEMUND-BROKA

VIKING

VIKING
An imprint of Penguin Random House LLC, New York

First published in the United States of America by Viking,
an imprint of Penguin Random House LLC, 2021

Copyright © 2021 by Austin Siegemund-Broka and Emily Wibberley

Penguin supports copyright. Copyright fuels creativity, encourages diverse
voices, promotes free speech, and creates a vibrant culture. Thank you for
buying an authorized edition of this book and for complying with copyright
laws by not reproducing, scanning, or distributing any part of it in any form
without permission. You are supporting writers and allowing Penguin to
continue to publish books for every reader.

Viking & colophon are registered trademarks of Penguin Random House LLC.

Visit us online at penguinrandomhouse.com

LIBRARY OF CONGRESS CATALOGING-IN-PUBLICATION DATA IS AVAILABLE

Printed in the USA

ISBN 9781984835864

10  9  8  7  6  5  4  3  2  1

This book is a work of fiction. Any references to historical events, real people,
or real places are used fictitiously. Other names, characters, places, and events
are products of the author's imagination, and any resemblance to actual events
or places or persons, living or dead, is entirely coincidental.

The publisher does not have any control over and does not assume any
responsibility for author or third-party websites or their content.

To the Classes of 2020

# One

I HOLD MY HEAD high, sitting up straight in the passenger seat of my mom's SUV. Whatever happens, I will *not* vomit in the next hour.

Mom eyes me suspiciously, like she's reading my mind and formulating the questions she would for one of her witnesses. I stare forward, focusing intently on the sedan in front of us in the drop-off zone for my high school. In hopes of resolving my expression into one evincing no intestinal distress, I rehearse the key facts for this morning's Shakespeare exam. *Thirty-seven plays, not including works of disputed origin. Seventeen comedies. Ten histories. Ten tragedies.* I try to picture the timeline I created listing each of them in order, which of course reminds me that I left the study guide next to the toilet in my bathroom between two and three in the morning. The thought brings on a new wave of nausea.

"You sure you're feeling okay, Alison?" Mom's voice is wary. "You look a little off."

I check my reflection in the window. It could definitely be worse. My glasses, which I'm only wearing because I was too sick to put in my contacts, do a commendable job of hiding the dark circles under my eyes. My skin is a little paler than usual, but nothing out of character for someone who spends most of her time indoors studying, and though I didn't have time to wash my hair, I pulled it into a respectable if lopsided bun. Instead of wearing the cozy Harvard sweatshirt I wanted to leave the house in, I put on a lightly wrinkled button-down blouse. But my mom's not wrong. There's a slick sheen of sweat on my forehead, my hair, typically a shiny dirty blond, is flat and unwashed, and my sallow cheeks don't give the strongest impression of health and well-being.

"I'm fine," I say. I'm lying.

The drop-off line crawls forward. Our car doesn't budge. I glance over and find Mom's hand inching in my direction. Realizing what she's doing, I reach for my seat belt.

I'm too late. Mom's hand finds my sweaty forehead.

"You have a fever," she says, sounding worried.

I don't give her the chance to finish her diagnosis. Unbuckling my seat belt, I jump out of the car. The cool morning hits my skin refreshingly, soothing the dull headache I'd been fighting to ignore.

The relief is short-lived. When I grab my bag, I catch my mom's expression. Irritation has replaced whatever motherly concern her face held. I pause, knowing not to ignore her outright.

My mom is fifty-seven years old, older than every one of

my friends' parents. Not that she acts her age. Unless she's in court, defending multimillion-dollar corporations like she's done for thirty years, she's remarkably unfiltered. "We're not doing this again," she says sternly. "What is it this time? You have a gov exam today?"

"Nope." I fling my bag over my shoulder.

In my defense, I *don't* have a gov exam. I have a Shakespeare exam. In ten minutes. It's completely different.

"I feel great, and I just want to go to school like a normal person." Despite Mom's grimace, I pack confidence into my voice.

The car behind Mom's honks, which she ignores. "You're a smart kid," she says, "but I'm not convinced you understand the concept of normal."

"Like mother, like daughter," I say with a smile, not entirely joking. It's true she fits in on paper with my classmates' parents. Her lucrative career, her SUV hardly three years out of the dealership, her frequent SoulCycle attendance. Having spent seventeen years with her, however, I've learned she's outspoken, easygoing, and the furthest thing possible from a helicopter parent. I don't know if it's because she has ten years on the other moms and she's over the whole parenting thing, or if it's just the way she is.

"Alison Sanger," she says, leaning over the center console. "I am not picking you up in the middle of the day."

"Great," I reply. "You won't have to. I'm not sick." I shut the door in one swift motion, hoping it will feel like a punctuation mark.

I immediately hear Mom rolling down the window. I wanted punctuation, and she's given me a semicolon. "If you had your license—"

"Bye, Mom," I interrupt her, waving behind me and heading for the locker hall. I know every inch of the Fairview High School campus—every bench useful for last-minute studying, every shortcut so I'm never late to class, everywhere people hang out, which is helpful when I need to hunt them down for quotes for the newspaper. I've walked up the stairs leading to the locker hall hundreds of times, and I could recite the names of the teachers in every classroom just like I could Shakespeare's seventeen comedies.

It's 6:52 in the morning, and the heavy fog coming in off the ocean hovers over everything, coating the campus in dew. Droplets cling to the needles of the pine trees outside the front gate. San Mateo is thirty minutes from San Francisco and ten from the water, and even in the first week of March we're fending off the Northern California winter of forty-eight-degree mornings and seawater-scented clouds.

It's zero period, and right now the only people here are those like me who needed an early extra hour to fit every class they wanted into their schedule. The half-empty locker hall echoes with the squeak of sneakers on linoleum, the clang of closing locker doors, and the mumbled conversations of Monday mornings.

I head directly for my locker, where I unload my physics and government books and pull the plastic bottle of Tums from my backpack. I chew and swallow down four.

There's no way I'm letting the events of last night interfere with this English exam. If it were up to me, I wouldn't have gone out on a Sunday night. When Dylan invited me to sushi with her and Nick Caufman, I wanted to say no. I only went because she begged me, and because Dylan is the only person in the known universe for whom I'd forsake a few hours of important test prep. Nick had invited Dylan to dinner, and she didn't know if she wanted the night to be a date. I was brought to third-wheel.

Of course, fifteen minutes in I could feel the dinner veering decidedly into date territory. While Dylan flirted and probably played footsie under the table, I prodded my hamachi with chopsticks. Dylan and Nick shared California rolls. Three hours later, I ended up hunched over the toilet, puking my guts out.

On the upside, I did plenty of studying between trips to the bathroom. I'm not the type to pull all-nighters before exams—I'm usually prepared by then, and I prefer to be well rested. While conditions weren't ideal, I made it work.

I close my locker, my stomach cramping ominously. Ignoring the pain, I head for class, rehearsing the history plays to distract myself. *Henry VI. Richard III. Richard II.* Whatever happens, there's nothing I'm letting keep me from this exam. Not even explosive vomiting.

# Two

THE REASON I'M NOT home recuperating is waiting outside the door when I reach English.

"Hello, Sanger," Ethan says casually. He doesn't look up.

"Molloy," I reply.

I wish there was a word worse than nemesis I could use *just* for Ethan. He's an un-popped blister. The splinter in your shoe from walking on woodchips. Your printer running out of toner when you're finishing your twenty-page final paper on the Hundred Years' War. He's your Kindle dying in the first hour of your flight to Boston, even though you're pretty certain you charged it, leaving you to sit through a random in-flight movie you never wanted to see. If this was the last time I ever had to look at Ethan's overly coiffed blond hair and obnoxiously piercing green eyes, I'd feel like the luckiest person on earth.

Unfortunately, it's not the last time. I have every class with Ethan, the regrettable effect of us both taking every

AP Fairview offers and the same electives. It's been this way for two years. Every class, every study group, every extra-curricular event. Ethan, Ethan, Ethan. I just have to endure the rest of our final semester of senior year. Then Ethan's out of my life.

Unless, of course, we both get into Harvard. It's not a possibility I permit myself to consider. Two students from the same California public school getting into Harvard would be exceedingly rare. I've studied Fairview's Harvard admissions history, and it's rare we have even one accepted student per year. Yet another reason for me to outdo him in every way I can.

I ignore the way he's leaning casually on the wall next to the door, not glancing up, reading his phone's screen. We stand in icy silence. Ethan is Kennedyesque via California. High cheekbones, sharp nose. He's rolled up the sleeves of the white button-down he's wearing under his forest green sweater, which, combined with the leather shoulder bag he uses instead of a backpack, gives him the look of a prep-school boy who's wandered off his high-hedged campus and onto Fairview's. I hate the effort he puts into his clothes, his hair, his everything. I hate how he does it to spite me, to show me he's not only prepared for this test, but he had the extra time to look "good."

Not that I'm attracted to him. Ethan's just objectively good-looking. His nearly constant stream of short-lived relationships proves his conventional desirability. I'm mature enough to admit it, although it gives me no personal pleasure to do so.

I resent the fact I've had to lay eyes on him this morning while he's not even spared me a glance. It's an upper hand, if barely. With Ethan, every loss counts. Even the infinitesimal ones.

Consequently, it's one I'm determined to rectify. "You're going to have to work late on the paper today," I inform the top of his head while he reads his damn phone. "Your piece on the gym funding was poorly organized, per usual."

I feel a rush of victory when finally he looks up, eyebrows furrowing. *Point: Alison.*

His story wasn't poorly organized, truthfully. They never are. I, however, will never forgo the chance to exert the dominance I hold over Ethan in the student newspaper. I'm editor in chief of the *Fairview Chronicle*, and Ethan's one of our strongest reporters, not that I'd ever tell him that. Consequently he's the writer most often assigned to exposés and complicated pieces. The one he's preparing on the construction of Fairview's new gym will undoubtedly be prominent in our upcoming issue, which I will be submitting for the National Student Press Club Awards at the end of the month. I want it to be perfect.

"*Poorly organized?*" he repeats. I hear the note of protest in his voice. "Honestly, Sanger," he drawls, "your ploys to get me to spend time with you have grown thinner and thinner."

I roll my eyes. Around us, our classmates have started to congregate. Everyone's concentrated on flashcards or notebooks, hoping to fit in a little cramming in the final minutes before Mr. Pham opens the door. Not Ethan and me. We're the only ones who look calm and collected.

"I wish you were a good enough writer we didn't need hours of in-person edits. I'm the victim here. You—" I clamp my mouth shut, the retort half finished. My stomach lurches uncomfortably. *Not now.*

He arches an eyebrow, no doubt surprised by my sudden silence. "Did—did you just nearly throw up on me?" Pocketing his phone, he smirks, his confusion fading. "Don't you think you're taking your revulsion act a little far?"

"It's no act," I reply, ignoring the rising wave of nausea in me. For a moment, I wonder what would happen if I just puked directly on Ethan, spattering his stupid sweater and his repugnant leather oxfords. I kind of wish I could, just to watch horror fracture the impassivity in his eyes. Except then, Mr. Pham would definitely send me home before the exam.

Instead, I lean on the wall, hoping the posture projects confidence, not light-headedness.

Ethan scrutinizes me. "You're *sick.*" There's no small measure of glee in his voice.

"No, I'm not."

"Your skin is unusually blotchy, even for you," he says, smiling now. "You know, Mr. Pham would let you make up the exam if you need to go home." It's not a well-intentioned suggestion, I know. It's a taunt. An *I win.* Which he will, if I retreat to the nurse's office now.

Ethan and I compete on every exam for the highest score. It started out informally—me peeking over his shoulder to check his grade, his intolerably smug face when he knew he'd done better. In sophomore chemistry, we made the competition official. Whoever scores worse on each exam does an unpleasant task of the winner's choosing, whatever comes up in the newspaper or Associated Student Government, where we're co–vice presidents. Fixing the printer in the newsroom, meeting with Principal Williams, picking up the work the student government president forgot or decided not to do.

If you miss a test, you forfeit on the grounds that makeup exams offer extra time for reviewing. Hence my coming to school with food poisoning.

"I'm fine," I say firmly.

"Sanger, seriously." Ethan is faux sympathetic, enjoying every minute of this. "If you have the flu, don't force yourself to be here. It's okay to forfeit. Self-care is important."

I glare. *Self-care? Please.* I've had a SLEEP IS AN INADEQUATE SUBSTITUTE FOR CAFFEINE coffee mug since I was fourteen. Ethan's crossing his arms, facing me. The feet separating us feel painfully insufficient for the size of his enormous ego. Pushing myself up from the wall, I match his nonchalance. "You're pretty eager for me to concede. What, not feeling prepared this morning?"

"Oh, I'm prepared." Ethan doesn't flinch.

"Good," I reply. The words fly out of my mouth like vomit. "I call a blitz."

Ethan's eyes widen. *Point: Alison.*

"Yeah, right," he ventures. "You won't get ten minutes into the exam before blowing chunks."

My stomach rolls over. I swallow hard, willing the ominous roiling to settle. "You don't have to accept." Of course, Ethan not accepting would be as good as surrendering.

The blitz is the most extreme twist on our competition. When either of us invokes it, the contest becomes one of speed. Whoever turns their test in first wins, regardless of score. However, since neither of us would forsake even a point of our perfect GPAs by turning in sloppy work, we both balance accuracy with the time pressure. It has a devious beauty.

"Nice try," Ethan fires back. He's no longer smiling. With the gradual crowding of our classmates, we've ended up closer together. Only a foot between us. "I'm calling your bluff," he declares. "Blitz."

Right then, Mr. Pham opens his door. "You'll find your exams facedown on your desks," he says while everyone files in. He looks bored, and it's not even seven. "Please have your pens and pencils ready and wait for the bell."

I push past Ethan in the doorway, not minding when my bag hits his shoulder. The room is organized with half the desks on one side of the room, facing the other half. Finding my seat, I wait while Ethan sits down in his, which is directly opposite mine.

Clammy sweat coats my forehead, and I reassure myself I have nothing left to expel. Despite my vigorous mental efforts, my stomach gurgles loudly enough for Ethan to hear. He looks straight into my eyes and winks. I vow I won't give him the satisfaction, not of winning the blitz and definitely not of seeing me vomit in English.

The bell rings.

# Three

I FLY THROUGH THE multiple choice.

Out of the corner of my eye, I watch Ethan, tallying the number of pages he's flipped. He has only seconds on me. I fight the discomfort in my stomach while I circle my responses, forcing myself to focus on the material. *What king's interest in the occult inspired* Macbeth? I choose *C) King James I.*

I can't let Ethan win. Not now, not ever. Beating him has become my primary goal in high school. Three and a half years of trading top grades, and neither of us has emerged the definitive victor.

I reach the essay. Despite Ethan having scribbled his first few sentences, I grin. I know this prompt. It's one I practiced during my two a.m. toilet bowl facial. I obliterate the question, interconnecting Shakespeare's mid-career themes with the political turmoil in his country through one concise thesis in my introduction, three perfect body paragraphs, and a thoughtful conclusion.

I burst out of my seat right before Ethan. He scowls while I walk in front of him to Pham's desk, where I present my exam with a flourish.

Pham eyes us unhappily. Ethan and I don't exactly have beloved reputations with the teachers of Fairview. With our constant challenging questions, well-reasoned rebuttals to classmates' points, and frequent feedback, teachers . . . kind of can't stand us. Pham is no exception.

"It's not a race, you two," he grumbles. "Take the remaining twenty minutes to check over your answers."

"That won't be necessary." I place my exam directly on his desk. Ethan follows.

"Good test, though," Ethan says.

Mr. Pham fixes Ethan with a droll glance. "Thank you, Mr. Molloy."

"The question on Shakespeare's possible Catholicism gave me pause," Ethan continues.

I turn to him, raising an unimpressed eyebrow. "Did it?"

"Seconds, Sanger."

"Sounds like they were important seconds," I reply, feeling bile biting the back of my throat. I face Mr. Pham. "May I please go to the restroom?" I inquire calmly, knowing Ethan's glowering behind me.

Pham waves his hand, dismissing me. I don't bother to linger for my traditional post-test gloating. Instead, I book it directly to the bathroom. I barely fumble into a stall in time to be spectacularly sick.

# Four

I'M CROUCHED DOWN NEAR the toilet when I hear Dylan's voice outside. "Alison, are you in here?" I moan incoherently. "Oh my god," Dylan says. Her bulky Doc Martens cross the room to the door of my stall. "You're ridiculous."

Flushing the toilet, I stand and walk to the sinks, needing to wash the unspeakable residue of the past ten minutes out of my mouth. Dylan waits behind me, holding my bag. She must've somehow collected it from Mr. Pham's class. She doesn't have zero period, which explains why she's not in class, but not how she knew I was in here.

Dylan hands me a paper towel, and I detect the slightest hint of sympathy under her stern demeanor. It's the way Dylan is, hiding her heart under her uncompromising exterior. Her dark hair cropped to her chin in a dramatic bob of harsh diagonals and daring curves, her baggy black T-shirts, her bold lipstick—I sometimes get the feeling they're efforts to challenge anyone who might otherwise take one look at her and only notice her magazine-cover beauty, her round face, porcelain skin, full lips, and supermodel height.

I wipe my mouth gratefully with the paper towel. Dylan frowns under the dim halogen of the bathroom lights.

"You have food poisoning, Alison," she says, disapproval written on her face.

"I'm aware, thanks," I reply. I wash my hands in the least gunky sink of the row. Last night, I texted Dylan after I first got sick, wondering if she had the same thing. She didn't. It was just me. Just the person with the early morning English exam. Granted, she did stay up until two, live-texting me her reactions to a Korean zombie movie in an effort to distract me. I eventually reassured her I needed to study and she could sleep. "How did you even know I was in here?"

"Ethan texted me. I was on campus early getting photos for your feature on the new swim coach." While, officially, Dylan does photography for yearbook, I enlist her whenever possible to take photos for the newspaper. I know she secretly enjoys working with me, even if she grumbles about the extra workload.

"Molloy texted you?" I narrow my eyes. "Why?"

Dylan pulls out her phone to read directly from it. "'Take Sanger to the nurse,'" she says, doing her best Ethan impersonation, disaffected and haughty. "'She's in the English quad bathroom. I'd rather not have to watch her barf in first period.'" She looks up, rolling her eyes. "God, he's bossy."

Like a dutiful best friend, Dylan shares my hatred of Ethan. Every time I've ranted to her about his incessant insults and usurping moves in the newspaper or ASG, she's listened, shook her head disapprovingly exactly when she should, and badmouthed him with enduring vengeance. I'm sure she has personal reasons to despise him—jerkish comments she's heard him make in class, unpleasant group projects, open disparagement of her work in yearbook. But the real core of her loathing I know stems from the front-row seat she's had to Ethan's and my own destructive discourse. According to her, we'd both be happier if we never spoke to each other again. I don't disagree, but I can't just let him win, either.

"Do you want me to get you a trash can from Mrs. Cordova's room to walk to the nurse's with?" Dylan asks.

"I think it's out of my system now. I'm going to class," I say decisively right as the bell rings. I reach for my bag.

Dylan blocks the door. "Either I call your mom now or we go to the nurse." She issues this ultimatum like she was prepared for me to want to return to class.

I eye her, weighing how serious she is. Her expression hardening, she meets my gaze.

"Fine," I say. "Let's go to the nurse."

Dylan turns toward the door, looking pleased. I follow her into the quad, where everyone's walking to their next class, catching up with friends, or heads down, reading their phones. It's chaotic, the fragments of conversation and countless patterns of cross traffic, in harsh contrast to how quiet the campus was when I left English and how quiet it will be in five minutes.

I notice Ethan, his head turned in my direction. His eyes find me, and he looks smug I'm not walking toward our next period. I meet his stare for long enough he knows *I* know he was looking, then face forward to show him I couldn't care less.

Dylan and I walk down the cement pathway leading to the nurse's office. "This is your fault, by the way," I remind her. "If you hadn't dragged me on your date, I wouldn't be sick."

She tosses her hair. "I'll admit I'm somewhat to blame. Did I mention how much I appreciated you coming?" she asks, nudging my shoulder.

I soften. Even if Dylan is demanding, I know she would drop everything for me, despite the cooler-than-thou version of herself she presents to everyone else. She did just two months ago during Winter Formal when the freshman class president forgot to help me with cleanup. Dylan ditched the yearbook after-party, opting to spend the rest of the night mopping and picking up trash with me. It ended up being more fun than the dance itself.

"It's fine," I say. "How'd things go after I left?"

"We kissed in his car." Dylan pauses, pursing her lips. "I don't know, though. It wasn't . . ."

I don't need her to finish the sentence to know what it wasn't. *Who* it wasn't. Dylan's ex-girlfriend Olivia dumped her unceremoniously a month ago when Dylan went to Berkeley to visit her. Olivia's a freshman there, but they started dating when she was a senior here. I can't say I'm not happy they broke up. The eleven months they were together weren't my favorite. Their relationship was intense for high school, fraught with fights and little spats, over which Dylan would inevitably be distraught. I watched her change into what Dylan imagined Olivia wanted her to be, wearing the clothes Olivia preferred, liking the bands Olivia thought were cool, hanging out with Olivia's cultish crowd of theater friends, all of whom have stopped inviting Dylan to things since the breakup.

When Olivia dumped her without explanation, Dylan was destroyed. But over the past weeks, I've gotten my best friend back.

Last night with Nick was her first effort to move on. I'm glad she went, regardless of the food-poisoning ramifications on my day. "Not that I have a wealth of experience to draw from," I venture, "but give it time."

Dylan's soft smile doesn't reach her eyes. "Yeah. I know."

We reach the nurse's office. Dylan holds open the door for me. Inside, Nurse Sharp's working on her computer, tattoos visible thanks to the pushed-up sleeves of her white Fairview sweatshirt. Her eyes flit up from the monitor when we walk in. "Nurse Sharp," Dylan starts, "Alison's—"

I rush to the trash can to heave into it.

"Sick," Dylan finishes.

When I raise my head, Nurse Sharp's watching me unhappily. "Sit on the table," she instructs me. "I'm calling your parents."

I protest immediately. "Couldn't I just—"

"No," Nurse Sharp and Dylan say in unison.

Scowling, I climb up on the exam table, the paper crinkling noisily under my palms. While Nurse Sharp takes my temperature, I sternly study the STD classification chart on the opposite wall.

"Slight fever," she says, "probably caused by exhaustion and a stomach virus."

"It was food poisoning," Dylan volunteers. Then she fixes me with a look. "Though I'm guessing the exhaustion didn't help."

Miserable, I say nothing. Nurse Sharp shakes her head. "I swear, Miss Sanger, you don't know how much easier my job would be if you and Mr. Molloy had the sense to stay home when sick."

I'd openly debate the recommendation if it weren't coming from Nurse Sharp. She's not someone to be messed with. In her thirties, she's younger than most Fairview teachers, and she's covered in tattoos from her years in the military, where she was a medic. Or possibly from whatever she did before—probably patching up broken bones and bullet holes for a biker gang. She's never impressed with my hyper-competitive efforts, in particular when I volunteered to fill in for a sports photographer for the paper sophomore year, and my pursuit of an award-worthy on-field shot of the soccer game left me with a ball to the face and a broken nose. I got the photo though.

Dylan grabs a tardy note from the desk. "Feel better, Alison." She walks out the door, waving behind her.

I wait, knowing I'm a prisoner here until Nurse Sharp decides my fate. She pulls up the directory on her computer. "How angry will your mom be when I call her this time?" she asks.

Even though I know it's useless to protest, I try nonetheless. "You could always not? I could call an Uber home."

"Nice try." Nurse Sharp picks up her phone. Instead of dialing, she pauses, glancing up with an unreadable expression. "Did you at least beat him on whatever had you here for an entire class with food poisoning?"

"Oh yeah," I say, proud. This is why I don't resent Nurse Sharp, despite her repeatedly sending me home and complaining about my "reckless disregard for my physiological well-being." While she doesn't condone Ethan's and my competition, she's definitely on my side. I don't know if it's because she understands how hard it is for young women to prove themselves intellectually, or if it's just because she knows Ethan's a dick.

Nurse Sharp nods, no longer looking entirely unamused. She picks up the phone and dials what I know is my mom's work number. We wait while it rings.

It's the first free moment I've had the whole morning. The weight of how punishing the past eight hours have been drops onto me hard, but it doesn't feel smothering. It's rewarding. The feeling of essay margins free of red ink, or the perfect interlocking of every variable in a complicated equation. Even though my mom will imminently be pissed at me, even though I spent more time than I ever wanted on the floor of a high school bathroom, even though I'm completely exhausted and could very well pass out without warning—it was worth it. Every nauseating, draining second. They were all worth it to beat Ethan.

Because beating Ethan doesn't just bring the rush of defeating my nemesis. It's something bigger, something I value even more than Ethan's personal injury. With every win, I'm showing myself, and everyone around me, that I'm capable of anything I set my mind to.

It's not arrogance pushing me. It's ambition. I'm not out to defeat Ethan despite everything, despite food poisoning or the stares and eye-rolls from our classmates, out of wanting to be better than everyone else. Only better than everyone else thinks I can be. There's a difference, one I wish the world would recognize.

It's why I've sometimes let this rivalry get the better of me. For every reason I have to despise Ethan, I'm grateful for the chance to prove my worth. To prove not that I *am* the best, but that I *can be* the best.

# Five

MY MOM DOESN'T PICK me up. It's worse.

After fifteen minutes of me hunched over the waste-basket while Nurse Sharp patches up the knees of a freshman who had limited success jumping over a railing, my sister walks in, dressed like she just woke up.

Which I'm certain she has. She's in sweats, her Columbia crop top, and the stained purple Uggs she bought when she was a sophomore in high school. The remarkable thing is, Jamie Sanger wears disheveled well. Though obviously uncombed, her hair, dark brown with the hint of a curl mine's never had, frames her face and falls over her shoulders perfectly. I haven't yet gotten used to the tan and the dusting of freckles I've noticed on her cheeks in the months since she moved home. Besides the difference in hair color and her being twenty-six, we're similar in our features. They're just packaged differently, Jamie's in couch-potato chic and mine in . . . me. A seventeen-year-old who shops exclusively at Nordstrom.

"Sorry it took so long," she says, sounding genuinely apologetic. "I was totally asleep when Mom called." Rushing over, she places her hand on my forehead, which feels weird and unnecessary. "How are you feeling?"

I slide off the table and stand out of her arm's reach. "I'm fine."

"Jamie Sanger," Nurse Sharp says, walking out of the supply room. "Is that you?"

Jamie straightens, facing Sharp with effortless enthusiasm. My sister's probably the only person in the known universe capable of feeling genuine joy at seeing the school nurse of her alma mater at eight in the morning. I honestly don't know where Jamie gets her endless reservoir of excitement. It's just the way she is.

"Nurse Sharp, it's *so* nice to see you." Jamie hugs Nurse Sharp, who looks surprised, if delighted. "How are you?"

"I'm great when I'm not dealing with stubborn students like this one." She nods in my direction. I pretend not to hear, resuming my examination of the STD chart. "What about you? What are you doing in town?"

Jamie doesn't wince. Her smile doesn't falter. I've watched Jamie handle this question half a dozen times and yet her reaction never ceases to surprise me. "Oh, I'm back home for a bit," she replies. "Figuring out what's next for me."

She couldn't sound happier. Couldn't sound happier her college fiancé ended their engagement three months ago. Couldn't sound happier she was let go from her dream job working in city politics in Chicago and now lives in her parents' house, sleeping under the same sheets she did when she was in high school. For all I know, it could be true. Everything is an *opportunity* to Jamie. Even failure.

It's one of many things we've never seen eye to eye on.

"Well. Wonderful," Nurse Sharp says. The effusive word feels out of place coming from the mouth I usually only hear issuing me gruff admonitions. "I hope you're taking whatever time you need."

Jamie just beams.

Turning to me, my sister's expression transforms, concern filling her eyes. "Do you need help to the car?"

I clench my jaw. "No. I've got it."

Jamie nods, sympathy undimmed. If she caught the edge in my voice, she doesn't react. Nurse Sharp intercedes, giving me a warning look. "Take the trash can," she orders me. "Don't even think about coming back until you've kept two meals down."

I brusquely grab the trash can, knowing Nurse Sharp will follow us into the parking lot with it if I don't. "I'll take care of her," Jamie says over her shoulder as we're walking out the door.

This nearly pushes me to remind her I don't need or want her *taking care of me*. While I'm eight years younger, I'm hardly Jamie's baby sister. I haven't been since before she went off to college. Instead, I'm the future valedictorian, the head of an extracurricular that produces hundreds of pages of publication-worthy content, the vice president of the student body—not to mention the reliable competitor to one very pernicious nemesis. I'm capable. I don't need babying.

We walk in the direction of the parking lot. I notice Jamie studying the science hall, which is one of the newer buildings on campus, the clean concrete facade contrasting with the beige stucco of the other classrooms. "It's weird how different the campus is," Jamie comments, a rare note of wistfulness in her usually cheerful voice. "I hardly recognize this place."

"Yeah, a lot can change in eight years," I reply neutrally. Jamie says nothing, and I wonder if she's reflecting on how different Fairview is—how different *I* am—while she's functionally exactly the same. No job. No cute one-bedroom in Chicago. No plan.

I'm not scornful of Jamie. I'm not even judgmental, except in the sense of having evaluated her response to life upheaval and *judged* it to be extremely confusing. I remember the dinners she spent scrolling through pictures of her and her ex-fiancé on her phone, the nights she was curled on her comforter, clutching her pillow like a life preserver. I understand she's been hurt and left with new and scary uncertainty. I just don't understand how her response is doing exactly *nothing*.

Passing the chain-link fence on the edge of campus, Jamie inhales deeply, like she's relishing the sea-scented air hanging over campus. "I'm so happy I'm here for your final semester," she says, exuberance returning. "I'll get to be here when you go to prom, when you come home from your last day of school, when you graduate . . . The next few months will be huge for you. I'm really happy I'll be around to see it."

"Yeah," I say, hiding everything I would voice if I weren't worried I'd insult Jamie. Really though, the next few months will be no different from the months before now, with the exception of getting into Harvard in April. I've already done the work. I've applied to colleges, I've gotten perfect AP scores, I've defeated Ethan on everything from chemistry exams to Mrs. Cohen's Greatest US President debate competition (defending Rutherford B. Hayes, no less). What remains is sitting in classes, waiting for the real world to start.

Jamie just wants to relive her days here through me. Why, I have no idea. It's just high school.

# Six

I'M FINALLY READY TO admit I'm too sick for school. When we get home, I head directly upstairs, the grinding in my gut and the dull pain everywhere else pointing me toward bed. I know without checking the house is empty—my dad's dermatology clinic keeps him until five, and my mom comes home from the firm in time for dinner.

Our house is quiet, the stillness of spaciousness. So is our suburban street of cream-stuccoed homes and wide lawns. My family is fortunate, with my lawyer mother and doctor father—I know we're privileged to live where we do, to worry about what we worry about, to afford any and every college we could want to. It's part of why I work as hard as I do for my every goal. I don't want to waste a single one of the many chances I have.

Jamie closes the front door, the click clear and audible. I drag myself into my bedroom, where I collapse on the bed. Jamie follows, her footsteps in her Uggs padding on the carpet. I can practically feel her watching me with concern from where she's leaning in the doorway. Facedown on the comforter, I wait for her to leave.

"Can I get you anything?" she asks. "Soup?"

I groan, the sound muffled by the rumpled fabric. The idea of food is not a particularly pleasant one.

"We could watch Netflix," she suggests, undeterred. "It might distract you."

I roll over. "You don't have to entertain me." In reality, I'm somewhat suspicious Jamie doesn't want to entertain *me*. She wants to entertain herself. I just happen to be here. I know her days probably feel long, formless, even empty—mine are just too full to add anything to.

Jamie brightens. "I know," she replies. "I want to. It'll be fun."

"You think watching me run to the bathroom every half hour will be fun?"

She rolls her eyes playfully. Walking into my room, she sits down next to me, leaning on one elbow like she's done this hundreds of times before. "I want to spend time with you. I feel like it's the whole point of this year for me," she says contemplatively, looking around my room like she's found her epiphany in the space between the comforter and the ceiling. "You know," she continues, "we've never had a chance to be in the same place together. When I was a senior in high school, you were in, like, fourth grade. By the time you were a teenager, I was away at college. This feels like our opportunity to get to know each other."

There's her favorite word. *Opportunity.* I don't resent what she's trying to say, though. We never had a normal sisterly relationship growing up—Jamie was closer to a babysitter. I remember wondering what it was like to have siblings only a couple years older, like Dylan's brothers. Siblings who would steal your dolls during playdates, or crank the volume up on their video games until you just *had* to come watch. Instead I had Jamie, whose weeknight rock concerts in the city and occasional boyfriends brought over for dinner felt endlessly distant from elementary-school me.

In theory, I wouldn't mind getting to know my sister for the first time. It's unfair, though, to turn my life into "The point" of her year just because she has nothing else going on. I'm not Jamie's new project, not the job she's giving herself, not the role she's cast me into. I'm me. I'm *busy.* I'm not a replacement for the plans she once had for herself. Getting to know me would look like conversations about school and college, my workload, my goals for the newspaper. It wouldn't look like TV on the couch when I'm already behind.

"Honestly, I think I'm going to try to get ahead on homework," I tell her. The words come with their usual combination of excitement and anxiety. I do have a ton to do. Editorial emails from writers with questions, the hockey-puck physics lab I have to double-check, the essay I'm outlining for AP gov on constitutional review . . .

"Come on," Jamie implores gently. "Take a break. I'll give you a pedicure."

I feel my brow furrow. Yeah, I've had Dylan do my nails

from time to time, before dances I'm obligated to go to for ASG and the handful of dates I've had over the past couple years, but they were distinctly un-busy days. Not days like today.

Jamie's watching me expectantly. I gesture to the wall of my room near the door. "I have things to do, Jamie," I say.

She doesn't need to glance in the direction I'm pointing to know what I'm referring to. On the opposite wall of my room hangs one of my honest-to-goodness prized posses-sions. It's a whiteboard six feet long and six feet high, every inch covered with information I need to remember. One edge holds the outline for my constitutional review essay. There's a quadrant for newspaper deadlines, *Chronicle* staffers' photo and story assignments. This month's issue is the one we'll submit for consideration for the prestigious NSPC Awards in every category: reporting, photography, editing, and my goal—publication of the year. The entire top half of the board is the ever-changing to-do lists I keep for the day and week.

It's a marvel of grids and connections, checklists and col-ored ink. Dylan said it made my room look like a classroom. I told her that was the point.

Jamie gets up from my bed. I know she's not pleased with my brush-off of the pedicure offer. She'd never show it, of course—ever the optimist—but I catch the strain in her grin, the new forcedness in her voice. "Okay," she says. "Let me know if you change your mind."

"I will," I promise.

While I know she's being friendly, I dislike the quiet

pressure in her efforts. I live my life like I organize my white-board, with carefully interconnecting lattices of responsibility and timeliness and thorough detail. With her invitations, her lightly imposing jokes, her eye rolls when I remind her how busy I am, Jamie, knowingly or unknowingly, is pry-ing those lattices into uncertain new geometries. I hate the feeling, the expectation I'll drop everything going on for me right now because she's got nothing else to do.

Wandering toward the door, she pauses in front of the whiteboard. "You know, slowing down wouldn't be the worst. I studied all throughout high school, and looking back, I just think, wow, I wish I'd let up on myself sometimes. The world is so much bigger. You just don't know it yet."

"Thanks for the advice," I say flatly. It's not the first time an adult—if Jamie qualifies—has told me to *slow down, enjoy high school*. I don't appreciate it. I have to conclude high school is the only time people feel free to give such intru-sive, unsolicited, condescending suggestions. As if I'm not capable of knowing what I want just because I'm young. It's rude when people give adults unwanted advice on how they should parent, decorate their house, or load the dishwasher, but when directed to a teen it's somehow "mentoring." I'm not interested.

Jamie closes the door on her way out, leaving me alone in my room.

Finally.

# Seven

I'M WOKEN UP BY knocking on my door. For a couple disorienting seconds I have no idea how much time has passed. I only remember getting thirty pages into the novel we're reading in French, before *le rêve* and *le désespoir* began to run together and I couldn't keep my eyes open. Frustrated with myself, I resolve to catch up tonight.

"Alison," Jamie calls from outside the door, "your friend's here to drop off your homework."

Peeling my face from the pool of drool on my book, I refocus. If Dylan's here, I slept the entire school day. Like, seven hours. I'm *screwed* on homework. I prop myself up on my pillows, rearranging the planner and books and pens I've scattered across my bed.

But Dylan doesn't walk in.

Ethan does.

He barges in, really, inspecting the room with his usual dismissiveness. Disinterested and judgmental, he waits, like he owns the place and every other house on the street. I sit up instantly, wondering if I'll need the trash can next to the bed. Ethan makes me sick even when I don't have food poisoning.

"Wow," he finally says. "You look terrible."

I scowl. I don't need the trash can. I need something to throw. Ideally something heavy or pointy. "My head's been inside a toilet bowl all day." I say, pushing my hair behind one ear. It's ineffectual, the straight brown strands falling to my face like they're taunting me. "What's your excuse?"

His lips nearly twitch. I have the feeling he's trying to engineer a witty reply and failing. Instead, he faces the whiteboard, where every single one of my plans and ideas is laid out for him. His eyes light up, a general in the war room of his enemy's stronghold.

"Your thesis for the gov essay is unmotivated," he says mildly, reading from the middle of my room with his hands in his pockets. "In my opinion."

I'm going to murder Jamie for letting him up here.

Gritting my teeth, I fight to keep my composure. "Why are you in my room?" I ask evenly. "Miss me that much?"

"Like I'd miss a hangnail, Sanger," he replies. "The day was rather pleasant after you left. Unfortunately, however, numerous teachers requested I deliver you today's assignments. Why they figured I'm the man for the job is beyond me."

I know he's not lying. It's no secret Ethan and I have every class together, not to mention our extracurriculars, and we're with each other nearly every minute of the day. As a result, everyone's always asking us to mention or deliver things to each other. *Tell Alison we need to redesign pages three and four. Remind Ethan to pick up the homecoming flyers from the printer.* In fairness, it's arguably their repayment for Ethan's and my endless verbal warfare. Even our teachers do it, to our immense irritation.

"I'm surprised you followed through," I say. "I wouldn't put it past you to tell them you would, then conveniently forget."

"Where's the fun in that?" Ethan walks to the whiteboard, where he does what my family members know never to do. He picks up the eraser. "Our competition's only amusing when I know I've beaten you fairly. Like I will when Harvard decisions come out." I hate his word choice. *Amusing.* Like I'm a game, a novel, a menswear magazine—whatever it is Ethan chooses for fun. I don't compete with him for his *amusement.*

Reaching up, he erases *edit Ethan's gym story* from my list with one swift swipe.

I glare. I'll rewrite it later. "You're capable of fun?"

"You have no idea." He regards his erasing handiwork. I won't give him the satisfaction of prying the eraser from his hands, letting him know he's annoyed me. Instead, I do the opposite, staring coolly and crossing my arms. Eventually, he puts the eraser down and pulls a pile of papers from his bag, which he drops on my desk. "This counts as my task for losing the blitz," he says casually.

"No way," I reply immediately. "You're going to the meeting with Principal Williams tomorrow." Every month, one representative from ASG leadership sits down with the principal and discusses funding and upcoming events over lunch. It's everyone's least favorite part of serving on student government. Because our president, Isabel Rodriguez, often flat-out refuses, it generally falls to Ethan or me. Whoever loses our first grade-related competition of the month, usually. I was excited to win today's blitz for this very reason. Neither Ethan nor I have a positive relationship with the principal, and we don't enjoy giving up a lunch period we could use for homework or other obligations.

"I don't think so," he replies, unflinching.

"The loser doesn't pick the task," I point out. It's been Ethan's and my rule forever, since the time in sophomore year he tried to fulfill his task by holding the door to chemistry open for me.

Ethan shrugs, shoving his hands in his pockets. "Well, you weren't at school today to decide. Really is a shame you were sick."

He wears mocking sympathy like he wears his stupid sweater—poorly. I sit up straighter. "You are going to that meeting."

Sighing, Ethan picks up the packet from my desk. I narrow my eyes, watching him shuffle the papers' edges straight in his hands. "I guess I'll be taking your homework with me then. Since it's not my task after all," he says.

"What happened to it's no fun unless it's fair?"

Ethan grins. It's never good when Ethan grins. It always, *always* means he's won something. The expression brings to mind dozens of tests he's bested me on, points on which he's out-debated me in US or English or gov, votes his ASG proposals have won instead of mine. It's amazing how overwhelmingly angry it makes me, this effortless gesture of Ethan's with the power to set my world on fire.

"It's your call," he says.

It hits me like lightning, this is exactly what he planned. The moment he's been leading up to ever since he walked into my room. It's why he brought my homework over in person instead of sending it over email. He's forcing me to pick the task he prefers. He watches me expectantly from the desk, papers in hand. His hostages, I realize.

I hold my hand out for them. "Get out of my room, please," I say when he places the packet into my outstretched fingers.

"Happily." He walks to the door, where he pauses. "Feel better."

I climb off the bed and close the door behind him. *Point: Ethan.*

Facing the whiteboard, I pick up the black felt-tip marker. I rewrite *edit Ethan's gym story* where he'd erased it, then examine the board. My eyes end up where they're usually drawn—the college checklist I've had since the start of junior year. It has everything: SAT schedules, the teachers who wrote recommendation letters, common app deadlines, and college essay ideas. There's only one item not crossed out. The important one. The Harvard decision date on April 1.

I applied Early Action and was deferred, which was okay because Ethan was too. I remember the feeling of opening the decision email in the newspaper room on the Friday before winter break. The dull rushing in my ears, the weird wobble the whole world gave when my goal was pulled temporarily out of reach. Instead of dwelling on the feeling, I set my sights on regular decision and focused on what was important—Ethan didn't get in, either.

Once I receive my admission letter and Ethan hopefully doesn't, I'll finally have the gloriously Ethan-free life I've fantasized about for years. Of course, I have to admit the possibility we both get in. It would be *the worst*. We'd inevitably be on the newspaper together, undoubtedly run into each other in the freshman dining hall, and probably sit in the same lectures. Should it happen, I've consoled myself with the thought I'll find plenty of non-Ethan people. I'm sure I'll even find a more bearable rival.

Right now, I just need to survive the rest of the year with the one I have.

# Eight

"SERIOUSLY?"

I'm eating breakfast the next morning, plain Cheerios, the only thing my stomach will withstand right now, while I work on AP calculus homework. Or I *was*, until my mom dropped a driver's ed course registration paper onto the conic-section diagrams I'm solving.

"Seriously," she says. She walks past me, circling the kitchen island and reaching for the Keurig. I notice she's especially dressed-up for work, wearing her new charcoal skirt suit instead of her usual colorful sweaters, which I'm guessing means she has an important client conference. Yet she doesn't seem stressed in the least. "You're signing up, or no more rides home from the newspaper at all hours. You got your learner's permit, like, six months ago. It's time for driver's ed."

"I don't have the time," I protest.

Dad walks in, holding his Nikes in one hand. He focuses

immediately on the coffeemaker, eyes bright under his thick brows. Lately, he's been growing an awful beard, which is coming in even grayer than his heavy crop of hair. We're on week three of the beard, despite repeated hints and eventually outright directives from me, my mom, and Jamie.

"You know," my mom says, "you don't actually have time for half the things you do, and yet you find a way." She closes the Keurig, piercing the plastic pod as if to put punctuation on this point. "Why are you avoiding this, baby girl?"

I frown. I hate the nickname, which is a relic from when I was a kid and would come home from third grade and read Jamie's Nancy Drew collection. "I'm not avoiding it. I'll do it. When I have time."

"Your mother's right," Dad contributes. "We're too old to be picking you up at one in the morning on production nights."

In fairness to my parents, production nights are ridiculous. The weeks we publish the newspaper, the editorial staff stays in the journalism room after school working late into the night, designing pages, placing stories and photos, editing with writers when necessary. While it's not strictly allowed under school rules—or strictly legal—our lackadaisical advisor, Ms. Heyward, provides the shallowest pretense of supervision, and the administration pretty much looks the other way.

Regardless of production night hours, I hate how my dad's playing the age card. Yes, my parents are closer in years to my friends' grandparents. I just don't like to be reminded of how incongruous I am with the lives of people nearly in their sixties.

"You should have thought of that before you had me," I reply. It's not like having old parents was my choice.

"Shoulda, woulda, coulda," Mom says, while the coffee-maker sputters and fills her mug.

"What's that supposed to mean?"

She lifts the cup and sips hesitantly, looking up with an innocent expression. "I got pregnant with you *seven years* after I had your sister," she says. "You think there was any forethought involved in your conception?"

I pull a gagging face. "Could you please not reference accidental pregnancies while I'm eating? Especially when they pertain to my very existence."

Mom and Dad share a mildly disturbing look. "Greatest accident of our lives, kiddo," Dad says. Walking over to where I'm finishing my Cheerios, he places one hand on my shoulder. I smell the familiar pine scent of his shampoo. "Right above the time I spilled soup on Harrison Ford."

I ignore him. It's the universe's only 100 percent proven way of deflecting his jokes. "You'd seriously leave your seventeen-year-old daughter to find her own way home from her exhausting extracurricular after midnight?" We're fifteen minutes from school, streets I've never wanted to walk post-production night even though they're empty and quiet with the safety of suburbia.

"Yes," my parents say together.

I don't know why I expected anything else. When it

comes to me, I'd characterize my parents' parenting style as "hands-off." Maybe they were different with Jamie. But by the time I arrived, they'd become easygoing on everything from curfews to SAT scores. They're not unsupportive—they've encouraged me in every way, praised me, paid for every extra-curricular and summer program I ever wanted. But because they're older, they're not invested in the higher-pressure behavior I've seen in my classmates' parents. They've done it already. Now they're just waiting to retire.

"You could always depend on Jamie," my mom adds, earning a laugh from my dad.

Everyone knows Jamie's not exactly dependable. I'm sure she's still sleeping right now. It's like moving back into her childhood bedroom has regressed her. She sleeps until noon, watches sitcoms at all hours, and eats junk food every day. When Mom sends me to summon her downstairs for dinner, I get glimpses into her room and inevitably see empty Frappuccino cups surrounding her wastebasket and sweatshirts and sweatpants strewn on the floor. The idea of relying on her for rides home is, to say the least, iffy.

"You're both incorrigible," I tell my parents.

"Just think," Mom says expansively, "with your own license you could sneak out and go to a boy's house."

Placing my dish in the sink, I frown. "I have other—"

"Oh, you mean Ethan Molloy's house," Dad interrupts. I close my eyes, sighing. I've heard this bit before. Hundreds of times, I would estimate. Ever since my parents encountered Ethan when I hosted an AP Euro study group and we debated the entire time, I haven't heard the end of their enthusiasm for the idea of me and my rival dating.

"I do mean Ethan Molloy's house," my mom replies, her face lighting up. "Speaking of accidental pregnancies . . ."

I turn a violent shade of red.

"What smart grandchildren we'd have," my dad says, putting on exaggerated wistfulness.

Grabbing my bag from the floor, I rein in the frustration in my voice. "Okay, I'll get my license just to end this conversation." I check the clock on my phone—*6:41*. I have to be in the car in two minutes. "Now, can one of you be a real parent for a second and drive me to school?"

Ignoring my parents' victorious smiles, I head into the garage. I open the passenger door of mom's car and sling my bag into the space under the dash, the heat in my cheeks starting to subside.

Objectively, I do want my driver's license. I don't like having to wait for my mom to pick me up from production nights or dances or to drive me to school in the mornings. It's just, getting my license requires giving hours I don't have. Hours I could be re-outlining my government essay or editing Ethan's gym story. Driver's ed will mean staying up even later on weekends.

But worse than the intrusion on my schedule, I kind of hate driving. Or rather, I hate learning how to drive. As much as I do want my license and everything that comes with it, I do not enjoy having my age and inexperience exposed to adults watching me fumble with lane changes and parallel parking. I'm not particularly used to being so objectively bad at things every other adult around me can do easily.

With my parents, it's worse. Driving lessons expose me as the "kid" of the household. It's not a feeling I relish, nor is it one I need reminding of. Not when I constantly feel hopelessly behind the curve of where their lives would be without me. It's left me working to conceal my seventeen-ness wherever possible, chasing to catch up with who I should be in their nearly retirement age. Someone older. Someone independent.

Because I am independent. I am mature.

I just also have to wait five minutes for my mom to get in the driver's seat and take me to school.

# Nine

I IGNORE ETHAN AS much as humanly possible. It's not easy, considering he sits next to me in half of our classes. But I love a challenge.

I've always chosen seats in the front of the class, obviously. Ethan started copying me sophomore year. I'm pretty sure he doesn't do it for the reason I do—to be called on more often. It's definitely just to irritate me. Even sitting in the front row, he's usually on his phone. This morning, he DMs under his desk and reads news on his phone, raising his hand only when he's evidently unsatisfied with what he's finding on *The Washington Post*. Teachers don't call him on it because they know Ethan occupied with his phone is preferable to his full attention—and criticism—of their lectures.

In fourth period, I can't ignore him—and his phone reading, and his incessant rotation of messaging conversations—any longer. We have Associated Student Government in one of the expansive multipurpose rooms near the cafeteria, the open-plan linoleum floors perfect for painting posters or folding programs. Honestly, ASG is an easy class. Unless we're convening a quorum on an issue or preparing for an event, the period is free for homework or hanging out with friends.

The makeup of the class is markedly different from my others, which include the same group of overachievers I've shared APs and Honors courses with since everyone got serious about college apps in sophomore year. Every position on ASG is elected, which means my classmates in here are considerably more popular. While my name is known to most of the student body, it's not because I'm friends with everyone. I have Dylan, and the majority of my staff in the *Chronicle*. But beyond that, I don't get out enough to be invited into other social spheres.

Ethan, however, with his looks and superficial charm, flits between girlfriends and friend groups frequently enough to be semipopular. Whether he grows bored of people or chooses to keep them at a distance so they don't realize he's a jerk is an open question. Ultimately, he and I only won the vice president positions due to expertly run campaigns. Neither of us entertained running for president, knowing we couldn't defeat someone students actually enjoy hanging out with.

Someone like Isabel Rodriguez. Isabel was homecoming queen, and what she lacks in fulfilling her ASG responsibilities she makes up for in genuinely getting students excited about events and other initiatives. On occasion I wonder if she's realized she can take advantage of Ethan's and my unique position. Our rivalry comes up in every ASG vote, where each time, Ethan and I are on opposing sides. Isabel has no patience for it, and I get the sense she delegates more of her duties to us, knowing we'll do everything we can to show the other up. It's a savvy leadership strategy, I have to admit.

I'm not surprised when she walks over to me in class. She's straightened her long black hair, and her signature red lipstick is bright against her brown skin. Today is the Williams meeting, and I'd wager my GPA on Isabel "having a thing" during lunch and needing Ethan or me to fill in. Since Ethan wriggled out of his task last night, it's only a question of fighting him over who's going to go.

Isabel clicks her perfectly polished red nails on my desk and looks over her shoulder. "Ethan, could you come over here for a second?" she calls out. He's working on the other side of the room, and we make commiserative eye contact when he glances up from his laptop. He wanders over and perches on the desk next to me. "Williams wants to meet with both of you today," Isabel says.

I frown, not expecting this.

"So we're just entirely dropping the pretense this is your job?" Ethan replies.

Isabel smiles the way someone does when they know they've got a good excuse. "She asked for you both specifically. I was actually planning to go today."

Ethan scoffs, skepticism in his eyes. He crosses his arms over his crisp oxford.

"I was!" Isabel insists. She stomps her foot for emphasis, causing her skirt to flutter up a little.

I catch Ethan's eyes flit down her leg, his expression changing. It's only for a moment, an unguarded flash. Then his gaze returns to her face, his symmetrical features relaxing into their Ethan Molloy combination of arrogance and apathy.

*Uh-oh.* I know that look. It's the intrigued glance I caught from Ethan when Christina Cheng and the girls' a cappella group came into the ASG room singing Christmas carols, and when we were forced into a group project in AP US and he kept asking Rebecca Markey about her upcoming Model UN conference. He promptly started dating each of them, and then he promptly stopped. I've watched Ethan progress through numerous girlfriends over the course of our rivalry. I'm always delighted when one of them dumps him, not that he ever appears broken-up about it. Still, I like to fantasize about him lying on his bed, listening to some sad white-boy music as he struggles not to cry over his heartache.

"Isabel, you haven't gone to a single meeting," he says. "Why would I believe you were starting today?" I know when Ethan's genuinely irritated or impatient. This isn't it. There's playfulness in his tone. I recognize it because I literally never hear it when he's talking to me.

"I guess you didn't hear," Isabel says casually. "I dumped Jared over the weekend. My lunches will be a lot freer from now on." She flips her hair, looking pleased with herself.

I, on the other hand, close my eyes in pain. Usually I

enjoy when Ethan enters a relationship. He's way easier to beat when he's distracted. However, never in the past have I had quite so close a front-row seat to the proceedings. I've shared classes with Ethan and his girlfriends, sure—watched them eye-flirt and exchange stupid little smiles. But student government has a fair amount of after-class obligations. I'll have to interact with Ethan and Isabel up close and personal in class and outside of school. I don't know if I'm over my food poisoning enough to start now.

I cut in before this conversation can go where it's obviously headed. "Why does Williams want *both* of us?" I ask.

Isabel shrugs. "She didn't say. Oh, and do you have your bonfire volunteers?"

*Shit.* "Working on it," I say. It's a generous characterization. By *working on it,* I mean finding volunteers for the baseball kickoff bonfire that ASG's putting together remains near the bottom of my very long to-do list.

"Ethan's already signed up four people. I need yours by Friday," Isabel says casually, knowing exactly what the comparison does to me. "Thanks, guys," she adds. Her gaze lingers on Ethan a fraction of a second before she walks away.

Ethan's eyes follow her—or more precisely, follow the hemline of her skirt. Without turning, he says to me, "Lunch with Alison Sanger and Principal Williams. I'm being punished for something, surely."

"Feel free to blow it off," I reply.

Finally, his eyes flit from Isabel. He cuts me a dry glance, then walks off to follow her.

Isabel's on the opposite end of the room, talking to Kristin Cole, the treasurer. I watch Ethan come up next to Isabel and effortlessly enter their conversation. Ignoring them, I return to my English homework. We have to read the first half of *Macbeth* by the end of the week. With three hours of meetings with reporters and editors after school, I need to read ahead now, and I immerse myself in the pages of Scottish rulers and sinister prophecies. I don't resent my packed schedule, of course. I don't particularly like unstructured time. Ethan, on the other hand . . .

Isabel laughs loudly, and I look up. It's obvious from Ethan's pompous expression he's just said something funny. Something Isabel finds funny, I mean.

I know he's not actually interested in her. He's never interested in his romances, not in a real way or in a way that extends beyond three months. It's just how Ethan is— flighty, distractible in everything from relationships to class lectures.

I don't understand him. The flirting, the extracurriculars, even the rivalry. Sometimes I think Ethan only works hard in school because he has nothing better to do, and not because he truly wants the things he achieves. It's infuriating, knowing I'm spending endless hours feuding with someone who's probably only playing with me. He's using our rivalry just to pass the time, interchangeable with chatting up the newly single student body president. However hateful it would be to know he was working his hardest out of the unshakeable desire to destroy me, this—this petty, throwaway opposition—is worse.

I want the things I achieve. Student body vice president, editor in chief of the *Chronicle*, Harvard, valedictorian. Ethan competes with me in almost everything, but does he even want any of the achievements he'd take from me? Or is it just fun for him to say he did?

I move to a desk without a direct view of him and return to work.

# Ten

PERPETUALLY UNIMPRESSED WITH HER students, Principal Williams is scarily silent, with a stare capable of rooting class-cutters and freshmen goofing off in the hallways where they stand. She's in her fifties, Black, of medium height, and partial to pantsuits. I think of her in bullet points, in organized punches of information, because it's the way she requires you speak when you're in her office.

We don't have the friendliest relationship. To be fair, we got off on the wrong foot when I complained to her that my freshman English teacher was too easy. I wasn't wrong—we went the first week of school without a mention of homework while Dylan's class was five chapters into *Lord of the Flies.* I returned to Williams's office every day until she finally relented and switched my classes. Since then, we've crossed paths whenever Ethan and I publish unflattering stories about the administration in the newspaper or petition the PTSA for funding for the humanities department.

Right now, I'm waiting in her office. I don't know when I'll eat lunch. I definitely won't try it in here. Once when I brought my prepackaged salad in, Williams watched the little plastic fork disapprovingly until I threw the whole thing out.

Ethan sits silently in the chair next to me, once again scrolling aimlessly on his phone. He clicks off the screen with practiced deftness and returns his phone to his pocket. "You're quiet," he observes.

I frown. "You're literally equally quiet."

"Except I'm the one who spoke first," he points out. "Just now."

"I wish you hadn't," I reply. I hate this fight. I hate it on a conceptual level. We're fighting about fighting. It's grossly married-couple, the whole framework. Worse, Ethan's now smiling, elbow on his armrest, chin on his palm.

"What, Sanger?" he inquires slowly. "You don't enjoy our conversations?"

"They're not conversations, they're hostage negotiations," I inform him. "You holding me captive until I've paid your ransom of pithy remarks and retorts. Enough for you to feel important."

Ethan *hmms*. "I wonder why you extend them, then?" he drawls. "A negotiating tactic, I assume?"

I'm fuming over my reply when Williams walks in. Deliverance. She's wearing black, and her hair is cut close to her head. It's a straight-to-the-point look, which is like Williams.

Sitting down smoothly, she picks up the papers on her

desk. "My favorite students," she says drolly without looking up.

I say nothing. Ethan says nothing, which is rarer. This is when he'd fire off some sarcastic comment with one of our teachers like he's on a Netflix comedy special instead of at school. With Williams, though, he holds his humor in.

"Any disasters I need to know about in ASG?" Williams inquires in sharp syllables.

I exchange a confused glance with Ethan. "Not at the moment," I say, hearing the uncertainty in my voice. If this is just our normal ASG meeting, I don't understand why she wanted both Ethan and me.

"What about the upcoming paper? Anything I'll want to know about?" she asks distractedly, reading the papers she's holding.

I'm fully puzzled now. We never discuss *Chronicle* issues in student government meetings. Whatever the purpose of this meeting is, it's unusual.

"Nothing I can think of," Ethan replies, like he's the editor in chief. Williams fixes him with a hard look. I do too, though mine's less skeptical, more *don't tell the principal everything in the upcoming issue, please.* Clearly ignoring me, Ethan elaborates. "We're publishing the budget for the gym renovations."

"Where did you get those numbers?" Williams's stony stare intensifies. It's not a curious-sounding question.

Ethan smirks, undaunted. "I can't reveal my sources, Ms. Williams. But if you'd like to comment on whether there'll be funding left over for the long-discussed library remodel, I'd be glad to get you on the record."

I clench my jaw and keep from rolling my eyes. It's a miracle Ethan gets *anyone* on the record with what a butt-hole he is.

Williams checks the calendar on her wall. French bull-dogs. It's the only piece of décor in her office. "Only three and a half months to go," she says emotionless.

"Until the remodel?" I ask. Ethan's story said July. If he got this fundamental detail wrong, I'm going to love rubbing it in.

"Until you two graduate," Williams corrects me. "I'm counting down the days."

"Aren't we all?" Ethan replies. I wonder if he means it. When I watch him flirt with Isabel or debate our teachers, I honestly don't know whether he's enjoying himself, if he's engaged in high school or eagerly awaiting next year. Even his comment to Williams feel like just something to say, a placeholder instead of a real sentiment.

Williams sighs, setting down her papers. "I need you to do something for me."

"You know we can't pull the story," I tell her. We've fought before over her requesting I "refocus" negative reporting.

"Not that." Williams waves her hand. "Do either of you know who Adam Elliot is?"

Ethan jumps in. "Fairview alum, listed last year on *Forbes's* 30 Under 30 for finance—"

"Harvard alum as well, graduated Phi Beta Kappa," I

interject. There are plenty of successful Fairview alums, many who've gone on to graduate from nearby Stanford or Berkeley and found their way into the tech bubble thirty minutes south of here. Adam is unique even among them, with his cryptocurrency startup earning headlines for its high-profile Series A financing. We've requested interviews with him for a *Chronicle* profile a few times, but we've never gotten a response.

"A 'yes' would have sufficed." Williams raises an eyebrow. "Adam was supposed to be in charge of his class's Fairview reunion to be held in May."

Of course he was. He was president of his class, which happened to be two years ahead of Jamie's. In researching him for a prospective profile, I found out he was also editor of the newspaper, president of numerous clubs, and valedictorian. Pretty much everything I aspire to be.

"What does this have to do with us?" I ask.

Principal Williams crosses her arms, her features hard with displeasure. "Despite *Forbes* calling him an 'organizational genius,'" she practically growls, "it seems some of his reunion obligations slipped his mind. He paid a nonrefundable deposit for a venue the weekend *after* the reunion. Then he only figured out the problem when alumni across the country had already bought their tickets and booked their flights. This is all off the record, by the way," Williams interrupts herself, firing me a warning glance. "We can't move the reunion," she continues, "and now we're out $2,000 of our $10,000 budget."

Ethan is expressionless. "Okay," he says. "Why are you telling us?"

"I can't find anyone from the ten-year class to take over planning the event with only two months left, and clearly Adam does not have the time." Williams picks up a pen like she's preparing to return to work. Like this conversation is nearly over. "Which is why you're going to do it."

The office goes quiet with Ethan's and my collective surprise. There's only the hum of the fluorescent lights, the rhythmic whirr of the copier in the hall. I imagine the work the reunion would entail—the visits to venues, the vendor coordination, the chaos of everything on the night itself. When my cousin Stephanie got married, I was a bridesmaid, and I remember the enormous effort involved in planning a worthy event for one-hundred-fifty people who wouldn't have been content with hand-painted banners and folding tables with punch bowls.

I open my mouth, pause, then say delicately, "I'm going to have to decline. Between the newspaper and finals . . . I really don't have the time."

"I hate to say it," Ethan adds, following my reply quickly, "but I'm with Sanger on this one."

Lining up the papers she's holding in one crisp motion, the edges snapping when they strike her desk, Williams proceeds to ignore us. "Here's everything Adam's done, as well as Adam's contact information since the finances are still under his name." She holds the papers out in my direction. "I'll need you to deal directly with the venue and the vendors."

Notwithstanding the fact she's totally disregarded Ethan's and my very reasonable, school-related reasons for declining, I'm thrown by Williams's nonchalance requesting us to "deal directly" with every party involved. She's forgotten what everyone with teenage-hood far in the rearview mirror forgets—how little respect you get.

Even if Ethan and I did end up in charge, I know how the planning would go. Vendors won't want to hear complaints or deal with requests from high school seniors. No matter how hard I work or how much I achieve, adults only ever see a young person, someone easy to ignore or underestimate. I've encountered it on the newspaper, where sources speak patronizingly and the printer tries to disregard prices and deadlines. Wherever possible, I fight it. I act as mature as I can, with my parents, with the clothes I wear, with my orderly goals. It never quite works, frustratingly. This reunion would be nothing but more of that very frustration.

I want to point this out to Williams. "Don't you think teenagers shouldn't be in charge of a project this important?" It pains me to say, but this might be the only way to keep the reunion off my very full plate.

"You and Mr. Molloy are very capable. I'm sure you'll be fine," Williams says easily. I grit my teeth. She's not listening, not really.

"Can't you give this to ASG?" I press her. "Why us?"

For once, it's Williams who looks a little uncomfortable. "We're already in a difficult position with the Ed Foundation over this. Class reunions are extremely lucrative for donations.

Without the money we'll raise for the ten-year, we'll never get that library remodel." She shoots Ethan a pointed look, her discomfort gone. "While you two annoy me, you're undeniably competent. I trust you won't phone this in. What's more—" She pauses. "I've received complaints regarding both of you."

"From *who*?" I sit up sharply.

"About what?" Ethan's eyes narrow.

Possibilities fire through my thoughts. I wonder if PTSA representatives have bemoaned the pressure we've put on them for interviews, or it's possible classmates have charged us with giving teachers unrealistic expectations for essays and projects.

The furrow in Williams's brow deepens. "Teachers," she says, looking miserable. "They're complaining about the toxic and disruptive nature of your rivalry. Certain teachers have asked me to change your schedules to avoid having you both in their classes."

Ethan leans back in his chair. I recognize his expression. Under the veneer of neutrality he's contemptuous. "Is Pham behind this?"

"I won't disclose the teachers who complained," Williams replies, "and it's not one teacher. Giving you a *collaborative* project is my attempt at conflict resolution. The pair of you planning the reunion fixes two of my problems at once."

*The pair of you.* I've been so busy trying to wrestle out of this obligation I didn't consider this part of Williams's request. She wants us to plan the reunion *together*. I reimagine every reunion-planning responsibility with Ethan involved, figuring out every detail with the person who fought me for a full thirty minutes over the use of one em dash. With Ethan, organizing this event wouldn't just be frustrating. It would be torture.

"You can't require us to do this," Ethan ventures. His sliver of sarcasm has disappeared, replaced with wariness. "It's not for a class or an extracurricular. We don't just work for the school."

Heaving a sigh, Williams puts her folded hands on her desk. "I didn't want to have to do this," she starts, "but I should have known you would be difficult. You both want to get in to Harvard, right? As you pointed out, Miss Sanger, Adam went to Harvard. I'll ask him to put in a good word. Besides, you're both obviously in the running for valedictorian," she continues with strained concession in her voice, like she resents validating Ethan and me. Like it's a burden having two overachievers reaching the uppermost heights of every class and extracurricular. "Whoever takes on this task will find themselves looked favorably upon by the teachers' committee."

"I'm in," Ethan and I say simultaneously.

I hate the echo of his voice under mine. It doesn't matter, though. All of my objections have vanished in an instant. There's no way I'm letting Ethan win valedictorian or get into Harvard over something as inconsequential as planning a party.

This reunion will be nothing. I've spent sleepless nights

studying, pulled together powerfully written profiles with a week's notice, unraveled complicated chemistry equations even our teacher got wrong on the whiteboard. For years I've crested academic and extracurricular Everests without needing to catch my breath. Writing a few name tags and wrangling a few vendors won't be what holds me back.

Williams frowns. "Wonderful."

# Eleven

"I'M SCREWED."

I'm whispering to Dylan in sixth-period government. Ethan's a few rows up, his back to us. We're supposed to be discussing the pros and cons of the presidential veto, but when Mrs. Warshaw told us to pair up, I promptly told Dylan what happened in the meeting with Williams. It's unlike me to disregard teachers' instructions. "Group discussion," however, is different. I've never been interested in unstructured dialogues with classmates, especially when it's obvious our teacher only wants time to check her email.

"You're not screwed," Dylan says, and I know it's not idle reassurance. Dylan's reliably straight with me, whether she's telling me my hair bun is crooked or reassuring me I don't need to practice my vice presidential campaign speech for the tenth time.

In the hours since Ethan and I met with Williams, I started to realize just how much planning the reunion would entail, how many pieces remained undone or out of order. It's like someone started building one of those enormous one-thousand-piece puzzles, the type my mom loves, with scenes of Italy or wildlife, except they've put even the easy corner pieces in the wrong places. What's more, we're ferociously behind. It's already March and the event is in May. Two months out and we have no confirmed venue, no catering, no nothing. From the wedding planning calendar I googled in the *Chronicle*—not exactly comparable, I know, but I'm working with what I've got—we need way more components in place by now. This very scenario is why I plan everything on my whiteboard, where I'm going to have to incorporate a reunion checklist. With enough preparation, I avoid being haphazard or hurried. Instead, I'll need to rush the reunion, praying the whole while that my frenetic pace doesn't produce problems.

And I'm going to have to do the entire thing with Ethan.

"Overlooking the very real issue of who I'll have to work with on this," I say to Dylan, glaring at the back of Ethan's head. "I'm really behind, and I know nothing about party-planning. Especially not when the party's celebrating returning to *high school*. I mean, I barely go to high school stuff and I'm actually a high school student."

Dylan chews her lip, considering.

"Well, when you put it that way . . ." she says, the first unconvinced waver in her voice. I hang my head in my hands. "I'll help, of course," she adds quickly.

"You don't have to help," I protest automatically. The

reunion's my job. Well, mine and Ethan's. I'm not in the habit of passing off responsibilities to my peers, especially not my friends.

"Ethan's going to try to make you look bad," Dylan points out. "Don't turn down my offer."

She's not wrong there. Ethan will try to outdo me or compromise my efforts in every way imaginable. When he's not reviewing for exams or finding ways to annoy me, he's somewhat popular with social groups on campus known for occasionally throwing parties. Or so I've heard. It'll give him an edge in planning the glorified party that is the reunion. Despite the discomfort of taking my friend's help, Dylan would be useful in this regard. She has a whole group of yearbook friends who host regular pregames and ragers.

"Fine," I say. "You're right." I try to focus on my discussion worksheet. *The presidential veto is the power to . . .* The drone of classmates' halfhearted conversations crowd in on my efforts. I promptly give up, turning back to Dylan. "I just don't get it."

Dylan's lips purse in puzzlement. "The assignment?"

"No. Obviously. High school reunions," I say. "Like, why do we ritualistically reunite every decade with this group of people connected to us only by geography and four arbitrary years? It's not like we chose who we go to high school with. Why do we care? Why can't we just graduate and move on with our lives? We don't place this emphasis on the people in our first office or our first neighborhood." I know I'm kind of ranting, but I've had the thoughts building in my head since the conversation with Williams. "Why don't we have reunions with them?"

"I don't know. I think high school is special," Dylan says contemplatively. "It's where we'll have experiences we'll remember for the rest of our lives. The kind of epic stuff you only do when you're young."

I'm not convinced. "Like what?"

"Sneaking out to a concert, staying out partying until five a.m." I can hear the memories lacing every word. I remember the stories, relayed to me in long strings of texts the next morning. Stuff she did with the yearbook clique or Olivia and the drama kids. "Hooking up with someone even when you know it's a horrible idea."

Frowning, I reach into my own high school memories. They're less *epic* in the way Dylan describes, more sneaking off campus past midnight on production nights, staying up all hours studying in my room, and competing with Ethan every waking moment. I'm about to reply when Mrs. Warshaw calls our attention to the front of the class. Returning to my desk in the first row, I permit my mind to wander from the discussion of the presidential veto.

The truth is, there are very few things I'll regret leaving behind in high school. There's having Dylan in my classes. We've been in school together and best friends since second grade, and having a friend like her in middle school, where a nerdy girl who wore collared shirts would have ended up reading on her own every lunch otherwise, was invaluable. It's not like our friendship will end when we go to college, though. Then there's the newspaper, into which I've poured thousands of proud and meaningful hours. But I'll have a bigger, better newspaper in college. Maybe I'm meant to regret not having done the things Dylan said. The epic nights everyone else chases. I just . . . don't.

If I did, maybe I'd understand high school reunions.

# Twelve

**WHEN SCHOOL GOT OUT,** I went directly to the *Chronicle*, where I'm waiting for Ethan in my office. Everyone who's had my position over the years has decorated the editor in chief's office differently. Windows overlook the newsroom from two walls, but the other two are an empty canvas. I've opted, obviously, for purely professional décor, with past years' prize-winning headlines hanging next to my desk and nothing but dictionaries and style guides on the shelves.

What I can see through my window, however, is in stark contrast to the orderly oasis in my office. In the high-ceilinged space, half-finished homework, lunch left-overs, and the last issue's penciled-up page designs litter the folding tables running the length of the *Chronicle* room. Printouts of memes and funny typos paper the walls over the row of iMacs we use for design. Under the wall clock hangs the *Fairview Chronicle* sign we pasted up at the beginning of the year over the paper's previous name, *The Paw Print*. The old name was derived from Fairview's mascot, the puma. In a rare instance of agreement, Ethan and I found it offensively stupid, and I changed it immediately upon becoming editor in chief.

In my head, I review the edits I'm going to give Ethan. *Reorganize opening paragraphs, return to construction consultant source for follow-up questions on cost estimates. Reduce pretentiousness overall.* I don't usually directly edit reporters' work. It's not in the editor in chief's job description, which typically consists of keeping section editors on track and dealing with bigger-picture questions like the website we launched this year.

Ethan's the unfortunate exception, for a few reasons. One, Ethan's impossible to edit. When I've put his work under the purview of the news or features editors, they've inevitably stormed into my office on the brink of tears. Ethan's not shy about telling editors he finds their ideas dumb. The problem is, he's often right.

The other reason is the stories Ethan writes. He takes on the longer investigative reports and narrative features, the kind we submit for state and national journalism prizes. Despite how little I enjoy contributing to his success, I care about the paper. Everything we win reflects well on the *Chronicle* and on me.

The room outside my office is quiet. In the days before production weeks, nobody comes in here when school's out. I'm jotting down headline ideas for Ethan's piece when he walks into the journalism room. *Write a headline for the devil, and what do you know.*

He strides through the newsroom and enters my office without knocking. He never knocks. Either it's ingrained into his psyche that the rest of the world's just waiting for him to show up, or, likelier, he knows it annoys me specifically.

"I've gone over the structure, and you're wrong," he says, depositing his bag on the floor. "It's as it should be."

"Your lede is in the sixth paragraph, Ethan," I say automatically, having anticipated his resistance on this point. "This is a *news* story, remember?"

"It's hardly unconventional to organize long-form reporting like a feature," he fires back, dropping into the chair opposite me and crossing one ankle over his knee. "Read *The Wall Street Journal* every once in a while."

"This is *not* the *Journal*. It's my paper. I'm your editor." I lean back in my chair, relishing the moment. I can't imagine even sex holds a candle to pulling rank on Ethan. "And while we're on the subject of improving this piece," I continue, "I'm not convinced you've done the research on every angle here."

Ethan bristles. "I have what I need."

"Do I have to remind you of the paramount rule of journalism?" I ask. I know I don't. Ethan and I have gone to the same journalism conferences and summer camps for years. This past summer, we were both in DC attending an elite twenty-person rotation among major media groups. But besides pulling rank, patronizing Ethan is my other great joy. "You can't just decide you know the story, then incorporate or ignore facts to fit your framework. You need to find every important fact, and *then* you'll understand what the story really is."

Ethan looks directly into my eyes, glaring. He says nothing. I smirk.

"You're enjoying this way too much." His voice is a dry edge.

"I don't know what you mean." I do, though. He's not wrong. Which I would never in a hundred years admit. In between us, my open laptop hums like a third uncomfortable member of the conversation.

"Just because you're technically the boss here doesn't mean you're my superior," Ethan says. He's visibly trying not to let his frustration tighten his shoulders. I know because he's failing.

"Doesn't it, though?" I raise an eyebrow, innocently quizzical. "I decide what is and isn't published in the *Chronicle*. If you have an issue with that, you're welcome to write for another, lesser publication."

He can't, of course. Publication in the *Chronicle* is the only way he'll be eligible for the National Student Press Club Awards. Ethan's won every year, and not winning his senior year would embarrass him. Ordinarily, Ethan's embarrassment is something I'd encourage and wholeheartedly endorse. But every award the *Chronicle* wins is important to me, and Ethan's reporting contributes to the paper overall. In this, unfortunately, I need Ethan and he needs me.

Granted, I don't think Ethan actually cares about the

award itself. Not what it represents. He's never talked about studying journalism in college, or pursuing a career in media. He only joined the *Chronicle* sophomore year after I did, and to this day I'm convinced it was to spite me. No, what Ethan cares about is *winning* the award.

"I'll do more research," he concedes grudgingly. *Point: Alison.*

He's fuming. I'm accustomed to Ethan's varying levels of vexation, and this one's near the top. I recognize the way he fidgets with the collar of his shirt, the tendon shifting in his neck.

I can't blame him. Knowing we'll have to work together planning the reunion has raised my own blood pressure. I don't know if Ethan feels it too, but for me this added component of Ethan in my life feels like one more link in the chain of competition and obligations encircling my neck. It's going to fray my nerves in new ways, I can tell.

Ethan's features relax into their practiced neutrality. He pulls his laptop from his bag. Wincing the way I do whenever he produces the computer, I regard the cluster of stickers decorating the back. The name of a Thai restaurant, the logo for the San Francisco Short Film Festival, the campaign graphic of a candidate for the city council election four years ago, a quote from *The Little Prince*.

There's no rhyme or reason to them. I don't think even Ethan cares what they say. It's easy to imagine people handing him each one and him sticking them on senselessly. The only one with the remotest connection to his personality is the sticker of the posturing and egomaniacal Kylo Ren. Still, it perplexes me, the lack of care he shows with his computer and the complete incoherence of what he purports to be interested in.

"Do you mind if I eat while we discuss the rest of your feedback?" His voice is nonchalant. "I didn't have lunch because of the Williams meeting."

Instantly suspicious, I narrow my eyes. It's not like Ethan to ask for permission. In fact, he's usually outwardly rude in our edits. I've watched him put his feet up on my desk while we're working. I can't deny him without reason, though, especially not when I have half a smooshed PB&J next to my computer.

"Go ahead," I say warily.

Ethan extracts from his bag a plastic container holding his lunch.

It's sushi. The sight's bad enough. Then the smell hits. My stomach flips over.

"Want some?" he offers.

*Of course.* I don't know how he even found out what caused my recent food poisoning, not to mention how he somehow obtained sushi in the ten minutes between the end of school and this meeting. It clearly took effort—effort that's paying off in the grimace of revulsion I'm undoubtedly wearing. *Point: Ethan.*

"No, thank you," I reply. Ethan happily pops one into his mouth, chewing for an exaggeratedly long time. I ignore him, focusing instead on my computer. "We're going to push this information to the second through fourth paragraphs. Then the anecdote."

While I talk, he continues eating, typing notes into his computer. He doesn't object to any of my edits, which leaves me feeling uneasy. Ethan never lets anything go. I stifle the suspicion there's a devious explanation for his cooperativeness.

He closes his computer. "I'll have the revision done next Friday," he says. I nod, and he stands up, sliding his laptop into his bag. "Oh, and for the reunion," he adds, "it'll be best if we divide up responsibilities. We see enough of each other already, wouldn't you say?" There's no hint of an insult in the proposition. It's just a statement of fact.

"Absolutely," I agree. Anything to avoid even a minute of extra interaction with Ethan on the weekends.

"So I'll handle the venue, the music, and the menu. You do the decorations, the registration table, and the slideshow."

"You're joking." It's not even the implicit order in his phrasing that's making me mad.

"I know, I know," Ethan starts, leaning on the door-frame. "Slideshows are inherently stupid, but I'm pretty sure Williams will put us in detention if we don't—"

I stand, irritated by how it feels like he's like literally speaking down to me. "You just gave yourself the most important jobs."

"And?"

"*And* I'm not letting you take all the credit for the reunion." I know what he's planning. He'll take the complicated jobs, the ones involving multiple meetings and large-scale coordination and creativity, and then tell Williams I'm shirking my responsibilities.

Ethan sighs dramatically. "Fine," he relents. "Which jobs do you want?"

"I'll do venue, music, and decorations," I offer reasonably.

Ethan's reply is immediate. "No way. You can do venue and slideshow."

"Ethan!"

"Alison!" he echoes, imitating the register of my voice. It's such a horrible impression I'm half ready to drop the argument right here just to mock him for it.

"You're not even trying to compromise," I say instead.

Ethan shrugs, sweeping errant blond strands from his forehead. "Have you ever known me to compromise?"

I should have predicted discussing this with him would be entirely futile. Even so, I try one last time. "I'll do menu, music, slideshow, and registration." I'm being very reasonable. I'm honestly really impressed with how reasonable I'm being.

"No," Ethan says. His eyes sparkle. I realize how much he's enjoying our ill-fated negotiation, and it takes everything in me not to upend the container of sushi he's picked up. Everything's a game with him. Everything. I wonder if he's keeping score the way I am.

"You know this means we'll end up doing it all together," I say in exasperation.

"I guess it does." He pops the final piece of sushi into his mouth, looking satisfied. No, smug. *Satisfied* is the fulfillment of community service or the humble pride of a day's hard work. Ethan looks *smug*. It's like he knew this would be the outcome, and he enjoyed goading me there.

Knocking once on the doorframe, signaling the end of the conversation, Ethan turns to leave.

I refuse to permit him the last word. "Don't forget, I'll expect your revision next Friday." It's not my strongest parting shot, but it's something. Wordlessly, he waves away the reminder. I watch his retreating back exit the newsroom.

Sitting back down, I mentally douse the fires of frustration heating my face. I turn to the next item on my to-do list, replying to editors' emails regarding upcoming stories. But I'm still spiraling on the discussion with Ethan. I close the email I'm writing, knowing I'm getting nothing done. If this conversation was anything to judge by, collaborating with Ethan is going to be painful and utterly useless.

I should have worked harder to compromise on dividing responsibilities. In the quiet of my office, though, I know why I didn't. I feel the familiar pull of the volatile thing I hide underneath and within outward professionality. There's a recklessness in me when it comes to Ethan, one I see in giving up on test questions to win a blitz, and in dragging myself to school with food poisoning.

And in my dangerous refusal to compromise with him. It's one way I'm unfortunately like Ethan.

We've never compromised in our lives when it comes to each other.

# Thirteen

IT'S FRIDAY NIGHT, AND I'm in my room, studying. I have everything exactly the way I prefer when I'm working. My computer plays Beethoven from Spotify in hushed swells. I've organized papers and folders in neat piles on my long desk, and I've lit the ginseng ginger candle I got from the neighborhood independent bookstore. It's this cocoon of calming productivity I create, the perfect environment for thinking clearly and shifting seamlessly from one task to the next.

Open on my desk, next to the candle, is my calculus textbook. I'm reviewing for the differential equations exam we have next week. In between problems, I reply to texts from Dylan, who's in San Francisco, going to some concert with Grace Wu, her friend from yearbook. She knew better than to invite me.

I'm turning the page to find new review problems when there's an earsplitting screech.

Wincing violently, I spin around. It's the wavering shrill

of something mechanical, and it's coming from somewhere in the house. I wonder if the smoke detector is on the fritz. It disturbs the tranquility of my room, to say the least. It's frankly unbearable, and I close my book and rush into the hallway.

The sound is coming from Jamie's room. Plugging my ears with my fingers, I hurry down the hall, then throw open her door.

I find my sister sitting on her bed, strumming the shittiest-looking electric guitar I've ever seen. One knob is missing, the pegs for the strings are chipped, and countless dents and scratches mar the candy-apple red paint. With her other hand, Jamie's fiddling with the fat cable running into the amp on the floor.

Irritation replaces whatever smoke-detector-related concern I momentarily had. "What are you *doing*?" I ask.

Jamie glances up. When she stops strumming, the harsh wail ceases. "Oh, hey, Alison. Isn't it cool?" She waves her hand down the guitar. I think it looks more like garbage and sounds worse. Jamie is dressed with her usual carelessness, wearing a gray hoodie, her hair in a sloppy knot at the top of her head. "I'm going to learn how to play."

She shifts the guitar, and feedback screams from the amp. I walk over and unplug the cable, yanking the metal head out with a little more force than is necessary. "Maybe learning can be a quieter activity," I propose, marshaling my voice into patience. "Where did you even get this stuff?"

"I was walking to Starbucks and saw a sign for a garage

sale." Jamie crosses her legs on her comforter, and I get the feeling she wants me to sit next to her. "I just *had* to check it out."

I push past Jamie's very generous use of the phrase *had to*, not to mention my perplexity for her unstructured day. "I didn't even know you were interested in playing guitar," I say lightly.

"Neither did I!" Jamie replies. "But when I saw it, this whole vision of me on stage in a band flashed before my eyes. It was totally a sign. Besides, I used to love violin."

"You mean when you played in middle school?" I remember being dragged to those middle-school orchestra concerts as a kid, as well as the two hours a week Jamie would agree to practice at home. Not fond acoustical memories. Back then, our parents forced Jamie to pick up an instrument—something they'd given up by the time it was my turn. In high school, Jamie dropped orchestra in favor of the *Chronicle*, knowing it would look better on her college apps.

"The strings are different, but the logic is similar. I think I can pick it up pretty quickly." She plucks one of the strings, then another, twisting the knobs at the head like she's tuning them.

I feel the minutes passing, knowing I have calculus waiting in my room, and yet I can't help pressing the subject. "So you're going to teach yourself guitar and find a band?" Having retreated toward the doorway, I pause, unconsciously toeing the little pile of *New Yorker* issues on the carpet. "That's the new plan?"

"It might be." Jamie shrugs. "Hey, do you want to learn piano?"

I finally lose hold on my incredulity. "Yeah, in all my spare time I'm just going to learn piano to be in the band you decided to form, like, fifteen minutes ago."

Jamie's lips flit up. "I'm picking up your disparaging sarcasm loud and clear, Alison," she says sweetly. "But I won't be deterred. We're *going* to hang out." She points a playful finger in my direction, then resumes plucking the strings of the guitar.

I don't reply, not knowing how. What's infuriating about Jamie is how intelligent she is, despite the new slacker sensibility she's slumped into. She went to Columbia and graduated with high honors in philosophy while working on the newspaper. She uses words like *disparaging* and *deterred*. I remember the Jamie who had goals and plans and dreams founded on firmer stuff than garage-sale pickings. She's hard to reconcile with the older sister in front of me who just wants to *hang out*.

"Aren't you at all eager to get out of our parents' house?" The question jumps out at me.

"Why? Should I be?" While her voice remains light, for once I catch an undercurrent to her easygoing friendliness. She doesn't sound upset. It's more like she's challenging me. Daring her little sister to tell her she knows better.

I know it's not my place. Jamie's her own person, and I have no right to judge her or direct her on how to lead her life. Even if I find her choices entirely baffling. What's more,

I have enough to keep on top of in my own life. "No," I say. "Just curious. Good luck with the guitar."

I leave her room, wracking my memory. I'm trying to recall if I ever knew this version of Jamie when she lived here before college. When I was in elementary school, Jamie was definitely larger than life, vivacious, with plenty of friends and interests. I remember her running the Fairview literary magazine and submitting poetry to state contests, biting her nails before Ivy League decisions, canvasing for our representatives in elections for Congress. The memories I have don't include this freewheeling nothingness.

It's frightening, in a way. I return to my room, closing the door and reopening my calculus book. My memories of Jamie in high school don't differ much from what my own high school days look like, filled with projects and pursuits. If it's possible for Jamie's life to implode into Netflix and neighborhood walks, it's possible for *mine* to, despite my every effort. I don't want to work this hard to be mature in high school only to end up a perpetual teenager.

I shut my door just in time to hear my dad walk into Jamie's room. I hear laughing, then he must plug the amp back in, because a moment later, the guitar screeches to life.

# Fourteen

**I CHECK MY PHONE,** irritated. My driver's ed instructor is late. I'm not pleased I'm doing this with my Saturday in the first place, not when I could've used the coming hour to research reunion venues. Driver's ed will consist of three hour-long lessons over the next three weeks, each one consuming priceless weekend work time. Last night, I stayed up scouring YouTube for everything I could find on past Fairview reunions. Venues, decorations, the works. When I got used to the nauseating shaky-cam footage of the videos, what I found wasn't encouraging. These reunions have a high standard for extravagance and formality. It's not like they're black tie, but Fairview alums will expect more than some streamers in the San Mateo Community Center.

I don't know how Ethan and I will pull this off. I *do* know driver's ed won't help.

Compulsively clicking my phone screen on and off, I sit in the front room, watching the driveway from the cushioned bench under the windows where the sun filters in from the front yard. Wandering past from the kitchen, Mom frowns when she notices me. "You're sure you don't want to practice with me before your lesson?"

"We practiced over the summer," I say shortly.

"Oh, baby girl, you were so bad." She's trying to sound sympathetic, but she can't hide the bluntness of her honesty.

"I was not."

Mom shifts, watching me dryly. She's in head-to-toe Lululemon, fresh from the yoga she does to unwind on weekends. "You almost crashed when there wasn't anything even near you," she says.

I grimace. That did happen. It was intimidating the few times I got behind the wheel. The perspective of everything felt off-kilter from the driver's seat of Mom's SUV, leaving me with the irresistible impulse to veer into the middle of the road. The memory is contributing to my nerves, and I restlessly lock and unlock my phone screen on the couch. "You're exaggerating," I protest, not needing the reminder of my inexperience before my lesson.

"I've literally never exaggerated in my life," my mom declares.

I cut her a look. "Say I *was* bad. It was probably because of your teaching. I need a professional."

Just then, the dented and dinged vehicle I'm guessing will be mine for the next hour pulls into the driveway. From the rolled-down windows, Bon Jovi blares. The car is missing both hubcaps on one side, and the sticker for IN THE DRIVER'S

SEAT is faded and peeling. A Latino man wearing a red Spider-Man shirt is driving. He looks to be in his late twenties.

I walk outside, Mom trailing behind. When I reach the car, the guy turns down the volume barely low enough to be heard. "Hey," he calls. "You Alison Sanger?"

"Yeah," I say, examining the interior of the car. It's clean up front but a battleground of water bottles and sweatshirts in back.

"Sorry I was late. The girl before you had a minor panic attack on the off-ramp. We're cool, though. My name's Hector. You ready to go?" Hector taps the wheel with his thumb.

Mom walks up beside me, giving the dented car a once-over. "This'll be great," she says brightly, then heads back toward the house, clearly not at all concerned with the visible evidence of the accidents the car's been in.

Hector exits the car, holding the door for me. "Oh," I say haltingly, "am I driving?" The prospect hits my stomach with a little lurch. I hate that learning such an everyday skill is making me nervous.

"Yeah," Hector confirms. "Wild, right?"

I pause in the driver's door. "I don't have a ton of experience. What if I kill you?"

Hector opens the passenger door and gets in. "How about you don't, though?"

I sit down in the driver's seat. The cloth scratches my shoulders, and I awkwardly place my hands on the worn rubber of the wheel. I can handle college interviews with CEOs and three-hour exams, but driving? It's been a while since

I've done something I didn't already excel at. I don't love the feeling of incompetence stealing over me.

"Nah, you won't kill me," Hector says. "I have my own gas and brakes. See?" He shifts his feet, gesturing. I glance under the dashboard on his side and notice he's wearing Birkenstocks with his basketball shorts. "First step, turn on the car. Oh shit, sorry," he adds, realizing the car's already on. He reaches over and removes the keys, then hands them to me. "Okay, first step. Turn on the car."

I rotate the key in the ignition, feeling the engine hum to life.

"Now?" Hector prompts.

"Mirrors?" I venture.

Hector nods. "Rad. But also put him in reverse."

"Him?" I repeat.

Hector places one hand lovingly on the curve of the door handle. "It's kind of creepy every dude refers to his car as a 'she.'" I don't have the chance to agree. "Okay," he continues, "so now you're going to ease him in reverse down the driveway while looking for cross traffic and pedestrians." Hector speaks quickly, one thought proceeding fluidly into the next.

I peer into the mirror, concentrating, and lift my foot hesitantly off the brake. We start to roll down the driveway.

"Was that your mom?" Hector asks.

I don't reply, focusing instead on the reversing. The movement is at once familiar, the prologue to hundreds of mornings driving to school with Mom, and incredibly alien.

Finally, I reach the street, stopping on the pavement. "Yeah," I answer him.

"Okay, now you want to shift to drive, and we're off." Hector's fingers drum on his knee, and I can tell his reckless energy isn't well contained within work days cooped up in this little Honda. "Anywhere you want to go?"

"What do you mean?"

"Shit, like"—he shrugs—"if you have errands or whatever. Or we can just drive in circles. Hey, you hungry?"

"I guess," I say. I'm not, really. I'm just hoping the reply quiets Hector. Right now, I'm working very hard to avoid veering into the curb. Pressing the gas pedal down gently, I feel fortunate the wide avenue is free of other cars. Nevertheless, every familiar feature of the neighborhood, the knotted trunks of the trees, the BMWs and Range Rovers in the driveways I'm passing, feels newly intimidating, obstacles to watch out for instead of the comforting imagery of home.

"Awesome. You want to go to Dairy Queen?" Hector proposes this like it's what he's had in mind all along. "You ever had a Blizzard?"

I wrinkle my noise, wishing Hector would let me concentrate. "No," I say. In truth, I'm not 100 percent certain what a Blizzard is.

"Then you have to try one. Turn left here," he instructs without warning. We've come to the first traffic light of the drive, the one leading to the Starbucks I walk to. A couple cars have come up behind me. I roll calmly into the intersection,

my blinker on, and one of the cars honks as I gradually finish the turn. Hector doesn't comment on the honking, which
means he's either not concerned or not paying attention.
"Your mom seemed laid back," he says.

I'm guessing moms usually interrogate the driving
instructor, wanting to know routes and vehicle details and
whether the freeway will be involved. Not my mom. "You
could say that," I reply. "She's been pushing me to get my
license since, like, the day I turned sixteen."

Hector nods, chuckling. "Turn right here," he commands.

I do, feeling grateful there's no one behind me.

"Nice. Much better than last time. Feel free to step off the
gas and let him coast to stops instead of braking. Reluctant
driver?" he asks, returning to the previous conversation
without pause. His fingers continue their incessant rhythm
on his knees, and I have the feeling he wants to reach for the
radio and is deferring to my painfully obvious discomfort in
the driver's seat. "I get it," he continues. "Let me guess. Honor
roll kid?"

"Yeah," I confirm—a little annoyed to be called merely
*honor roll*, but whatever. I'm too concentrated on the road to
explain I'm going to be *valedictorian*.

"It's always the overachievers who put off driving. Okay,
the DQ's up here." Hector points. "We're going to do the
drive-thru."

The Dairy Queen emerges on my right. The plastic sign
with the red-and-white logo occupies the front wall of the
nondescript building. White metal fences encircle the low

hedges, with openings for the drive-thru. On the front patio, a kid in a hoodie fiddles with his phone at one of the blue tables. I'm familiar with the Dairy Queen's reputation for being the hangout for band kids and burnouts.

"I'm a Royal New York Cheesecake man," Hector starts while I guide the car into the drive-thru. "It's all about the strawberry center. I also like the Rocky Road, and the Oreo is classic. I wasn't into the Peanut Butter Cookie Dough Smash. It could just require a couple more tries, though."

I say nothing. I'm realizing it's easier with Hector to just let him talk instead of following the conversation.

We roll up to the ordering window. The employee working the register doesn't look in our direction. "What're you having?"

Hector leans over the center console to speak out the window. "Daniel, hey," he says. "Good to see you." I wonder if Hector read Daniel's name tag, or if he comes here often enough to be on a first-name basis with the employees. Either way, it's weird, but not the weirdest thing I've noticed about Hector. "I'll have the Royal New York Cheesecake," he tells Daniel, then turns to me. "What do you want? I'm not going to buy it for you, obviously, it'd be kind of inappropriate. If you have cash, though . . ."

"I'm okay. I don't know if I'm up for eating while driving on my first day." If Hector hears the light judgment in my voice, he doesn't react.

"I got you." He nods. "Next lesson." I honestly don't know if he's joking.

He pays, and Daniel reappears with the Blizzard, flipping the paper cup upside-down robotically before handing over the ice cream. I drive forward. Hector's quiet for once while he eats.

"I went to high school with that guy," he says out of nowhere after some minutes have passed.

"Who?" My confusion distracts me, and I nearly roll past the stop sign into the intersection. The car shudders to a halt when Hector hits his own brakes. With the lurch comes a little jolt of fear. *This is why I don't like driving.*

"Daniel," Hector says, ignoring our sudden stop. "The Dairy Queen guy. I had ceramics with him junior year."

I remember Daniel's distant demeanor. It's kind of odd he betrayed no recognition of Hector. Then again, I reconsider, I probably won't remember every random classmate in ten years. It's Hector who's unusual for remembering this dude from one ceramics class he took.

We keep driving. With every turn and lane change, I find myself feeling more comfortable. Hector gives me random directions and sporadic instruction while peppering me with questions on what TV shows I watch. When I say I don't watch TV—which is true, not just me trying to prevent further conversation—he proceeds to recount the entire first season of *Westworld*. It's confusing, but it's not bad background noise while we circle endless streets of small supermarkets, veterinarians, and churches, and every possible view of the country club's golf course.

At the end of the hour, Hector directs me into a residential neighborhood I distantly recognize. "Pull in here." He nods toward one of the houses on the right. "We're picking up the next student."

I effortfully navigate into the driveway. "Why don't you just pick them up after you've dropped me off?" I press the brake hard, then put the car into park, a bit proud of myself for finding the right gear.

"Because then I'd have to double back," Hector informs me. "His house is on the way."

I grudgingly understand the logic in what he's saying, despite my displeasure at having one more person in this car chatting with Hector while I drive home. My antipathy is nothing in comparison to what I feel when the house's door swings shut and I look up.

Ethan walks out. *Of course.*

Without driving to distract me, I realize I recognize the house. The white clapboard with white trim, the large square windows, and a wide lawn. I definitely don't visit Ethan's house frequently—I don't remember Dante popping habitually back into Hell in *The Divine Comedy*, either. The times I have been forced to Ethan's home were for group projects and ASG work. Watching him walk onto the porch, I'm filled again with the feeling I got in our meeting with Williams. Like I'll never escape him, no matter what I'm doing.

I note his expression before he sees me. He's his usual blend of bored and skeptical. Then his eyes find mine, and his grimace mirrors my own.

Solemnly, he walks to the back seat. When he slides in, he

says nothing. I say nothing. It's like everything with Ethan. We're even competing over who can say the least.

"Hey, Ethan," says Hector.

"Hector," Ethan replies, like an asshole.

Hector twists in his seat, facing Ethan. "Excited for the freeway?"

"Thrilled. What's she doing here?" His voice is distinctly *not* thrilled.

"She's just my previous session," Hector says easily, oblivious to the nuclear war of disdainful passivity I'm currently waging with Ethan. "She's driving home, and then you'll be behind the wheel."

"Oh, it's okay," I say. "I'll walk home." I don't mention it's nearly a thirty-minute walk to my house. Exercise is good for me, and so is limiting my exposure to Ethan.

"No can do." Hector shakes his head. "You have to finish your lesson."

I fume, formulating my rebuttal. It's Ethan who finds one first. "Is she really going to learn anything in ten minutes of surface streets?" It's strange having Ethan on my side. In this, however, we have the same objective.

Hector looks from me to Ethan, Ethan to me. Understanding flits into his eyes, and I prepare for the worst. "Do you two know each other or something?"

Ethan doesn't respond. I don't either for a moment. "We go to school together," I say shortly when it's clear Ethan's just going to sit there stone-faced. I glance in the mirror, catching his eyes. "Why don't you have your license yet?" I can't comprehend my misfortune that we're in driver's ed at the exact same time.

"My parents won't let me until I turn eighteen," he replies coolly. "I've timed this course to line up perfectly with my birthday."

This checks out. Ethan's birthday is in a couple weeks, on March 27. He throws himself a party every year, no doubt to revel in his popularity with the incongruous segments of the school who like him. Rebecca Markey hosted a year ago, two months into her and Ethan's relationship, only for Ethan to dump with her weeks later.

"Why don't you have yours?" he asks, studying me in the rearview mirror.

"None of your business," I snap. Ethan smirks, evidently delighted with the weakness of my retort. I focus firmly on Ethan's driveway in front of me, knowing if I dwell on the laughter in Ethan's eyes, I'll leap out of the car immediately.

Hector smiles. "Oh, I get it," he says.

I'm confused for an instant until I realize exactly what he thinks he's gotten. Then I'm filled with horror anticipating the conversation we're about to have. Glancing in the mirror, I confirm Ethan's come to the same conclusion. His posture's rigid, one hand clenched stiffly, like he's just heard someone laugh at a funeral.

"What exactly do you get?" he grinds out.

"You're exes, right?" Hector says.

Ethan and I speak simultaneously, a chorus of disdain and denial. "*No*," I say. "Of course not," Ethan says.

Hector's grin widens. "Oh, good. I would have rearranged the schedule to avoid putting exes in the car together. Regardless, legally, I have to see you to your front door."

From the levity in Hector's voice, I know he's not convinced Ethan and I don't have history. While I very, very much want to dissuade him of this notion, I know continuing this conversation in the car will only waste time, not to mention give off the impression I'm working *too* hard to deny it. I've heard enough times how Ethan's and my rivalry masks some unfulfilled sexual tension. It doesn't. The only hope I have is getting home as soon as possible.

I put the car in reverse, preparing to back out of Ethan's driveway. Easy. I release the brake, reminding myself I've done this already today. Then I catch Ethan's eyes in the mirror. Everything goes to hell—I remember he's watching and judging everything I'm doing, and I'm distracted enough not to notice the car whizzing past the curb in front of Ethan's house. Hector slams on his brake, and we bump forward and back with the car's momentum.

"Always check your mirrors for cross traffic when you're backing out," Hector counsels calmly.

"Yeah, Sanger," Ethan says. "Check your mirrors."

I glare daggers dipped in sulfuric acid at him in the rearview. *You're the absolute worst,* I want to say. Instead, I hold firm in my resolve not to continue our war in front of Hector. Ethan seems to understand this, the corners of his mouth turning up when I leer wordlessly.

Looking in the mirrors, I pointedly avoid Ethan's

reflection, instead focusing on the road out the rear window. I head for home, finding my way to the main streets.

Hector speaks up, continuing with his constant chatter. "Do you guys have any classes together?"

"Some," Ethan says.

"*Every* class," I correct him.

"That's a lot," Hector says. His finger-drumming has changed into fidgeting in his seat, like there's no energy created or destroyed with Hector, only converted into new, disruptive forms. "How does that even happen? Wait, does that mean Alison is on the newspaper with you?"

The question gives me pause. I wouldn't have expected Ethan to discuss the *Chronicle* with Hector. Briefly, I wonder what he said. "I'm the editor in chief, actually," I cut in, wanting to head off whatever insulting characterization of our working relationship Ethan's surely about to offer, and to reassert my superiority in the wake of the driveway fiasco.

"I didn't want the job," Ethan replies casually.

I whirl to face him. "Whoa, eyes on the road, girl," Hector interjects. Guiltily, I revert my attention to the road, where I find I'm a bit close to the bumper of the Prius in front of me.

Recovering my composure, I ignore Ethan watching gleefully from the back seat. "As if you'd have gotten the job over me." Part of me is glad Ethan didn't go for editor in chief. Not because I have the slightest doubt I would've beaten him, but because I'm not certain the competition wouldn't have ended in homicide.

"I guess we'll never know," Ethan says.

"No, we do know. You wouldn't have won."

He shrugs.

"You're too self-absorbed to be editor in chief," I insist.

Hector laughs, interrupting us. "You guys remind me of myself in high school." I don't have to see Ethan's face to know his expression of doubt matches my own. Hector, fortunately, seems not to notice. "I was copresident of the Settlers of Catan Club with this guy AJ," he continues. "The power struggles were constant. We were best buds, though."

"I'm guessing you didn't keep in touch," I say, picking up on the past tense.

Hector's face falls a little. "Unfortunately, I haven't seen him in years," he says, something distant in his still-upbeat voice.

"Unfortunate," I echo, happily imagining a future where Ethan and I are as estranged. The feeling ranks right up there with the idea of getting my Harvard diploma, winning a Pulitzer, or establishing world peace. It's one more reason I won't be sorry when high school ends.

We round the corner onto my street, and I pull up in front of my house.

"Good job today, Alison," Hector says, sounding like he means it. Putting the car in park, I get out, eager to escape the confines of the vehicle with Ethan, who does the same. "I'll see you at the same time next week," Hector adds. "We'll work on unprotected lefts."

I speak up immediately. "Well, could we—"

Hector shakes his head. "We can't reschedule. You don't have to thank me now," he says, sounding extravagantly generous. "But one day, when you're eating Blizzards and perfectly executing unprotected lefts, you and Ethan will remember the ten minutes you spent together in Hector's car in driver's ed. You can thank me then."

It's a conversation-ender if I've ever heard one. "Right," I say glumly.

Ethan steps past me into the driver's seat and shuts the door sharply, probably hoping he'll slam my fingertips. He starts the car swiftly and drives forward. "Does Fairview still have the Settlers of Catan Club?" Hector asks before they're out of earshot.

Walking inside the house, I head directly to my room, overhearing the laugh track of whatever Jamie's watching and feeling relieved she doesn't intercept me. My work is waiting for me in my room. The items on my whiteboard remain imposingly undone. I pause in front of my desk, feeling something disconcerting. Usually I like the pressure of long lists of objectives, pages of reading, projects planned in need of execution. I like the hectic days, the demanding nights.

Right now, I'm just overwhelmed. The sunset cuts through my window, seeming to taunt me with the hour I lost getting nothing done. What I didn't need was to waste more time fighting with Ethan. His constant presence in my life is frustrating. Not the familiar frustration of Ethan, either, like traffic on the way to school and teachers with bad penmanship. *Really* frustrating.

It's exhausting. In the past, our battles were energizing, even occasionally inspiring. Tonight, I'm only weary from spending the last hour going in circles, literally and figuratively, driving miles and miles and going nowhere.

# Fifteen

HOURS LATER, I'M STARING at my whiteboard. Faced with my overburdened funk, I decided tackling my work was kind of like a fever—unpleasant, yet sometimes necessary. Each individual task will keep my mind off the enormous accumulation of them waiting for me.

I'm doing financial budgeting for the reunion, figuring out how we'll host two hundred people on $8,000. From my extensive internet research, I've learned costs stack up quickly. Every thousand dollars really counts. Which is why I need to know exactly what we have, not Principal Williams's estimate. Adam Elliot has not replied to my four emails, and he's the only one who knows the precise number.

It's time for me to change that. Dropping onto my desk chair, I open my computer and pull up the enterprising journalist's greatest ally—Google. Finding Adam's cell phone number requires resourcefulness and fifteen minutes of vigorous searching. I prevail when I have the idea to search his name in connection with Harvard student organizations he was part of when he was an undergrad. Finally, I find his number listed on the flyer for a Harvard Sports Analysts Club event.

I call the number. On the second ring, he picks up.

"Elliot here." The voice is low, round. Bro-y, basically.

"Hello," I say. "This is Alison Sanger from Fairview. I think Principal Williams mentioned me. I'm taking over the reunion planning for your class. I sent you a couple emails regarding current finances but haven't heard back." One thing I've learned from journalism—other than effective googling—is not to let people cut you off before you've explained your purpose.

"Oh, yeah," Adam replies distractedly. Hearing the whoosh of wind and the murmur of street conversation over the phone, I figure he's walking from his Uber to drinks, client facetime, et cetera, et cetera—whatever's keeping him from replying to my emails. "I think Williams left me a voicemail about that. What's your name again?"

"Alison," I repeat.

"Right. Why don't you ping my assistant with your ideas. We'll make final decisions and handle booking."

I rub my eyes, forcing my voice level. "Actually," I say, "Williams was pretty clear we would handle everything."

"Look, kid—" Adam starts.

"It's Alison," I cut him off.

Adam pauses. I can practically hear him weighing his

irritation with proper phone decorum. "Alison," he amends, "I'm sure you're bright, but I'm not certain a high school student should be in charge of an event this big."

Fuming, I pace from one end of my room to the other. I'm grateful we're on the phone, because if we were face-to-face, I wouldn't have the wherewithal to hide my fury. Adam's only ten years older than I am, and even he acts patronizing and reads incompetence into my youth. I wish I had a recording of this conversation to rub in Williams's face.

Except it would get me nowhere with our obstinate principal. Just like it would only piss Adam off to point out I'm not the one who booked the wrong date with a nonrefundable deposit. I remind myself of the purpose of this call. I need information, and Adam won't give me the numbers if I insult him.

Working my hardest not to hate this part, I put on the voice I use for college interviews and uncooperative sources. "Mr. Elliot, as such an influential and successful alumnus of Fairview, you surely have much more important demands on your time. I read in *Forbes's* 30 Under 30 you're expanding your cryptocurrency to the nonprofit world."

Adam's voice changes, becoming more welcoming. "Wait, I remember now. Williams mentioned wanting me to put in a good word for you at Harvard."

"I would be . . ." I swallow. "Honored."

"How about this," Adam continues brightly, like of course I'd be honored, like it's a foregone conclusion. "You handle the booking, then hit my assistant with regular reports on your purchases. Just to check your numbers. If everything lines up, you'll get your recommendation."

"Wow. Thank you," I say, watching myself in the mirror through the doorway to my bathroom. While I force my voice into reverence, my expression remains flat. "So . . . if you wouldn't mind, can you give me an exact account balance?"

"Hold on," he says. I hear rustling over the line, which I'm hoping is Adam searching his email. His voice returns seconds later. "$7,855.66. I have a call coming in," he continues hurriedly. "Follow up if you have any questions, kid."

"Thank you—" I begin, but he's already hung up.

Ignoring Adam's parting comment, I return to my whiteboard. Once I've written the number in the reunion quadrant in heavy, clear numerals, I bite my lip. It's even worse than Williams told us. We're going to have to budget *very* conservatively. I begin outlining breakdowns on the board, putting projections to each item.

While I'm working, my phone buzzes. I ignore the faint noise, focusing on my mental math. Then it buzzes again, humming on the desk next to me. I exhale, annoyed to be interrupted. With the numbers in front of me, the task feels even more daunting. Nevertheless, I check my phone's illuminated screen, surprised when I find Ethan's name on the messages.

Curiosity gets the better of me. Ethan and I don't text unless strictly necessary. I pick up the phone, flicking Ethan's messages open with my thumb.

Found a venue I'm interested in. The
Willingham Hotel.

I have a walkthrough scheduled with the
coordinator tomorrow. I'll let you know how it
goes.

I reply immediately.

What time?

My message floats up into the conversation window not even a minute from when I got Ethan's. I know he's there. I know he's reading. But there's no reply. Not even the typing bubble on his end. With queasy anger, I realize what's going on here. What Ethan's orchestrating. He wants to meet with the events coordinator on his own, establish the relationship, and usurp me from securing the venue despite our uneasy compromise to plan everything together.

He's made one mistake, however. He told me the name of the hotel.

I walk quickly to my computer and google the Willingham Hotel without bothering to sit down. It's nearly eight, which means the events coordinator won't be in the office. Instead, I find the front desk number—no Harvard undergrad organizations required—and call.

When the receptionist picks up with a calmly welcoming "Willingham Hotel," I check whether the events coordinator went home, the thought occurring to me this is exactly why Ethan chose to text me now. The receptionist confirms the coordinator is gone for the day, which is when I unravel a version of the truth. My partner *forgot* to write down the time of the walkthrough he scheduled tomorrow—he's *awful* with numbers—and could the receptionist please find the events coordinator's calendar and check when Ethan Molloy is supposed to come in?

It works. Following one very obliging "Hold please" and several minutes, the receptionist's voice returns to the phone. She tells me our appointment is tomorrow at eleven. I thank her profusely and hang up, a little thrilled I got what I needed.

Refocusing on the finances, I feel myself smiling. Despite how much I don't want to be working with Ethan on the reunion, the thought of his face when I meet him in front of the Willingham Hotel right on time tomorrow is the tiniest sliver of a silver lining.

I feel a quiet rush of validation. Whatever Adam Elliot thinks, I'm clever and professional enough to coax cooperation out of him, and to outthink Ethan. I pick up my dry-erase marker, filling in blanks and checking boxes. Right now, the numbers on the board don't feel quite so daunting.

# Sixteen

I HEAD INTO SAN Francisco the next day for the Willingham Hotel walkthrough. My Uber driver, Robert, remains quiet, nodding his head to the easygoing R&B he's playing. In the back seat of his 2013 Honda Insight—I've learned more varieties of compact consumer cars from riding Uber than I ever wanted to know—I focus on meditative breathing in preparation for meeting with Ethan. The freeway flies by in the window.

We're passing the Bay on the right. It's beautiful, the spring sunlight glittering on the water, the wakes of boats crisscrossing foamy lines on the surface. Heading into the city, I watch the fences and greenery of the suburbs gradually cede to hectic street corners and finally the skyscrapers of the Financial District. It's funny how I live close to the city, yet I feel like a tourist. It's not uncomfortable, though. I find it refreshing to remember there's a wider world out there than Fairview and fighting with Ethan.

We pull up to the curb, and I tip Robert on my phone. I have a small monthly allowance from my parents that goes almost entirely toward Uber rides and desperation coffee. When I run out of funds, I generally have to plead with Dylan to drive me to ASG events and study sessions. She got her license the second she could, and while she used to love any excuse to drive, now she's started giving me lectures on how she doesn't like to "enable" me.

When I get out of the car, the Willingham Hotel looms in front of me. Right away, I know the meditative breathing was for nothing. Ethan should have known this hotel is way out of our budget. I note the elegant columns flanking the front entrance, the carved stone ornamentation over every window, the spiraled hedges out front. The Willingham caters to investment fund managers courting clients, not overworked high schoolers organizing a reunion for inebriated alumni. Which Ethan could've deduced from reading the hotel's website even once, like I did, instead of rushing in to outdo me.

I'm watching the valet gingerly open the doors of a Rolls-Royce when I hear my name behind me. "Sanger?" Ethan's voice is skeptical, not quite surprised. I turn, finding him wearing one of his interchangeable preppy outfits, white shorts, canvas sneakers, and an untucked sky-blue button-down. His features are rigid, like he's hiding frustration. "I'm almost certain I didn't tell you when this meeting was," he says.

"You didn't," I reply simply, then walk past the doorman holding the door into the hotel.

The lobby is no less obviously opulent, with high ceilings, marble floors, and elaborate rugs with swooping geometric designs. I approach the front desk. While I tell the receptionist we have an appointment with the events coordinator, I feel Ethan fuming, his resentment practically palpable. But at this point, he can't kick me out.

The coordinator, a fashionable woman named Sarah, escorts us into the ballroom, describing features other events have incorporated into the wide, chandeliered space. Photo booths, live bands, chocolate fountains, specialty top-shelf cocktails. I nod like they're not way out of our budget. When the tour ends, I ask the price, and Sarah says $7,000—with no bar or food. From her haughty tone and bland expression, I know she's not taking us seriously. It annoys me because I know she was disappointed when she saw how young we are, but truthfully I can't be too upset. She's right. We can't afford this. I thank her and walk outside, Ethan following me wordlessly.

When we reach the patio in front of the hotel, I round on him. "Are you out of your mind?" I ask incredulously, earning a startled glance from the doorman. "$7,000 without any food or entertainment or anything?"

Ethan doesn't meet my eyes. "In my defense, they didn't put the price online."

I wave in the general direction of the hotel's facade. "Come on, Ethan. Did you really need the price written out for you? This place has Kylie Jenner in their photo gallery."

He half shrugs, his expression empty. Not the forced

emptiness of someone hiding their emotions, either. Ethan looks apathetic.

It infuriates me in the way only Ethan's capable of. I charge on. "Why don't you just let me handle the venue? It's not like you actually care about any of this." I'm not just saying it to usurp him, but because I honestly don't understand.

Ethan's eyes flit to mine now, glinting gray-green in the sun. "I don't?"

"You don't," I repeat. "Sometimes I think you don't care about anything." It's the puzzle of Ethan, the enigma he's encircled with walls of clever retorts and constant competitiveness and his overly polished appearance. I don't know what he *wants*. It's absurd to imagine he works endless hours on homework, *Chronicle* articles, and ASG motions just for fun, but I've seen nothing to suggest he has any real goal outside our competition.

Standing in front of the Willingham Hotel, I realize I didn't mean to present this existential inquiry directly to him. His apathetic reactions and carelessness in planning this obviously wrong walkthrough just sparked something in me, and the words exploded out.

Ethan's watching me harder now. "I care about beating you," he says.

"That's not caring about something," I reply. "That's what you use to fill the absence of caring about something. It's a pastime, not a pursuit."

He scoffs. "What would you know about it?" I read defensiveness in the way he shoves his hands in his pockets.

"I could be wrong." I raise an eyebrow, wanting now to press him. "Name me one thing you care about other than our rivalry?"

Ethan opens his mouth. I wait for his proof I'm wrong, wait for him to reveal he's really into international diplomacy or collecting vinyl or underwater basket-weaving. Nothing comes out, and he closes his mouth a moment later. His eyes narrow, the vehemence I find in them unusual even for us. "We're not friends," he declares. "I don't need to satisfy your curiosity. It doesn't matter what you know or don't know about me."

He's deflecting, and flimsily. It bothers me. Not because I *at all* want to be his friend, but because I want an answer to my question, and I know I won't get one. The uncertainty bothers me more than I'd like to admit. However much I hate Ethan, I'm invested in our rivalry, and I fear it's nothing but a game to him, interchangeable with his other empty whims. I don't like to imagine I've sunk hours of my life competing with someone who sees me and everything I care about as just *fun*.

"Obviously, we're not friends," I fire back. "But we still have to plan this ridiculous event together. It took me thirty seconds on the Willingham website to know this place would never work. Fortunately, I scheduled a walkthrough with a more *realistic* venue for fifteen minutes from now. Come with me or don't," I say. "I don't care."

Ethan furrows his brow. "Come with you where?"

# Seventeen

**THE MILLARD FILLMORE HOTEL** is—well, it's not the Willingham. We stop in front of the shady edifice fifteen minutes later, and even I'm discouraged when I see the state of the place in person. It's a stout Victorian hotel, and from the paint peeling off the shingles on the gaudy spired roofs and the warping of the window glass, I have no doubt the place was constructed in the literal Victorian era. The building's unique appearance could theoretically be cool if anyone had taken care of it in the past hundred years.

We walked over from the Willingham in acidic silence, the kind you can *feel* corroding your emotional fortitude and patience. I distracted myself by resolutely studying the streets, realizing I'm unfamiliar with the heart of San Francisco. For a city focused on creativity and innovation, it wears history well, stone multistories sitting proudly among the skyscrapers and a quick gradient from steel and slate into quaintly colorful Victorian houses. I could comfortably ignore Ethan until we wound up here, in front of the Millard Fillmore.

It's his turn to throw me a disbelieving look, which I ignore. Holding my head high, I walk in, Ethan on my heels. Grayish carpet that could have been any color twenty years ago runs end to end in the small lobby, and on my right there's a wide arch opening onto the ballroom. What I realize is a senior citizens' speed-dating event is underway in the unadorned room, elderly people in pairs crossing from table to table in a sort of slow musical chairs.

"You can't be serious," Ethan says next to me.

"I am serious. And fiscally responsible." I head for the empty reception desk, passing the archway where couples are now exchanging loud introductions.

Leaning on the reception desk, Ethan inspects the room, his expression dubious. His eyes settle on what even I will admit is a very weird piece of art, a portrait of people with insect limbs protruding from their coat sleeves. "What even is this place?" he asks, looking a little revolted.

I don't have the chance to reply. Someone steps out from the office behind the reception desk, his face lighting up when he sees me. "You must be Alison." He extends his hand warmly. He looks like he's in his sixties, wearing clothing coherent with the overall aesthetic of this hotel. "I'm Clint."

"Hi, Clint," I say, shaking his hand. "This is my partner, Ethan." Ethan shakes Clint's hand with visible hesitancy.

"Welcome to the Millard Fillmore," Clint says.

Ethan snorts. I close my eyes, wishing he could for once not be a dickhead.

"You think our thirteenth president is a joke?" Clint scrutinizes Ethan, his voice defensive.

"The joke is naming a hotel after one of the most forgettable presidents in history," Ethan replies, looking unfazed. Consciously, I know this should mortify me, but I've known Ethan long enough to become desensitized to his impressive rudeness.

Clint makes the wise decision to ignore Ethan and faces me instead. "You're a lot younger than you sounded on the phone."

I grit my teeth, really hoping this won't come up with every single person we deal with. "Will that be a problem?"

"Not at all. It's refreshing to find young people with this kind of commitment." He gestures to the two of us. I nod, uncomprehending. Commitment to event planning? "I married my Annabelle right out of high school," Clint continues.

Not following, I stay silent. Ethan's expression, however, shifts viciously.

"Sanger and I are *not* getting married," he says.

*Oh no.* The implications of Clint's words crash into place in my mind. *Married out of high school. This kind of commitment.* In a rush of images that rival the car-crash footage they have on the online driver's ed course, I imagine walking gracefully into my wedding to find Ethan waiting there, smirking, hoping he outdid me by writing more poetic vows. We wouldn't be able to agree on a honeymoon location. He'd likely choose somewhere with history he'd insist he knew in more detail, while getting facts wrong left and right. It would be insufferable.

Not to mention the wedding night. We'd critique each other endlessly, rush to finish, fight over who got to do what. I shut off the picture before the very idea of sex is ruined for me for life.

While I'm corralling my thoughts to correct Clint's very wrong impression, Clint preempts me, looking confused. "This isn't a wedding you're considering booking here?"

"You have weddings here?" Ethan asks doubtfully. He glances around the room like he's unable to imagine a pair of humans on earth who would celebrate their union at the Millard Fillmore.

"All the time," Clint replies genially.

Ethan turns to me, his horror changing to indignation. "You told him you were planning a wedding? *For us?*"

"Yes, Ethan. I told him we were getting married, because we're just so in love. I can't wait to spend the rest of my life with you," I deadpan. "*Of course* I didn't say we were planning a wedding."

Clint chimes in. "Come to think of it, you didn't mention on the phone what type of event you were booking. When you introduced your partner, I put it together."

"Well, you put it together incorrectly." Ethan's voice is beyond typical levels of exasperation. He sounds genuinely offended.

Clint's eyes narrow. "You'd be surprised how many couples

come in here trying to convince me their wedding is an intimate gathering, family celebration, or whatnot. Anything to
avoid the extra wedding vendor fees."

"It's not a wedding," I protest. "Honestly. It's a high school
reunion."

This seems only to increase Clint's suspicion. "You don't
look old enough to have a high school reunion."

"But we look old enough to get *married*?" Ethan interjects.

"We're planning the reunion on behalf of our school," I
say calmly, not wanting Ethan to scare off the one hotel in
our price range. He's done enough damage. "It's not for us."

Clint eyes me, seemingly unconvinced. Before he has the
chance to question my explanation, Ethan jumps in, help-
fully for once. "Could we just have the walkthrough?"

Clint nods. "Follow me." He leads us into the ballroom,
where the seniors' dating event continues. I examine the
room from an economical, logistical perspective, imagining
the bar on one end, the name tag table on the other. "Our
great room can fit two hundred and twenty guests," Clint
continues, "with plenty of room for a DJ or live band, ban-
quet dinner . . ." He throws us a meaningful look. "Sweetheart
table."

Ethan closes his eyes, clearly wishing for death.

"The hotel kitchen can cater, or you can use your own
caterers," Clint goes on. "We won't even charge a cake-cutting
fee."

I force my voice level. "Reunions don't typically involve
cake cutting."

Clint shrugs noncommittally. With a small swell of hope, I notice Ethan looks like he might really be considering the venue. He walks into the center of the room, facing the far wall. "Is there room for a photo booth here?" he asks.

I startle. "Wait, what? We're not doing a photo booth." I realize a second later he's gotten the idea from the Willingham coordinator and abruptly decided it's worth pursuing. It's just like the stickers on his computer, like everything he does, like the collection of whims he calls himself.

"We are, actually," he replies simply.

"We don't have the money for a photo booth." I'm giving him the fakest cheery warning voice, the one your parents use when they're reminding each other of a fight not to pick in front of the guests.

Ethan pretends to consider. It is 100 percent certain he knows exactly what fight he's picking. "If we host the reunion here we'll have enough money." The reasonableness in his voice is as pretend as my own.

"Money we'll use on other, *necessary* things." I feel my resolve not to alarm Clint fraying, the composure in my voice wobbling precariously. Ethan's done everything he could to ruin this meeting short of lighting the hotel on fire, while I've kept it together in hopes of checking the venue item off our list without blowing our budget. I don't know how much more I can handle while maintaining my composure. There's something about Ethan that makes me work twice as hard to be mature.

Having evidently had enough of this conversation, Ethan

turns to Clint. "Do you have the room for a photo booth or not?"

"Don't answer," I instruct Clint, glaring at Ethan. "It's irrelevant. It's a ridiculous question."

When Clint doesn't reply, I pull my eyes from Ethan and find Clint regarding us with concern. "You know, like I said, we have couples come through here often. It's not difficult to tell which relationships have real foundation. Watching the pair of you . . ." He pauses, then continues gravely. "You two may want to consider counseling."

# Eighteen

**WE LEFT THE MILLARD** Fillmore with Ethan in denial despite the $6,000 price tag, including food and drink. Exasperated, I issued him a challenge. Either he finds a comparably priced venue not booked on the date of the reunion in two months, or I'll put down the deposit with Clint. It's not like I care where we have the reunion. While I don't love the idea of Ethan finding the place we end up using, I honestly don't think he'll succeed. I did the research, and I know there aren't many options.

On Monday, I've put reunion planning out of my head in order to work on the homework I didn't finish over the weekend. It's only been a week since we got the reunion assignment, and I already feel myself slipping in my classes. I'm catching up on calculus in ASG when Isabel walks up.

"Alison?" she asks, and I reluctantly look up. "I wondered if you had your bonfire volunteers. We needed them Friday."

My chest constricts. I completely forgot. With every-thing I have going on, and especially this week with the new impositions of the reunion and driver's ed, Isabel wanting me to find help for the upcoming baseball season kickoff got buried under the thousand other things I had to do.

I'm not used to forgetting things. I don't like the feel-ing. "Um, yeah," I say, deciding to bluff. "Of course. Dylan Giordano's doing it."

Isabel waits while I pray she drops the subject and leaves me to my calculus. "Okay, great," she replies. "I need two vol-unteers. Just give me the other name when you have the chance." Her voice still holds her usual friendliness, but now with an unmistakable passive-aggressive push.

"I will." I smile, my teeth clenched.

Behind me, I hear Ethan laugh.

I face him. "Can I help you?"

He's looking relaxed in his chair, legs crossed, phone in his hand. "Can I help *you*? Overwhelmed, Sanger? Not enough time to devote to your duties as vice president?" He turns to our president, who's still standing over me. "Isabel, you really ought to file a complaint."

Isabel examines her nails. "Why don't you two collabo-rate on getting volunteers? Then no one has to complain."

"You don't actually think forcing us to collaborate would create less complaints, do you?" I ask.

"Yeah, we do better with open hostility. Honestly, it's healthier this way." Ethan uncrosses his legs and fixes me with a glare.

Isabel rolls her eyes. "I swear, you two are worse than an old married couple."

"Sure," I say. "One of those old married couples who fight constantly and would be much happier if they got a divorce but they can't until the kids are out of high school."

"Who exactly are our kids in this scenario?"

I sigh. "The reunion, driver's ed, the *seven* classes we share."

Ethan's eyes go comically wide. "Nine children. Wow. I assume we got married at the illustrious Millard Fillmore?"

Isabel walks off, clearly tired of this. "Speaking of the Millard Fillmore, have you found any other realistic venues?" I ask.

"I will."

"You won't, but please do waste your time trying."

I close my homework folder and leave the room, giving myself the final word. I know I need to talk to Dylan now that I've signed her up to do work during a party I know she'll want to enjoy. With the hallways empty, I cross campus quickly in the direction of yearbook.

I cringe entering the yearbook room. It's not the clutter I object to—like the *Chronicle*, the yearbook room is decorated with incongruous pieces of furniture and wallpapered with random printouts. What earns my distaste is the cloying sentimentality of everything. The faux-inspirational quotes imploring us to REFLECT and LIVE EVERY DAY, the notes on the board for yearbook pages on "The Freshman Family" and

"Pumas Forever," even the dumb *Puma Pride* yearbook title painted over the door.

Mr. Pham, the advisor, looks up and acknowledges my presence, then returns to grading papers. I speed past his desk, still suspicious he's the one who complained to Williams and indirectly stuck Ethan and me with the reunion.

I find Dylan in the far corner of the room. The yearbook desktop in front of her displays the "Seniors Reflect" page I've seen her working on. But Dylan's attention is fixed on the laptop open on her knees. When I walk up behind her, I'm surprised to recognize the window she has open. It's Naviance, the portal that compiles Fairview students' statistics and their college admissions. Over the summer I used it to compare myself with every Fairview student admitted to Harvard.

"Hey," I say. Dylan looks up sharply. Momentarily abandoning my purpose here, I can't help my curiosity. I nod in the direction of the laptop screen. "Why are you on Naviance?" I examine the window closer and find Dylan's on the page for UC Berkeley, which charts GPA and SAT scores for admitted and denied students. Berkeley is Dylan's first choice, I know. It's an hour from home and close to the San Francisco "scene"—and of course, it's where her ex Olivia is a freshman now.

"I'm never getting in." Dylan's voice is flat, with an unusual worried undercurrent. It's not that she's careless when it comes to college. She's just never fixated on her chances before. "I'm *here*," she says, pointing to a place on the graph undeniably in the red.

I wince. The graph is not reassuring, but I know that's not what Dylan needs to hear. "You're not just your GPA and your SAT score," I say delicately. "You have photography, and . . . other things."

"Colleges don't care!" Dylan's eyes, wide and urgent, dart up to mine. I sense she's close to freaking out.

I recognize the feeling. It brings me back to my own nights dwelling on my college chances, working myself up over Harvard threads on College Confidential, imagining worst-case scenarios. The nerves weren't something I could be talked out of. I decide to redirect the conversation instead. "Why are you checking this now?" I ask. "College apps are in. There's nothing you can do."

Dylan pauses. Then she closes her computer. "No reason." There's no waver in her voice, no echo of her previous panic. I know she's not being honest, but if Dylan doesn't want to talk, it's not for me to force her. "Why are you here?" She stows her laptop in her bag and spins her chair to face me fully. "I know how much you hate the yearbook room."

"I need a favor," I say. "I was supposed to find volunteers for the bonfire ASG's throwing for the first baseball game, and I sort of . . . signed you up."

Dylan looks peeved. "Seriously, Alison? Am I your only friend in this entire school?"

"I deserve that," I reply. "Please?"

"Nick's on the baseball team," she says, emphasizing his name disdainfully. "What with how our second date went this weekend, I really don't want to build a bonfire in his honor."

I didn't even know Dylan went out with Nick this weekend, which makes me feel guilty. "Second date didn't go well?" I ask sympathetically. I wasn't exactly rooting for Nick himself, but I was hoping he would help Dylan move on from the hurt of Olivia dumping her.

"Second and final date," Dylan confirms, indignant revulsion in her voice. "He kept asking questions about my relationship with Olivia."

I frown, understanding what she means. Dylan's been openly bi since eighth grade. Everybody knows, and with our proximity to San Francisco, it's not like queerness is a foreign concept. But even in our liberal neighborhood, there are people who insist on making a thing of it. I guess Nick is one of those people. "I'm sorry, Dylan," I say. "Really."

Dylan sighs. "If I'm doing this"—she levels me a stern look—"you're doing it with me."

"I don't have time," I start to protest, until Dylan hits me with an imperious eyebrow. "Fine," I relent.

"Fine," she repeats. She faces her yearbook computer, studying the "Seniors Reflect" page like she plans on returning to work. I see her chewing on her nail, though, and the distracted nervousness has returned to her eyes. Remembering the fretful nights I had in October when I applied early, I think of how Dylan was the person I went to when the anxiety overwhelmed me. The person who distracted me with inane gossip and in-depth discussions of our favorite episodes of *The Office*. I need to be here for her the way she was for me.

"Hey," I say, my voice gentler. Dylan glances my way. "It's going to be okay. College and everything." I'm not faking the conviction in my voice. While I don't know if Dylan will get into Berkeley, I do know she's genuinely smart and a really talented photographer. One way or the other, everything *will* be okay for her.

She musters a weak smile. When she turns back to her computer, I leave.

Walking in the hallways, I put together the pieces of the conversation. I'm not dumb. I know Dylan's new fixation on Berkeley is because of Olivia. Having just gone on a disappointing date with Nick, Dylan's clinging even harder to the idea of her ex. Dreaming of Berkeley with Olivia is putting a pressure on Dylan's college decisions she's never experienced.

While Dylan was there for me when I needed distracting from single-digit admission percentages and intimidating College Confidential research—and while I can be there for her—the truth is, we're very different in our outlooks on college, even high school. Our priorities rarely align. I want ivy-adorned walls and opportunities in journalism, politics, finance, or whatever future I end up loving. Dylan wants more of the same, including, I guess, her ex.

Ethan is working on French homework when I walk into the ASG room. I purposefully don't look in his direction, instead observing him out of my peripheral vision. Eyes narrowed, he's highlighting in efficient, deliberate strokes.

It's ironic how the only other person I know whose goals line up with mine—like the moon covering the sun in an eclipse—is the person standing in my way of achieving them.

# Nineteen

IN THE *CHRONICLE* OFFICE on Friday, I'm reading Ethan's revision of his gym financing story. It's odd. He's fixed everything I pointed out, input every note and comment. He's even pushed the anecdote—his prized anecdote—to paragraph four and opened with the hard information, the way I often have to vigorously coerce him to on production nights.

What's more, he's done the edits sort of sloppily. Word-for-word copying of my suggested phrasing, extra spaces and periods left over from deletions. It's still excellent work, still probably worthy of the NSPC Award. I'm not complaining I didn't have to put him to medieval thumbscrews to get my way, either. It's just odd.

Outside my office, the room is chaotic, notwithstanding it being the middle of fifth period. Robbie Kang, one of our strongest sports writers, is showing some wide-eyed sophomores YouTube videos. In one corner, a group of Model UN kids debate on the couch. The news editor is making out obviously with the business manager, while our advisor is out of the room. Then there's Ethan, who's hunched over his government study guide, which I resent. I wish I had time to review for the exam we have next period.

I walk out of my office, directly to the desk where he's working. *Marbury v. Madison*, I notice on his study guide. *Established constitutional review*, the voice in my head reminds me, joined by the louder voice commenting, *stupid Ethan and his studying*. "Is this your final revision?" I demand, holding up the printout of his article.

He continues his reading, deliberately reminding me he's enjoying studying time that I'm not. When he looks up, there's confrontation in his eyes. "Yes," he says. "Why?"

I'm not surprised to hear the edge in his voice. Our conversations have started at unusual levels of hostility lately, even for us. It's not hard to intuit why. With this revision, every class, and now the reunion and driver's ed, Ethan's suddenly everywhere in my life. Every frustration he fills me with, every quality I find irritating, is a hundred times worse for my experiencing them a hundred times more often. I'm resenting this particular conversation knowing I have to see him again after school for a vendor meeting with our prospective DJ.

"It's just not as good as your pieces usually are," I reply. Instantly, I regret the phrasing. I hate when I pay Ethan unintended compliments.

He latches on to the opportunity I've given him.

Grinning, he cocks his head. "Well, I'm glad I've established a high standard for my work."

*Point: Ethan.*

I scowl, feeling my temper flare. If Ethan's and my relationship weren't especially volatile due to our constant proximity, I'd let the comment go. I'd leave the conversation and resume hating him from the privacy of my office. Unfortunately, I don't. I can't let anything go with him. My eyes flitting from his, I seize on the first opening I find. "You have . . . mustard on the sleeve of your oxford," I inform him. "You look ridiculous."

Ethan's upper lip curls, inflecting his features with unmistakable scorn. He rolls his pen in his fingers like a dart. "*Me?* What about you? Your wardrobe looks composed of hand-me-downs from my mom."

I glance down, regretting the gesture's self-consciousness. This morning, I chose my blue knee-length pleated skirt and white sweater because I thought the outfit looked cute but professional. Knowing Ethan doesn't like it just makes me happier with my decision. "Your mom's a marketing exec for Google," I say. I've met Mrs. Molloy once or twice. She's nothing like her noxious son. "I'm going to take it as a compliment."

"You're a high school student, not a marketing exec. Do you even own a T-shirt?"

I'm distantly conscious of how dumb it is I came out here to question Ethan about his revision and ended up in a heated debate about our clothing. Yet I can't help myself. "Do *you?*"

Ethan doesn't reply right away. In the pause, I hear a voice behind me. "I, um—" It's one of the junior editors, who I find watching me and Ethan with hesitation. "I need help with the page-design program."

I refocus, annoyed I needed the interruption from features editor Julie Wang to return me to reality. I notice a couple other staffers watching our conversation, their expressions variations of nervous and annoyed. The other senior editors generally regard us as a necessary evil for the awards we help the paper win. The underclassmen haven't gotten used to us yet. I fire Ethan a final glare, which he doesn't notice, having returned to his gov reviewing. The familiar tremors of something beyond competitiveness begin to quake, but this time, I'm just in control enough to put them to rest.

I settle for flicking the tip of my pen onto the paper he's reading. "Today," I say. "Blitz."

He doesn't look up. "Fine."

# Twenty

I LOSE THE BLITZ.

Fuming quietly on the curb after class, I pull out my phone to call my Uber, putting in the location of the park where we're meeting the DJ.

"I suppose we should ride together," Ethan says, walking up to me.

I don't look up. "Why?"

"We're literally going to the same place, Sanger. Seems wasteful."

Admittedly, I *have* run out of allowance for the month. I don't care. Dipping into my own savings is definitely preferable to eight avoidable minutes in a car with Ethan.

"Even the shortest recess from you is the opposite of wasteful," I reply, hitting the button to request my ride.

"Embarrassed about losing last period? I get it." He takes out his phone, presumably requesting his own ride.

"You didn't even write five paragraphs on the long-answer. Who turns in an exam with a four-paragraph essay?"

Ethan's fingers freeze on his phone. "Eyes on your own paper." His voice is low. I've struck a nerve.

"Hey, an A-minus is nothing to be *embarrassed* about, Ethan." I walk a few feet away, putting cool distance between us as I watch the 2010 Ford Focus's progress on my phone.

Ethan doesn't move. He stares at his own phone, presumably following the progress of *his* Uber. It pulls up first. Without even glancing in my direction, he gets in, flinging his shoulder bag into the seat like he's in some great hurry. I wait a few minutes for my Uber, which is navigating the complicated obstacles of students flocking to their cars and parents driving into the parking lot for pickups.

When I hop in, I feel my phone vibrate. I glance down, reading the message from the lock screen. It's from Ethan.

ETA 3:22.

I realize in a flash why he hurried into his Uber. The blitz is evidently *not* over. He wants to be first to the park. It's immature and idiotic, racing the mean streets of San Mateo County to reach our reunion vendor first. And right now, I'm all in.

I check the Uber app, which informs me my ETA is 3:24. "Turn here," I instruct the driver. "It's faster." We cut on to one of the residential streets near the school, and I write Ethan a quick text.

I'll be there at 3:21

Using every shortcut I know and crosschecking the route with multiple online maps, I find our way to the park, passing Dylan's house, the Whole Foods, and the elementary school. When we pull up, I catch sight of Ethan out of the corner of my eye. He's arrived at the exact same time.

I walk in the direction of the music I hear pulsing over the green inclines of the park, quickening my pace when I notice Ethan picking up his. We're supposed to meet the DJ at the food truck she's playing from, but I don't know where the truck will be, exactly. If I follow the electronic rhythms reverberating over the hills and past the people playing Frisbee, I'll end up where I need to be.

Ethan and I hurry in lockstep up the nearest hill, both of us stealing glances at the other's pace. I reach the top seconds before him. My thighs burn, which I ignore because from up here, I can see our destination.

Parked near the picnic tables, the food truck is drawing a small crowd for its signature product—dessert hot dogs. Parents with strollers and groups of teenagers leave the window holding Twinkies halved to resemble buns with pieces of licorice or strips of brownie down the middle. The truck is painted entirely white, except the name scrawled in black on the front. SWEET WIENERS, reads the thick, marker-like lettering.

I cut Ethan off rounding the back of the truck, where I find the DJ booth inside the open rear doors. Soulful vocals over a skittering beat vibrate from the speakers, and a twentysomething girl with dark hair and copper skin stands in between them, her hands deftly navigating the keyboard of her computer and the knobs of her turntable. She's slim, with big plastic glasses, and wearing a white, well-fitting SWEET WIENERS T-shirt.

I shove my hand out. "Avery Tran? I'm Alison."

Avery doesn't shake my hand. Hers remain working the controls on her station, like I should've realized they would. Feeling dumb, I withdraw my hand.

"You're the Fairview girl, right?" Avery asks. Her hat, I notice, reads DJ RAVERY. I nod. Her eyes dart to Ethan, who appears to be reading her shirt with faint amusement. "Yeah, yeah," she says dryly. "It's a job, okay? Getting gigs isn't easy in a white-dude-dominated industry. Which is why I was hype to get your email. The date's May ninth, right?"

"Yeah. May ninth," I say. "We haven't officially found a venue yet"—I glare at Ethan—"but we wanted to confirm important items. The music first and foremost."

"Definitely," Avery agrees. She describes her reasonable rates and hours and her electrical outlet needs, and while she speaks, I find I'm impressed. She's effortlessly professional. Multitasking with ease, she modulates the music as she runs through the details for us. "Reunions are awesome to play," she says once she's laid out the logistics. "Excellent throwback options, and a really drunk crowd."

I grin. Ethan, however, laughs. It's jarring, and I jerk involuntarily to look at him. I can't remember him laughing genuinely, without sarcasm, instead of as a cruel punctuation mark.

"Yeah, we're depending on you to make the night fun," Ethan says, his voice easy, light with flippant charm. It's a version of Ethan I rarely see, one that leads me to wonder who he is when we're not competing. "I mean, Sanger's not," he adds. "She's incurably dull."

I draw back, actually stunned by how harsh and unprovoked the insult is. Ethan cozying up to our cool prospective DJ is a normal level of mildly annoying for him. Insulting me in front of her is a different degree of shitty. It's unacceptable.

I can't let it stand. Raising my voice over the synthesizer noise now streaming from Avery's speakers, I lay into Ethan. "If people wanted your opinion, they would ask," I say. "But they don't because nobody wants to subject themselves to a conversation with you."

Ethan sneers. "I have plenty of conversations with plenty of people." He says it like it's obvious, but I hear combativeness straining his voice.

I face him fully, ignoring Avery waiting awkwardly to my left. "Really? I've spent practically every waking minute with you this week, and I haven't seen you have one conversation over five minutes long with anyone except me."

"Yeah, well, being around you doesn't exactly inspire friendliness." His nonchalance disappearing entirely, he feverishly runs a hand through his hair. "This week has been my idea of hell."

"If you're miserable, Ethan, feel free to drop out of the reunion. Why don't you just drop out of Fairview while you're at it too?"

"One more week like this one, and I just might!"

Ideas dance through my head of annoying Ethan enough he genuinely drops out. The thought is wonderful. I imagine my gloriously Ethan-free days, editing with only coopera-tive writers who never have controversial opinions on the Oxford comma, getting 100 percent on every test because I'm not racing him and the clock, not being infuriated at seven every single morning when I first see his face.

It feels like victory. Like freedom.

While I'm envisioning this new world, though, I notice Avery out of the corner of my eye watching us skeptically. "I'll send the contract over to you after my set, and we'll finalize location and hours later," she says stiffly, halting the retort I was preparing for Ethan. "Quick question. Do you have a supervisor I can correspond with on this?"

My victory fizzles out. I face Avery, shame rushing through me. "We're the ones who will be coordinating every-thing. I assure you, you can email or call us anytime and we'll be capable of handling your requests."

Avery studies us a moment longer. "Okay. No problem. There's one thing I forgot to mention, though. When I'm working for minors, I require a larger portion of the pay-ment up front."

I nod, mustering as much dignity as I can. I know what's happening here. Our DJ didn't *forget* to mention this deposit. She just saw Ethan and me fighting like kindergarteners, and she decided we were unreliable and immature. The horrible part is, I don't even fault her. We *were* immature. I'm instantly angry and ashamed of myself for behaving exactly the way people expect I will.

"Of course," I tell Avery, fighting to recover my composure. "Thanks so much for meeting with us."

Avery nods once and returns to work. Ethan and I walk away from the truck, not speaking as we cut through the crowd waiting for their candy-decked hot dogs. I feel his glare on my back, following me onto the path over the emerald grass of the park's hills. It's obvious he's not chagrined by our public outburst. I resent him all the more for it—silently this time.

Once again, it's Ethan not caring enough and doing whatever he wants despite the reasons or repercussions. I honestly don't know if I envy him for his detachment. The liberation must be nice, not holding himself to the cage of requirements and personal standards I confine myself in. On the other hand, without those requirements, I don't know who I'd be. The emptiness from which Ethan's impulsiveness seems to come is just a little terrifying.

A chilly wind is gusting over the park when we reach the curb, where Ethan and I instinctually separate and wait silently for our respective Ubers. Ethan stares at his phone while I watch the passersby, the dads in fleece vests walking golden retrievers and the kids playing tag. I don't give Ethan the gratification of glancing over when his Uber, again, arrives minutes ahead of mine.

In the car on the way home, I feel my phone vibrate with a text from Ethan.

> By the way, for losing the blitz, you're wearing a T-shirt to school on Monday.

He's obviously aiming to pick another fight. My fingers itch with the impulse to reply, to inform him what a short-sighted waste of a task this is.

For the first time, I don't. We crossed a line today. One I've toed with him a long time. Competing with Ethan has always been a high-wire act of proving my worth while not appearing unprofessional. I'm aware of how constant bickering and infighting makes me look. I've just always felt I gain more than I lose when it comes to our rivalry. Now . . . I'm forced to reevaluate. What's the point of beating Ethan if I end up looking *less* capable in the end?

It's time I recognize how childish our competition is. I can't allow another repeat of today.

My phone buzzes again. I flip it over, ignoring Ethan the whole way home.

# Twenty-One

I'M IN MY ROOM on Saturday, working on homework while Dylan edits a photo on her computer. Or I should be working. Instead, I'm mentally preparing for the ten minutes I'll have to spend with Ethan in driver's ed. It's my second lesson of three, and my nerves have lessened in comparison to my first lesson a week ago. My resistance to the idea of spending even one short drive with Ethan, however, has not. I'm fortifying the walls of my internal castle, constructing ramparts and a moat, raising the drawbridge, barricading the doors. Come what may, I vow I'll remain completely cool and collected.

"How about this one?" Dylan swivels the screen to face me. I'm treated to a bare-chested Jake Freedman throwing a water polo ball in the indoor pool. We haven't discussed her college worries since Monday, despite her having dinner here on Wednesday and us hanging out every lunch this week when I didn't have *Chronicle* work.

"It looks great," I tell her enthusiastically. "It looks a lot like the last three versions you've shown me."

"It has to be perfect," Dylan declares. She returns to editing, leaning in to examine her work. "This is the best photo in the entire yearbook."

I can't help smiling. I'd forgotten Dylan's open enthusiasm for yearbook, which fell into Olivia's "uncool" column. Dylan's love of yearbook was one of those things she dimmed to make herself into the girl Olivia wanted. Watching her return to herself hasn't been gradual or all at once, but rather in bright bursts like this one.

"I love yearbook." Dylan sighs contentedly. "Where else would I find the excuse to unabashedly study Jake's abs all day?"

"You need an excuse?" I raise an eyebrow. Dylan laughs.

I know what she said about yearbook was an oversimplification, though. While she's definitely enjoying her pièce de résistance portrait of Jake, I know she edits photos of the ecology club's spring cleanup with equal diligence, despite a distinct lack of abs.

I return to my physics homework, trying to refocus on rotational motion while Dylan clicks and studies her screen. It's quiet for a moment, each of us concentrating. While Dylan and I work in each other's company often, genuine silence is rare. Dylan usually wants to discuss the details of our days, or play me a YouTube video of whatever sweaty rock show she went to over the weekend, or—

"Okay, it's perfect. Coffee break?" she asks, sitting up

straight and unconsciously looping the longer side of her short hair over her ear. Checking the clock on my phone, I do the math and realize I don't really have time to finish the problems I'm working on before driver's ed. What's more, I could use coffee. The mug I made this morning is wearing off, leaving me an unpleasant combination of weary and wired.

I close my book. "Why not?" We head into the hall, Dylan following me down the stairs. On our way to the door, we pass Jamie, who's on the couch watching something in the living room.

She hits pause. "Where are you guys going?" she calls out.

"Just Starbucks," Dylan replies cheerfully. I hover near the kitchen, saying nothing. Ever since we were in sixth grade, Dylan's loved Jamie. My sister had just come home from college for winter break and her first night here, she hosted a huge party for her high school friends while our parents were out. It was surprising—Jamie was never a "partier" in high school. Looking back on it now, I guess it was the first indication of how Jamie would change. Of how growing up could look like growing sideways. Dylan was sleeping over that night, and I remember waiting to fall asleep while the pulsing music and the noise of the party kept us awake. I was furious. Dylan was enamored.

Jamie gets up, not bothering to turn the TV off. "Do you guys need a ride?"

"We're walking." I speak up, lightly annoyed Jamie just wants to insert herself in whatever I'm doing because she's bored.

"Oh, great. I'm craving a latte," Jamie says enthusiastically. She steps into her sandals and heads past Dylan and me to the door. I inhale and exhale. While Jamie inviting herself irritates me, it would be unforgivably standoffish to tell my sister she's not welcome, especially without good reason.

We walk outside. It's a perfect day, everything in pure colors Dylan wouldn't even bother to Photoshop. The fresh pavement of the road, the cloudless brilliance of the sky, the pattern of green and gray lawns and driveways. We follow the sidewalk in the direction of the mini-mall near our house.

"You guys been working on homework?" Jamie asks. Her languid pace sets ours.

"Yeah," I say, squinting and wishing I'd grabbed my sunglasses from my desk.

"On a Saturday? It's the weekend." Her voice is playful.

I glance sideways at my sister. Every day's the weekend for her, which I restrain myself from pointing out. I don't want to rub her face in her situation, and I certainly don't want to upset her. "Yeah," I repeat. "On the weekend." Jamie did homework on the weekend when she was in high school too. I don't know how she forgot, or maybe she just doesn't think it's important anymore.

If Jamie hears the edge in my voice, she ignores it. She turns to Dylan. "Who do you have this year?"

Dylan names several of her teachers. While they share horror stories of Mr. Murphy's excruciatingly slow lecturing style, I scrutinize the familiar scuffs and seams of the sidewalk.

We cross the street in front of the mall, and Dylan changes the subject. "Alison mentioned you're learning the guitar," she says to Jamie. By *mentioned*, Dylan means I texted her the other night complaining I couldn't concentrate over the metallic whine from Jamie's room. I choose not to clarify this detail.

Jamie brightens instantly when Dylan brings up the guitar. "I *am*," she says with her unwavering excitement. "I even met up with this girl from my graduating class who plays drums. We're thinking of starting a band."

This startles me from my silence. "Who?"

"Mara Naser," Jamie answers. "It's wild—I didn't even know her in high school, but we're in a Facebook group for Fairview people still in town." She pulls open the door to the Starbucks. The familiar smell envelops me, the sweetness of the flavored syrups and the bitter bite of the coffee.

"Now you're just going to start a band with this random girl?" I ask.

"Is it a crime to make new friends in the neighborhood, Alison?" There's a rare hint of irritation in Jamie's voice. Then her eyes soften, turning somewhat sad. "Everyone I was friends with in high school lives in other cities."

I don't reply, feeling kind of bad for my sister. Even so, her seeking out her old high school classmates seems like one more sign of regression. There are certain people in your life you're supposed to graduate from. Returning to them is like forcing yourself to play with the toys you enjoyed when you were in kindergarten.

We order our drinks from the register. Black iced coffee for me—the perfect combination of productivity and refreshment—a Frappuccino for Dylan, and a nonfat, sugar-free vanilla latte with an extra pump of syrup for Jamie. I follow Dylan to our regular table, where we wait for our orders. "So what does Mara, like, do?" I ask Jamie, keeping my voice light. I'm hoping Mara has more happening in her life and will be a positive influence on my sister.

Jamie shrugs like the question's uninteresting. "I think she's applying for her master's?"

"In what?" I'm coming off like a parent eager for her kid to make friends with the honor students.

"I don't really know," Jamie says quickly. "You can ask her tonight. She's bringing a friend over and we're going to practice."

I frown. I'd hoped the band idea was an unformed possibility, not one materializing in our garage in a few hours.

Jamie's eyes fix on Dylan, her face lighting up. "Maybe you could take some photos of us sometime. I'm thinking of making a website."

I want to tell Dylan not to waste time on this whim of Jamie's. But when I look over, Dylan's evidently elsewhere, gazing out the window with a distant and unreadable combination of emotions in her eyes. Following her gaze, I immediately know why she's distracted.

In the parking lot stands Olivia, having a conversation with a girl I don't recognize. Olivia's hair is different, cut short and dyed platinum from its natural blonde, and she's dressed with an effortless style I don't remember her having. She and her friend each hold their keys, lingering like they're meaning to leave and not wanting to. Clearly telling a story, Olivia gestures with her hands, a habit of hers I remember from hanging out with her and Dylan while they dated.

I knew Olivia well, having third-wheeled her and Dylan often. Olivia was likable in obvious, indisputable ways. Pretty, popular, and expressive, she's the sort of person who won friends easily, not to mention girlfriends. But I found her friendliness kind of perfunctory and universal, even performative. She's an actress, and sometimes, it was hard to know whether she was playing a role even when it was only Dylan and me in the room. It's the put-on quality I see right now in her enthusiastic laughter, her intense engagement in whatever conversation they're having.

"I didn't know she was in town this weekend," Dylan says to no one in particular. She adjusts her hair again and straightens her shirt, looking unusually self-conscious.

Watching her watch Olivia, I feel a punch of dread hit my stomach. I know this will only make it harder for Dylan to get over her ex. The place we're in isn't helping, either. This Starbucks is where Dylan and Olivia and I spent plenty of weekend afternoons. This very table, even. It's crisscrossed with memories, conversations, inside jokes, and old plans built into the architecture as fundamentally as the windows and ceiling beams.

Olivia and the girl hug, then head to their cars. I think

Dylan and I notice Olivia's silver Volkswagen simultaneously, and I catch Dylan's eyes flicker. Then, pretending she's fine, Dylan faces Jamie. Her voice is uneven when she speaks. "Sorry. What were you saying?"

"It's fine," Jamie replies, understanding replacing her excitement from moments ago. "Don't worry about it."

The barista puts out our drinks, and we pick them up on our way out the door. We're quiet for a while, using the pretense of straws and much-needed midday coffee for not saying anything. When we've crossed the street and walked halfway home, it's Jamie who speaks up. "I used to run into Craig all the time after we broke up. Splitting up didn't change that we both loved the same coffee shops, the same movie theater and restaurants. I had to give those up just to avoid seeing him. Then I realized I didn't need to run into him to be hit with missing him. Just reading a book I knew he'd like or talking to a mutual friend was enough." She pauses, like she's choosing her words carefully, speaking past a hurt in her chest I didn't realize was so deep. "I guess what I'm saying is it's hard living in the same place as your ex," she finally adds, her voice gentle.

Dylan nods, but she doesn't reply.

The remark gives me a moment of sympathy for my sister. While we walk, I imagine how Jamie's engagement ending undoubtedly felt. I didn't know Craig very well. They met in college, and I only saw him for every other Thanksgiving, and our occasional visits to Chicago and theirs to California. But my sister seemed happy with him. Their relationship collapsing must've upended Jamie's world, turning every place or routine into an unwanted reminder of what's over. I envision Jamie buying groceries for one, finding new neighborhood restaurants where she wouldn't risk running into her ex. Sitting in a Starbucks and seeing him out the window. While my sister moved home for a lot of reasons, I'm sure her heartbreak was one of them.

I don't want those painful reminders for Dylan. Which, I realize, is exactly what Dylan would set herself up for if she followed Olivia to college. Campus quads and dining spaces where she would see Olivia over and over. It would be today, every day, for the next three years. Instead of just wanting to recapture the last year of her life, I wish Dylan would let herself leave the past behind.

It's like the reunion. High school relationships, high school drama, high school rivalries—they're not meant to be revisited every ten years. They're meant to be outgrown.

"Did moving home help?" I ask Jamie.

I see the sadness in her smile. The uncertainty and lingering loss. "Yeah," she says. "Yeah, it did."

# Twenty-Two

I'M NEARING THE END of my driver's ed lesson without Hector having used his pedals at all. Once again we went to Dairy Queen, where once again Hector ordered the Royal New York Cheesecake, and once again Daniel evinced no recognition of him when Hector said hi. I pull out of the Dairy Queen parking lot, pausing for a couple skateboarders who cross in front of me, and focus on our next destination. Ethan's house.

I've been preparing all day for having to drive with Ethan. The mature way of dealing with him is to refuse to escalate our disagreements, no matter what. Simple. Easy, even. On the list of the hardest accomplishments in my life, this won't even rank.

I follow the newly familiar route, Hector complimenting me on how well I glide through the turn into Ethan's neighborhood. His street is lined with cozy clapboard houses in muted colors. I drive to the end of the block, my nerves calm, my breathing even. It's the feeling of total prepared-ness. When I reach Ethan's driveway, he's waiting out front.

He gets in without a word, the padded thud of the door echoing in the quiet of the car. I don't glance in the rearview mirror to meet his eyes.

"Hey, Hector," Ethan says after a moment's pause, like he and Hector are the only people here.

While Hector greets Ethan, and Ethan pointedly doesn't greet me, I pull out of the driveway. Keeping my eyes on the road, I don't acknowledge Ethan's silence toward me, which stretches into a stalemate, one I find welcoming in compar-ison to the fiery conflict I'm used to. Ethan and Hector chat about some superhero movie until they finally fall silent too, and we're left for a few minutes with no sound except the pumping of the pedals and the wheels on the road.

Suddenly, Ethan speaks up. "Oh, Sanger," he says, "I put the deposit down on the DJ. I decided this morning she was definitely the person for the job."

I purse my lips, pressure pounding in my temples. This is a clear provocation. Ethan went behind my back, making a unilateral decision he knew would piss me off. He wants me to reply, wants me to explode, possibly even wants me distracted. He just wants amusement, and fighting with me is his equivalent of having games on his phone or whatever normal, non-evil people do.

Part of me wants to gulp down the bait the way he expects. I'm itching to stop the car, chew him out, and put down a deposit on the Millard Fillmore as soon as I'm home.

I have a resolution, however. A vow. A strategy. I inhale evenly. "I agree," I say. It sounds strangled. "Thanks for taking care of the deposit."

I steal a glance in the rearview mirror at a stoplight and find Ethan visibly stunned. "Great," he replies haltingly. Then he recovers, composure settling over his pretty-boy features. "I found a photo booth vendor I'm going to talk to this week as well," he adds with renewed cockiness.

*Oh god, the fucking photo booth.* I feel my blood pressure rising. If I have a stroke behind the wheel, "death by Ethan" will be an interesting obituary. I remind myself this is his final driver's ed lesson. While I still have one more before my test next month, it won't be with Ethan. I'll be free. "Okay," I reply with herculean restraint. "Why don't you do some research and then we can have a conversation about it next week."

Ethan says nothing. I understand it's because he doesn't even know how to deal with me when I'm not fighting him on everything. In the mirror, I note he's fidgeting with the collar of his shirt—one of those crisp white polos with the crocodile logo. I would be pleased that he's obviously irritated, except I remind myself I'm not engaging in our warfare anymore.

After I pull up to the curb of my house, I say goodbye to Hector. I say nothing to Ethan. Getting out of the car, I glance in his direction, and I'm surprised to find his green eyes on me. He's not reading *The New Yorker* on his phone or gazing dispassionately out the window.

His eyes are a hurricane. I pause for a moment, caught in

their currents. There's his everyday vexation at our endless fighting, and the veneer of equanimity he works to uphold. Rising within them, though, there's a dissatisfaction I'm not used to.

I'm the one who breaks our eye contact. Walking to the front door of my house, I know I deserve to feel victorious. I conducted myself perfectly, exactly the way I'd hoped. But I'd be lying to myself if I said I didn't feel irksome hints of the same unfulfilled frustration I saw in Ethan. They tighten my chest, and despite accomplishing each of my goals, I feel like I lost something.

# Twenty-Three

INSIDE THE HOUSE, I hear voices. One is Jamie's. I don't recognize the other two. There's a girl, who I'm guessing is the Mara Jamie mentioned, and the other voice belongs to a guy. In a flash I remember what Jamie said on the way to coffee— *band practice.*

I'm in no mood to interact with Jamie's new Facebook friends. Rolling my eyes, I head quietly for the stairs, hoping to work on homework in my room *without* Jamie plugging in her guitar. I need to reorganize the reunion to-do list, read *Macbeth* for English, and finish my physics homework. Really, I need to do whatever I can to take my mind off this weird discontentment with Ethan.

I barely reach the first step before my sister's voice rings out. "Hey, Alison, is that you?" she calls from the other room. Holding my breath, I tiptoe up the stairs, hoping Jamie figures she was wrong and doesn't come to investigate. I'm halfway up when Jamie appears on the other side of the railing below me. "It *is* you," she says, sounding pleased. "I want you to meet the band. Mara and Ted."

"I'm pretty tired . . ." I lie.

Jamie's expression falters. "It'll only take a second."

I hear the undertone in her voice. Having brushed Jamie off a couple times this week without her protesting, I realize she might finally be fed up. If I dodge her now, I'm pretty certain I'll provoke a fight, which I'm definitely not in the mood for.

I draw on the restraint I just used with Ethan. "Yeah, sure," I reply.

Jamie beams. I follow her into the kitchen, where I find Ted, his back turned while he searches for something in the fridge, and Mara, who's leaning on the counter, beer in hand.

Mara waves. "Hey, Alison. I'm Mara." She's short, with thick black hair, wearing a gray oversized T-shirt. The rasp in her tone makes me think she might actually have a decent singing voice.

This looks nothing like a band practice. I don't see instruments. I doubt Jamie's new bandmates even brought them. Instead, this looks like three twentysomethings drinking my parents' beer in our kitchen. Jamie hops up on the countertop, perching on the granite and blissfully watching Mara and me. I wonder when I'm permitted to leave without pissing off Jamie.

The thought vanishes when Ted turns toward us, closing the fridge.

Because this random guy Jamie brought into our house

is *hot*. Ted is tall, his arms leanly muscled, his chin covered in more stubble than a high schooler is capable of growing. His eyes are green, a much nicer shade than Ethan's. Holding his beer in one hand, he rubs his corded forearm with the other.

I find myself fixating on those forearms. I don't often devote time to pursuing boys, or even to thinking in romantic or purely physical directions. It's not like I haven't enjoyed the relationships I've had in high school. Nate, with hipster glasses and insightful comments in English. Prateek, one of the *Chronicle* news editors who graduated last year, who I made out with after production nights over a couple months. They were nice guys. Our relationships were just insubstantial because of how fleeting I knew they were. Knowing I would leave home for college, hopefully for Harvard, I couldn't ignore how my high school relationships could only ever be that—high school. The reality made it hard to invest much of myself in dating.

None of which is to say I don't *think* about guys.

"Mara's our drummer," Jamie announces proudly, "and Ted plays bass."

This information doesn't register in any meaningful way with me. I watch Ted slide onto one of the barstools on the other side of the island. He places his elbows on the smooth granite. "Did you go to Fairview with Jamie too?" I ask him.

He nods. "I did."

"I didn't know him then, either," Jamie chimes in. "But he and Mara go way back."

"Jazz band freshman year," Mara says.

Ted's watching me from where he's sitting. "Do you want a beer, Alison?"

I don't, really. For one thing, I don't drink. For another, he's offering me beer from my own fridge. I'm ready to ignore both these points, however, in the pursuit of continuing this conversation with Ted.

Jamie cuts in, upending my plans. "She's seventeen, Ted." I close my mouth, fuming, and not just from Jamie interrupting my one-on-one with Ted. I know my age won't exactly further my flirting. It's not like I'm trying to sleep with Ted. I just don't want to be Jamie's *kid sister* right now.

"Oh, word," Ted replies, looking unbothered.

"Mara, Alison was curious what you're doing your master's in." Jamie's face has lit up, and I know she's loving me hanging out with her "friends." Despite presently having no interest in Mara's master's program, I turn in her direction.

"Well, I'm not in the master's program yet," Mara clarifies. "I'm thinking about applying to one in public policy or business or something. I'm not really sure."

The implication of what she's said surprises me. While I haven't decided if I'll major in English, government, or philosophy for an eventual career in politics or law, I'm seventeen. I couldn't imagine reaching my midtwenties and not knowing what subject of higher education I want to pursue.

"Cool." I offer Mara an encouraging nod, then turn to Ted. "What about you? What do you do?"

"I want to be a music producer," Ted says easily, like this career is not incredibly competitive and is instead equivalent to wanting pizza for dinner. "I make a lot of beats on my computer," he elaborates. It's a testament to his attractiveness this isn't a turnoff. But I look from him to Mara, both hanging out in my parents' kitchen, nowhere near pursuing the plans they each said. They're functionally no different from Jamie, who doesn't even have a plan.

Except Jamie did. She had a life. And now it's gone, like it never existed.

While I grab a soda from the fridge, Mara says she wants to see the garage to figure out where her drums will fit. Jamie offers to show her, and they walk out of the kitchen, leaving Ted and me alone.

I decide to capitalize on the opportunity. While I'm really not interested in the band, I'm definitely interested in Ted. I lean casually on the counter near where he's seated. Meeting my gaze, his green eyes leap out from his chiseled features. "What's your band going to be called?" I ask.

"Oh man." He rubs the stubble on his chin. "Such a good question. It's got to be genuine and memorable, you know? I was thinking Get Us Out of Our Moms' Houses."

He flashes me a grin, which, obviously, I return, my eyes straying to the sliver of his chest exposed under the open top button of his Henley. "I think the Beatles were originally called that."

He laughs. "It's just a bit wordy. Or, you know, I've always wanted a band with my name in it. Like the Jimi Hendrix Experience, Fleetwood Mac, Florence and the Machine."

"The Jonas Brothers."

"Exactly," he says smoothly, and now I laugh. It's really nice. His eyes sparkle, and I lean in a little closer over the countertop. This conversation's just fun, even flirtatious, not defensive or argumentative.

"You could be Ted and the Rough Riders?" I suggest.

His face clouds with confusion. Instantly, I'm mortified. If he doesn't get the reference, "Rough Riders" sounds like a definitely unintended innuendo.

"You know, Teddy Roosevelt?" I rush to clarify. It doesn't help. He's watching me, half frowning in puzzlement. "The Rough Riders? Theodore Roosevelt's cavalry unit in the Spanish–American War?"

He finally nods, but in the slow, lost way of students not following a complicated lecture. "Oh, yeah," he says. "He was president, right?"

It's instantaneous. The moment the question passes his lips, I feel like I'm looking at a different person. A way less attractive person. New details come into focus—the stain on his collar, his unwashed hair, the seed stuck in his upper teeth. It's like the weird experience of meeting someone you've only ever seen in pictures, and the lighting's off, and their features seem subtly out of place. I'm left with nothing except wishing I'd escaped up the stairs when I got home.

"Yeah. He was." I straighten up from the counter. "Speaking of which, I need to do my government homework."

"Homework? For real?" He laughs like I've just successfully told a joke. "You know homework isn't actually important, though. Like, the real world has nothing to do with that stuff."

Now I'm extremely ready to be done with this conversation. Obviously, Ted isn't the brightest, but his dismissal irks me. "I enjoy homework. Nice meeting you, Ted," I say over my shoulder.

"Oh. Yeah, you too," Ted says.

I head upstairs, closing my door when I'm inside my room. My whiteboard looms over me on the wall, reminding me of the work I have to do. When I try to focus, though, I realize I'm too worked up to get anything done. I'm not used to the combustible mixture of emotions distracting me. Lingering malaise from the charged moment with Ethan. Embarrassment, not to mention whiplash, from being very into Ted and then very *not* into Ted. Disappointment he didn't turn out to be even idle-crush material.

Needing easy, mindless preoccupation, I open my closet. I have to find a T-shirt to fulfill Ethan's blitz task. While I'm devoted to maintaining my mature decision not to feed into our rivalry, I refuse to balk on this task. Ethan would never let me. He'd heckle me endlessly for refusing, drawing out his petty victory interminably. It's better to just get it over with.

While I shuffle through my hangers, I decide I'm grateful I quickly fell out of infatuation with Ted. I don't need to waste time on errant crushes. I'm just months from being done with high school, moving to college, and starting my adult life. Now, if I could just find this T-shirt, I could be done with Ethan as well.

But when I reach the final hanger in my closet, I realize I don't have even one T-shirt. I've pawed past blouses and cable-knit cardigans, dress pants, and the dusty zip-up jacket from when I toured Harvard last year—nothing. Ethan was right.

Of course he was right. It's one of his greatest reporting strengths and one of his worst qualities on a list of expansive length. He's undeniably smart and observant, and he commits every fact and facet to memory. Recognizing this is yet another detail he's gotten right only makes me angrier.

Ethan would have gotten the Rough Riders reference. He might've even laughed.

Imagining him laughing at one of my jokes, I close my closet door with a bang, feeling dangerously on edge for too many reasons to name.

# Twenty-Four

**WHEN I WALK INTO** English, I immediately notice Ethan's eyes on the beige cardigan I'm wearing fully buttoned up. It's Monday morning, and he's no doubt preparing his pithy commentary on me not completing my loser's task. I file into the front row, sliding into my seat without meeting his gloating gaze.

We're discussing *Macbeth* and how the central couple needs each other to precipitate the events of the play. Without the prophecy given to her husband, Lady Macbeth could never have been queen, and without her ruthless ambition, Macbeth never would have been king. I listen and participate, but in the back of my mind, my thoughts are on Ethan. The way they always are. The tireless back-and-forth of our rivalry consumes too much time, too much thought, too much everything. It's like playing chess while giving a class presentation.

Nevertheless, I'm not going out without the final win.

Ethan raises his hand, which is the moment I was waiting for. "You're presuming the actions of Macbeth and his wife are entirely detrimental to themselves and to Scotland," Ethan says pompously.

Mr. Pham sighs, no doubt preparing for one of Ethan's long-winded diatribes. "Enlighten me, Mr. Molloy."

"It's indisputable the pair's plot harms their country and the people close to them," Ethan goes on evenly, obviously proud of the point and enjoying drawing the explanation out. "But they still achieve a greatness they never would have otherwise. Macbeth could have died in the next battle King Duncan ordered him off to, a glorified foot soldier. Instead, he died king."

I remove my cardigan.

"Lady Macbeth—" Ethan continues, then falters, his eyes falling on the shirt I've revealed I'm wearing. They fix there, on the white tee I borrowed from Avery yesterday with SWEET WIENERS emblazoned in black block text on the front. Ethan's mouth hangs open for a moment. Nothing comes out, not even his well-reasoned defense of his controversial viewpoints on *Macbeth*. The corners of his lips tip up precariously, like he's teetering on the edge of a laugh.

Checkmate. *Final point: Alison.*

Ethan looks away, evidently working hard to keep my shirt out of his eyeline. He finds his composure and his train of thought and continues. "Lady Macbeth wouldn't have been queen without having Macbeth to manipulate."

While Mr. Pham responds, I sit back in my seat, feeling

free. Watching Ethan return to his notes, pretending every-thing's normal, I smirk. I have the win I needed. Now I'm ready to move on from this ridiculous rivalry. From here on out, I'll treat Ethan with cool professionalism and dispas-sionate normalcy.

# Twenty-Five

I IGNORE THE STARES and hushed laughter I earn for my shirt throughout the morning. Only Dylan questions my wardrobe choice directly. When I find her in the fifteen-minute break between second and third period sitting on the blue benches where we usually meet outside the *Chronicle* and yearbook rooms, she levels me a dry look and asks if I lost a bet to Ethan.

Ethan, for his part, crows compliments, telling me the look suits me and wondering loudly where I found the fine T-shirt I'm wearing. I receive his remarks with indifference, often not even bothering to answer while we walk from class to class, crossing through the backpacked crowd. In ASG, when he challenges my proposal to run a s'mores booth at the bonfire this Friday to raise money, I calmly debate him until Isabel sides with me. During lunch in the newspaper room, he positions himself near me to talk to Christine Reed about how "unprepared" he feels for this week's French exam.

Naturally, he makes sure to mention how much he's studied, a typical, time-tested Ethan intimidation tactic.

Instead of joining the conversation the way I usually would, I focus on the news edits I'm working on. I enjoy the feeling of Ethan eyeing me, expecting a reaction that never comes.

By fifth period, the *Chronicle*, I can tell he's had enough. I'm meeting with the editorial staff to report on how everything's going before next week, which is production week for the NSPCA issue. We gather in front of the whiteboard while the rest of the staff works on writing their pieces on the computers in the back. This meeting is crucial, the final check of whether the editors have filed their photo requests, given writers deadlines for revisions, and planned for any content they'll receive last minute.

The editors pull chairs into a semicircle surrounding me. They sit in their usual order, with news on my right wrapping around to sports on my left. Ethan perches on the long table next to Julie Wang, who's playing idly with the drawstring of her Fairview volleyball hoodie. Ethan's not an editor, but he sits in on these meetings regardless, which I grudgingly permit due to the importance of his pieces in every issue. This month's is no exception, what with his fifteen-hundred-word gym-funding story.

When the discussion turns to the final meeting item, the front page, Ethan interjects, cutting off Tori Sundaram, who's itemizing the stories we'll need space for—the school board meeting, changes to campus security. "I'll be above the fold," Ethan declares. It's not a question, though it could have been. We haven't even begun discussing which story will occupy the prestigious above-the-fold position. Tori looks unamused.

I know he's being presumptuous on purpose. Nevertheless, I nod. "I agree." I turn back to Tori. "Then below, we'll probably do—"

"Oh, and," Ethan cuts me off, eyes narrowing, "I was thinking I'd have the above-the-fold photo and the jump to center."

"Yeah, we'll see," I say noncommittally, wanting to remain conciliatory.

Ethan's not having it. "I'll need the inside pages for word count, and color befits the story. We'll do graphics—you know, timelines, budget breakdowns—in addition to photo illustrations." He waves his hand.

I know he's expecting me to refuse. He has the glint in his eye he gets when he's preparing rebuttals to my rebuttals. While he's not wrong—his story will work excellently as pitched—he's only proposing his ideas this rudely because he wants the fight. Which I refuse to give him.

"Sounds good," I say. With Ethan's glare on me, I turn nonchalantly to the news editors. "Will you start designing the layout? Fifteen hundred words, graphs, photos, jump to center." The editors nod, jotting down notes. "I think that's everything. I'll be in my office if you have any questions."

I walk directly to my office, where I open my laptop on

my desk. Ethan appears immediately in the doorway. I pull up the photo request spreadsheet I was reviewing, hoping he'll go away.

Predictably, he doesn't. He picks up the blue Post-it note cube on my desk, peels a few off, then sticks them sloppily on my window.

Gritting my teeth, I keep my eyes on my computer. "Was there something else you needed to discuss about your story?"

"No," he replies. But I don't hear him leave.

"Great. Well, I have spreadsheets to review . . ."

Out of the corner of my eye, I see him pull off one more Post-it note. This time, he presses it to my desk, right next to my computer. I exhale. This is testing even my newly resolved patience. "You're ignoring me," Ethan says simply.

I look up, surprised. It's not what I expected him to say, not one of his provocations or passive insults. He sounds not exactly vulnerable, but not calculated, either. There's an implied question in his statement, one he genuinely wants answered.

But I'm not interested in explaining myself. "I'm not ignoring you." I keep my voice lukewarm, the epitome of neutrality. "We've had every class together, and I've spoken to you seven times today. Eight, if we count right now."

Ethan's features flatten with displeasure. "You know what I mean."

"No, Ethan. I don't."

"You're . . ." He gestures emptily.

I wait for the end of the sentence, prompting him with raised eyebrows when he doesn't continue.

"I'm what?" I ask. I could finish the phrase for him. I'm *working*. I'm *wishing you'd put down my Post-its*. I'm *honestly wondering what you're hoping to get out of this conversation*.

"You're . . . cool toward me. I don't know."

I try to repress the tiny thrill of hearing Ethan awkward and ineloquent. "Have I ever given you the impression I'm *warm* toward you?"

His gaze darts from me, flashing furiously. "It's—it's not—" He folds a Post-it in half, creasing the center with one harsh motion. "This is different. You've been *agreeable*."

I watch him pace in the doorway, stopping to scuff his dark suede shoe into the carpet, reaching one hand up to the white metal doorframe like he doesn't know what to do with himself. "Let me get this straight," I say slowly. "You're complaining to me because I'm being too nice to you?"

His eyes snap to me, and I'm kind of unprepared for the intensity in them. "Yes, exactly," he says.

The honesty in his tone and the fervor in his expression hold my voice prisoner for a moment. It's the head-spinning sensation of taking a practice exam before you've even begun studying. Of finding evidence that upsets the entire thesis of your research paper. It's paradigms shifting. I feel like we're close to something. What it is, I don't know.

"Look," I start, "we have three months of school left. We work closely with each other on the newspaper, ASG, the reunion. Don't you think it'd be better if we were mature about this and *tried* to get along?"

Ethan's expression shutters, and he drops the folded Post-it onto my desk. "No," he says. "I don't." He walks out into the newsroom. Against my judgment, I let my eyes follow him.

It's a retreat. Ethan came in here and left without getting what he wanted. I'm not even playing our game anymore, and somehow I've stumbled into the way to win. The irony almost makes me laugh. If I'd known not engaging would bother him so much, I'd have tried it months ago.

Instead of returning to my spreadsheet, I remove the Post-its from my desk and window and drop them into the plastic recycling bin by my chair, suddenly exasperated. Without meaning to, I'm *still* taking pleasure in Ethan's losses. It makes me question myself entirely. What if I'm not mature enough to end this? How will I know as long as not competing with him leaves me with the upper hand? I don't trust myself enough to believe there isn't a small corner of my brain enjoying exactly what I'm doing to him.

Three more months of this. I sit, hating the idea. Not fighting with Ethan is going to be as strenuous as fighting with Ethan. I remind myself it's for the best, and I can handle three months.

Except, I realize, it won't really be three months. The thought rushes over me like a wave of exhaustion. I've noticed hints of this one unnerving truth in Jamie's new friendships with her old classmates, in the reunion I've been forced to plan—even in Hector's reminiscences and hellos to Dairy Queen Daniel. High school holds a unique immortality for everyone. It clings on to your identity the way elementary and middle school don't, or first boyfriends or first jobs. For whatever reason, high school lingers.

For me, every memory of Ethan will linger with it, haunting me even while I move on to college and what comes after.

# Twenty-Six

"WHO'S GOING TO BE there?" Mom asks from the passenger seat. The sun isn't yet setting, the sky the gray-blue of the hours before dusk. It's Friday night, the night of the bonfire. I'm driving to the beach because Mom insisted I needed the practice, what with my driving test in only weeks, and I feel out of place in Mom's sleek SUV when I'd gotten used to Hector's small sedan. Despite the differences, though, I can't deny parts of driving are starting to come more easily to me.

"There are going to be teachers, if that's what you're asking," I reply.

She makes a dissatisfied sound. "I don't mean supervision. I mean, like, people you're interested in seeing," she says leadingly. When we pull up to the stop, I glance right and find her eyeing me inquisitively. She's wearing her black blazer and skirt from the office, having come home early, the way she often does on Fridays.

"You mean guys," I correct, slightly annoyed.

"There's a guy you're interested in seeing?" Mom asks immediately.

I recognize the witness-stand trick she's pulling on me. "You're putting words in my mouth." My phone vibrates in the cup holder, where it rests on an empty granola bar wrapper and the collection of change my mom keeps for meters. The interior of my mom's car reflects her perfectly, professional in its clean cream-colored leather, yet with over-it details of empty water bottles and a hectically packed glove compartment.

"You going to get that?" Mom asks.

"No, Mom. I'm driving."

She nods, looking satisfied. "Good answer." She eyes the phone with an interest, even an eagerness, I really don't like. "Besides, you probably don't want to read your hot hookup plans for the night right next to your mom."

"I do not have hot hookup plans." I flush. It's just like my mom, openly wishing her daughter would have an enthusiastic sex life. When she only smiles knowingly, I gesture to my phone. "I don't. Really. Here, read me the message." Hopefully it's from Adam. We've been trading emails on updating the reunion website, which Adam refuses to give me the login for.

Mom needs no more invitation. She grabs my phone and keys in the password. I don't dwell on how she knows it. While the light changes and I drive into the intersection, she reads the message. "It's from Dylan," she says. "She's leaving in ten minutes, and she wants to know if you have a towel." Mom looks up. "Why would you need a towel?"

"I don't know." I rotate in my seat to check for cars, then change lanes. It feels harrowing, but no one honks. "I'll ask her when I'm not driving."

"I'll just ask her now," Mom says. I don't have the chance to protest. Out of the corner of my eye, I watch her type and send the message. When Dylan responds a moment later, Mom looks up. "There's going to be skinny-dipping," Mom informs me excitedly. "Did you know there was going to be skinny-dipping?"

"No, and I don't care." We're close to the coast now, on residential streets of houses with tennis courts. I'm not surprised there will be skinny-dipping. While it's not like I've been to plenty of bonfires over the years, the experience I've had throwing them for student government has taught me they have two parts. First there's the school-spirit part, with cheerleading, red and white beaded necklaces, and of course, teacher supervision. Once the teachers leave, the bonfire turns into a regular party for whoever wants to stay. I guess this time with skinny-dipping.

"Oh, come on," Mom chides. "Don't be like that."

"You're welcome to go if you want."

Mom rolls her eyes. "It could be fun. For *you*, not your fifty-seven-year-old mother."

"Is Jamie going to be picking me up tonight?" I ask sharply, having had enough skinny-dipping encouragement.

"I think she has band practice," Mom says. I'm grateful

she let me change the subject, and grateful I'm out of the house instead of running the risk of further conversation with Ted and Mara.

I make a face. "Is it called band practice if no one ever plays an instrument?"

"Fair point." Mom returns my phone to the cup holder. "Although I'm not complaining. I know I'll miss her when she leaves, but right now her guitar is driving me bonkers."

"Oh, we think she's leaving?" I don't conceal the skepticism in my voice.

Mom shrugs. "Eventually."

For reasons I can't identify, her empty response irritates me. I try to put the feeling into words. "Don't you think it's just a bit weird she's behaving like a teenager?"

Mom crosses her arms over her white blouse. "What do you mean?"

I reach for the thoughts echoing in my head the past weeks of having Jamie home. "Remember Jamie in high school? And college? She earned top grades. She was on the newspaper and got a good job and everything. She had her plan. She had her life figured out. I just . . . I don't understand what she's doing right now. She keeps wanting me to walk to get coffee, or watch some Netflix show, or just . . . I don't know." I hear my own exasperation. "Like, what, she's going to stay in the house for however long she wants, doing nothing? Shouldn't you be worried?"

I hit my turn signal and guide Mom's SUV into the drive down to the beach parking lot. Following the gravelly pavement surrounded by painted wooden posts, I find a parking spot next to a Mini Cooper where girls heft bottles of Coke from the open trunk. I'm unbuckling my seat belt when my mom speaks. "You leave the parenting to me."

I look up, surprised to hear the seriousness in her voice.

She continues, watching me unwaveringly. "I know you're seventeen going on thirty-five and you think you have everything figured out, but guess what, baby girl?" I grit my teeth at the nickname. "You're a teenager," she says. "I know you don't like to admit it, but you are. In this, be the teenager. I'll be the parent. Me, a woman with multiple degrees and an excellent career, who's raised two wonderful, intelligent, independent girls. Jamie just needs time and space, and that's my call. Not yours."

Stunned by my mom's rare reprimand, I say nothing. I don't like being told my opinion's worth less because it has only seventeen years behind it. Nor do I like conceding defeat in an argument. Most of all, I dislike the reminder that my plans and aspirations could crumble the way Jamie's have and my mom wouldn't push me to pull myself together. I know it intuitively, of course. It's why I'm hard on myself. If I'm not, no one will be, and then what's to keep me from being in the exact same place I am now in ten years? Life feels like a tightrope walk, but I want to reach the end, not lounge in the net.

"Sound good?" Mom's words refocus me sharply.

"Yeah."

When she next speaks, her voice softens, if only slightly. "Text me when you want me to pick you up."

# Twenty-Seven

I STEP OUT OF the car. The small parking lot overlooks a hill speckled with patches of grass and sloping down to the sand, which stretches out in a flat expanse pocked with footprints. The water is navy in the evening light, distant waves curling lips of foam and collapsing on themselves. I see the crowd forming for the bonfire halfway up from where the surf meets the shore.

When I reach the spot where people have started to congregate, I find the bonfire half built. The twenty-ish members of ASG members and volunteers here have started heaping wooden pallets onto the high pile we'll ignite when the sun sets. Early partygoers wander up, receiving their necklaces in Fairview colors from Kevin Young, our enthusiastic freshman rep.

I know I have to set up the s'mores stand. First, however, I want to find Dylan. I search for her in the line of volunteers hauling pallets from pickups in the parking lot. There's no sign of her, and I figure she's not here yet or she's finding parking.

Returning to the bonfire itself, I find Kristin Cole, our treasurer, who's co-running the stand with me and who brought the ingredients. Dressed in leggings, flip-flops, and a windbreaker, she's setting up the folding table on the sand. She straightens up when she sees me. "Hey," she says.

"Hey." I'm on friendly if somewhat removed terms with Kristin. She's in my physics class, she plays soccer, and she's been dating Bryce Wilson for two years. It's funny how in the close-quarters, endlessly interconnected environment of high school, it's possible to know fundamental details of a person's life without being close to them.

I help Kristin set up the table and tape on the S'MORES SUPPLIES $2 sign Isabel painted in class yesterday. It's lettered in dramatic gold-glitter paint, and it looks good, which isn't surprising. You don't get to be student body president without being an excellent sign maker. "You brought everything," I say when we finish. "I'll run the stand."

Kristin's eyebrows go up like she wasn't expecting the offer. "Thanks, Alison. Text me if you change your mind." I nod. Kristin doesn't linger long, like I knew she wouldn't. I saw Bryce in the crowd gathering, and I'm sure Kristin's eager to enjoy the bonfire.

Opening packages of marshmallows, I search the sand for Dylan. It's harder now since people have begun to fill the beach, some in Fairview face paint and color-coordinated clothes who've started an off-key rendition of the fight song, others forming loose groups near where the fire will be. The sun is setting, bathing the beach in orange.

Instead of finding Dylan, my eyes settle on Ethan. He's dressed in "casual Ethan," which consists of a crisp white polo under a gray quarter-zip fleece and chinos cuffed to the ankles. While I watch, he carries one of the wooden pallets with Isabel, who laughs at something he's said. Ethan looks irritatingly pleased with himself.

When they toss the pallet onto the pile, Isabel's phone slips from her pocket. Ethan springs to pick it up, earning him a smile from Isabel before she walks in the direction of the parking lot. Ethan's eyes linger on her.

Since our conversation in my office, Ethan's been his usual self toward me for the rest of the week—goading me, one-upping me, contradicting me every chance he's gotten, and frowning whenever I've happened to glance in his direction. We're a month and a half out from the reunion, and items seem to constantly come up—lighting, parking attendants, whether we'll need extra servers. Ethan's done everything he could to fight me on each and every one. Right now, though, he looks like his resentment's entirely gone, like the footprints the wind's covered over in the sand. I don't know why, but it bothers me.

Instead of spending even a millisecond more focusing on Ethan, I distract myself. I pull out my phone and text Dylan.

Where are you?

I wait for her response as the sun sets, slivering into nothing on the horizon. The temperature sinks, making me glad I brought the vest I'm wearing over my sweater. While the fire's unlit, the beach is packed now. Laughter and errant shouts echo up from the dense crowd of my classmates. Already people have started coming over to purchase pre-emptive s'mores supplies, and I hand them paper trays of graham crackers, marshmallows, compostable skewers, and squares of Hershey's.

When I feel my phone vibrate, I finish serving Jackson Parker and his freshman sister, then check the message.

It's from Dylan. Finally. I frown, reading.

> Ran into Olivia. I'm not going to make it. I'll explain later.

I stare at her words, feeling uneasy. I'm not even frustrated that she flaked on me—with how many volunteers there are here, Isabel won't notice. What gets me is the thought of Dylan dropping everything for Olivia. I don't know if they're fighting, or if this is like Starbucks and Dylan's just rattled to have seen Olivia. Whatever it is, the fact her ex was enough for her to completely bail on this plan doesn't bode well. It's unnervingly in character, given how Olivia kind of consumed Dylan's life. While I sympathize with Dylan post-breakup, it's better for Dylan to leave Olivia in the past.

I'm composing a reply when I hear Principal Williams's voice. "You supposed to be texting while running the stand?"

Looking up flatly, I find Williams watching me with amusement. The Fairview jacket she's wearing appears impeccably clean, possibly new. Of course even her school-spirit attire is polished. Pointedly, I place my phone on the table. "Can I get you a s'more, Principal Williams?"

"Yes, thank you." Williams nods once.

I hand her the paper tray of ingredients, then wait for her to leave, which she doesn't. Instead, she watches the stretch of sand in front of us, her eyes sharp and unreadable. They narrow when two boys charge past us, one tackling the other until they crash into the sand, laughing.

"Knock it off or detention!" Williams shouts. They get up, dusting sand from their clothes, and rejoin the crowd, shooting her sullen looks. She shakes her head. "It's unbelievable the stupid shit kids will get up to under your nose," she says to me, then shoots me a glance I could possibly consider respectful. "Except for you, of course."

"Of course," I say. I can't explain why she's being candid with me right now. "Future valedictorians need to hold themselves to higher standards."

Williams huffs a laugh. "Well, I hope *future valedictorians*, which I might say is pretty confident of you to declare in March—" I shrug, nonchalant. "I hope even future valedictorians let themselves have fun from time to time," Williams continues, gesturing to the beach. "Enjoying a bonfire, for instance."

"I'm enjoying it." It's true. While I probably wouldn't spend my entire life selling s'mores on the beach, I like the feeling of contributing to student government and executing something I planned.

Williams looks unconvinced. Her gaze roams to the unlit pyre. "We didn't have bonfires when I was in high school. We did have football games. I loved marching in the band." Her eyes refocus on me, the spell of nostalgia gone and the Williams I know returning. "You and Mr. Molloy have done a competent job with the reunion, from what I understand. Just remember, it'll be your ten-year reunion before you know it. You might want memories of high school to look back on besides studying, and exams, and . . . selling s'mores."

I bite back instantaneous annoyance. I don't know why Williams is suddenly reflecting on her time in high school or why she feels the need to talk to *me* about it, but I'm not interested in her projected regrets. You would think working on an actual high school campus would make her immune to teenage reminiscence. Apparently not. It's like the very fact that *I'm* about to graduate makes the adults around me long for what's behind them. Jamie, Hector, Williams—they all think they have some perspective I lack on my own life.

Will I have regrets? Possibly. I don't really care. Right now, I know what I want. I'm decisive and capable, and every choice I make is with conscious thought. If I wanted to enjoy the bonfire or study less, I would.

"This future valedictorian happens to like selling s'mores," I say, keeping my voice upbeat.

I'm distracted when I see Ethan behind her, heading this way. His expression is all conceited lines and haughty lips, his eyes restless, like they're looking for something worthy of a glare. The knowledge I'm the intended target quickens my pulse, sending a confused concoction of emotions through my veins. Anticipation, anger, even a strange kind of relief, like walking into an exam I know I'm prepared for.

Williams must notice my expression sour, because she follows my gaze to Ethan. "It looks like Mr. Molloy is approaching," she says, facing me once more. "I think I'll reach a minimum safe distance." I nod, and she walks off right as Ethan steps up to the stand.

He looks right at me, his eyes flickering side to side, searching. Before he opens his mouth, I know he's desperate for a fight.

"You should have sold them for three dollars," he finally says, pointing to the s'mores sign. His gaze remains fixed on me, and I wonder what other opening strikes he considered, then discarded.

I feel the undimmed itch to debate him, to play into his game, to allow my blood to boil. It's been days, and the urge hasn't faded. It hasn't even weakened. Like I have all week, I fight it, repressing the impulses I wish I could change. Behind Ethan, the baseball coach is standing in front of the bonfire speaking to the assembled crowd. I catch only every other word through the crackle of his megaphone, but it's clear the fire's about to be lit. There'll be a rush on the stand once it is, and I'll be spared Ethan by a line of hungry classmates.

"Isabel and Kristin picked the price," I tell Ethan, my voice meticulously measured. "It wasn't my decision."

Clearly not having a retort, Ethan circles to my side of the stand. I don't budge, but I don't order him out, either. "What did Williams want?" he asks, examining the system of trays and supplies I've arranged.

"Just a s'more."

Ethan rearranges the box of graham crackers and the bag of marshmallows, reaching in front of me and reordering my precise assembly line without permission. "Looked like a pretty long conversation over a s'more," he says, leaning on the table with lips curled. "I swear, Sanger, only you would come to a party and end up hanging out with the principal."

I reply without thinking. "Were you watching me, Ethan? It's like you're obsessed with me or something." The moment the words fly out, I kick myself. I feel betrayed by my brain. It's a relapse in the direction I promised I wouldn't go. I need to pull it together and keep things detached.

"Of course I'm obsessed with you," Ethan replies easily, catching me off guard. "Besting you is all I think about. Come on, Sanger. Tell me you're not obsessed with me."

*Of course I'm obsessed with you.* This isn't the way our conflicts generally go. Ethan's brought a rhetorical knife to a fistfight, though I'll walk out before I concede this to him. I look sideways, knowing I need this conversation over—*now*. "I'm not," I say firmly.

The lie feels hollower with every empty millisecond Ethan watches me, facing me while I keep my eyes on the unlit fire. Deep down, I know obsession lives within my relationship with Ethan. The times I've strategized how to one-up him, or resented something he's done, or reveled in some victory over him—they're uncountable, like the grains of sand on this beach.

I preoccupy myself sorting the change in the cashbox, expecting Ethan to retort.

He doesn't. I feel him drop his gaze to the ground. There's a fragile pause before he walks out of the booth without a word.

The realization washes over me, cold and uncomfortable. This isn't fun. It's not the consumptive fire of fighting with Ethan, the exhausting push-and-pull of every day spent feuding. Instead, it's discontented emptiness, equally distracting and unpleasant. I'm not working myself into a sweat, I'm standing soaking in the cold. I was sure ending our rivalry would make me feel mature, even fulfilled. The fact it's not working is one I don't know how to deal with. But suddenly I'm scared that I've really ended the feud I've followed for years.

In front of me, I watch Ethan's steps slow, then stop. Like he's gotten a second wind, he spins and marches toward me. "You know," he says when he reaches me, "it's not easy to hear that you're not obsessed with me, Sanger. I've worked hard." His voice is light like he's joking and slightly strained like he's not.

I'm unequipped for how my heart leaps knowing he hasn't thrown in the towel. Familiar muscles come to life in me, stretching, ready. I don't stop them this time. "Well,

Ethan, surely you're no stranger to working hard and falling short of success."

Slowly, Ethan grins. It's wide, victorious, and elated. Behind him, the bonfire leaps into flame, and there's fire in Ethan's eyes. "There she is," he says. The heat hits us, rolling over the sand and covering my skin. "If I wasn't sworn to hate you until graduation, I'd say I missed this."

"Good thing you're sworn to hate me then," I say.

His grin shifts into a smirk. "Good thing."

"Hey, um," I hear someone say, "do you sell s'mores or what?" Pulling my gaze from Ethan, I realize a long line has formed for my stand while he and I were locked in our staring match.

I spring into action, handing Benjamin Polinski a tray. Wordlessly, Ethan joins me behind the table, counting out change from the cashbox. We work in instinctual rhythm, this unlikely mirror image of our constant clashes. I can't help myself once we've served five or six students. "Hey," I say to Ethan, "remember when you thought this s'mores stand wouldn't be a good idea?"

Ethan's eyes narrow, but he looks pleased. "Still should have priced it at three dollars."

"I told you. It wasn't my decision."

While we work, I'm conscious of every time Ethan bumps me with his elbow, closes the cashbox while I'm reaching for it, or preempts me in passing out a tray. They're familiar nudges, peace offerings in the form of tiny declarations of war. The heat doesn't fade from my cheeks until we've served nearly the whole line. I don't know what just happened between us, but I know what I'm feeling now isn't discontented emptiness. It's not consuming exhaustion I remember, either.

It's that, *and*.

And what, I don't know.

# Twenty-Eight

I **WATCH THE FIRE** department check to make sure the final embers of the bonfire are out. In the past hour, I've sold countless s'mores, worked until my hands were numb and we ran out of chocolate, and once elbowed Ethan hard enough he actually smiled. He left the stand half an hour ago to check on the cleanup crew, which left me to work double time to serve everyone. While I pack the s'mores supplies into the Trader Joe's bags Kristen left, students and teachers walk in the direction of the parking lot, leaving a smattering of cups and s'more skewers on the soot-streaked sand.

The firefighters finish and haul their equipment off, and the students who remain walk farther down the shore. It's nearly ten. The water is inky in the night, the moon reflected in luminous ripples. Watching a guy pull off his shirt and run into the waves, I remember Dylan's text about skinny-dipping. Sure enough, a group of girls shrug off their jackets and strip down to their underwear. I shiver just imagining it.

"I'll take this to my car," Kristin says, bouncing up to the stand, Bryce in tow. He gazes in the direction of the waves, obviously wishing for skinny-dipping.

"It's okay." I hold up the bag. "I'll—"

Kristin cuts me off with a humorously cross look. "No. You worked the stand all night. I'll handle this part," she insists. "I'll see you down there. The water's *freezing*," she says, eyes widening for emphasis.

I choose not to mention my disinterest in skinny-dipping. "Thanks, Kristin."

Leaving her and Bryce to the stand, I walk toward where the bonfire used to be. I feel unsettled, if not exactly in a bad way. I don't know how to do this part. The unscripted, impromptu part of high school. The parties, the group messages, the endless wandering conversations in fast-food restaurants or the house of whoever's parents have a hot tub. It's one of the variables I'm not interested in solving for in the equation of high school. Ethan's stubborn smugness is my only constant.

Instead of doing nothing on the sand, I decide I'll text my mom for her to pick me up. I head for the parking lot, up the empty stretch from the party to the pavement. It's dark, the streetlights of the neighborhood small in the distance. When I'm halfway there, I notice a figure walking a few yards from me in the same direction.

I see it's Ethan the same moment his eyes fall on me. We're nearing the same point, our paths converging like the sides of an angle. Soon, we're walking in step.

"Not skinny-dipping, then?" I ask.

"Unfortunately for our classmates, no," Ethan replies. The wind whips past us suddenly, rustling the hair curling onto his forehead.

I roll my eyes, loving the familiar feeling of the gesture. "Everyone looks really disappointed," I say dryly.

He laughs lightly, imperceptibly enough I'm not sure I didn't imagine it. "What about you?"

"I'm *definitely* not disappointed," I say quickly. It's ridiculous, the idea I would enjoy him skinny-dipping. Him removing his fleece, his polo and chinos, folding them neatly on the sand so they're not wrinkled when he puts them on later. Him rushing into the waves. It's nothing I enjoy imagining.

"I meant"—Ethan's voice is heavy with derision—"why aren't *you* skinny-dipping?"

I pause, not volleying back the way I usually would. "I don't know," I say honestly. "It's just not interesting to me."

Ethan doesn't reply. We walk the next steps in silence. The sand slopes upward, narrowing into a path lined with rocks. On either side, wildflowers grow, the short-stemmed plants' white and orange petals fluttering in the wind.

While we walk, I feel compelled to continue. "Do you think we'll regret not doing it?"

"Not doing what?" Ethan's question holds no skepticism or scorn.

I gesture in the direction of the water. "Skinny-dipping," I say. "You know. The things they do while we're studying.

The romanticized high school experience everyone says we should have."

Ethan thinks for a moment. I find myself feeling pleased he's not rushing his response, not speeding to formulate some discussion-ending rebuttal the way he would if we were debating in English or student government. "I don't know," he finally replies. "I don't regret it right now. Do you?"

"No," I say, not hesitating. It's surprising, the relief of hearing my own sentiments in Ethan's voice.

"Then why do you wonder if you'll regret it later?" he asks, and even though I'm not looking at him, I can feel his gaze on me.

I don't know why we're speaking so honestly, or why it feels like Ethan's actually interested in my thoughts for once. I wonder if it's the free feeling of the open night sky, far from the confining classrooms where we're constantly in each other's faces, or if he just missed me while I was playing hard-to-piss-off.

I think back on Williams's warning, on Dylan theorizing high school was the only time you could have certain experiences. I hope I'm not the only person in the world who disagrees. "I guess I don't," I say. "In ten years, when I look back on high school I'll be reliving long nights of studying, early mornings getting last-minute reviewing in, icing my hand from hours of note-taking."

Ethan's lips twitch. "I don't see anything wrong with those memories."

I feel piled-up thoughts tilt precariously, ready to tumble

out. "I just wonder if I'm . . . overlooking something. I don't understand why everyone thinks high school is special. Why is now the time to go skinny-dipping or we'll regret it? We could go skinny-dipping next year or the year after or when we're sixty. But it's high school everyone holds up like it's this epicenter of your life. This milestone we feel compelled to revisit every ten years for the rest of forever."

Ethan remains quiet. When I'm done, he nods. We've reached the parking lot, and we stand under the amber ring of one of the lampposts. "I think it's probably because high school is where you start to figure out who you really are," he says, his voice taking on the quiet deliberateness it does when he's delivering one of his more insightful comments in class. He looks past me, his eyes on the waves. "Sometimes, I guess you need skinny-dipping to find out."

"Why aren't you in the water, then?" I ask. "Do you know exactly who you are, no skinny-dipping required?" His comment catches on the questions I've had recently, the suspicion Ethan's a shiny, smart package surrounding a center I can't see into.

"No," he says.

I note the non-elaboration of his reply. Like all his evasions, it does nothing to unwrap the riddle he is, the boundary between real and fun, and what's beneath them both. The lingering unfinished feeling I'm left with raises more questions I'm sure he won't answer.

I don't know if I accept his explanation, either. High school isn't the time everyone figures out who they are.

People like me have known for years, and plenty of people won't until years later. Jamie, for example.

Ethan interrupts my contemplations. "The reason I'm not skinny-dipping is because I have to Photoshop a few graphics tonight." His posture has changed, his hands shoved cavalierly in his pockets, his shoulders shifting into their usual combative slant. His teeth flash. "Honestly, Sanger, you wouldn't have a newspaper without me."

The squeals and laughter of our classmates echo up from the water. I face Ethan squarely, putting the shore behind me. "You haven't finished those yet?" I cross my arms. "Very unlike you, Ethan." In tossing jabs back and forth, I realize they're the first punches I've thrown in the past ten minutes. I still don't know how to fill in the *and* I felt earlier, but those ten minutes haven't been terrible.

While we're watching each other, waiting for each other's next move, my mom pulls into the parking lot, the gravel grinding under the wheels of her car. The cool white of her headlights sweeps over the pavement, blinding me and Ethan in the glare.

"See you on Monday," I say, walking in the direction of the car.

"I'm dreading it already," Ethan replies dryly, but in his eyes there's the hint of a smile and a flicker of fire.

# Twenty-Nine

HECTOR'S TALKED NONSTOP FOR the duration of my third and final driver's ed lesson, telling me how he learned his friend AJ is coming into town. While Hector polished off his Cotton Candy Blizzard, I've heard for the past forty minutes every AJ anecdote I could ever want to hear. Their decision to found the Settlers of Catan Club, when Hector helped AJ mount a campaign for class president, how they fought over AJ changing the club meeting schedule so he could join the Young Entrepreneurs Club.

Eager to change the subject, I head off his next wistful recollection. "Hey, how's Ethan's driving? Do you think he'll pass?" I check the crosswalk for pedestrians. Ethan's finished his lessons, and with his birthday this week, I know his test must be soon. "Who's better, him or me?"

Hector peers into his Blizzard cup. "You're pretty much the same." He looks up, pointing with his spoon. "Turn right here. I wonder if AJ misses our friendship at all," he continues without skipping a beat. "It's not like we had a friend breakup or anything. It's just hard to keep in touch in college. You'll see."

I push down my frustration with Hector's answer and execute a perfect right turn. *Pretty much the same?* I continue past mall complexes and a Costco, a Starbucks and a Safeway. We're farther from home this lesson. Hector had me drive on the freeway, and we're currently going in circles in a stiffly suburban neighborhood I don't recognize. "Look, if you miss this guy so much, text him," I say.

"I don't know if I even have his number anymore."

I shrug. "What do you and Ethan talk about?" The question flies out of me. Once again, I realize what I'm doing. Once again I'm trying to figure Ethan out. After our conversation at the bonfire, I'm even more fixated on understanding him.

Hector, finally distracted from AJ, considers this. "He describes his plans to destroy you," he replies.

I sit up straight until I realize Hector's joking. "Hilarious."

Hector chuckles. "Nah, we just listen to music or run errands." He catches my incredulous expression. "I know you think he's demon spawn, but he's really a pretty average kid."

This information leaves me with no reply. What Hector's saying is unexpected, nonsensical. Honestly, I wouldn't be surprised if Ethan *had* described his plots to destroy me. But just listening to music? Being called average? They're new pieces in a puzzle I don't know the full picture of. Ethan's not just inscrutable, he's inconsistent. He's smart and driven, obviously, yet he flirts casually and enters relationships without real commitment, and he's oddly ordinary with Hector. Despite how visibly upset he was when I was ignoring him, our rivalry can't really be important to someone like him. I've long suspected it, and it's getting harder and harder to deny. Competition with me is as meaningless to him as checking out Isabel or running errands with Hector.

"You know," Hector says out of nowhere, "you're right. I'll just talk to AJ at the reunion."

I'm half listening until the final word. "The what?"

"It's our high school reunion. That's why he's coming into town," Hector replies.

I nearly roll through the stop. "That wouldn't happen to be the ten-year Fairview reunion, would it?"

Hector taps his brakes. "Yeah. Why?"

"I'm planning the Fairview ten-year reunion. With Ethan," I reluctantly add a moment later. Hector notices the pause, no doubt.

"No shit," he says. Rubbing his couple-days' stubble, he continues contemplatively. "You know, you and Ethan say you hate each other, but you sure do a lot together."

"Not by choice!" I protest.

"Right," Hector replies, nudging humor in his voice. "Neither one of you made any choices. Not in choosing your electives or your schedules, or in agreeing to plan this reunion. You just *end up* together, against your will, every time."

I open my mouth, ready to fire back with the first argument I think of. I'm not choosing to do everything with

Ethan, I'm choosing what I want to do, and Ethan happens to be there. I joined the *Chronicle* first, and he followed *me*. It's not my fault Ethan's interests and mine collide with unfortunate frequency. In the part of my brain trained for in-class debates, I know it's a convincing, rational explanation.

Except it's wrong. The falseness of it feels vaguely, even worrisomely unsupportable, like houses constructed on crooked foundations. If I'd wanted, I could have switched zero-period English and sixth-period government in my schedule to avoid Ethan. I could've chosen to continue with Model UN at the end of freshman year instead of joining ASG. I could've even declined to plan the reunion, if I'm really honest. Williams wouldn't have actually excluded me from the running for valedictorian, and one alumni recommendation won't be the thing that gets me into Harvard.

The fact I didn't make those choices sits with me for the rest of the drive. It's a question I can't answer. Or one I'm just not willing to.

# Thirty

I'M WAITING IN FRONT of Michaels, the craft supply store, scrolling College Confidential. It's nearly the end of March, which means my Harvard decision is right around the corner. In some years, Harvard has released their decisions a couple days early. I'm hunting for clues in other hopefuls' posts, dropped hints from interviewers or admissions officers, anything.

The clock in the corner of my screen reads 2:58. Two minutes until Dylan's meeting me here. Finding nothing on College Confidential, I click off my screen.

I'm here to pick up components for the DIY decorations I'm planning on making for the reunion. Dylan volunteered to help out. I'm guessing she's feeling guilty for ditching the bonfire on Friday, though she didn't mention it. It'll be just me and her—I'm excluding Ethan as payback for him putting the DJ deposit down without consulting me.

With everything going on between him and me, the

question of Harvard feels even more urgent. It's more imperative than ever I get in over him. Because despite the doubts Hector left me with, *I* want Harvard, no matter whether Ethan's there with me. I want to work on the number one college newspaper in the country. I want to learn in the oldest lecture halls, want to prove I'm worth my dream.

While I'm waiting in front of the store, I hear car doors closing. I look up and find Dylan.

And Olivia. Dylan's ex is wearing casually cool high-waisted shorts and a vintage band tee, her expression flat. Her eyes scan the craft store parking lot, like she wishes there were, I don't know, a music festival there or something.

"Surprise," Dylan says eagerly. "Look who's going to help us."

Olivia waves, unsmiling.

I can't say it's a welcome surprise. My plans for the day didn't involve forcing polite conversation with my friend's ex or dealing with whatever hanging out with Olivia will mean for Dylan tomorrow. Not wanting to be unpleasant, I iron friendliness into my voice. "I didn't know you were still in town," I say to Olivia.

"I'm going back to Berkeley tonight," she replies with an edge to her cheerfulness. "How's everything with you, Straight-As?"

Hearing Olivia's old nickname for me, I clench my jaw involuntarily. If it were a compliment instead of a joke, I wouldn't mind. It's definitely not a compliment, however. Olivia's habit of turning people's passions into pressure points, things to feel uncool for, is one of her worst qualities.

Frankly, with my studiousness putting me on the periphery of social status, I'm not popular enough for Olivia. I never went to enough parties or had enough romantic drama for her, and she made sure I knew it, referencing inside jokes of her and Dylan's theater friends while I sat stupidly with nothing to say.

"Super," I say flatly. "How's Berkeley? I feel like you're home a lot."

Olivia shrugs. "My parents miss me." Looking distracted, or like she's working hard to project distraction, she pulls a cart from the line in front of the store. "Shall we?" she asks, then walks in past the automatic doors without waiting for a reply.

I start to follow, resetting my expectations for the day. It'll be fine, I reassure myself. Hopefully, Olivia gets bored and leaves halfway into shopping. I'm nearly to the door when I feel Dylan grab my elbow, stopping me. "We're back together." Her voice is furtive and full of excitement.

"What?" I fight to control my expression. "How?"

If I fail to hide how flustered the news makes me, Dylan doesn't notice or respond. She's practically glowing. "She was going to the bonfire, and we just ran into each other in the parking lot. Like it was meant to be. We started talking, and then I went to her house and we hooked up. I kind of can't believe it."

In other circumstances, I would be happy to see Dylan

this excited. She's not exactly effusive. If this much joy is shining through her usual demeanor, she must be elated. I want to share her feelings, I do. It's just, this is happening too fast to end well. I settle for forcing a smile. "Did she explain why she broke up with you in the first place?"

"College is an adjustment," Dylan reassures me, no hint of uncertainty in her voice. "I understand she was just figuring herself out. Now she knows what she wants."

Maybe it is as simple as college adjustment. But part of me wonders if Olivia was totally honest in her explanation, or if it was something else. The possibilities quickly present themselves in my head. Olivia said her parents missed her, but I'm convinced Olivia is just too cool to confess she's homesick herself. If she *is* homesick, getting back together with Dylan might just be a facet of missing the familiar. When she gets enough of San Mateo, she'll move on, leaving Dylan crushed. Or it's possible Dylan's just something to occupy Olivia whenever she's here, for spring break, weekend visits, whenever, and she'll just ignore Dylan when she's enjoying her life at Berkeley.

I don't know how to tell my friend she's watching the clouds with her feet on shaky ground. "So you're going to do long distance again?"

"It's hardly long distance," Dylan says easily. "Besides, maybe I'll get into Berkeley."

She tugs me toward the store, which feels indicative, like she's cuing the end of the conversation. I don't press the point. We rejoin Olivia in the crafts section, and I redirect my thoughts to what we'll need for the reunion. We ended up booking the Millard Fillmore, Ethan having failed to find anything available and comparable. I envision the event in the hotel's ballroom. Avery's DJ booth will occupy one corner, and we'll find a place for guest sign-in. Cocktail tables on the worn carpet near the dance floor. We'll need centerpieces, ribbons in Fairview colors for the white hotel walls, and other decorations around the room.

I walk the aisles with Dylan and Olivia, picking out mason jars, candles, ribbons—whatever's within the budget. Which is not much, following our other expenses. Adam Elliot explained this when we exchanged emails yesterday, like he didn't think I could subtract 6,450 from 7,855.66 and figure out what's left.

Unable to help myself, I watch Dylan with Olivia while we walk. When Dylan proposes we make photo collages for the tables, Olivia rolls her eyes. I catch hurt flicker on Dylan's features. She's no longer into the idea when I try to tell her I like it.

The rest of the shopping turns into Dylan doing her best to please Olivia, who barely pays attention. I hate seeing Dylan like this. "Maybe we could bring the yearbook theme from their senior year into the décor," I say, inspired by Dylan's collage idea. "Dylan, do you think you can find old copies in the yearbook room?"

"Oh my god," Olivia interjects. "So cheesy."

I feel my temper flare. Fortunately, I'm experienced in restraining my resentment. "It's a reunion," I reply lightly. "It's going to be cheesy." I indicatively face Dylan.

"If you want, I'm sure I can hunt it up, Straight-As," she says.

Hearing the use of her nickname for me, Olivia looks satisfied. Then her phone rings. "It's my roommate," she says, reading the screen. "Give me a minute." She walks off and promptly starts FaceTiming, leaving Dylan and me standing in an aisle of chalkboard signs.

Dylan inspects the shelves like nothing's wrong. Like I'm not stung. While I felt Olivia's scorn for my social remove constantly, Dylan's never judged me for focusing on schoolwork or for having no close friends except for her. I watch her, formulating the question I've wanted to ask for the past hour. "Do you really think getting back together is a good idea?" I keep my voice gentle, hiding my hurt. "I mean, remember how you felt when things ended before?"

Dylan's expression closes off. Her reply comes out harsh. "Of course you assume this won't work out. I knew you wouldn't be supportive."

"Dylan, it's not about that." I fight to keep my expression sympathetic. Dylan doesn't look over. Her eyes remain fixed on the small chalkboards, their unfinished wooden edges ready for decoration. "I just don't want you to get hurt."

"I won't," she replies. Her gaze finds mine, her whole demeanor confrontational. "You just don't think we can last. But I love her."

I can't help my growing irritation. Doesn't Dylan remember their petty fights? The whipsawing of crying over the phone one night and then having a "perfect date" the next day? I *don't* think their relationship can last. It's immature—it just is. I cross my arms reflexively. "You guys met in high school. Come on, the odds are—"

"God, Alison." Dylan cuts me off, her voice rising. "Could you just not act like you know more about relationships than me? You've barely even been in one."

It's a low blow, and one I can't object to, but it still doesn't feel great. This has turned into more of a fight than I expected, and I don't want to fight with Dylan. I soften my voice. "All I'm saying is take things slow. Especially if you really do want to go to Berkeley, you guys will have so much time to be serious." Hesitantly, I smile. Mentioning her and Olivia going to Berkeley together was an olive branch.

Dylan looks only half convinced. "Yeah. I guess."

It's obvious she's still upset, and honestly, so am I. Neither of us says anything. The music on in the store, some outdated radio hit, underscores the emptiness of the moment. In the midst of our silence, Olivia walks up, oblivious. Stowing her phone in her bag, she eyes the chalkboards disdainfully. "This place is so boring," she says. "I have a friend who's an amazing artist. You should hire her."

Dylan laughs, which I ignore. "I don't have the budget to hire anyone, Olivia. But thanks for the idea." I grab a couple chalkboards for the sign-in table and walk to the checkout, pointedly not watching how Dylan drapes herself over Olivia, giggling in her ear.

I feel like I don't know my best friend. Or really, I feel like she's returning to the version of herself I remember from months ago. The thought presses painfully on the walls of my chest while I go through the motions of handing cash over to the clerk.

We're graduating in less than three months. We're supposed to be moving on, moving out of our homes and our high school selves. It's what I know waits on the horizon for me. With every mention I hear of Olivia, every rebound like this one, I worry Dylan won't graduate the same way I will. If she doesn't, I don't know what happens next. Maybe we'll end up like Hector and AJ, wondering in ten years if we'll reconnect.

Maybe we won't even have that.

# Thirty-One

PRODUCTION WEEK FEELS LIKE real newspaper journalism, like working long hours, juggling reporters, editors,
and photographers, feeling the pressure of actual deadlines
and responsibilities. It's the opposite of the *Chronicle* during
the school day, one hour of fifth period with everyone eating
their lunches and doing their math homework. On Monday
night, the first night of production for this month's issue,
I'm in my office, loving every minute and allowing the reunion to fade temporarily from my thoughts.

In the newsroom, everyone's working on the iMacs lining
the walls, the wide screens emanating cool computer light.
It's half past eight, and the windows frame dark views of
the empty campus. Ms. Heyward checks in every hour from
grading papers next door. Nearly the entire editorial staff is
here, only one of the sports editors missing to cover an away
match. The trays of takeout tacos someone's mom brought sit
picked-over on one table, and repetitive hip-hop plays quietly from the speakers in the corner.

I'm fact-checking Ethan's story on my computer, googling figures and cross-referencing notes. Ethan's out in the newsroom, engaged in conversation with one of the features editors, who's supposed to be working.

When I search the spelling of one of his source's names, I have to scroll through several results to find the confirmation I need. The name's complicated enough I nearly don't notice the headline of the result I find it under, instead focusing on the placement of every *e* and *i*. What catches my eye is the phrase preceding the name. It's the exact wording of the quote I just edited.

Then my eyes flit up to the headline. My blood freezes.

I check my computer window a couple times. Google Chrome, not Microsoft Word. I scroll down and up a couple times, my mind numb, not comprehending. But I know what I'm reading. It's *this* story. My story. But it's on the *San Mateo Daily Journal*'s website. Ethan's byline sits under the headline, tauntingly professional and perfect in the *Daily Journal*'s font.

Immediately, I realize what he's done. He's sold his story to a larger publication. School issues are community issues, so when Ethan presumably approached the local newspaper with a fully researched, well-reported story on Fairview High's gym funding, the *Daily Journal* editor would have shrugged and gone for it.

The first time we discussed his coverage, Ethan fought my edits and I threateningly suggested he take his story elsewhere. Which is exactly what he did.

It crosses every line. It escalates our warfare past casual

insults and competing on exams. He might think he's made a nice move in the game of our rivalry, when really, he's flipped the board. I feel my emotions cascading unstoppably, from confusion into sheer shock into rage.

I hardly even hear my door fly open when I charge into the newsroom. Ethan's standing behind the center spread editor, reaching over his shoulder and pointing at some text on the screen. "Drop the word *important*," Ethan instructs the editor. "It's unnecessary, and it's why the caption's running over."

"Ethan." I raise my voice. "What the *fuck*."

I feel quiet descend over the room. Everyone's looking. Whoever's working near the speakers even lowers the music. While the *Chronicle* staff is used to the level of hostility in Ethan's and my relationship, it's never like this. Even I've rarely heard the stony fury solidifying my every syllable.

Ethan turns to me, and I know he's the only one in the room who knows why I'm angry. His eyes sparkle. "What's up, Sanger?" The casualness in his reply is calculated, intended to irritate.

I cross my arms. Right now, I'm not interested in games. "You know exactly what," I say.

Ethan says nothing. He maintains our eye contact, and the silence practically echoes in the newsroom. His lips twitch. Erin Goldberg, the managing editor, stands up abruptly, the metallic screech of her chair on the linoleum punctuating the moment. "Everyone out," she says, forcibly upbeat. "Five-minute break."

She ushers the gawking staffers into the hallway, and I shoot her a grateful glance. When I return my gaze to Ethan, he's leaning on the desk, hands in his pockets. He looks hatefully delighted with himself, a Ralph Lauren magazine model who's gotten away with murder. "The *Daily Journal*, Ethan? Seriously?"

"They were really eager for the story," he replies with a shrug.

"I assigned you that story," I say, fighting to keep my response focused on real points instead of flinging playground insults. "I gave you the resources to write it. I fought to get you in with the Ed Foundation. It was my piece."

"Yet it's my name in the byline." The first hint of spite enters his voice.

I fume. "Were you ever going to tell me?"

"I knew you'd find it." He's flippant, having erased whatever malice I just heard. He pushes his hair back with one hand, and I'm reminded of our walk on the beach. I can't believe I had a halfway respectful conversation with him then.

"And now I'm supposed to, what? Pull together some unfinished crap and put it on the front page of the issue we're required to send to the NSPC?"

"Don't be ridiculous," Ethan says. "You can just syndicate my story."

Ethan's strategy suddenly fits into place in my head. I hear it in the leading way he proposes syndication. It's not a suggestion—it's the whole point. I remember Ethan's pushiness in the editorial meeting the other day, the way he pressed for the front-page position and the jump to center. He was ensuring I made his story the focus of the issue, knowing it would be impossible to replace. When he decided to take his piece elsewhere, he didn't tell me so I wouldn't have time to prep a new feature. Which, of course, he doesn't want. Ethan *needs* his story in a high school paper to be eligible for the National Student Press Club Awards.

Beneath my fury, I admit I'm impressed. I have to hand him this one. It was carefully planned and perfectly executed. The flicker of respect I have for him pulling it off is yet another insult. Nevertheless, I can't help grudgingly admiring him.

"I can't win best newspaper with a syndicated story," I say.

Ethan cocks his head, pretending to consider. "You might. It's better than being disqualified for having an insufficient number of pages. Let's face it"—his eyes narrow on mine—"my story could be enough for you to get an honorable mention. If you replaced it, though . . ." He leaves the sentence unfinished, forcing me to play out the scenario myself.

He's right. I hate how right he is. If I replace his piece with unpolished filler, we'll win nothing. There's a slim shot at *some* prizes with his syndicated story, but it would reflect badly on me, the editor in chief. The judges, some of the best journalists in the country, would know I centered our issue on something syndicated from the local news.

It's why he did this. Not the prestige of having his reporting in a professional paper, not the production week curveball it'll cause. He did it just to make me look bad. What's more, I realize, remembering Erin and everyone in the hallway, he's done it without regard for the rest of the *Chronicle* staff—some of whom, the sophomores and juniors, could've put our publication-of-the-year award on their own résumés and college applications. I don't know if he's overlooked how his move will affect them, or he just doesn't care. Either way, it's just like him.

"You've crossed a line." My voice vibrates with fury.

"No." Ethan steps forward from the desk, closer to me. He's slightly taller than I am. I don't know why I notice it now. He's wiped the smugness from his expression and watches me with a mask of determination. "I've won," he says. The hint of a grin flits over his lips. "I hope you're *mature* enough not to be a sore loser about it, Sanger." He flings the word in my face, repeating the reason I gave him when he wanted to know why I wasn't competing with him.

He looks down on me, eyes electric, enjoying his victory. I hold his gaze. I refuse to show him how defeated I feel. When finally he walks past me, crossing close enough our shoulders nearly knock, I realize I was clenching my jaw so hard my teeth hurt.

I hear the door close, the sound harsh in the empty room. *I've won.* Working over his declaration in my head, I reflect on the past few weeks. I've been so focused on Harvard and valedictorian that he was able to hit me out of nowhere on this new front. My chest heaves. My pulse pounds furiously enough my veins ache.

While I'm wounded, though, I'll never concede Ethan's won. Not to him, not to myself. I'm left with one goal.

Forget maturity. I'm getting revenge.

# Thirty-Two

IN ZERO PERIOD THE next morning, I feel awful. The pressure of an impending headache pounds in my forehead. My eyes refuse to focus, warping the writing on Pham's whiteboard into colorful nothings. In my stomach, hunger and nausea fight, like I swallowed static electricity. In short, I have every symptom of an all-nighter.

I spent literally the entire night in the newsroom. When I told my parents I wouldn't be coming home because there'd been a *Chronicle* crisis, they didn't object. They told me to call them in the morning and joked I didn't need to use the paper for cover, reassuring me they wouldn't tell Ethan Molloy's parents. I was too overwrought to dispute the insinuation. Ms. Heyward went home a little past midnight, ordering the editors to leave with her. I hid in the bathroom until she was gone, then used my keys to get back in.

Under the eye-watering fluorescents, I worked for hours rearranging the page designs so I could remove Ethan's story before deciding it was impossible. There was no way I could come up with enough lengthy headlines, extra graphics, and creative margins to replace fifteen hundred words. More desperate measures would be required. With the clock in the corner of my computer monitor reading 3:58 a.m., I started a new story—one without interviews or original reporting. We'll never win publication of the year, but in my resolution for revenge, I decided I didn't care. What's important is Ethan doesn't win.

It's one thing he'll never expect. Mutually assured destruction.

I wrote five hundred words of a year-in-review piece, nonsensical in the middle of March, while running on nothing except the can of cashews I keep in my office drawer. Ignoring the sky changing in the windows from black to the depressingly light blue of the early morning, I wrote and deleted, revised and reworked this hopelessly mediocre story. Finally, it was seven. To the sounds of students trudging onto campus and the custodians unlocking the doors, I forced myself to close my computer and walk to zero period.

Knees shaky, I find my desk in Pham's room and sit. Ethan strolls in, smirking when he sees me.

"Nice blazer, Sanger," he says. "It looked great yesterday too."

I'm too tired to come up with a pithy retort. "Drop dead."

Ethan doesn't reply, no doubt considering my exhaustion a victory. When the bell rings, Pham passes out the day's AP practice questions. Reaching me, he doesn't drop the paper on my desk. "Miss Sanger, no. Nurse," he orders.

"What? Why?" I ask.

"You look like you're about to collapse." Pham's watching me flatly, not even pretending to sound sympathetic.

Ethan leans over his desk. "I'm worried for her as well."

"I'm fine," I say forcefully, shooting Ethan a look that a court could consider evidence of intent to commit murder.

Pham shakes his head. "Did you think I didn't notice when you sat through an entire exam with food poisoning? Either you're lying and I can't trust a word you say, or you have no idea when you're sick. Which means I can't trust a word you say. If Nurse Sharp clears you, you're welcome to return."

I wait stubbornly, hoping he'll reconsider. When the moment stretches into a standoff, I grab my stuff with a huff and walk out of the room. He thinks I shouldn't be allowed to determine when *I* go see a medical professional? It's infantilizing. Not pleased to find myself crossing the empty campus to the nurse's office the second time this month, I scowl the whole way there.

I push open Nurse Sharp's door. She looks up from her computer, then sighs. "Again, Alison?" she says, walking over to the exam table and removing her thermometer from the drawer.

"I don't have food poisoning," I reply quickly, not wanting her to send me home. Nurse Sharp narrows her eyes, and

I know I need to explain the dark circles under mine. "I was just up all night working on the newspaper."

Nurse Sharp looks even less pleased. "Sit," she orders.

I drop my bag and climb up onto the exam table. "Come on," I implore. "I can't be the only student here who's sleep-deprived."

She fits the plastic tip to the thermometer pointedly. "Did you know sleep deprivation can cause heart disease? It's not something to be treated lightly."

"I *had* to stay up. Ethan sabotaged the paper, and there are two days until the final version is due to the printer." Before I can keep complaining, she slips the thermometer into my mouth. If she takes my blood pressure, I know what she'll find. Just the thought of the deadline hits me with a new rush of panic. Part of me still can't believe Ethan did this. He's upped the stakes of our rivalry to hazardous heights, turning competition into torture. The thermometer beeps, and Nurse Sharp pulls it out. "I don't know why he would do this," I go on.

She huffs. "Don't you? It's constant with you and Ethan." She returns the thermometer to the drawer without commenting on my temperature, which I consider a victory. "Tell me, honestly," she continues, "you're not planning your equally ugly revenge."

I say nothing. Of course I'm planning revenge.

Nurse Sharp shakes her head. "I don't understand it. I mean, I understand needing to prove yourself. When I was in the military, even in nursing school, I was constantly trying to show up the guys. There's a difference between proving yourself and fighting every chance you get, though. Why keep this rivalry up?"

It's obviously rhetorical, but the question leaves me thinking. While she washes her hands with practiced efficiency, I imagine my days without Ethan's and my fights. Plenty of people go through high school or do great things without this constant feuding. Why has ours gotten so out of control?

"Why don't you just not have your revenge?" Nurse Sharp asks. "Wouldn't this war of yours die out?"

I've wondered the same thing on occasion. When I've received a grade short of perfect on an exam we blitzed, or when Ethan's insults really hit their mark and I had to ignore the embarrassment singeing my cheeks. They've never been enough for me to bow out. His newspaper victory is no different. If I syndicated his story, it wouldn't be the end of the world. I could let it go.

But I know I won't. I tried. Ethan pulled me right back in, and I let him.

When I shrug emptily, Nurse Sharp writes a note on her chart. "Okay," she says, her voice gentler. "I won't send you home. But I will force you to take a nap."

I nod, grateful not to be going home. "Fair," I say. While Nurse Sharp returns to her computer, I curl up on the comfortable cot in the office. With the rough pillow under my cheek, my final waking thought is of her question. Why do I keep up this feud with Ethan? Being an overachiever means jumping through hundreds of hoops—why do I insist on lighting them on fire?

The answer, I know, is immature. Unprofessional. Everything I wish it wasn't.

Even right now, with my head pounding ferociously and exhaustion running ragged through me, I recognize the undeniable thrill I get from the thought of besting him. The truth is, I fight with Ethan because I *like* it.

# Thirty-Three

IN MY MOM'S CAR on the way home from school after production night, I close my eyes, collapsing into the cool
leather of the seat. After napping in Nurse Sharp's office, I
returned to class and even managed to supervise four hours
of production on the newspaper until I finally decided I was
exhausted and useless. Miraculously, in that time, I finished
the year-in-review story. Leaving Erin in charge, I decided I
would regroup by heading home, resting my eyes for a few
hours, and then starting the revisions the story desperately
needs.

When I got in the car, Mom looked me over, no doubt
observing my disheveled hair and red eyes. "I won't ask,"
she said. For once, I was grateful for her laissez-faire
parenting.

I think I nodded off in the ten minutes it took to drive
home, only waking up to the sound of the garage door.
Heading into the kitchen for a water, I hear the noise of

the TV. I close my eyes ruefully. Just my luck. As I pass through the living room, I find Jamie, Ted, and Mara watching *Easy A*. The volume is egregious. I'm exhausted, but I'm not exhausted enough to sleep while Emma Stone's voice blares up from downstairs.

I pause close to the TV. "Hey, could you guys turn it down?"

Jamie, legs crossed on the long section of the sofa, looks up. "Hi, Alison. Yeah, sure." She reaches for the remote and lowers the volume. When I turn to trudge toward the kitchen, Ted calls out.

"Wait, Alison, watch with us." He's propped his bare feet up on the coffee table, and I notice his soles are suspiciously filthy. I have no difficulty imagining the Henley he's wearing hasn't been washed in days. There's a rip in one knee of his black jeans, a carabiner on one belt loop from which his keys dangle.

I shake my head. "I'm going to bed."

"Whaaaaaat?" Ted draws out the word playfully. Jamie and Mara glance up, questioning, and I regret not coming up with a more normal explanation for not dropping everything to watch *Easy A*. "Come on," Ted says. "It's like seven!"

"This is backwards," Mara says, laughing. "We're the adults, and we're literally pressuring a teenager to stay up late."

Ted throws a piece of popcorn into Mara's curls. "Dude, we're not adults."

I'm halfway out of the room when I stop. His words hit

me with a flicker of inspiration, which unfurls into an idea. Adrenaline rushes into me, and I'm wide awake. I return to the living room, where I face Jamie and her friends.

"Hey," I say, "could I interview you for a story?"

# Thirty-Four

ON FRIDAY IN FIFTH period, the *Chronicle*, it's distribution day for the new issue. The process involves the whole class, with parcels of the paper wrapped up in cable ties lining the long tables in the newsroom. Everyone takes their package and removes copies of the paper one by one, counting them into the right number for each class. The room is filled with the mechanical odor of ink and the rustle of newsprint.

It also happens to be Ethan's birthday today. When he opens the new issue, he'll discover I've left him the perfect gift.

While staffers file in and out of the room for classroom deliveries, I'm in my office working on the reunion slideshow, catching up on the work I neglected this week. I hear my door fly open, and I know it's him without looking up. He drops a copy of the issue on my desk, the paper hitting the keys of my computer harshly.

"What," he seethes, "is this?"

The replacement story I wrote headlines the front page. "Eight Years Out and Living Back Home: Three Fairview Alums 'Figuring It Out.'" I'm proud of the piece. It took me nonstop effort on Wednesday, not to mention four coffee runs with Dylan in which we both dutifully avoided the topic of her and Olivia's relationship. I interviewed Jamie and her friends Tuesday night, slept for six hours, then worked the entirety of Wednesday—including a second nightlong effort—writing the fiteen-hundred-word story to replace Ethan's. It was five in the morning on Thursday when I submitted the issue with my story to the printer.

The only good thing about the accelerated pace is I've managed to keep the drama from the staff. I passed off his and my fight the other night as a personal one, offered the news editors a vague excuse regarding unprintable flaws in his reporting, and assured them I would handle their pages. The last thing I needed was one of the editors taking this issue to Ms. Heyward, who would have forced me to syndicate the story and robbed us of the slimmest chance of major awards. As it is, we probably won't win publication of the year, but we won't be humiliated, either. And Ethan has lost.

His expression at this very moment easily makes it all worth it. "You knew I needed my story in this issue to be eligible for the NSPC reporting award," he says, his face redder than I've ever seen it. His hair sticks up a little in the front, like he ran his hands through it in shock and didn't remember to flatten the light golden waves back down. It's perfect.

I hold in my grin, maintaining an unaffected expression. "Oh, whoops." I widen my eyes, the picture of facetious innocence. "I guess you should have thought of that before trying to screw me over. It really was a nice effort, though. Next time, maybe." I get up and walk past him, knowing he'll follow. I plan to wring this moment for everything it's worth, including gloating in public.

He speeds ahead, rounding on me. "I deserved to win that award, Alison." It's weird hearing him use my first name. I enjoy the uncommonness of it, the way it shows how obviously flustered he is. Like we've left behind schoolyard games and entered something real. I wouldn't mind hearing it from him more often.

"You know," I reply, "you did deserve it. Your piece was probably the finest high school reporting I've read. Pity the judges won't ever see it."

The staffers sorting papers have fallen silent. Some pretend they're not listening, while others watch with unhidden interest. When two sophomores return from delivering papers, they notice us and their conversation dies instantly. It's exactly what I wanted. Ethan provoked me into making a scene on Monday—now I'm returning the favor.

Meeting Ethan's eyes, I reach past his waist for the stacks of papers on the desk behind him. When I lift them, the folded newspaper edges brush his belt. He watches me heatedly. I head into campus and immediately hear his foot-steps following me.

"Where did you even get this half-assed replacement?" he asks, quickening his pace and coming up next to me as I cross the hallway outside the *Chronicle*. I duck into the first classroom, where I drop a pile of the papers on Miss Cho's desk. When I come out, Ethan's right in front of the door-way, perilously close. I sidestep him.

"Check the byline," I tell him.

There's a pause while he does. I don't need to be looking at him to imagine his grimace.

"It's sloppy," he says. "I should've—"

"No." I pivot to face him, and he stops abruptly right when he's about to collide with me. I abandon my indif-ference and finally let my anger fly. "No, what you *should've* done is remembered I'm your editor. The *Chronicle* is my paper, and I *always* have the final say on every story on every page."

Without waiting for him to reply, I leave him in the hallway and drop off another stack of papers. When I walk into the next hall, it's empty until Ethan joins me. The sharp sound of him pushing open the door resounds down the rows of lockers. He cuts me off, planting himself in my path.

"Is beating me really that important to you? That you would jeopardize your own newspaper?" he asks.

He's close to me now, inches separating us. Hatred rolls off him in waves, but I don't step back. It's exactly what I feel coursing through me. I'm fully in the grip of what Ethan does to me, the consuming drive that makes me reckless.

"Yes," I say. "It is."

His eyes harden. "Are you enjoying this?" he asks, a dangerous edge in his voice.

"Isn't it obvious? Don't be a sore loser, Ethan." I throw his words back at him and am rewarded by a scowl.

"Four years of seeing your face every day," he says like it's a prison sentence. "Of hearing your voice in every class. Graduation can't come soon enough."

"I fantasize about it frequently," I fire back.

"Just imagining the day I never again have to look upon your endless array of pretentious blazers—"

"Your obnoxious shoulder bag," I interject, standing my ground as he steps closer.

"Your ridiculously narrow handwriting."

"Your grating laugh."

"Your noxious perfume."

We're fully in each other's faces now. My gaze roams over every inch of the features I've learned to loathe. I could draw Ethan from memory, if only to light the portrait on fire when I'd finished and watch his long jaw and cheekbones go up in flames. "Your eyes," I say contemptuously, nearly under my breath.

His green irises drop to my lips. "Your mouth." It comes out in a rasp.

Within heartbeats, I'm conscious of the distance closing between our faces. I don't know what to do with this knowledge. Everything I remember, every rational thought in my head feels far out of reach. I'm picking up velocity, brakes cut, heading for collision. Without thinking, I drop the newspapers and reach for his waist at the precise moment his hands find my face.

Our lips crash together.

# Thirty-Five

I SINK INTO THE kiss for an incinerating moment. The rush is overwhelming, high-altitude dizziness in the middle of this empty locker hall. Ethan's lips are hurried, frantic almost, his hands frenzied in my hair. My hands aren't conducting themselves any more respectably. They clutch him desperately, without reason.

Ethan walks me back until I'm pressed to the locker behind me. Our legs tangle, his chest heaving against mine. Distantly, I'm surprised how strong Ethan feels. His arms hold us together, and I don't object.

It's like our hatred has ignited, changed state. Water into steam. We hit the point of transition, our atoms vibrating, energy and heat building between us, until suddenly we're something new. My mouth meets his every movement, and my brain can't keep up. I abandon arguments and comebacks in exchange for lips and hands, gripping his back while he deepens the kiss. The fight hasn't stopped, only moved to new fronts.

When his tongue brushes my lips, it's like it triggers whatever instinct the intensity of the moment overwhelmed. We break apart, eyes wide, and fly to opposite sides of the hallway. My mind unlocks. Realization slams into me, knocking the wind I have left from my lungs. I just kissed *Ethan*.

Daring to lift my eyes, I find him looking like he's having an identical reaction. "You . . . kissed me." He gets the words out past heaved breaths. With an agitated hand, he thumbs his lips, and I notice how uncharacteristically disheveled his hair and shirt collar are.

"No," I reply hotly. "*You* kissed *me*. Why would you do that?"

"I wouldn't. I despise you." There's an unconvinced waver in his voice, a forced quality. He averts his eyes when the words pass his lips, like he's aware of how wrongly they landed.

"Likewise," I manage to say, my lips stinging. They're probably swollen. I lift my hand to check, and Ethan's eyes follow the movement, mesmerized. His expression is one I don't entirely know how to read. I'm not sure I want to, either. Like he's been slapped, he suddenly blinks, then spins sharply on his heel and storms out of the hallway.

I watch the door swing shut behind him, my nerves jumping under my skin. *What was that?* I'd almost believe it never happened were it not for the lingering burn on my lips and the scattered newspapers at my feet. I bend down to pick them up, straightening edges and refolding pages with shaking hands.

The kiss was an anomaly, I tell myself as I make my final deliveries. An outlier. Data sets allow for outliers, and they don't have to destroy years of careful research and analyses. I reassure myself of this repeatedly. My lips on his—nothing more than a quirk of nature.

Except I *enjoyed* this anomaly. The feeling of his hands in my hair, his mouth harried and heated. It fed a flame in me, one I'm finding it impossible to ignore. Just admitting to myself that I didn't hate it infuriates me. I don't even like Ethan, not as a person, and certainly not as someone I'd choose to kiss. The fact that we did kiss, that for a breathless moment I wanted nothing but to keep kissing him, is something I can't reconcile with everything I know about myself.

So I won't, I decide. The kiss and the feelings they sparked don't matter. I simply need to return to my life as it was thirty minutes ago. To a world governed by gravity and the laws of nature.

I pull myself down the way I do whenever Ethan threatens to push me out of control. I hold on to what's real—goals, plans. Logistics. This day's requirements, and the next day's. Ethan will be seeking revenge for my newspaper coup, and I have to be prepared. We've both upped the ante. Now I have no choice but to play for keeps.

# Thirty-Six

HOURS LATER I'M ON the couch sandwiched between my dad and Jamie while my mom scrolls Netflix. I don't typically join in for family movie nights, but when I tried to work on homework or the reunion alone in my room, I couldn't focus. I grit my teeth, hoping my mom finds something to put on before I lose control of my thoughts completely.

"How about a drama?" Mom asks.

"Only if it's not sad," Jamie replies. "No crying. What about a comedy?"

"A rom-com!" my dad interjects.

"No," I say too quickly. All eyes turn to me.

My mom stops scrolling. "Okay, so what would *you* like to watch, Alison?"

"Just. Not that." I feel heat in my cheeks. There's absolutely no reason why I shouldn't be able to watch a rom-com right now. None. Except the idea of watching characters who don't get along eventually realize their love for one another turns my stomach. Worse, having to see actors passionately make out will frankly make it impossible to not think about the way Ethan's hands tangled in my hair, his chest heaving against mine—"How about a documentary?"

"Seriously?" My dad frowns. "What is wrong with you?"

"Let's just watch . . ." I scramble. "Something about revenge."

"I'd watch an action movie," my mom adds.

I sink deeper into the couch, letting my family debate what movie will have the highest explosions-to-frame ratio. When they finally agree on something, I don't object. The opening sequence plays, and I try to focus on the international crime setup. It doesn't work. One question plays on repeat in my brain, consuming me. *What was that kiss?*

I remind myself the most important thing right now is not letting Ethan get an edge on me. I have absolutely no doubt in my mind that Ethan's obliterated the kiss from his memory. He's probably finishing assignments, gloating over how distracted I must be.

But I can't help it. My thoughts stray to the locker hall, his lips, his body pressed firmly to mine. It's infuriating.

Surreptitiously, I slip my phone out of my pocket, earning a glare from Jamie, which I ignore. This is *Ethan* I'm daydreaming about. Something is very, very wrong. I open Instagram and search Ethan's profile. I don't follow him, obviously. Hoping the sight of his hateful face will set me straight, I select his most recent post. He's sitting on the wall outside the *Chronicle*, glancing sideways at the camera and wearing a Harvard sweatshirt. It's stupidly vain. I select another. This one's a selfie. His hair is pushed up from his forehead, his eyes cool and distant. The caption is dumb. *The face of a man studying for finals.* I select another. Then another.

I hate everything about them. It's not helping, though. I keep noticing things I shouldn't. The broad square of his shoulders. The fullness of his lips. The way his hair curls on his forehead. When I woke up this morning I found absolutely nothing about Ethan Molloy attractive. Now . . . My throat is dry, and I'm pretty sure I haven't blinked in minutes. Something is seriously wrong with me.

It's because I haven't kissed anyone since last year, I reason. That's all this is. I've put Harvard and valedictorian first for too long, and now my hormones are desperate. I ignore the part of my head pointing out the times I kissed other guys don't even compare to the overwhelming rush I felt this afternoon with Ethan.

I open his Stories and watch the clip he posted an hour ago. He's walking through his house, which is clearly being readied for a party. Ian and Cole, the senior sports editors, are setting up speakers and putting out chips in the background while Ethan speaks to the camera. *Birthday party tonight. My place,* Ethan says.

Out loud. Really loud. The sound explodes from my phone speakers, cutting right into the film's quiet scene. I fumble to switch off the audio, but my finger slips. *Counting on it to make up for the day I've had,* phone Ethan declares. He grins cheekily, and finally I successfully mute him.

The damage is already done.

"Alison," my dad says slowly, "was that Ethan's voice?"

"Hey, look"—I point to the screen—"The, um, bad guy is . . . doing stuff."

My mom pauses the movie. Evidently, I'm more entertaining. "Have you been paying attention at all? That's one of the *good* guys."

"Right. That guy. Let's keep watching."

"Were you just playing Ethan's Insta Stories?" Dad asks, a dangerously keen look in his eyes.

"By accident."

Dad turns to Mom. "Something's going on with her."

"I agree. She's been jumpy since she got home."

"She's definitely been distracted," Jamie says.

I stand up. "I'm not—jumpy."

"With all due respect," Dad says gently, "you literally did just jump up."

This was a mistake. I should've stayed in my room. "Not because of—anything. Especially not Ethan."

"*Especially* not Ethan?" Mom repeats. "Did you hear that? It's definitely not, in any way, about Ethan."

"I'm just getting some water. How about we all drop this interrogation when I get back?" I head into the kitchen, ignoring the audience of smirks behind me.

Standing in front of the open fridge, I let the cool air chill my cheeks. With a quick glance into the living room to make sure my family's turned back to the movie, I replay Ethan's video three times, with the sound off. He doesn't look bothered. His comment about his day could refer to our kiss, but it could also just refer to his story being left out of the paper. Not because he's actually upset about the journalism recognition. I took a victory from him, one he'd counted on.

I realize I'm desperate for some indication of how he's responding to what happened. Is he as confused and disturbed as I am? His easy smiles in the video betray no hint of a deeper agitation. If he hates me, I'd expect to find the regular manifestations of his anger, but I don't. If he *doesn't* hate me, then surely he'd seem less confident, more uncertain. I can't read him at all, which is unusual.

A horrifying thought enters my mind. What if he's already started his revenge? What if kissing me was nothing but his next mind game? Just a way to ensure I'm distracted and not getting ahead on homework while he's off enjoying his party. It's just the kind of awful thing I should expect from the guy who lied to me about his story. The possibility lodges in my stomach with more discomfort than I care to admit, making me question everything about myself over one heart-stopping, incredible—

No. I won't let his retaliation work. I click to replay the video, hoping I missed something, but before it starts, a text from Dylan drops into the screen.

I'm outside. Busy?

I close Instagram immediately, suddenly hyperconscious of just how long I've spent on Ethan's profile alone in this kitchen. I have to get over this, put Ethan out of my mind, forget every memory I have of the kiss. Focusing on Dylan is the perfect diversion, better than this disastrous movie night. Dylan doesn't drop by unannounced without drama to share, usually of the Olivia variety.

I reach the front room, the sounds of my family's movie drifting down the hall, and peer through the window to find Dylan leaning against her car door. Things have been a little off between us ever since our argument in Michaels. Neither one of us has brought up Olivia, and part of me is relieved she's decided to confide in me again despite knowing what I think of her relationship. When I open the front door, Dylan practically jogs to the house, her eyes bright and her cheeks flushed.

"I got in," she squeals before we're inside.

I blink, trying to connect her words to Olivia. "You got into what?"

"Berkeley!" Her face breaks into a wide grin. "I just checked my email! My parents aren't home yet, and I had to tell someone."

"Oh my god." My mind empties, all thoughts of Olivia—of everything with Ethan—vanishing. Dylan got into *Berkeley*. Her dream school. I feel her elation in my own chest, as real as if I'd just heard from Harvard.

Dylan's eyes are almost glassy, like she hasn't accepted this is real yet. "I know," she says dreamily.

"Berkeley," I repeat, just because it's wonderful to say out loud. "This is amazing, Dylan. I'm so happy for you." I'm not what one might call a "hugger." I don't hug friends goodbye when I'm not going to see them for three days, and I don't like to look like the little kid constantly running into her parents' embrace. But right now, a hug feels more than called for. I sweep Dylan into my arms. She's stiff for a second, evidently surprised by the gesture, then quickly squeezes me back.

"It's all because of you," Dylan says when we separate. "If you hadn't edited my essays and helped me study for the SAT, I'd never have gotten in."

"No way," I reply firmly. Dylan always does this. She looks for how to downplay her success and achievements. We're opposites in this way, among others. I don't press her when I know she's trying to protect herself, like when she acts like photography is a joke and not her passion. I know her reticence comes from not wanting to expose such a personal part of herself to rejection and ridicule. It's a habit Olivia encourages. The difference is Olivia is so good at acting like she doesn't care that sometimes I wonder if she even does. I know Dylan cares, though. With this accomplishment, I don't want her to hide her achievement from the world or herself. "This is because of *you*," I tell her. "And because Berkeley was smart enough to recognize how incredible you are."

Dylan averts her eyes, but her lips twitch, and I know she's pleased. She collapses onto the blue armchair near the window. "I haven't even told Olivia yet," she says. "She's in an evening lab until ten. I can't believe it. We're going to be at the same school next year. No more long distance. It'll be just like last year."

My stomach twists. I can't ignore how quickly this

achievement has been put in terms of Olivia. Getting into college is supposed to be a new chapter in Dylan's life, not just a repeat of one that should have been closed by now. But I don't want to fight again. "We should take a trip up to Berkeley," I suggest brightly. "Maybe we can view their art and photography program." I'm hoping a campus tour can show Dylan just how much there is to be excited for at Berkeley other than her former ex.

"Yes! Definitely!" Dylan agrees, enthusiasm pitching her voice high. "Wait, what are you doing tonight?"

I check the clock on my phone. "You want to drive to Berkeley tonight? It might be a little late."

"No." Dylan stands up. "Tonight, I want to celebrate with my best friend."

I smile. It doesn't matter that I feel Olivia becoming a bigger and bigger wedge in our friendship. Right now, Dylan is happy and she wants to share this moment with me. Everything else can wait while I help Dylan enjoy the evening.

Possibilities of what we can do to celebrate flit through my head. We could grab dinner at the taco place Dylan's been wanting to try, sing at the top of our lungs in her car, drive to the ice cream parlor in Palo Alto that Dylan maintains is worth any amount of time stuck in traffic. Just the thought of ice cream has me thinking about Blizzards with Hector, which sends my mind to driver's ed, then to Ethan and finally the kiss, where the whirl of my ideas gets caught. I can't move past him. Even the most tenuous of connections is bringing this afternoon right back into vivid and exasper-ating detail.

I need to know how Ethan's reacting to today, and not just from the videos and photos he posts online. I need to see him, to read his subtle displays of emotion the way only I can and confirm this afternoon was nothing more than a perfectly executed ploy on his part. Then, when I know that the kiss was nothing, I'll be able to move on. It's the puzzle I'm fixated on, not the kiss. Obviously not the kiss.

"Let's go out," Dylan says, clearly impatient.

In a flash, I realize the perfect way to celebrate *and* fig-ure out Ethan at the same time. I grab my purse from the table and jog a couple feet down the hallway toward the liv-ing room.

"I'm going over to Dylan's," I say to my parents over the sound of explosions and gunfire.

"What about the movie?" Mom asks.

"You guys finish."

My parents exchange a look. I know they have questions, and I'm not interested in hearing them.

"Bye, have a good night," I preempt them, heading back down the hall to the front door, where I face Dylan. "How does a party sound?"

# Thirty-Seven

"MY GIRL ALISON," DYLAN says while driving, "suggesting we go to an actual party. You really are excited about me getting into Berkeley." She makes a left, following the directions from her phone leading us to Ethan's house.

I laugh off her comment. I neglected to mention exactly whose address I plugged into her GPS, only explaining vaguely I heard about the party from someone in ASG. She's not going to be pleased if she figures it out, but I'm hoping the allure of a party will supersede her hatred of Ethan. Besides, there's no reason for her to recognize Ethan's house. She avoids all possible interaction with him even more than I do.

"This is Ethan's house," she says suddenly. She's parked the car on the street and is glancing from the house to the GPS map in her phone like she's searching for an error.

"How do you know that?" I realize a moment after speaking that it was the wrong thing to say. I should have acted surprised.

Sure enough, Dylan narrows her eyes. "I had to do a *Beowulf* project with him sophomore year, remember? He made us work until two in the morning because he was obsessed with our project scoring higher than yours." I cringe. They did beat me by three points, and Ethan made me supervise the winter formal as my task. "Why are we at Ethan's house, Alison?" Dylan asks pointedly.

"Because it's the only party I knew about tonight," I reply, keeping my tone innocent. "Does it matter? We probably won't even see Ethan. Look how crowded it is." I gesture to the line of people crossing Ethan's lawn to the front door. The windows to his living room are lit up, and inside I can see a crowded makeshift dance floor. Frankly, I'm surprised this many people want to celebrate his birth. I would rather commemorate it the way one would a natural disaster or other unfortunate occurrence—somber social media posts, vows to stay strong on this dark day. Either our classmates are indiscriminate with their partying or they like Ethan even more than I'd known.

Dylan's expression wavers. She glances at the crowd, and I can see her hopes for the night warring with years of vows and rants against Ethan and our "unhealthy" rivalry. I know it won't be long before she presses me further on why *I* opted to come here. It's a conversation I don't want to have, at least not until I've rationalized the kiss better.

I preempt her questions. "Come on. Let's have fun. We're already here, aren't we? Might as well go in." I flash my most convincing smile.

Her skepticism seems to reluctantly fade. "Fine," she says, unbuckling her seat belt. "I'm going to need a drink if we end up talking to Ethan, though."

I don't object. We join the line of people heading to Ethan's door, and as the low pulse of the music gets louder, Dylan's step brightens. Dylan loves parties. It's something I've known about her for years, but rarely seen in person. Personally, I don't get it. I felt like I had grown out of high school parties by the time I turned fifteen. It's just hard for me to see the point. But the same side of Dylan that signed up for yearbook and wanted to go skinny-dipping loves a raging house party.

We barely get inside before a group of Dylan's yearbook friends finds her. They swarm us, and I step to the side while Dylan exchanges hugs with Grace Wu and Molly Goldbaum. The entire space is packed. We're in the foyer, which overlooks a large living room and behind that, an open kitchen. Everything is impeccably furnished in a modern Cape Cod style under white paneled walls and dark wood ceiling beams. Gray armchairs flank the fireplace currently covered in red cups and empty bottles. From the drapes to the surely expensive rug under my feet and the pristine built-in bookshelves, it's easy to imagine Ethan in his polos and suede boots reading something obnoxious like *Ulysses* in here.

I put the image out of my mind. I absolutely refuse to be attracted to such a preppy stereotype.

When I turn back to Dylan, she's telling the small circle around her about Berkeley. Immediately, Grace grabs Dylan's arm and pulls her away. Dylan shoots me an apologetic look, and I wave her on.

The yearbook crowd moves into the living room, and I'm given a clear line of vision into the kitchen. Ethan's leaning against the slate-gray countertop. He's wearing a white button-down untucked from his jeans with the sleeves rolled up his forearms. A group of guys I don't recognize stands around him, eating chips and laughing at something he's said. I notice Ethan, like me, is without a drink. While I don't drink, mainly because I would never want to get caught doing anything that could jeopardize getting into Harvard or winning valedictorian, I can't help wondering why he threw a party like this if he's not interested in participating in the main event. Why does Ethan choose to do anything, though? If I had my answer, I wouldn't be here trying to find out.

While I'm staring, he glances in my direction, his eyes immediately finding me. I wait, watching his face for hints of emotion. He doesn't blink, his smile doesn't slip, not a single muscle in his jaw tightens. Then, like he never saw me in the first place, he turns back to the nondescript dude in front of him and rejoins the conversation.

It's abnormal behavior. Reassuringly abnormal. If I had shown up to Ethan's party uninvited on any other day, he never would've passed up the opportunity to make a snide comment. Ethan glories in making a scene at my expense. The fact that he didn't has me thinking he's feeling as weird as I am. Either that, or he's taken his mind games up an obsessive notch.

I'm distracted from the quandary by Dylan reappearing at my side. She tugs my arm, pulling me into the living room. "Let's dance," she pleads.

I don't know the song playing, and I can't think of the last time I danced in public, but for Dylan, I'll give it my best shot.

Immediately, I'm rewarded. Dylan is a hilarious dancer. She exaggerates everything, throwing her hips in wide arcs, then switching dramatically to subtle head bobs. It's intentionally ridiculous. She'd never behave like this with Olivia, I find myself thinking. Even if she was having fun, she'd never let herself look funny, wacky, uncool. Not while Olivia is obviously judging her. It's nice, watching her feeling free to have fun.

I copy her movements conservatively, stiffly bouncing my knees and shoulders in time with the music. Out of the corner of my eye, I notice Ethan walking languidly onto the dance floor, Isabel following him. They dance, close together but not close enough to be overtly romantic.

Ethan looks confident, swaying in sync with the rhythm. He's not touching Isabel, but I keep watching, waiting for their hips to connect, for his hand to find the small of her back, for their fingers to intertwine while the song shifts into a faster tempo.

I'm not jealous. Not at all. In fact, it would be ideal if he were to date Isabel. There's one semester of grades left in high school, one semester in which Ethan, distracted with a new girlfriend, could get an A-minus. I would get valedictorian,

Ethan would get to second base if he's lucky, and high school would end exactly as it should.

"Hey." Dylan's voice pulls me into the present.

"What?" I shout in reply.

"Chips." She points, and I follow her off the dance floor, losing sight of Ethan. While I walk with her into the kitchen, past portraits of Ethan's family and minimalist paintings of the ocean in crisp black frames, I find myself fighting the feeling that I'm going through the motions. It's in jarring contrast to my goal-oriented days. But this isn't one of my goals. This is a party. For the next half hour, I watch with forced enthusiasm while Dylan eats Cheetos and chats with inebriated classmates.

It's hard to believe Ethan really enjoys this. But when I next catch sight of him, it's hard to imagine he doesn't. He's doubled over laughing, his eyes watering, one hand clasping the shoulder of the dude next to him.

It doesn't look fake. I wonder with Ethan from time to time, whether his popularity and partygoing are just him playing the persona he's intuited people want. It's irrefutable watching him now. He's loving this.

The questions I've wrestled with today—this week, this month—come rushing back. With the memory of his lips lingering on mine, I'm even more eager now to unravel what's real with him and what's a game. It's overwhelmingly convincing that the kiss was a tactic at best and a game at worst, so why can't I just accept that realization and move on?

It comes to me paralyzingly swiftly. I know who Ethan is.

I know what our competition is to him. It's *me* I'm puzzled by. When I wonder what Ethan wants, really I'm wondering what *I* want. It bothers me to think this is a game to Ethan, not because it's not a game to me, but because it might be. I've always told myself I compete with Ethan to prove my capability, but time and time again, our rivalry has made me appear *less* capable. And yet, I do it anyway.

I don't know how to make my peace with that, to accept that Ethan and I might be more similar than I'd thought possible. I don't know where that leaves this kiss. Did I do that because I *enjoyed* it? Did he?

The questions spiral, not helped by this party. Needing a minute to myself, I retreat upstairs while Dylan is sitting on one of the couches talking to a guy in a Cal sweatshirt. The party hasn't overflowed to the second floor yet, and I find an unoccupied bathroom at the top of the stairs. I notice the glass in the shower is damp, the barest trace of Ethan's shampoo still in the air. The smell calls to mind zero periods, Ethan's hair lightly wet as he takes a seat beside me. An empty locker hall, my fingers clutching his neck—

I shut down the thought. I need to find Dylan and hope she's ready to leave.

After using the bathroom, I exit and find myself faced with an open bedroom door. There's a desk clearly visible through the doorframe. It's cluttered with books and binders, pens and loose papers. A very familiar leather shoulder bag is slung over the chair. This is Ethan's room, I realize in a hot jolt.

I can't help it. I should leave, but curiosity gets the better of me. It's only fair, I rationalize. He came into my room without my permission when I was sick. I step in.

The room is nondescript. No posters or photos or battle strategies. It's even somewhat messy. The bed's unmade, and the corners of clothes stick out the top of his dresser drawer. There's something disorganized about it, like he's not committed to anything enough to decorate.

"Why did you come to my party?" I hear his voice behind me and turn around, my cheeks red. "I specifically remember not inviting you." Ethan's leaning against the doorframe, arms crossed. He's watching me, his expression hard.

"You put it on social media, dumbass."

His eyes flatten. "I didn't know you followed me."

"I . . . don't." I don't care to elaborate, so I change the subject. "You avoided me downstairs." I will my posture to be casual, confident, and not like he just caught me snooping.

"I was busy."

"You've never been too busy to confront me before." I keep my voice even, not betraying how much I want him to respond.

He shifts, a challenge entering his eye. "You're implying something, but I'm not sure what."

He thinks he has me cornered. Neither of us wants to voice what happened, and Ethan's trying to trap me into being the one to bring it up first. Fine. I adjust my strategy, opting for directness. "Did kissing me affect you that much?"

I ask, like the topic is not at all terrifying. "That you're afraid to speak to me?"

His expression darkens. *Point: Alison.* "I'm talking to you now."

I press my advantage, pleased by how rigid his shoulders are. "You're evading my question."

He drops his gaze. "Of course it didn't affect me," he replies quickly, clearly annoyed to have lost ground. "The kiss was meaningless, inconsequential"—his eyes find mine—"Totally unremarkable." He delivers the insult with the perfect enunciation I recognize from his closing arguments in classroom debates. "Wouldn't you agree?"

*Point: Ethan.* His jab lands, bruising my pride more than I thought possible. But I remind myself I knew he only kissed me out of revenge—not one iota of wanting—and I don't let my expression waver. "Obviously," I reply, refusing to break eye contact.

"You say that a lot. Obviously. It's like you think you're the first one to have every answer." His posture's relaxed again, but there's a charge to his words I don't recognize. My face feels flushed, and I hope to god I'm not blushing under his stare. I need out of this conversation.

"I often am," I say easily, heading for the door.

He doesn't move from where he's leaning on the doorframe. I step closer, waiting, not touching him, expecting him to withdraw. But his body blocks the doorway. There's fire in his eyes, his lips sharp and challenging. The sound from the party has faded completely beneath the rush of blood in my veins, and I feel my fingertips tingling, itching for action. I'm suddenly hyperaware of all the air around us, like I could light a match and send this whole room up in flames. It's uniquely tempting.

"You're in my way." My voice is embarrassingly uneven. We're toe to toe. My chest would brush his if I were able to take a deep breath, but his gaze has me pinned. To be the center of his ever-shifting focus feels intoxicatingly dangerous. Ethan's eyes flicker over me, his expression pained. "Are you all right?" I ask.

"No, Alison. I'm not." I've never seen him look so defeated.

I open my mouth to order him out of my way, but the words never leave my throat, swallowed by his lips. They meet mine, hot and insistent, our bodies hurtling together.

It's somehow more electric this time. The surprise is dulled, the kiss no longer a total shock to my system, allowing me to feel everything more acutely without the distraction of disbelief. My thoughts shut off, and I savor the weightless tug in my stomach, the perfect dizziness brought on by the brush of his tongue. I've been kissed before, but never like this. Never with this much intensity, like we both know it's only a matter of time before someone breaks this off, and we want to get as close as possible before then.

It's a blitz. Not raced across pages with pens and printed ink. But urged on with fingers entwined, heartbeats colliding, lips pressing deeper, harder.

He tears his hand free long enough to swing his bedroom

door shut behind us, his mouth never leaving mine. If this is just for revenge, it feels like Ethan's *really* into revenge. I grab his collar, pulling him tightly to me. So, it appears, am I. His hands fist, then smooth down my back as he tugs my shirt up from where it's tucked into my pants. When his fingers brush the bare skin of my stomach, I make a noise like a moan or a sigh, and I can feel Ethan's lips turn smug under mine. *Point: Ethan.*

His conceited satisfaction flames the heat in me. "This," I say, breaking off between breathless kisses, "is"—I pant— "meaningless."

His mouth twitches. I think I've almost made him laugh, but he kisses me again. "Inconsequential," he adds, his voice gravelly.

"Totally—"

He cuts me off with tongue. "Unremarkable," he finishes, forcing emotion out of the word.

I grip him harder, annoyed I can't get the upper hand. I kiss him more fiercely, tangling my hands in his hair. His breathing is ragged, but it's not enough. When I feel the tremor in his hand as he explores my midriff, I realize how I can win. Keeping my eyes on his, I draw back just long enough to pull my shirt over my head. I drop it at our feet. The moment his gaze dips down to my chest, his expression tightens. He doesn't look away until I bring his mouth back to mine.

*Point: Alison.*

His kisses come faster. I can feel him losing control.

The fervor in his touch, his pounding heartbeat, his shallow breaths. While this may have started as payback, I don't think he was prepared for *this*. For wanting me as badly as I know he does. This isn't the Ethan with the perfect detached comeback, the impassive expression, the dry glance. This is Ethan on the edge, fighting desperately to right himself. He's skidding on wet pavement, knowing if he brakes he'll spin out, flip, crash. So he doesn't, he rides it, waiting, hoping to feel the road under him again.

I don't object when he walks me back to his bed. His hands leave my hair, darting to the buttons of his shirt. I feel his knuckles at my chest, fumbling to undo one button, then the next. Impatient, I knock his hand aside, unbuttoning three buttons, exposing a triangle of skin at his chest I've never seen before. His hands move to the bottom of his shirt, working his way up, racing me. We meet in the middle, and I shove his shirt from his shoulders, my skin singing at the new contact.

Heat is building between us, and I don't know how far we're planning to take this. We fall into his unmade bed, the smell of Ethan suddenly everywhere. It's like my thoughts have stalled, unable to keep up with the contradicting desires coursing through me. Distantly, I know I should have a hundred questions right now. *Important* questions. What this means, why now, whether this is somehow real—they're obliterated under the brush of his fingers on the curve of my rib cage.

He's kissing my neck when I feel my phone buzz in my

pocket. I ignore it. Ethan hesitates, though. We're pressed so close together, he must have felt the vibration. I make no move to check whatever text I've received, already feeling the pull between us fading. I don't want it to, not yet. I reach my chin up, catching his bottom lip between my teeth, and he makes a rough noise in the back of his throat. Everything inside me leaps when his hand grips mine on the pillow above my head.

My phone buzzes again.

We both still. The interruption is enough. Without the heady distraction of his kiss, his hands' slow exploration of my skin, my mind can finally form complete thoughts. *What did I just do?* Horror cools my heated blood.

"Maybe you should get that," Ethan says above me. His voice is rigid, his expression stony. He's realized what I have, and he's equally displeased.

"Right." I scramble out from under him, ignoring the fuller view I'm given of Ethan's shirtless chest. His chest that was just pressed sweaty and hot to mine. I'm dreaming—no, having a nightmare. This cannot possibly be happening.

I pull out my phone, finding texts from Dylan.

Where are you? We have to leave.

Alison??

I don't know what's going on with Dylan, but I have absolutely no objection to getting as far from this house—this bedroom—as possible. I send off a quick reply, telling her I'll meet her at the door, then stand and reach awkwardly for my shirt on the floor. Ethan does the same, turning his back as he gets dressed. Neither of us says anything. I can't even look him in the eye. I may never be able to look him in the eye again.

I head for the door, then pause. The sounds of the party are louder here, no longer muffled by Ethan's sheets. My classmates are down there. The thought of them, or anyone, finding out what we just did . . . I can't imagine it.

"This," I begin, turning back to Ethan, "can't leave this room."

"For once I agree," he replies quickly. "And, Sanger"—he looks away from me, like he's ashamed—"This *won't* happen again." He says it like he's commanding himself.

I know better than to trust Ethan, even if I want to. And I'm not certain either of us knows what this has become. But I'm not going to contradict him. I nod and walk out, hoping Ethan's smart enough to wait five minutes before following me.

My legs feel unstable as I descend the stairs. My heart is pounding, my face feverish. I cut through the crowd, flattening my hair when I catch my reflection in the decorative mirror in the hallway. I look wild. A dangerous edge in my eyes. Something has changed, but I don't know quite what. *This is the reflection of a girl recently kissed by Ethan. A girl who wanted more of him.*

I quicken my steps, continuing toward the front door,

making my way through classmates who are blissfully unaware of what just transpired ten feet above them.

"There you are," Dylan says. She finds me in the living room and immediately takes my elbow to usher us outside. "I'm so screwed. I posted a photo from the party, and Olivia saw. She was super jealous. When I told her I was celebrating because I got in to Berkeley, she just got pissed I hadn't told her first. I need to get out of here and call her."

I don't trust my voice to be steady enough to reply. I settle for nodding sympathetically. Thankfully, Dylan seems too emotionally preoccupied to take in my disheveled state. She checks her phone, which is lighting up constantly with a stream of texts. It's classic Olivia. She doesn't always want to be with Dylan, but the moment Dylan does something without her, she snaps, making Dylan a villain for doing nothing more than what Olivia does on a regular basis. I don't comment on how selfish and controlling Olivia is being, though. I don't want another fight. Besides, after what I just did upstairs, I no longer think I'm qualified to give even remedial romantic advice.

When we reach the door, I catch sight of Ethan out of the corner of my eye. He's entering the living room, heading to join Isabel and a crowd of ASG people talking by the fireplace. I can't help noticing he hasn't tucked his shirt in fully on his side, revealing a sliver of skin at his waistband. My hand was on that skin. I shiver at the memory, feeling the whisper of his breath on my neck.

Ethan says something to Isabel, who laughs. Just

twenty minutes ago I was hoping they would get together and clear my path to valedictorian. Now . . . I don't know what I want. Every truth I'd believed unshakeable is wobbling in my mind, threatening to crash to the floor, bringing down with it the very core of who I am. I *hate* Ethan Molloy. I can't wait to be free of him, to leave him behind and never look back. Our relationship is nothing but competition with the only objective being showing my superiority at his expense.

But there's more now. I . . . want him. I like the way he kisses me. I feel flushed remembering how close our bodies were. With every recollection, I recognize my detail-oriented brain betraying me. I'm used to compiling the components of student government funding proposals, of chemistry rules, of the War of 1812. This is *not* the War of 1812. This is me and Ethan in his bedroom. There's definitely chemistry, but not the type I got the highest grade on in Honors sophomore year.

I'm furious with myself for the realization, but I know there's something between us. Something other than rivalry or winning.

Something I don't understand. Not even close.

The problem is, I don't want to figure out this new whatever-it-is right now. I don't have time, and I don't know if I even want to follow my thoughts down this path. I have very real reasons for disliking Ethan—insults he's flung my way, the self-satisfied way he carries himself, his attempt to screw me over with the newspaper. What's more, I don't know how much of what we did upstairs was one of Ethan's games.

I decide I hope he does get together with Isabel. It would fix everything, close off every question. Then I wouldn't have to wonder what our surprisingly heat-filled collision was to Ethan.

Or what it was to me.

# Thirty-Eight

ETHAN AND I DON'T return to normal on Monday or on Tuesday. To outside observers I'm sure we look like nothing's changed. Ethan reads on his phone in class, spends ASG scribbling notes in his copy of Hamlet like his thoughts have outpaced his pen, and jokes with staffers in the newsroom during lunch. I throw myself into my rituals and routines, making sure I don't waste even a single minute.

When we're called into Ms. Heyward's room during the *Chronicle* class period on Monday for complaints from the *Chronicle* staff about the latest issue, we both do our utmost to push the other in front of the firing squad. Apparently, some of the editors took issue with me writing a new story in one night and publishing it without running it by anyone.

I explain what Ethan did, and Ethan gives a speech to Ms. Heyward about how I should have syndicated his story. Ms. Heyward isn't moved by either of us. She lectures us on professionalism and assigns us each a five-page paper on journalistic standards as if we're freshmen who've forgotten to cite their sources. To be talked down to by a teacher who wouldn't have even known about my story unless someone complained to her would normally frustrate me beyond measure. But it's a testament to how much making out with Ethan has messed with my head that I take Ms. Heyward's lecture without a fight.

Only when Ethan's alone with me do I know he's as uncomfortable as I am. It's obvious in the little inconsistencies. He doesn't goad me or get competitive when Mr. Pham announces a graded practice AP exam at the end of the week. He doesn't even make eye contact with me. I know why. Neither one of us wants to risk reigniting whatever happened in his room. We know if we did, it might finally consume us. *Mutually assured distraction.*

I have one very fortunate, if nerve-wracking, diversion. Harvard decisions come out on April 1—two days from now.

On Tuesday night, the eve of the decision, I'm in my room scrolling through College Confidential. In the past days, I've found it hard not to obsess over the threads where people inquire about their chances, posting résumés of extracurriculars, grade point averages, service programs in other countries, or inspiring charitable work. I'm chewing my nail, reading the post of one Hailey in Ottawa, when my email chimes.

The message is from Adam Elliot. I open it without reading the opening lines of the notification in the right-hand corner of my computer screen. I've continued to send Adam comprehensive updates on the reunion planning—he continues to rarely if ever reply. I have my doubts he reads them, doubts the cursory opening of this one hardly remediates.

From: adam@blockr.com
To: alison.sanger@fhs.edu
Subject: Fairview Reunion

Glad you're managing to stay within budget.

I roll my eyes. Adam never misses a chance to condescend to a high school student.

I know Harvard decisions are tomorrow. I wish
I could tell you something reassuring, but
admissions are very competitive. While I put in
a word for you and Ethan, it's ultimately going
to come down to how qualified the admissions
officer finds you.

There's nothing else. I close the email, wishing I hadn't read the reminder of how difficult achieving my dream is. I don't need reminding. In general, and especially when I'm with Ethan, it's easy to tell myself I'm going to get into Harvard. Easy to outwit and out-reason the possibilities my college hopes won't go the way I've planned, to knock them down before they grow fearsome. I'm not faking. I really am confident. Just . . . no one is confident all the time.

Alone in my room on the eve of decisions, I can acknowledge it's entirely possible I could fail. And I'm not practiced at failing.

I close out of College Confidential and grab my homework. While my desk lamp casts slanted shadows on my floor, I inhale and exhale, forcing Harvard and Ethan and condescension and uncertainty from my head. I open my French folder and reach past the neat pile of notebooks on my desk for a pen.

Before I've had the chance to conjugate one verb into *passé imparfait*, my bedroom door flies open. Jamie barges in, holding the most recent issue of the *Chronicle*.

"What the hell, Alison?" She holds up the paper, displaying my front-page story.

I don't react, stunned into silence. It's the first time in a while I've seen my sister anything but perfectly upbeat. Pink splotches stain her cheeks, her eyes narrowed and accusatory. I put together she's read my article, and she's not happy. "I told you I was writing a feature on your band," I say defensively.

"Yeah, you did," Jamie replies. "I thought it was going to be about Fairview alums reconnecting. Not how pathetic and lost we all are."

Instincts for debate, inherited from my mother and

perfected on Ethan, rear up within me. "In fairness, I never used the word *pathetic*—"

"Is this what you really think?" she cuts me off, shaking the paper.

"Jamie," I say delicately. "You moved back home with your parents. You're not even applying for jobs. If you're not a little lost right now, then . . . I don't understand what's going on with you."

"You're right. You don't understand, because you didn't ask. This piece is bad writing." Her voice flattens, her indignation fading into what looks like disappointment. "You may have forgotten that I worked on a collegiate paper, but I can tell you this wouldn't have made it to print in the real world. You didn't ask us one question about how *we* felt to be living at home or why we're doing this. You decided on the story you wanted to tell, and only included the reporting that fit your own ideas. Maybe one day you'll want my perspective. Maybe you don't care. I certainly don't have to justify my life to someone who shows so little interest in it."

She drops the paper on my desk and moves to leave without giving me a chance to reply. Then she pauses near the door, her eyes on my whiteboard, where the Harvard decision date is prominently written.

"Good luck tomorrow," she says. "I hope everything works out exactly the way you want."

I start to stand when she exits into the hall. Part of me wants to follow her. I regret hurting her feelings, I really do.

It was never my intention. Truthfully, I didn't think she'd ever read the story.

But I sit back down. While I didn't mean to hurt her, I don't think she's right. She's just upset I inadvertently forced her to confront the reality she's living in. I wrote nothing judgmental in my story. I just wrote nothing untrue, either. If she's uncomfortable facing the facts of her life, I don't think it's entirely my fault. When she's cooled down a little, I hope we can have a conversation about the story. Right now, however, I have enough to deal with without hearing Jamie try to defend every choice making her insecure.

I find my eyes returning to the Harvard date on my whiteboard. If Jamie doesn't know who she is by now, I certainly can't help her.

# Thirty-Nine

I'M HOLED UP IN my office the next day, computer on my desk with my email open, phone displaying Harvard's Twitter account, thumb compulsively refreshing the page. It's three forty-five. The latest tweet says decisions will be posted at seven p.m. eastern, four p.m. for us. I set an alarm on my phone, more out of wanting to feel proactive than fearing I could possibly miss it. The newsroom is empty, the hallway outside echoing faintly with the orchestra rehearsing for their upcoming concert. It's like a movie score playing over my anticipation. I'm fifteen minutes from the biggest moment of my life, and yet I'm unable to fully focus.

When I glanced over to Ethan in government today, I found him already looking at me. I held his gaze. Neither of us had a reason to stare at each other—we weren't checking each other's progress on a quiz or glaring just because. We stared anyway. We'd done okay pretending nothing had happened between us, but in that moment, I could practically feel his lips on my skin, his hands on my hips.

I haven't stopped feeling them since. It's funny. I honestly wish I was entirely devoted to freaking out about the Harvard decision instead of replaying memories I should find nauseating.

I refresh my email, hoping I can refresh my thoughts with it. The strategy works, my fear creeping back in. What if I don't get in? What if I did everything right just to fall short? Who will I be if I fail at my biggest goal, the truest test of my abilities?

I'm contemplating dismal possibilities when, in my peripheral vision, I catch sight of Ethan outside through the window in my office. It's like I conjured him from the effort of not thinking about him. He walks past the newsroom, then doubles back and hesitates in front of the door. I don't know what he's been doing on campus for the past forty-five minutes or why he's here now. Regardless, I'm certain he knows when the Harvard decision is happening.

Despite myself, I wonder if he's going to come in. I wonder if I want him to.

Before I have the chance to decide, he pushes the door open. I watch him walk toward my office, his eyes roaming the room purposelessly like he's just wandered in here, one hand tucked thumb-out in the pocket of his chinos. Finally, he reaches my door and pulls it open. Without knocking, of course.

I look up, pretending I'm lightly irritated instead of on

the verge of—I don't know what. "Is there something you need, Ethan?"

"Harvard decisions come out in thirteen minutes," he says simply. He drops his bag on the floor, then drops himself into the other chair in my office.

"Nervous?" I ask.

He scoffs. "I just want to see the look on your face when I get in and you don't." He props his white sneakers on my desk, which he knows I hate.

I get up and walk to the front of my desk, shoving his legs aside. It was the wrong move. With even the fleeting contact, I'm hit with images of the other night, the party, Ethan's room upstairs. Sheets and hands and lips parted and—*nope*. "You can stay if you don't try to make out with me," I say, searching for scathing and landing on stilted. I'm prepared for some pompous denial.

Instead, Ethan somehow looks even more relaxed. "Yeah, we should probably discuss that."

"*Now?*" My eyes widen. "Twelve minutes before Harvard decisions?"

"Did you have other plans?" He studies his nails, his whole demeanor dismissive, like this is just one more inconvenient edit I've given him.

It makes my pulse pound. Not just with heated memories. With jealousy. With competitiveness channeled into an increasingly familiar direction. I want to be the way he is right now. Unmoved. Careless. "There's nothing to discuss." I keep my voice lofty, so lofty I'm dizzy from the height.

Ethan pauses, one eyebrow rising in mocking disbelief. "Nothing?" He leans forward, and I swear the mocking shifts into something else. His features become intent, inquisitive.

I don't trust the way his expression urges my heart to beat faster. "Kissing you—"

He interrupts me. "I'd call it hooking up. Clothing was removed, Sanger."

*Yeah, I'm very aware clothing was removed, Ethan.* I furiously fight the flush in my cheeks, trying to act unmoved. "*Hooking up* with you was merely proof I'm still subject to hormones and reckless decision making. It's something I hope to mature out of promptly."

Ethan merely *hmm*s, considering. It unnerves me. It's very un-Ethan. I wait, in disbelief of how intensely I'm watching him for the slightest hint of what he's thinking. "It's irritating," he finally says, his eyes meeting mine, "how often I find myself thinking about that night. How often I find myself thinking about kissing you again." He wets his lips. "Worse, it's distracting me from school. I could hardly get through a practice AP Physics exam last night for how often my thoughts turned to you."

His words, and their precision and formal deliberateness, light a dangerous fire in my chest. I hope sarcasm will stamp it out. "Maybe we should hook up before the real exam, then. Make sure you're distracted when it matters." I lean against the desk facing him, our legs inches apart.

"Maybe we should," he replies. "I'm confident I could leave you more unfocused than I."

"Doubtful."

"I've noticed you noticing me in class, Alison," he says, no longer haughty. His green eyes haven't wavered from mine. "This isn't one-way."

"I've been *glaring*."

"You've been fantasizing."

I pretend I'm indignant, instead of deeply guilty. "Like you could be the object of my fantasies." I remember with grating fondness when my only fantasies of Ethan were academic. Watching him see me win valedictorian. Him confusing the War of the Roses with the Hundred Years' War or fumbling to remember which play Polonius comes from. Good fantasies. Nice fantasies. "We kissed, hooked up, whatever you want to call it. It wasn't exactly earth-shattering," I lie.

The remark hits Ethan right where I'd hoped. His whole expression darkens. "Yes it was," he replies immediately.

"You're so full of yourself," I say, pleased to have found a weakness. "You really think you're that good a kisser."

"I know I am." His mouth flattens.

I laugh. Pushing myself off the desk, I put distance between us, unable to face him. "Honestly, Ethan, your skills are average." It's not true. Just saying it is forcing me to recollect how not true it is. I've kissed enough people to know Ethan's, well, above average.

"Fine. Redo," he says. "Right now." I whirl, incredulous. He's standing up now, on the other end of the office. The old *Chronicle* copies and awards I've hung up frame his confrontationally crossed arms. I don't understand until he continues. "Kiss me, and then try to tell me it's average."

I open my mouth and find I have no response. He's actually affronted. What's more, he's not joking. He wants to kiss me right here, in my office at school, despite days of avoiding any reference to what's going on between us. He walks forward, slowly and deliberately coming closer.

"What happened to 'this *won't* happen again'?" I ask, repeating his promise from his bedroom.

He stops, then, like he's testing something, he carefully runs his hand all the way down my arm, lightly twining his fingers in mine. "I did try," he says softly. "Every night since, I've tried. I don't—you know this"—his lips curl—"I don't enjoy failing, Alison."

I meet his eyes, taking my time trying to parse the emotions in them. There's disappointment, but larger than that, yearning. I don't find the satisfaction, the calculated poise that accompanies his tricks. He's being honest. It terrifies me, electrifies me. My chest is so tight, it hurts to breathe. I don't step away.

"This is failing," I whisper, brushing my other hand against his. He catches my fingers, both of our hands clasped together.

"Is it? I'm beginning to wonder. For a little while, it might be . . ." He leans closer, his breath tickling the corner of my mouth. *"Fun."*

Every cell in my body is at war with itself. I want to turn him down, or I *want* to want to turn him down. I don't know which. Either way, I don't have the chance to muster the strength. In my head I hear, like a weeks-old echo, the clang of us making contact with the metal locker doors in the empty hallway. I smell Ethan's off-white sheets, feel the uneven folds of his comforter under me while he pressed us chest to chest and kissed me. I—

My phone chimes on the gray plastic surface of my desk. Four p.m. In the same moment, I hear Ethan's phone go off in his pants pocket. *Of course* he also set an alarm.

I say nothing. Neither does Ethan.

It shatters whatever spell was drawing us closer. I rip my eyes from him and reach for my phone, heart pounding in a whole new way. Out of the corner of my eye, I see Ethan pull his phone out. In synchrony, we log into our portals. I don't let myself hesitate. I click through to the decision.

I am delighted . . . On the third word, I know. The rest of what's written vanishes in a haze of euphoric realization.

Every exam I reviewed for until my eyes watered, every project I put hours into polishing, every night in the newsroom and resolution I fought for in ASG—it worked. I was as confident as possible facing impossible odds, and yet, it's kind of incredible that I decided what I wanted and proved I was worth having it.

When I look up, I find my wild exhilaration mirrored in Ethan's eyes, and everything changes. I'd been counting on graduation to end this rivalry. Counting on Harvard to free me from our competition. But I know from the way Ethan's eyes dart now from his phone, to me, to mine—both of us got in. There's no winner, only four more years together and no end in sight. It's not just our competition we'll have the alarming chance to continue, either—it's the impossible attraction I'm fighting to pretend doesn't exist.

"Congrats," I say.

"Yeah, congrats," he repeats.

We're both awkward and uncomfortable. I don't need my Harvard-worthy GPA to know it's because he's realizing exactly what I have. There's no escape from each other now, no easy out. Ethan's eyes, which had been fixed on mine for the past five minutes, now point determinedly everywhere else. He's holding his phone, his whole posture off.

"Well," he says, "I should probably call my parents."

I nod. Without saying more, he walks out.

I don't move, paralyzed under warring elation and foreboding. In the past whenever I felt pressured by my workload or frustrated with Ethan, I would imagine myself on the opposite coast under the towering trees and redbrick walls of Harvard Yard. Now I have no choice. I have to imagine Ethan there with me. It's one more kind of fantasy he's invaded.

He was right. We do need to talk about whatever *this* is. But I don't know how, not when I was ready to kiss him again, thoughts of Harvard temporarily obliterated from my mind.

# Forty

I'M HEADED FOR THE baseball field, for whatever reason.

When Ethan left, I called my parents, who were predictably delighted, and then Dylan. Over the sounds of cheering,
I could hardly hear her telling me to meet her in the baseball
bleachers where we would celebrate. While I don't understand how Fairview baseball could be celebratory, I decided
to join her. Today, I'm in no rush to return to the homework
waiting for me. I've just achieved a nearly lifelong dream, and
I plan on reveling in the feeling.

I walk in the gates to the field, finding classmates and
parents lining up for the concessions stand and chatting in
groups. Continuing into the bleachers, I hear the umpire
calling pitches, the Fairview coach on the first base line beck-
oning players to the bat. People hold hot dogs and pretzels or
play with their phones in the crowd. Dylan's in the front row
in an oversized black sweatshirt, camera raised to her eye,
rotating the zoom lens with effortful precision.

"I admit," I say, sitting down next to her, "This isn't how I expected to celebrate getting into Harvard. Do we even like baseball?"

"I know." Dylan's camera shutter snaps several times in quick succession. "I'm sorry. But I have to take photos. Plus, I have a surprise for you later," she adds.

I rub my arms in the midafternoon cold. "What?"

"Patience," Dylan replies.

I know it would be useless to try to pry more from her. When Dylan digs her heels in, she's immovable. Instead of wasting the effort, I settle in, turning my attention to the game. I read the names on the uniforms of players walking to the plate, recognizing Josh Campos from government and Noah West, who's going out with Jason, one of the *Chronicle* sportswriters. When Nick Caufman strikes out, I cheer, earning laughter from Dylan and glares from the rest of the Fairview crowd.

Dylan elbows me gently when the inning ends. "Alison, you got into *Harvard* today."

I watch the field, remembering the moment I read the letter. There was an instant of undimmed, worry-free excitement, free from the implications of Ethan following me to college. "I know," I reply. "It feels weird. I mean, I know I put in the work. I know I deserve it. But I can't believe college—Harvard—is really happening."

When the words leave me, I recognize it's not just *weird* I'm feeling. Away from Ethan, I'm finally able to be excited. While I wanted to definitively beat him, I have valedictorian to fight for. Besides, now I can actually start making plans and goals for college. I'll want to be president of the *Harvard Crimson*, of course. Graduating Phi Beta Kappa is a must. I could even win a Rhodes Scholarship.

"We have a couple months left here, though," Dylan says, cutting off my thoughts. "We need to make the most of them."

I hear her nostalgia and find I'm unable to feel the way she does. When I imagine the next couple months, they're formless. It's the first time since the Harvard decision that I've contemplated the end of the school year, and I'm unnerved how empty it is. In the past I've had deadlines driving me, grades to gun for, extracurriculars and the overarching question of college to structure my minutes.

Without them, I feel like the pressure's been released from my life, and the color's fled with it. With nearly every goal met and no new ones impending until I go to Harvard, I don't really know what I'll do with the final months of high school. It's easy to imagine what *making the most of them* means for Dylan, or Isabel, or Josh Campos. What does it mean for me? There's valedictorian, but what else?

"I wonder if Ethan got in," Dylan says, not helping matters.

His name fills me with the flush of emotions his presence did in my office, his eyes locked on to mine, his challenge echoing in the room. *Redo. Right now.* It's half horrifying. I don't want to identify the other half. "He did," I say. "We were together when decisions were posted."

Dylan's quiet for a moment. I'm guessing she knows me well enough to hear past the effortful neutrality of my voice. "Wow," she says carefully. "That must've been intense." I nod, though the intensity in my office wasn't the type she thinks. "I'm sorry, Alison." Camera in her lap, she loops her arm in mine. "I know you were hoping you wouldn't have to deal with him once we graduate. Maybe you can treat Harvard like a fresh start and stay as far from him as possible."

"I hope so," I say.

It's not necessarily an honest response. Faced with the void of the next couple months, the idea of competition—even competition as ruthless as Ethan's and mine—isn't unwelcome. Not to mention the unnameable reasons, the newer . . . *interactions* we've had recently.

"Yes," Dylan says. "Finally."

Not knowing what she's referring to, I follow her eyeline and find the Fairview puma mascot walking onto the field. The large polyester cat hypes up the crowd with exaggerated hand motions. I pull out my phone to reread the Harvard letter, not interested in watching Christian Schwartz, the junior class president, do his mascot routine.

"Speak of the devil," Dylan singsongs.

The implication of her words doesn't hit me immediately. When I understand, my head leaps up from my phone, finding the puma doing jumping jacks on the rust-hued dirt of the first base line. "No," I say. "No way."

Dylan's facing me, no doubt reveling in my expression.

"Christian had some family obligation. I heard the cheerleaders mention it before the game," she explains while I'm putting the pieces together in my head. If Christian's not doing his usual mascot duty, Isabel would have needed to find a replacement fast. One of the only people whose elongated frame fits the suit is—Ethan. "My gift to you for getting into Harvard," she concludes proudly.

In fascination and delight, I return my gaze to the dancing puma, now loving every part of its ridiculous routine. It's obvious Ethan has no idea what he's doing. He's making this up on the fly, choreographing every wave and clap of his gawky paws without rhyme or reason. I'm honestly impressed Isabel strong-armed him into this. With this on her résumé, I think she's the greatest class president in history.

He must have gone directly from my office to the equipment shed. It's why he was on campus so late in the first place, I realize. I join the crowd in egging him on, cheering when he gives the kids in front high fives and laughing when he nearly stumbles over his own feet.

When the game resumes, Ethan walks over to the cheerleaders' water station right in front of us. He removes his puma head, and I smile so hard my face hurts. His usually perfectly coiffed hair is flattened down and disheveled, his neck slick with sweat. I wonder if he's wearing his blue button-down from earlier under there.

"Looking good," Dylan calls out.

Ethan spins. His eyes narrow when he sees us.

"Sanger thinks so," he says.

He's smirking. I'm stunned by how direct the comment is, how public, and it doesn't help he's looking right at me. I can't think of a reply.

"Gross," Dylan fires back. "As if."

His eyes flash to my friend and immediately return to me. I know with unnerving clarity he's guessed exactly what's implicit in Dylan's reply. He knows I haven't told her he and I hooked up. The knowledge is dangerous in Ethan's hands— what knowledge isn't?—and I'm flooded with momentary fear he's going to drop the reveal on her right now.

Instead, he only shrugs, leaving me frustratingly grateful before he picks up his puma head and walks toward the cheerleaders congregating on the sideline. I'm 99 percent certain I'm out of the woods when he looks over his shoulder and winks.

I glance at Dylan, hoping she didn't see, but she just rolls her eyes. I relax, reassured by her overt exasperation.

"He is definitely not one of the things I'll be sad to leave behind with high school," she says, picking her camera back up.

I cringe. For a moment, I imagine confessing Ethan and I hooked up. Hooked up twice. I couldn't even blame her for how horrified she'd undoubtedly be.

"Sorry." She frowns sympathetically, evidently misinterpreting my expression. "Maybe he won't go to Harvard. Maybe he'll go somewhere douchier. Like Yale."

"Yeah, maybe," I say, forcing hopefulness into my voice.

It's disingenuous, just like every time I pretended there's nothing going on between me and Ethan. My nemesis puts his puma head on, returns to the sidelines, and picks up his impromptu cheerleading.

It's no longer much fun to watch.

# Forty-One

MY PARENTS ORDER MY favorite pizza to celebrate Harvard. The three of us eat in the backyard, the cardboard boxes piled on the ground in front of the firepit my dad decided to build three years ago and which we've used approximately twice. Jamie was at Ted's house when I came home. Honestly, I was relieved she wasn't there. We haven't spoken since yesterday, and the thought of announcing my success to her definitely won't help us reconcile.

Except for Jamie's absence and the memory of Ethan's . . . everything, the evening is exactly what I've been dreaming of.

"So, Alison," my dad says, licking sauce from his fingers, "you happy?"

"I am." It's the truth. Even Ethan can't change that. I'm proud of myself.

"No reservations about leaving California?" Mom asks.

"None."

"What about leaving Dylan?" She leans back in her chair, passing the crust she doesn't want to my dad.

I eye them, suspicious of this line of questioning. "We'll visit each other."

"How about your amazing parents? Will we be allowed to visit you?" She raises an eyebrow.

"She doesn't have a choice," Dad answers. "I'm looking forward to parents' weekend already. We'll get to hang out with her roommates, talk to random students in the dining hall . . ."

I roll my eyes, but it doesn't sound terrible.

"Meet the people she's made out with," Mom adds.

"Oh, she'll *hate* that," Dad says.

The thought is mildly terrifying. "You think I'll have multiple hookups by parents' weekend? Isn't that like a month into the semester?"

"We went to college once," Dad says. "Hey, *completely* unrelated question, but where will Ethan Molloy be matriculating this fall?"

I grit my teeth. I knew the moment was coming. For the rest of my life, talking about Harvard will be tied to Ethan. "I don't know where he'll commit, but he got into Harvard if that's what you're asking."

My dad's face splits into a grin. He turns to my mom. "Pay up."

To my horror, my mom pulls a twenty from her pocket and hands it to my dad.

"You *bet* on us?"

"On whether you'd be at the same school or not." Mom shrugs. "Statistically, it seemed unlikely."

As much as I desperately want to change the subject, a worse thought enters my mind. "Wait, have you bet on other things?"

"You'll need to be more specific," Mom replies.

"Related to my life. *Specifically* related to Ethan in my life."

They exchange a glance that tells me everything.

"I could cut you in—" my dad starts, then stops when the sliding door opens and Jamie emerges.

"What's going on out here?" Jamie asks. She doesn't look in my direction.

"We're celebrating!" Mom nudges my shoulder. "Alison, tell her."

Jamie turns to me, perfectly polite. "I got into Harvard," I say to her feet.

A day ago, Jamie would've rushed to hug me. Instead, she just plasters on a pleasant smile. "I'm happy for you."

"Pizza?" My dad offers.

Jamie shakes her head. "Maybe later. I'm going to take a shower." She leaves, sandals scraping the gravel loudly in the warm night.

"Are you guys in a fight?" my mom asks when Jamie closes the sliding door.

Watching the light go on in Jamie's bedroom window, I push down the hurt that she won't even celebrate Harvard with me. "A little one," I say.

I do feel bad for how I upset her, but I still maintain she's not looking at herself objectively. I don't think me getting into Harvard helps. If anything, it's going to remind her of what she could be doing right now but isn't, and I don't need to hear how she sees my sacrifices as a waste just because she didn't like her own direction.

"Some unwanted parental advice," my mom says. "Go easy on her. It's difficult to watch your baby sister outpace you."

I frown. I don't like being told to diminish what I'm proud of. "I'm hardly outpacing her. She went to Columbia."

"She did, and right now she's living with her parents while her much younger sister is about to move out. It's not like she's happy she's here."

"She certainly acts like she is."

My dad gives me a stern look. "You're smarter than that. She may have recognized the job she had, even the relationship she was in, weren't right, but that doesn't mean she's happy in this house, unsure of what's next."

"We're all so proud of you, Alison," my mom says. "Even Jamie. She's just going through a lot right now, and we have to give her time. She'll come around and be happy for you about Harvard. You know she will."

"Fine." I pick up my pizza. Even if my sister won't celebrate, it doesn't mean I shouldn't.

My dad faces my mom. "Over-under on how long their fight lasts?"

# Forty-Two

THE MILLARD FILLMORE IS just the way I remember when Ethan and I meet there the following evening for the design consultation we scheduled with Clint. We're a little over a month out from the reunion. There's been no unexpected remodel, no visit from one of the renovation shows on HGTV, not even the pleasant uplift of realizing we'd only had a negative first impression. It's fine with me, of course. I only hope Williams overlooks the chipped paint and the exposed wiring where a power outlet once fit.

Ethan and I are walking up and down the room with Clint, pointing out the placements for tables and decorations, the awkwardness between us practically palpable as we *don't* compete with each other. This morning we even had a downright respectful discussion of *Crime and Punishment* in English.

It's undeniable where this nonconfrontational confrontation is going. We're headed for a conversation I don't know how to have. While Ethan points out where we want the bar, I watch him, the things he told me in my office in the *Chronicle* echoing in my ears. He wanted to kiss me again. He thinks about me often enough it distracts him from class-work. The memories fill my cheeks with fire.

Of course, right then Ethan catches my eye. I turn quickly to hide my blush, pretending I'm considering his bar positioning proposal.

What's frustrating is I've never felt *confused* by my own feelings before. Not the way I do now. I know what I want and why I want it. In my previous relationships, I could rationalize why I dated the guys I did. They were nice, easy-going, not overwhelming commitments. Ethan and I, we're nuclear fission. The explosive energy of pushing apart. We're messy, disruptive, uncontrollable. I don't understand why this infatuation with him hasn't run its course.

Yet here I am, enjoying lingering glances at his lips, his hands, wondering when we'll next find ourselves alone.

"You want the Millard Fillmore signature lemonade, right?" Clint asks. His words snap me from my reverie. I glance over and find Ethan grimacing.

"You have a signature lemonade?" Ethan's voice is weighted with skepticism.

"Best in the city," Clint replies. I'm ready to end this discussion and confirm we'll have whatever constitutes the Millard Fillmore lemonade when Clint continues. "Give me a moment," he says. "I'll fetch you a couple cups from the kitchen."

I realize seconds late what this will mean. Ethan and me

alone, without classmates and *Chronicle* writers and Clint to keep us from the conversations I'm desperate not to have. "Oh, we don't need—" I start to say. Unfortunately, Clint's already on his way to the kitchen. I'm left with my nemesis-with-benefits, who leans on the dark brown wooden archway near him, watching me curiously.

"Well, Sanger"—he's obviously enjoying this—"what should we talk about while we wait?"

"Nothing?" I offer weakly. "I've been meaning to incorporate more silence into my life." There's discomfort I don't hide in the way I finger the hem of my cardigan.

"What other schools did you get into?"

I startle. His question is competition, and competition, I know how to do. It's a respite, a removal from biting flames into the pleasant pain of an overheated bath. "Princeton, Columbia, Amherst, Northwestern," I reply haughtily. "You?"

Ethan's expressionless, evidently unimpressed. "Yale, Stanford, Brown, NYU."

"Any chance you're committing to Yale?" I ask, glancing into the hallway where Clint left, hoping to find him returning. I'm dismayed to find only the Millard Fillmore's mottled-flesh-gray carpet and incongruous collection of framed photos.

The harsh laugh I hear from Ethan in answer is one I've heard often. He stands a couple feet from me, one leg hooked lankily over the other. "No," he says. "I'm guessing you're committing to Harvard as well?"

"Obviously."

His lips twitch at the word. He cocks his head and crosses his arms. "So," he says.

I wait for him to continue. In a combination of horror and delight, I wonder if he's come up with a contest for who'll claim his or her Harvard place and who'll commit elsewhere, giving up our dream college to the other. It would kind of be the ultimate loser's task.

Ethan doesn't elaborate, however. "So what?'" I prompt him.

"Four more years of this." His shoulders seem more squared, his posture more posed instead of comfortable. I can't read his expression and decipher whether he's unhappy at the prospect or weirdly excited to mar our college experiences with immature fighting and needless one-upping.

"You know," I venture, "we could leave the competition at Fairview. Find new rivals at Harvard." Part of me feels like the proposal is conceding defeat. The other part feels like it's worth fighting for a well-rounded, freer college experience.

"I wasn't referring to our competition," he replies, eyes on me, emerald with whatever intrigue or anticipation lights them.

I steel my nerves. We're edging toward the subject I've been dreading. There's no use putting it off, pretending we can compare and compete with no other context. "What, then?"

Wry self-satisfaction infects Ethan's smile. "Four more years of you pretending you aren't into me."

"Four years of *you* pretending you had a shot," I say too quickly. Realizing I don't sound confident, I continue. "How could I possibly be into you? I've hated you for years." It's a question for myself, and unfortunately not rhetorical. I'm desperate for the answer.

Ethan's eyes narrow, his smile disappearing. I know immediately I've pissed him off. "You know what I think? I think you *are* into me." He pushes himself off the archway and steps closer to me. "Right now, this very minute, you're wondering about us and you're afraid to admit it."

"Why would I be afraid? I don't care one iota what you think." I hear venom in my voice exceeding even what I usually reserve for Ethan.

He flashes me an uncommon grin. It's not a game move— it's an emotion. "You're right," he muses, like he's realizing. "It's not my judgment you're worried about. It's your own. You're afraid, after all this time, this whole rivalry, of your feelings changing. You're afraid of who you'll be if they do." He's close enough now he could reach out and touch me. I know he won't.

I have no response. I hate that I don't have a response.

"Admit it," Ethan says.

The demand pushes me too far. Hot resentment rushing into me, I decide this entire discussion was a mistake. "I don't have to admit anything to you," I bite out. "We're not friends, remember?"

I don't owe Ethan any explanations. What we have isn't real. It's not worth interrogating or diagramming or reconstructing. It's not worth a minute more. I grab my bag off the floor and walk directly out of the room.

# Forty-Three

I RETREAT INTO THE lobby, where I drop onto the elaborately gaudy green couch. There's a pale, redheaded boy on one end, reading, and in front of the check-in counter, a young woman waits for Clint. I ignore them, needing to cool off. I shouldn't let Ethan's words get under my skin the way I did. I should have had a comeback ready like I usually do. It's clear to me why I didn't. He was right. Everything he said was right. I don't know what it means to like Ethan. How could I, someone so driven, so mature, develop feelings for someone I hated?

*Hate.*

The question unfolds into many. Can it possibly be real? What if it isn't? What if it is? How could I start a relationship at the end of high school?

I'm interrupted in my introspection when the girl comes over from the desk to the boy reading near me. "I don't know where the clerk is," she says. "We have to check in, though, because we only have thirty minutes before we need to leave if we're going to see the Golden Gate Bridge during sunset." She has light brown skin, and her dark curly hair is in a ponytail. She's looking around the room like she has a hundred other places she wants to be.

The redheaded boy glances up and smiles. I notice he's reading what looks like a dictionary. "Patient as ever, Juniper," he says. "Why don't you just arrogate to yourself the check-in process?"

The girl—Juniper—scowls. I see right through the expression. Under her frown, there's something softer, like she's charmed and trying to hide it. "Now's not the time to be cute, Fitzgerald."

"Hey, we have five days together," Fitzgerald replies. "I'm not forgoing a single opportunity for cuteness."

I stifle a groan. The last thing I needed while fighting off feelings I don't want is front-row seats to whatever this is. I grimace when Fitzgerald grabs Juniper's hand. She snatches it back, blushing. "No flirting," she says.

"None?" He eyes her playfully. "But I've stored up a plenitude of prurient comments for this sojourn in particular." He's got to be doing the SAT-word gimmick on purpose, I find myself guessing, a little annoyed with myself for letting their conversation draw me in.

Juniper shakes her head. "Still impossible, I see." She spins suddenly, searching the check-in desk with frustration. "Seriously, where is the receptionist? We don't have time to waste."

I chime in, wanting to help out despite my dark mood. "Clint, the manager, went into the kitchen. I'm sure he'll be out here soon."

Juniper faces me, her scowl disappearing. "Oh, thanks. Are you staying here?" she asks me.

"No, I'm just here for a meeting." Already, I'm regretting interjecting. On the other hand, I reason, conversation with these two is definitely preferable to returning to Ethan, or worse, the doubts occupying my head.

Juniper's expression lights up. "Ooh, a local! Hey, any tips?" She gestures to Fitzgerald. "We're on a road trip up the West Coast, and we have twenty-four hours here."

Fitzgerald's now watching me too, blue eyes set in freckled features. I wonder what their relationship could possibly be. They're definitely flirtatious, and taking a road trip just the two of them feels romantic. Yet Juniper ordered him not to flirt with her. I don't know why they've caught my curiosity when I have other things to concentrate on, but they have. Maybe other people's inscrutable romances are easier to figure out than my own.

"Um, what do you like to do?" I ask.

"Everything," Juniper promptly replies.

I kind of love the response. It's in keeping with the restless energy underwriting this girl's every move. However, it is somewhat unhelpful. Fitzgerald appears to understand this. "We're into food, desserts in particular," he elaborates, amusement dancing in his eyes.

"Oh, uh." I pause, realizing I'm out of my depth. I don't

know the restaurants in downtown San Francisco. There could be a world-famous bakery nestled under the stone and stucco skyscrapers five minutes from here—I'd have no idea. It feels childish to admit it, though, like I'd be betraying the fact I have neither a car nor disposable income and eat my parents' home-cooked food every night. I offer the only idea I have. "You could check out where the Sweet Wieners food truck is tomorrow."

Juniper diligently makes a note in her phone. Right then, Clint comes out to the counter, and Juniper rushes over to check in.

"She takes traveling seriously," I say to Fitzgerald. "Is she your girlfriend?"

He watches Juniper, fondness in his eyes mixed with something searching. "No."

"Oh, sorry," I say. "It just looked like—"

"It's fine." From the lightness in his voice, I get the feeling it really is. He closes his dictionary. Everything about his manner and clothes is Ethan's opposite, from the endearing way he gently joked with Juniper to the denim jacket he's wearing over his T-shirt. "We're just friends. We might be more if we went to college together. She's in Rhode Island, and I'm in Pittsburgh right now, but I'm transferring to New Hampshire next year."

"Did you go to high school together?" Wondering if they're a high school pair who stayed in each other's lives, I feel my thoughts stray back to Ethan in the other room.

"No. But we met in our senior year on a road trip,"

Fitzgerald says. "We've decided to make it a tradition, taking road trips together whenever we can. Last year we did the South—Charleston, Atlanta, New Orleans. It's like our annual reunion."

The word resonates with me. Everyone and their reunions, carrying people from the past into the present and on, no matter how much changes. They felt forced to me, like stuffing yourself into a childhood sweatshirt. Like grabbing on to old pieces of your life, ignoring how they don't fit.

But Fitzgerald and Juniper don't look like they no longer fit. I catch sight of Ethan lingering in the ballroom, rubbing his heel on the flat carpet. Does Ethan fit into my life now or in the future? I don't know. I've realized, however, being here with him isn't helping.

Because there's no figuring Ethan out. Regardless of what I feel, I can't be certain of how he feels. As long as I don't know what he wants, what our competition is, I'll never know what this unnerving evolution of it represents to him. If he's only ever found our rivalry to be a game, then this new phase is nothing more—just changing the board from checkers to chess. Maybe he's bored of competing over exams and class discussions, and he's only hooking up with me to entertain himself for a couple more weeks or months. Isn't that what he told me seconds before Harvard decisions came out? *For a little while, it might be fun.*

I know it's not the only explanation. It could be expertly executed payback, or a combination of the two. The *one* thing it definitely isn't is real.

My head clears. The way I need to deal with Ethan is no longer confusing. It's obvious. I refuse to feel something for him, plain and simple. Not while I don't know if I'm just one more empty pursuit of his. One more preoccupation, one more impermanent cure for his boredom. Every time we've talked about what's going on between us, he's treated it like just another chance to beat me at something. Conversations built on tactics and superiority aren't going to get me the answers I want, but I don't know if we're even capable of having a conversation founded on anything else.

In the ballroom, Ethan's not looking at me anymore. He's surveying the room with his usual skepticism, hands in his pockets. *I don't have to be here.* The thought comes like it's from outside me. I grab on, enjoying the crisp clarity, the freedom. Ethan can finish the design meeting without me.

I get up from the couch. "I hope you have a nice trip," I say to Fitzgerald.

He smiles. "Thanks."

I walk past the wooden table in the lobby, decorated with a full vase of flowers, and head for the door. On the way, I overhear Clint checking Juniper in while she waits in front of the ornately carved counter.

"Would you like a room with two double beds or one queen?" he asks.

"One bed is fine," Juniper replies.

# Forty-Four

I HAVE MY DRIVING test on Friday. In the front seat of Mom's car, waiting outside the DMV, I compulsively rehearse in my head the controls I'll need to know. *Wipers. Defroster. Hazard lights.* The way I do before tests in class, I remind myself I've practiced and memorized. There's no reason to be nervous. I feel prepared. Three weeks of lessons with Hector and I'm a fairly capable driver.

My mom's in the passenger seat, and my dad's in the back. Annoyingly, both of them took off work and insisted on coming. They decided to schedule the test during an ASG postering party at Isabel's house, where I wish I was. It's not like I enjoy postering or am particularly good at it, but I hate to fall short on my commitments, especially when Ethan will be there, making sure to remind everyone of my absence.

The car ahead of me moves up, and I roll forward in the line. We've formed a procession from the drive-thru to the parking lot, in which we've waited for the past twenty minutes. It's like the interim in class where they've passed out the exams facedown and you're not permitted to look, except it lasts for half an hour of *pedal, brake, pedal, brake.*

"Where are you going to drive first?" Dad asks.

"The ASG thing I was supposed to be at twenty minutes ago," I remind him, permitting irritation to enter my voice. He's used to it.

"You have to pick something more exciting than that," Mom protests.

"Yeah, this is your first drive on your own. You can have my car for the rest of the day." In the rearview mirror, I catch Dad wink. "Do something you'll remember."

I received the same exhortation from Dylan when I explained where I was going after school. I was urged to meet her and Grace in downtown San Francisco for a night out, which I declined.

"I thought being able to drive was supposed to mean freedom from your parents telling you what to do," I say, inching forward once more in the interminable line.

"We'll still tell you," Mom says. "It'll just be easier for you to ignore us."

"Not that she doesn't do that already," Dad adds to Mom.

I wish they would end this comedy routine and let me quiz myself on where the latch for the gas is. Out the window, the DMV itself comes into view on my left. Ugly, squat square hedges surround the cinderblock office, with walk-in visitors waiting single-file out the door hemmed in by posts and white plastic chains. "I don't understand why you both took off work for this," I mutter to my parents.

"This is a big day, a step into adulthood," Mom replies. While I know she doesn't mean her praise patronizingly, her words rub me the wrong way. Like graduation, having a license is one more marker people use to measure maturity. But it's not entirely accurate. Some people don't really reach adulthood until years later, while others of us are already there, chafing at the restrictions of our numerical age. I'll be glad to have my license, though. As long as people do respect those markers, they're worth having.

My phone vibrates in the cup holder. When I look down, I immediately wish I hadn't. It's a text from Ethan.

ASG is boring without you. Hurry up and pass.

I might know how to celebrate . . .

My mouth falls open. I can read between the lines and deduce what's happening here. I just wouldn't expect it of Ethan. Or, I would expect it of him with plenty of other girls in my grade. Just not with me.

He's *flirting*.

Not even the bickering flirting I've gotten used to in the past week. Genuine flirting. If I had to put words to the intolerable pull I find in his message, I wouldn't want them uttered out loud.

The line isn't moving, and my parents are engrossed in a discussion of what movie they're going to watch tonight. I pick up my phone, my fingers flying over the screen.

How exactly?

He doesn't make me wait, which is somehow so much worse than if he had. *This* conversation is clearly occupying all of his attention. It's thrilling.

However you like it.

I stare at his reply, my pulse pounding. Surely, he doesn't mean . . . I can't even finish the thought.

Is this flirting?

Wow, Sanger, I knew you were inexperienced but this surprises even me.

My cheeks flame as I rush to reply.

Inexperienced? Careful.
I do love proving you wrong.

His reply comes even faster.

Now you're getting it.

Please, do continue.

I toss my phone back into the cup holder, feeling far too many things at once. My face feels unbearably flushed, my hands suddenly hot. Dozens of replies come to mind, but I refuse to even type them.

I'm distracted—fortunately—when I hear tapping on the window to my left. I roll it down, finding the DMV examiner outside. "Alison Sanger?" she reads from her clipboard. I nod, and my parents open their doors and climb out.

"Good luck!" My mom waves.

As the examiner circles the car and gets in the passenger seat, I find myself unable to stop thinking about Ethan's text. What's happening with us keeps changing state, shifting faster than I can keep up with. First, we kissed, then we kissed twice, then I accepted I might want to kiss him again. Now he's upset the dynamic further, threatened the tenuous equilibrium I've hung on to. I can't imagine he meant what he said. I picture getting to Isabel's house, him and me sneaking off somewhere, him saying he missed me. It's unrealistic, farfetched, like when a friend flatters you with what you want to hear.

I follow the instructions of the examiner robotically, pointing out the parking brake, turn signals, headlights. When she tells me to exit the DMV lot, I turn on the car, pointedly check my mirrors, and shift the car into drive. Keeping my speed reasonable, I smoothly steer toward the exit, braking when a couple crosses the pavement in front of me.

I can't stop picturing Ethan. Ethan sitting with everyone, thinking of me while ignoring their conversation. Ethan pulling out his phone, typing in my name. Ethan waiting, wondering what I'll say next or when I'll knock on Isabel's door. The detail of the mental images embarrasses me, yet they keep coming. Ethan—

"Okay, take a right here, then circle back to the DMV," the woman says.

"Really?" Her words don't register. "Already?"

"Incomplete stop upon exiting the lot. Not leaving enough room for the approaching car. It's an automatic fail," she replies. Her voice is neither gentle nor incriminating. She writes notes on her clipboard without looking up.

"Fail?" I repeat, feeling the first wave of nerves.

"It's very common," the examiner explains, like it's reassuring. "Roughly 50 percent of people fail here. You can retake the test in two weeks."

I circle the block, stunned and slightly sick. Neither of us speak. I have nothing in my head except formless disappointment starting to coalesce into frustration. When I park in the parking lot, the examiner gets out of the car. I don't. *Fifty percent* of people fail? I've never been in the fiftieth percentile in my life. In the corner of my vision, I see my parents walk up to the car. I can't move. While my mom opens my door, I wait with my hands on the wheel, stock-still like a crash-test dummy.

"That was fast," she says. "Do you need to go inside to take your license photo?"

"I failed," I reply quietly.

"What?" Dad asks, coming to stand beside Mom.

"I failed." I raise my voice, and I hear everything the declaration means. It unlocks me. I get out of the car, movements rushed with humiliation. "You should drive."

While they pause, presumably not knowing how to respond, I crawl into the back seat. My mom gets behind the wheel.

She's the first to recover. "You know, hon, failure is natural," she offers, twisting around in the driver's seat. It's forced, like she understands why I'm upset but can't comprehend how this is a big deal to me.

I can't reply, a lump forming in the back of my throat.

"You've gone your whole life with never failing anything," my dad joins in, equally off-kilter. "Honestly, you should be proud."

"I'm brimming with pride right now, yeah." Facing the window instead of my parents, I wipe my eyes. It's ignominy on top of ignominy. I feel childish for getting this upset over a test I don't even care about. I remember what the examiner said. I'll retake it in a couple weeks.

"Don't worry about it," my mom says, sounding half consolatory and half uncomfortable. "You're young. You're going to fail hundreds of times in your life."

I close my eyes. I can't believe I made such a basic error. Four stupid texts from Ethan, and everything I practiced and worked at crumbled. If it only takes a handful words from him to throw me off—

My eyes fly open. What if Ethan *planned* this? He knew exactly where I was, what I was doing. I had to tell all of ASG why I wouldn't be there on time to paint posters.

It's instantaneous, the reaction the realization causes in me. Fire hitting dry kindling. Every ounce of furious hurt in me converts in a flash into resolve. I face forward. "Can you drop me off at Isabel's?" I ask Mom. "I have to go help ASG."

Ethan's promise from earlier rings in my head, fusing with the pounding in my ears into an uncomfortable cacophony. He'd said he could distract me, and he succeeded.

He wasn't flirting. He was competing.

# Forty-Five

**I CLOSE MOM'S CAR** door and head up the path to Isabel's house. It's one of those modern walkways of concrete squares spaced out on grass, with decorative cacti on one side. When I reach the frosted glass front door, I ring the doorbell, the sound echoing into Isabel's entryway. I see her form vaguely outlined behind the door before she opens it.

"Alison. You made it," she says, a hint of judgment in her voice. She scrutinizes me, looking perfect despite the paint-speckled sweatshirt she's wearing.

I ignore how harried I must look, frustration still fresh in my cheeks. Swiping one strand of hair from my forehead, I play the part of someone who's late for non-embarrassing reasons, someone who didn't just fail her driving test. "Of course," I reply. "You know I would never shirk my ASG responsibilities."

Isabel's expression doesn't change. "Well, you're not exactly an asset when it comes to making posters."

I frown for a moment. Admittedly, Isabel's not wrong. I know we're remembering the same incident. Last year, I was responsible for several homecoming posters. They ended up resembling kindergarten artwork, which I know wasn't the look Isabel had in mind since she frantically repainted them the day of the dance. It was not one of the finer moments of my distinguished career in student-government service.

"I'm dedicated to improving," I say, stepping into the entryway.

Isabel watches me. "I just want to make sure you and Ethan won't disrupt our work. There's such a collaborative energy in the room right now." She pauses delicately. "You guys sometimes turn things a little . . . toxic."

I blink, realizing Isabel just repeated Williams's complaint. It's an unnerving reminder of how caustic our relationship can get. "I promise we won't be disruptive," I say, knowing if I were Isabel, I wouldn't be convinced.

Isabel gestures with resignation down the hallway. "Everyone's in the kitchen."

I follow her farther into the house. Isabel's home has a minimalist design, with white marble floors, austere furniture, and wide windows revealing the modern landscaping outside. We enter the kitchen where a dozen members of ASG work on posters in various stages of completion. Parchment paper is laid down on the kitchen island, the expansive dining table, even the floor where people paint ASG FOOD DRIVE on red rectangles of cardstock.

Ethan's leaning by the sink, looking bored. I notice a fleck of white paint on his cheek. It's irritatingly cute. I push the observation to the very back of my head. Knowing him, the paint fleck is probably part of a facade designed to further distract me, offsetting his crisp wardrobe with just the right dash of unruliness.

His eyes fall on me slowly.

"You're here early." He sounds . . . pleased? It's a trick.

"I hurried. Didn't want to miss this," I say evenly. Whatever push-and-pull we're engaged in right now, I'm not giving him an inch.

"We're not letting you paint, you know." Pleased turns to patronizing in his reply.

I grit my teeth. We're not even fighting about the right thing now. "You look hard at work." Ethan gestures to the poster on the floor next to him. I inspect what he's done, doing my best to look unimpressed. When I open my mouth to critique his letter spacing, Isabel clears her throat. Plastering on a pleasant expression, I hold in my comment. "Ethan, could I have a word with you? In private?" I ask.

Ethan raises an eyebrow. "Am I in trouble for something?"

I laugh. "Don't be ridiculous," I say, keeping my gaze narrowed for only him to see. Without giving him a window to reply, I walk out into the hall.

I hear the soles of Ethan's sneakers on Isabel's marble floors following me. In the middle of the hallway, I spin to face him. He pauses purposefully close to me, his hands resting casually in his pockets. When he grins, the fucking fleck on his cheek winks. "So, we celebrating?" he asks.

I can hear chattering from the other room. If I'm going to lay into him for his stunt with my driving test, Isabel's hall-way won't work. I step into the nearby bathroom, holding the door for him. I'm already forming my points, organizing my arguments.

He walks past me, eyeing me curiously. Maybe even eagerly.

The moment I close the door, his lips hit mine. His hands find my waist, long fingers encircling my hips with deliberate urgency. I kiss him back, because goddamn it, I kind of knew we were going to do this regardless of how mad I am. Possibly because of it. How drawn I feel to Ethan is intertwined enough with my hatred for him that I'm no longer entirely sure when my desires are fighting each other or feeding each other. I let my hands skim the skin under his shirt, the outlines of his hipbones. It's great he's not wearing one of the oxfords he typically tucks in. *Really* great.

I know I have reasons to not want him. Enough that I could fill dossiers or hour-long debates. He's almost defi-nitely doing this to mess with me. What's more, it's a stupid cliché, hooking up with the guy you were convinced you hated. This can't possibly go anywhere real—it's just a com-bination of hormones and restlessness.

But those rational reasons don't hold up while Ethan's kissing me like there's nothing he'd rather be doing.

It's magnetic. We're pressed to each other, skin and lips and breaths aligned, like the pages of a closed book. I feel his fingers on my back, in my hair, trailing shivers with his touch. His mouth is hot on mine. I cling tighter, wanting the heat.

I've known Ethan's got a couple inches on me. I'd resented the height difference, hating how nature itself decided to give him the upper hand. Right now, I don't dislike the opportunities it presents. The unconscious necessity of raising my chin to kiss him, giving him room to bring one hand to the curve of my neck.

It's unlike the locker hall or the party. While our first kisses felt like collisions, this one feels like running hand-in-hand into whatever we're going to be.

His lips part from mine for one moment. "This skirt is nice," he says. He runs his hand up the fabric of my pleated skirt, planting his next kiss on my neck.

"You hate this skirt," I murmur, remembering the last time I wore it, he specifically commented that he loathed my wardrobe.

"*Hmm.* I like it now," he replies immediately, like he's hardly registered what I said. His fingers move up to trace the V-neck of my sweater. "I like this too."

Surprise surfaces above the sensations overwhelming me. I pull away, heart still racing while confusion seeps in. "What did you just say?"

"I said you look nice," he says. I feel his hand on my waist, pulling me closer again. "Is that a problem?"

I stay where I am. "What are you playing at?" I'm searching for his next trap, struggling past how dizzy my head still is with him. But I don't find it. It feels striking how fast my emotions shift, passion spiraling into skepticism.

"Shit, I'm just complimenting you," Ethan says, lightly indignant.

"Why?"

Impatience hardens his features. "I need a reason?"

I step out of his arms. "Yes, Ethan. You do."

"I don't know what you want me to say." He shoves the hand that was just moments ago sliding up my thigh into his pocket.

"I want a straight answer." I push aside his fervent kisses, flirtatious texts, his invitation to have fun. "Did you kiss me that day in the locker hall as some sort of payback?"

His eyes widen. "Payback?"

"For pulling your story from the *Chronicle*."

He laughs, short and bitter. "First, *I* didn't kiss *you*. Second, how could our kiss possibly figure into any kind of payback?"

"It's not payback to make me think I might *want* you?" The word gets strangled in my throat, but I don't drop his gaze. "To mess with my head that way, then pick the perfect time to drop me when it'll humiliate or cost me?"

Ethan's silent for a moment, his shoulders rigid. "Not everything is about our rivalry, Alison," he finally says, his tone dangerous.

"You know it is." His denial sends my heart pounding. For years, absolutely everything has been about competing, winning. Endless late nights, obscenely early mornings, frantically written essays—it's all been for one thing. Hasn't it?

"Not this."

"Then why?" I ask. I'm desperate now, more so than ever. I thought I understood, but his words have destroyed every conviction I've been clinging to, leaving me defenseless.

He doesn't say anything. His eyes leave mine, dropping to the floor.

My blood freezes. *No.* It's not possible. It can't be. "Why, Ethan?"

Green irises flick up. His jaw is squared, ready for the impossible, and I already know.

"Why?" I ask. I need him to say it.

"Because, despite everything, I'm attracted to you." He reaches for my elbow, caressing with some combination of urgency and frustration. Half resistant, half enthralled. In the bright bathroom light, I catch every uncomfortable flicker of his expression. This confession isn't a victory, it's a vulnerability. Ethan's *never* vulnerable. "Because I like you. There. Are you happy now?"

"You . . . like me." I'm mute except to repeat his words. It's unthinkable. Nothing, none of it was a game. This . . . is real. Or it could be. If I let it.

Ethan's irritation visibly increases. "Unfortunately," he says. I pace the floor from the sink to the window, glancing up every couple steps, studying him like a formula I don't recognize on my homework. "Do you have anything to say in response?" he prompts when I've stayed silent for too long.

I stop, facing him. "I failed my driving test."

Ethan opens his mouth, the instinctive way he does when we're mid-fight. Then he closes it. "I'm sorry, did you just say you *failed*?" he finally asks.

"Yes. I failed, Ethan. Texting with you left me completely distracted." It feels like I'm reminding myself. The heat coursing through me isn't the good kind. It's annoyance and shame I keep letting myself hook up with the source of my every misfortune. Predictably, Ethan's stunned expression splits, and he laughs. He literally laughs right in my face. My cheeks redden further. "So hilarious," I say, crossing my arms. "Alison Sanger failed something. You win."

I head for the door, passing him. He catches my arm.

"I didn't text you to mess with you," he says. I search his eyes. "Honest. I really was just trying to flirt with you." He pulls me toward him, reaching for my hands. I let him. What's more, I believe him. While sabotaging me would be fiercely in character, deflecting the credit for it isn't. If he's not gloating, something is very different. "Not that I'm *not* amused you failed," he adds, humor in his voice now.

I shove his shoulder. "You're serious." I say, softening. "You like me."

He nods.

I narrow my eyes. "When did you know?"

Ethan grins wryly. "You're going to keep rubbing it in my face, aren't you?"

"Wouldn't want to disappoint," I confirm.

"I guess I realized after my party," he says eventually, neither humorous or resentful. "When we first kissed, I was . . . surprised. I'd *never* thought about you like that."

"Is this still flirting? I can't tell," I reply dryly.

"Like you'd ever thought about me that way, either."

"Fair," I say, resting my hips against the marble counter behind me. Ethan's hand moves to grip the ledge, his waist pressing mine. "I knew you were objectively attractive, but not in a way that interested me."

"*Objectively* attractive, huh?"

I roll my eyes and hook a finger into his belt loop. "I'd like you to continue declaring your feelings now."

He laughs. "Like I said, I was surprised. Then confused, then angry. I didn't want to accept it."

His sincerity sobers me. "And now you're not angry about it?"

Ethan leans in, the white paint on his cheek brushing my skin. "Only a little," he says close to my ear, then pecks a quick kiss on the curve of my jaw.

I bring my lips to his in reply. Every day is full of hundreds of decisions—priorities, organizational efficiencies, editorial choices—and they're often not easy. This one, right now, isn't exactly easy, either. It's not impossible, though. I know what choice I'm going to make and what choice I *want* to make, and they're the same. It's like someone's illuminated neon lettering I could already read.

I kiss Ethan, deciding I want this too much to worry what it means for the future.

# Forty-Six

WE LEAVE THE BATHROOM after ten frenetic minutes together. I flatten my hair and straighten my clothes, feeling unlike myself. I guess I'm now the kind of person who steals away from ASG events for spirited make-out sessions. Ethan, walking with me, adjusts the collar of his shirt with what I have a hunch is practiced casualness.

When we enter the kitchen, everyone's cleaning up. I guiltily notice the finished posters on the dining table.

"Wow," Isabel says. "Looks like you guys really went at it." I startle, turning red. Her eyes sweep over our evidently still-disheveled appearances. "Let me guess," she goes on, "you had a disagreement over where to hang these posters."

Relief replaces my panic. Isabel doesn't know. The reprieve only lingers until I realize it's inevitable my classmates will find out. Ethan's and my rivalry was so public, the idea of people knowing what it's turned into fills me with embarrassment. Especially Dylan. She hates Ethan, and I can't blame her. I hated him for years too. I decide I don't want the knowledge getting out until I've determined how serious Ethan and I will be.

"Something like that," I say to Isabel.

Ethan catches my eye, his expression smugly playful. "You know Sanger," he says. "Vigorous when she wants something, with the stamina to see it through."

I hold his gaze and shrug. "I don't quit until I'm satisfied." I see the shadow of a smile cross his impassive expression. He says nothing. It feels like a small win. There's a new playing field for one-upping opening in front of us, and I plan to capitalize on it.

"Sometimes I wonder how you two even get through class together," Isabel says, shaking her head.

Ethan's eyes sparkle. "With determination and restraint, Isabel."

While the members of ASG walk to their cars, I wait in Isabel's driveway, holding my phone. It's dusk, and the sky is the flattering lavender gradient of suburban nights under the ungainly shadows of streetlights and power lines. We've packed up the posters and paint in Isabel's kitchen, and I'm writing a text to my mom to pick me up when Ethan walks past me.

"Need a ride?" He sounds friendly, which will require a little getting used to. "I mean, since you failed your driving test, and I passed mine, so I can drive you," he adds, and it's the old Ethan.

I roll my eyes, but I put my phone away. "You'll pay for that," I say, joining him.

"Will I?" He raises an intrigued eyebrow.

I walk to his passenger door. Ethan drives a white Mercedes. It looks new, and I find it hard to imagine it's his instead of on loan from his parents. Opening the door, I slide into the leather seat. "I do actually have to go home and study," I say when Ethan gets in.

"Did you think I had something else in mind, Sanger?" His nonchalance doesn't convince me.

"Yes," I say.

Ethan grins and starts the engine.

"So . . ." I know we need to get this out of the way. Defining our relationship. Not to mention the public-relations issue of when to disclose to our classmates.

"I'm not giving you my notes for the English exam," Ethan says.

I face him, insulted. "Like I'd want them! Your notes are always sloppy." I'm appalled whenever I glance over and read what he's written. His journal is a forest of arrows, stars, and footnotes.

"We'll see about that when we get our scores," he replies.

"Yeah. We will." I guess Ethan finds my comeback weak, because he only smiles once again, which obviously will not stand. "You know, *you* could probably benefit from reading *my* notes, though. I'm happy to help."

"Pass," Ethan replies, eyes on the road. "I will say I had no idea you'd be such a helpful girlfriend."

I feel my eyes widen, my spine straightening. It's like the word has vacuumed the air out of the car. Ethan looks similarly shocked.

"Ew," I say. "Did you just call me your girlfriend?"

The white of his knuckles on the wheel and woozy expression on his features lead me to think he didn't intend the word to leap out. I wonder from where in his subconscious it surfaced. Is he so used to picking up girlfriends that the label comes easily? Or . . . is it something he's considered before in reference to me. "It slipped out," he says stiffly.

I fold my hands in my lap, the habit one of high-pressure college interviews and tense newspaper meetings. Except in those situations, I knew what I was supposed to say, what I wanted to say. I clear my throat. "Do you—"

I'm grateful for the reprieve when he cuts me off. "No. Yes. I don't know." In other contexts, I'd be thrilled to witness Ethan so ineloquent. Maybe I should make him a promposal sign and display it during his next ASG motion. "The idea of being your boyfriend is simultaneously deeply upsetting and . . . not," he says. The final word falls heavily, like furniture on your foot.

"Let's table it," I suggest.

"Great. Yes," he agrees hastily. We stop behind the car in front of us, waiting for the light to change in the intersection. Ethan has a looser way of driving, I've noticed, coasting to stops and gentler turns. "What about at school. Do we tell people?"

"Tell people what? We're hooking up?" I ask. Ethan raises an eyebrow. "We can barely admit what this is to each other. I don't think getting more opinions on it would be helpful."

"Our secret then." His words thrill me more than I like. Glancing over, I see his expression's grown serious. "Harvard complicates this," he continues. "If only I'd gotten in and you were heading to Princeton or something, these decisions wouldn't be so weighted."

"First of all, if only one of us had gotten in to Harvard, it would have been me. But yes, I know what you mean." It's ironic, really. Our classmates hesitate to enter relationships right now for the opposite reason. With only a couple months before graduation and college in different cities, they know they'd be facing fast-approaching, definitive end points—which I'd wish for right now. Instead, we'll both be in Cambridge. There's no convenient out for our relationship, and going to Harvard with my high school boyfriend paints a very different vision of the future than the one I'd imagined. Holding on to this piece of high school feels wrong while I'm supposed to be starting this new, adult phase of my life.

"How about rivals with benefits?" Ethan proposes out of nowhere.

I pause, realizing what he's saying. I laugh, which seems to surprise him. His eyes flick to me, then return to the intersection. "What kind of commitment is that, exactly?" I ask.

"I don't know," Ethan replies. "But I've always been more committed to our rivalry than anything else."

I feel a pleased flush stealing into my cheeks. It's flattering. I remember every hour I've devoted to besting him, every night he's been my final thought before bed. There's an odd pleasure to imagining the comparable hours for him, the times he's heard my name echoing in his head while he's working. I know it's true. Our rivalry *is* his first and favorite commitment.

It raises the usual questions with Ethan, though. If our competition is his number-one focus, what occupies the lower places on the list? "What do you want to study at Harvard?" I ask. "I realize I don't even know." I half expect him to dismiss my curiosity defensively the way he's done before. Instead, he only looks thrown by the change in topic. We're really in uncharted waters now.

"I'm not sure." It's one short sentence of uncertainty before he flashes me a sharp smile. "Maybe I'll study whatever you do, just so you're not the best in your department."

I return the expression, my heart not in it. "Very funny. I know pestering Williams until she switched you into my AP US period last year didn't actually affect your future, but don't you think taking this to college might be too far? You could graduate with a degree you don't even want. I mean, you joined the *Chronicle* only because I did. Do you even enjoy it?"

"I was joking, Sanger," he says. I recognize the flippancy in his voice. It usually only provokes me into formulating carefree comebacks of my own. I don't let it. I want an answer, not a fight.

"Okay," I say evenly. "What concentrations are you interested in? Regardless of what I do." I've done enough research to know no Harvard student would call programs of studies *majors*. They're *concentrations*, for whatever reason.

Ethan says nothing. It's the longest pause of the drive, including the one after he called me his girlfriend. We're in my neighborhood now, and Ethan rounds the corner with deliberate focus. He fixes his gaze forward. "I guess I don't know yet." His voice is quiet.

We pull up in front of my house. It's gotten dark outside, the light over my front door dimly streaming through the windshield. I don't get out or unbuckle my belt. Today we've broken down boundaries with each other. This feels like my opportunity to put my toe over one more. "Ethan," I start gently, "why do you compete with me? Do you have a goal, or is it just fun for you?"

He doesn't look at me while he answers. "I don't know." His expression is drawn, his features emptied of their imperiousness. The car's interior feels intimate, this leather- and freshener-scented space just large enough for everything we wouldn't say otherwise. I swear I'm memorizing every detail of the black dashboard while I wait for Ethan to continue. "Sometimes I feel like our competition is the only thing driving me, and without it, I don't know what I want," he says. He rubs his neck uncomfortably, like his confession scares him.

I nod. His explanation makes sense. I could never figure

him out because *he* hasn't figured himself out. "What does that mean for us?" I ask into the heavy quiet. "Am I just another thing you don't know if you want?"

"Alison, if you think having feelings for you was something I *wanted*, you're a lot dumber than our four years of rivalry have led me to believe."

I fire him an unamused glare. "Charming. I feel great about this."

Ethan grabs my hand.

The gesture is incredibly tender. Until now we've only touched through fevered kisses, volatile embraces, high-contact fireworks of skin on skin. This almost innocuous clasping of hands is so much less, and yet so much more.

"What I'm saying is," he begins, "I know what I want. Not in everything. But with you, I know. If there was any room for error, I would have taken it as reason enough to never admit any of this to you. Because believe me, telling my nemesis I like her was not something I would have elected to do if given the choice."

I lean over the console and kiss him. "I like you too," I say.

It flies in the face of everything I thought I knew about myself, everything I expected of this year and of us. I probably wouldn't have recognized my feelings if Ethan hadn't said what he did. His certainty is contagious, however. The words feel right yet foreign, like picking up a new pen and knowing instantly it's your favorite.

Ethan smiles. Not smirks. Really smiles. I reach my other hand to his bicep, finding soft fabric on muscle. He straightens, evidently not having expected the touch. He looks sheepish, or sheepish on the Ethan scale. "This is going to take getting used to, isn't it?" he says.

"Obviously." I lean back in, closing the distance between us, but pause before my lips meet his. His chin tilts consciously or subconsciously, like he's ready for the kiss. "Up to the challenge, Molloy?"

He doesn't bother replying. When he kisses me, it's different. Careful. Delicate, even. With every brush of lips, we're feeling out what we're becoming. I decide I prefer this kind of kissing—which is definitely saying something. Typically, I thrive on efficiency, economy of time, but here, in Ethan's car outside my house, I'm okay with slowing down. I close my eyes and let the minutes slip by.

# Forty-Seven

WHEN I WALK INTO the house, Jamie's playing guitar in the front room. I'm probably feeling good from the pleasant tingle lingering on my lips, but her playing doesn't sound half bad. I hear traces of melody, complete chords here and there. It's possible she really is improving.

"You sound great," I say spontaneously. "You've been practicing."

Jamie's head snaps up like I've startled her. "Thanks. Yeah, I have. You should hear the band sometime."

"Sure," I say. I continue toward the stairs, then pause, hit with a pang of regret from our fight. We haven't spoken much since she found the *Chronicle* story, only pleasantries when we run into each other outside the bathroom. With Ethan's confession of not knowing what he wants ringing in my ears, I remember Jamie saying I didn't ask her enough questions. I never heard her side.

I return to the front room, where Jamie looks up

quizzically. Her strumming hand drops from her guitar, and I'm hit with guilt recognizing how ready she is to talk. She hasn't congratulated me on Harvard yet, not really. But I hurt her first, and it was wrong of me. "Hey, Jamie," I say. "Did you know what you wanted when you graduated from Columbia?"

Jamie puts down her guitar. Her expression is serious, her carefree enthusiasm gone. She pauses, really considering the question, and I'm grateful for her entertaining what is admittedly an out-of-nowhere existential inquiry on a Friday night. "I thought I did," she says finally. "But when I got those things, I realized they didn't make me happy. Then I started questioning all of my decisions."

I nod. Like Ethan's explanation, it fits. It's just not what I expected. Part of me wants to leave the conversation here. I've done what I should've done when I wrote the story. I understand Jamie better. The other part knows, I haven't gotten all the facts yet. "Like your relationship with Craig?" I ask.

The ghost of regret crosses Jamie's features, the first such reaction I've seen regarding her engagement. "Yeah, maybe a little. I think he realized I wasn't who we both thought I was. I don't blame him for breaking it off." Her voice is resigned, not rueful. "But everything I thought was a constant in my life was suddenly gone, and the worst part was that I didn't miss it. Not as much as I should have, anyway. So I wondered if I'd gotten any of it right. What I studied in college, things I'd sacrificed to achieve my goals, friends I'd made, the city I was living in. Was any of it what I wanted?"

I sit down on the window seat next to her, trying to put myself in her position. It's difficult. I can't imagine regretting my choices. But, then again, here I am, starting something with Ethan. *Ethan.* Will I regret the years we spent fighting? Or will I regret this? I've seen how changes can ripple into every corner of your life, shaking up what you once thought permanent.

"Has moving home helped you figure it out?" I ask. The house feels huge and empty in a way I can't explain. The lights are off in the rooms past this one. I don't hear Mom or Dad, who I figure have gone upstairs to catch up on work. It's just me and Jamie. I wonder if she ever feels lonely in the house when everyone's gone during the day.

"It has and it hasn't." She gazes into the dark dining room. "I think in high school and college, we're told what to want and aspire to. With grades and degrees, I had these obvious signs of success. It became easy to mistake them for what I really wanted and easier to let those markers guide my decisions. When I was in the real world, I had to choose for myself what success should mean."

Her words hit close to home. While I enjoy working hard, I've never exactly felt fortunate for the immediate, comprehensible checkboxes of grades and graduation. It's unnerving, recognizing for the first time I'll reach a point in my life where I won't have them defining my days.

"Back home, I can figure it out without distraction," Jamie

continues. "But I kind of feel like my life's on pause. I don't want to rush my decision, but I don't want to get comfortable, either."

I say nothing, feeling stupid. When my sister graduated from college, I figured her life was just one never-ending series of Instagrammable moments. Her Chicago neighborhood, brunch on the weekend with Craig, the shiny new job she'd gotten out of college. Then she came home. I read a newfound lack of motivation into her unscheduled days, not realizing she was dealing with a very real existential upheaval.

She laughs. "I guess you wouldn't really understand." There's no judgment in her voice, which I'm realizing is one of my sister's greatest virtues. There never is. "You've always known exactly who you are."

"You were just like me in high school," I argue. "What if I'm wrong about myself?" I wonder if the rest of my life will feel like Jamie's first year in Chicago did for her. It wouldn't be dissimilar to this conversation, relearning and revising the impressions I wrote about in the *Chronicle*, except I would be rewriting my understanding of myself. Even when you think you've found your story, you might need to change it later if the one you're living doesn't work. It would require finding new "facts"—what Jamie's doing now—and conceiving of a new narrative. I could be a completely different person in ten years. It scares me.

"Maybe," Jamie says. "But you're constantly seeking out new challenges for yourself instead of settling for the ones in front of you. I think if anyone knows who they are and what they want, it's you."

Touched, I feel grateful I have Jamie. I had no idea she was this insightful. For once, I don't resent being the younger sibling. I'm fortunate to get to peer through Jamie into a possible future.

"I mean, you got into Harvard, Alison. That's freaking incredible." She smiles, and I know it's genuine.

"Thanks. I'm really happy about it, but I don't want you to think that just because I'm excited means you have to regret the choices you've made."

She looks at me curiously. "You think I was upset you got in? Jealous?"

"Not exactly. But I'm younger than you, and I'm embarking on the exact path you've walked away from. It's sort of a reminder of what you've given up." I speak slowly, choosing my words carefully. I want to be honest with her though, and I'm starting to realize Jamie's a lot tougher than I gave her credit for.

She laughs. "Sure, but I'm *glad*. Seeing you do all of this and with such passion and determination . . . I never felt that. It makes sense to me now, why I wasn't happy."

It's a relief to hear, not only that she's figuring out what she wants, but that she believes in me and trusts me to make the decisions she regrets for herself. While she clearly understands me, I realize I haven't returned her careful consideration, not until too late. "I'm sorry about the *Chronicle* piece I wrote," I say.

"Thanks." Jamie stands, and I know it's behind us. Leaning her guitar on the seat, she eyes me, her usual enthusiasm returning. "Starbucks run?"

Homework waits for me in my room, hours I'm behind on. I don't hesitate. "Let me drop off my bag."

Jamie grins, and I know the two hours of sleep I'll lose will be worth it.

# Forty-Eight

I'M CONTENT FOR THE next week enjoying the ill-defined relationship Ethan and I have. It's definitely not dating, not the way our classmates do. We don't hold hands or make out in the halls, he doesn't meet me in front of my locker or eat lunch with me, and I don't doodle his name in my notebooks or, god, change my phone background. Really, our relationship doesn't much differ from before the kissing. We compete on every quiz, debate in every discussion. It's perfect.

The only difference is sometimes I catch something hungry in his glares in class, and, on occasion, when our classmates are distracted, we find a private place and pause our reviewing for fifteen minutes.

Which is what we're doing on Friday after school. We're in my *Chronicle* office, where we went to check our grades online for yesterday's calc midterm. Unfortunately, or fortunately, the newsroom was empty, and we got distracted in my office.

I'm perched on the edge of my desk, my legs on either side of Ethan's waist. With Ethan's lips pressed to mine, I murmur, "You're stalling."

"You're the one who closed the blinds," he replies instantly, his breath hot on my neck.

It's a valid point. I hate when he has valid points. One more way our relationship hasn't changed. I use a reliable countermove, changing the subject. Pulling back, I narrow my eyes suspiciously. "What will your task for me be if I score worse?"

Ethan's eyes light up. "Now there's a fun thought."

I realize what he's implying. While I don't *not* enjoy the goading charge in his voice, I drop my hands. "I think we need to establish some new ground rules," I say, picking his hand off my hip pointedly. "Nothing sexual."

He glances down at where my legs are wrapped around his waist.

"Not for our tasks," I clarify.

"So sexual stuff outside the competition is okay?" His lips curl. I grimace, realizing I walked right into his reply. My cheeks flame. *Point: Ethan.*

Instead of getting flustered, I scramble for the higher ground, lowering my hand to his belt buckle. "Obviously," I say.

Ethan's eyes widen. I'm highly conscious of where we're positioned, the edge of the desk digging into my thighs, his hand on the wood next to me, him watching me intently from his height above me. I've pushed the conversation in this new direction, not knowing exactly where it leads. None of my previous relationships went this far, but it's definitely not something I'm opposed to. Outside of school, that is. I think. With my hand on Ethan's belt, I'm 99 percent sure I'm bluffing.

I don't have the chance to confront the other one percent. Ethan and I jump apart when we hear the newsroom door open, the noise resounding through the wall of my office. I drop into my desk chair, pretending I'm working, right when my door opens.

"Dylan, how nice to see you," Ethan says, slightly breath-less.

Dylan doesn't seem to notice. Walking in, she stands on the opposite side of the office from him, sparing him a sneer-ing look. "Surely there's someone else you could be bothering right now."

Ethan picks up his shoulder bag. I notice he positions it strategically in front of his waist. "But Sanger is the most fun," he says.

I imagine my cheeks changing from pink to fuchsia. Working very hard not to catch Ethan's eye, I focus on Dylan. "Is it time already?" I ask.

"Um, yeah. You were supposed to meet me ten minutes ago." Dylan's voice holds irritation I now realize isn't only reserved for Ethan. "It's not like you to be late." Her brow furrowed, she watches me with commingled impatience and curiosity.

"I take full responsibility," Ethan interjects humorously.

Dylan's eyes cut to him, visibly loathing. It makes me uncomfortable. While Dylan and I have practically made a two-person sport of hating Ethan, I'm suddenly no longer interested in her looking like she's lining up shots on the goal.

I preempt her hurriedly. "Sorry, let's go." I give Ethan a final glance while I'm walking out with Dylan, which he receives with a flicker of the corner of his lips, playfulness in his eyes for only me to see.

I follow Dylan into campus. It takes effort to ignore how much I wish Ethan and I could continue where we left off. However, I promised Dylan I'd come with her to the final dress rehearsal for the drama department's spring musical, *The Wizard of Oz*, which she's photographing for yearbook. Figuring I could dust off my reporting skills, I decided I'd write the feature for the *Chronicle* since I'd be there anyway.

Dylan's camera bag bounces on the hip of her black jeans while we walk. As we pass an underclassman couple on one of the benches, holding hands and sharing earphones in their hoodies, she turns back to me. "What did Ethan want this time?"

"Oh, nothing," I reply, feigning carelessness. Dylan raises an eyebrow at my vague response. "We were just comparing calc scores," I elaborate.

We fall into step on the short set of stairs separating the auditorium from the rest of campus. "I don't know how you stand working with him." Dylan shakes her head. "The extra time you have to spend with him on the *Chronicle* must be torture."

"It's . . ." I search for the right description. I wouldn't call what just happened in my office *torture*. Nor what went on in Isabel's bathroom. Nor the greatest make-out of my life in Ethan's car on Wednesday. "Challenging," I finish noncommittally.

"I'll say." Dylan laughs. She opens the auditorium doors, and we walk in. The theater is empty except for the crew members working the lighting board in the back and the director in the front row, jotting notes on his clipboard. Dylan and I slide into seats on the aisle. The musical's just starting. Amy Davidson stands on stage, singing "Over the Rainbow." Next to me, Dylan starts snapping photos. "Did you ever find out if Ethan's going to Harvard?"

"He is," I say. I still don't know what we're going to do when we're on the same campus next year. He and I haven't discussed it since our talk in his car.

Dylan frowns, face to her camera's viewfinder. "My condolences."

I'm eager to change the subject. "Hey, have you checked out Berkeley's programs for photography?"

The question seems to confuse Dylan. She looks up, reading my expression. "A little," she says. "Olivia says I should focus on requirements first."

"Do *you* want to focus on requirements first?" I can't conceal the judgment from my voice.

Her expression clouds over. "Honestly, I can't even think

about classes right now. First, I have to fix things with Olivia. Then I'll worry about everything else."

"What's happening with Olivia?" I guess I was kind of caught up in Ethan this week. It occurs to me I haven't had a real conversation with Dylan in days. If I'd had, I'd know what drama Olivia was causing now.

"Over the Rainbow" ends, and the stage falls silent while the lighting drops into darkness. Dylan lowers her voice, her words pinched like the subject pains her. "We're just going through an adjustment period. I know it'll be fine when I'm on campus with her. Everything will go back to the way it was."

I wonder how it would feel, envisioning next year the way Dylan does. Looking into my college years and wanting nothing but a revival of high school with improved production values and a couple new cast members. I've watched Dylan wait for what she already has increasingly often in the past weeks, my frustration growing with everything she ignores while she focuses on Olivia. On *the way it was*. "Are you sure that's a good idea?" I ask, unable to hold the question in. "College isn't about reliving high school."

"I'm not reliving high school." I hear hurt in her whisper. "I'm making it work with a person I really care about."

"Dylan, come on." I wrestle down the impatience in my voice, knowing I'm pressing a sensitive subject. "You're holding on to a relationship that isn't good for you. It's not even what you remember. You and Olivia were always tumultuous, but now—I haven't seen you happy with her since you got together. Next year at Berkeley, you have a real chance to start fresh, but not if you're stuck on something that should be over."

When I finish my speech, the director in the front turns in his seat, gesturing for us to be quiet with an annoyed finger to his lips. I mouth an apology, then hide behind my notebook. We'll have to finish this conversation later. I turn to whisper as much to Dylan, but she stands. I assume she's going closer to the stage to take more photos, but instead she storms out the back and into the lobby. She punches the exit doors so forcefully Amy breaks character to frown in our direction.

I grab my things and follow Dylan, doing everything I can not to make a sound. Dylan's waiting in the empty lobby when I ease open the theater doors. She's glaring. I'm caught off guard, not having expected the force of her reaction. I say what first comes to mind, my voice sounding strangely small in the quiet space. "Not every relationship is meant to last."

I intend it consolingly. But with the change I watch come over Dylan's expression, I know it didn't come out well. "You're right," she replies waveringly. I know Dylan well enough to recognize when she's furious and fighting to keep her composure. "But I don't mean Olivia. I mean you. You're who I'm clinging to even though our relationship's not what I remember."

I flinch. "You don't mean that."

Dylan pauses, and I wonder if I'm right that she didn't mean it. I wait, hoping she'll withdraw her words and we'll figure this out. While neither of us speaks, people on their way to the parking lot wander past the wide windows of the lobby, laughing loud enough for us to hear.

"You're so judgmental," she finally says, softer now. "You think you're so much more mature than me, and I'm tired of it. You don't have all the answers, Alison."

Fear drains into me when I realize she's not retreated from what she said. My mind frantically replays a hundred memories simultaneously, Starbucks dates, studying and sleepovers and just doing nothing in my room, homecoming dances and trips to the beach. I hadn't realized I was holding on to them until they crumble in my fingers.

I don't want to have to say I was wrong about Olivia. I wasn't. Everything in me hopes—wills—Dylan to recognize it.

She doesn't. Shaking her head, she spins and heads for the doors. It sparks frustration in me. I guess those Starbucks runs and sleepovers aren't enough for her to dignify them with a discussion. "Real mature, walking out in the middle of an argument," I say to her back.

"I have enough shots of the show." She waves her hand flippantly. "I'm done here." Slamming open the doors, she leaves the lobby and me and everything we should have said.

Half of me wants to follow her, wants to force her to finish the conversation. The other half roots me in place. What's the point? Dylan was clear about how she felt. I won't indulge in the needless drama she's used to.

Instead, I work to reduce the problem rationally, replacing

panic with probabilities and heartache with objectivity. While it hurts, maybe Dylan was right. We'll be on opposite coasts next year. The odds are our friendship wouldn't have remained intact. It'll be better this way.

I turn and head back into the theater, ready to do the job I said I would.

# Forty-Nine

PRODUCTION WEEK IS COMING up the week right after spring break. Knowing I have to get a jump on the issue because my staff will be useless over the vacation provides welcome weekend distraction from my fight with Dylan. I don't text her, and she doesn't text me. Instead, I hurtle headfirst into my work. It's the middle of April, so I assign stories and photos while reviewing for AP exams coming up at the start of May. Sunday morning, I get up early to "help" the designers format the front page, which really involves me micromanaging and reworking layouts they had finished.

The whole weekend, it's not unclear to me what I'm really doing. I'm running. I pretend I'm running in the direction of the next *Chronicle* issue, when really, I'm running away from how Dylan and I left our friendship. When I send in my commitment to Harvard, I'm fully ready to move on to the next period of my life, leaving high school behind.

It edges resentment into every moment I devote to

working on my *other* gigantic obligation, the reunion. As if the *Chronicle* and APs weren't enough. It's in four weeks now, and while we've paid for the major pieces, the small details have started stacking up. I force myself to focus on making decorations, charting attendees, and, of course, emailing the rarely responsive Adam.

In my work-fueled haze, I haven't seen Ethan outside our classes and normal routines. I'm surprised when he shows up in my office on Monday after school. On my desk, I've organized in rows the name tags I've printed for the reunion, which I'm cutting to fit the laminated clips I ordered.

"You started without me," he says.

I glance up, remembering suddenly we'd planned on doing the name tags together. Evidently, I overlooked the detail in my workaholic frenzy and the fight with Dylan.

"You forgot," Ethan continues. He walks into the room. "I'm insulted." He doesn't sound insulted. Picking up one of the finished name tags, he inspects the laminated pouch, pinching the clip a couple times with passive interest.

"Sorry. I've been busy," I say. I'm pretty sure I've never said the word *sorry* to Ethan in my life.

He cocks his head, then sits down next to me, crossing one leg over the other expansively, one shoe perched on his knee. I feel his gaze on me while I finish cutting the row of name tags I'm holding. "You have been. Busy, that is," he says. "I didn't hear from you this weekend, and I looked for you during lunch."

"I was in the library," I reply, pushing hair past my ear compulsively. "I had to focus."

Ethan doesn't pick up a name tag. He just watches me, and I'm on the verge of ordering him to pitch in when he finally speaks. "What's wrong?"

"*What's wrong?*" Now I look over, my eyes wide like he's just declared he's dropping Harvard and becoming a priest. If Ethan Molloy wants to know what's wrong with *me*, I should ask him the same question.

"Yeah, Sanger," he says impatiently. "What's wrong? You look upset. You can tell me about whatever's"—he gestures awkwardly in the air—"bothering you."

Shifting in my seat to face him, I search Ethan's face. He seems sincere, which is weird. "We don't . . . do this," I start, not finding the vocabulary for what *this* is. His question is nothing I recognize from his lips on my collarbone or his hands under the hem of my shirt, nothing I remember from glares over group projects or class discussions. His surprising care warms me in an uncomfortable way. "Shouldn't you be taunting me or something?" I prod his knee with mine.

His expression doesn't change. "We *could* do this."

I frown. "Three years of fighting and rivalry and a couple weeks of hurried hookups doesn't lead to us discussing *what's wrong.*"

Ethan looks stung, and for a moment I regret my harshness. It's just, I spent the whole weekend ruminating on Dylan, and Dylan and Olivia. It left me with the unsettling suspicion their fraught relationship is exactly like what I have with Ethan. Everything I said of her and Olivia, I realized I could say of Ethan and myself. It's what Dylan's always maintained—Ethan and I aren't healthy for each other. We're tumultuous, we're unstable, and we're facing the prospect of carrying a high school relationship into college exactly the way I told Dylan not to do.

Ethan crosses his arms. "Thirty minutes in your office after school isn't exactly hurried." When I don't reply, the playful fire in his eyes goes out. He continues, his voice earnest. "What's happening right now? You're very eager to oppose whatever we have here. Why?"

If he were interviewing me in one of the reporting clinics the *Chronicle* holds for new staffers, I'd commend him for the precision and directness of the question. In present circumstances, though, it makes me shift my eyes to the door.

"Because what we're doing is immature. We don't make sense," I say. If my friendship with Dylan wasn't real enough to last past high school, this flammable new thing with Ethan definitely isn't. We're founded on intermittent hookups and furious competition. That's not a real relationship. That's nothing. "We hate each other, Ethan. Remember? Just because we've warped our hatred into whatever improbable chemistry we have doesn't mean it's worth moving forward with. We're going to Harvard next year. We need to think long-term."

Ethan's indignation fades into disappointment. "What

even was this past week to you? Just a new kind of mind game?"

His question, an echo of exactly what I suspected of him when we first kissed, is enough to prove just how wrong what we have is. It doesn't matter how intently he's leaning forward, waiting for my response. It doesn't matter how much being with him sometimes feels right. This is my nemesis. It would be painfully naive to have faith in a relationship constructed on top of the gunpowder we've stockpiled for years.

"Wasn't it to you?" I ask.

I can practically watch Ethan's expression closing up, becoming unreadable like a heavy book slammed shut. What enters his eyes is much more familiar. It's dispassionate determination, his favorite facade when dealing with me. He's watching me through the mask he's worn when he's not just ready to have one of our fights—he's ready to win.

"Obviously," he says coldly. If his reply didn't hurt so much, I'd applaud him for the impeccably placed blow. I fight the impulse to explain I don't *want* to do this—I just know, rationally, I have to. What would be the point in explaining? While I'm stuck silent, Ethan stands up, swinging his bag over his shoulder. "You'll finish the name tags, then? I have a list of places I'd rather be."

"I'll finish them," I say. I start routinely shutting off the possibilities of what Ethan and I could have been. Unrealistic possibilities, I remind myself. It does nothing to dispel the new wedge pressing into my heart. I fight the feeling, and when it wins, I clench my jaw and focus on the name tags. I guess I'm still not practiced at failing. "I work better alone."

"Yes. You do." He opens the door to the newsroom and walks out without looking back.

# Fifty

"EXIT HERE." HECTOR POINTS, indicating the freeway off-ramp where he wants me to return to surface streets. It's cloudy, the parallel strips of highway matching the sky in gray. When it starts drizzling, I switch on the headlights without needing to be told.

Having failed my driving test once, I scheduled this session with Hector because I couldn't bear the humiliation of failing when I retake the exam in a couple weeks. In part it's due to Ethan. In the days since we ended our non-relationship, he's been ruthless, seemingly determined to beat me even in the littlest contests. Getting to English earlier every morning. Disputing every one of my comments in class. Ignoring every edit I give him on his feature for the upcoming *Chronicle* issue. If our teachers thought we were toxic before, I imagine they're on the verge of issuing Fairview an environmental hazard warning now.

If I were to fail the driving test a second time, I don't

know what Ethan would do. He might quite literally rewrite his *Chronicle* feature to focus on my incompetence behind the wheel.

This imperative is lost on Hector, however. My instructor repeatedly reassures me I'm driving "fine" while detailing his excitement for the upcoming Fairview reunion. In between yielding for pedestrians and making loops of the Whole Foods near my house, he comments no less than three times how he's looking forward to getting together with AJ.

His enthusiasm for reconnecting with a lost high school friend stings. It forces me to remember how the split with Dylan and the new conflict with Ethan hurt, a reality I've worked to ignore.

When we're waiting under the overpass on the edge of the city and I'm hearing some new story from Settlers of Catan Club, I've had enough. I interrupt Hector harshly. "Don't you think the fact you fell out of touch might mean you shouldn't be friends anymore? Maybe there's a reason you haven't talked in ten years."

I press the pedal, continuing through the overpass. There *has* to be a reason they're not friends. I need Hector to recognize that and move on, because I need to know that in a decade *I'll* have moved on. I can't be coming up on my own reunion and longing for people in the past. I can't feel the way I'm feeling now.

Hector falls silent. I can feel him studying me, like he knows I'm not talking about AJ. I'm grateful when he doesn't call me on the clear undercurrent in my question. "You could be right," he says carefully. "But I miss him, which I think means something."

"People get nostalgic for the past. It doesn't mean you should turn back time," I say. "Sometimes people just outgrow each other." The drizzle patters the windshield while I drive.

Hector nods. He folds his hands in his lap. "Sometimes. But sometimes you only think you outgrew someone when really you let them go."

I don't say anything. If Hector has a point, it's not one I'm ready to consider right now. It's nearly the end of the hour, and I want this conversation to be over. The rain rattles on the roof. I wish it would let up, irrationally resenting the noise of wet rubber on pavement.

"Hold up, you should turn left," Hector says. "We're not picking up Ethan today, remember?"

I turn the wheel sharply. Lost in my thoughts, I'd instinctually driven in the direction of Ethan's house. Of course he doesn't have a lesson now. I'm frustrated I forgot. Navigating out of Ethan's neighborhood, I cross the city in the direction of mine. While I steer onto the streets close to my house, Hector says nothing. With memories of Ethan's overcompetitiveness this week caught on repeat in my mind, I for once wish Hector would pick up his high school stories where he left off.

The rain is relenting when I pull into my driveway. "Tell Ethan hi for me," Hector says congenially.

I cut him an unamused glance. "I will not."

Hector laughs lightly. "You're going to be fine."

"On my driving test? You think I'll pass?" It occurs to me I planned this extra hour with Hector intending to fine-tune my driving. Instead, I spent the entire time hearing his yearbook signatures in story form and dwelling on where I've left everything with Ethan and Dylan. It makes me freshly nervous for retaking the test.

Hector hums noncommittally, which I interpret as reassurance. "Try not to let thinking about where you're headed distract from what you're doing," he says. "I'll see you and Ethan at the reunion."

I nod, unbuckling my belt. Walking up to my front door, I wave goodbye, replaying Hector's final words of guidance in my head. They're definitely helpful for driving. I could forget details like signaling and full stops if I'm overly focused on getting my license.

Somehow, though, I don't think he was talking about the exam.

# Fifty-One

**OVER SPRING BREAK THE** next week, I focus on AP exams, feeling increasingly overwhelmed with the quantity of reviewing hours facing me. I repurpose an entire half of my whiteboard into a color-coded nightmare of a plan for the next two weeks. No minute is wasted. Whenever I'm eating breakfast, I'm reading my *Princeton Review* guides. When I walk to get coffee, I'm listening to an audiobook for AP English. When I'm home, I rarely leave my room, permitting myself only half-hour dinners with my family, repeating presidential powers and differential equations in my head the entire time.

I make flashcards in the garage while Jamie practices with her band, who have dubbed themselves the Stragglers. They're not horrible. Jamie's middle-school orchestra skills have set her up to be fairly capable, if not amazing. I could imagine the band playing open mic nights or something. Their Green Day covers don't provide the worst studying soundtrack ever, although sometimes their practicing devolves into Jamie helping with Mara's grad school application essays.

The highlight of my vacation is I manage to pass my driving exam. When I do, Jamie and I celebrate by driving to the Sweet Wieners truck, where we consume horrendous hot dogs covered in chocolate chips and graham cracker crumbs.

I'm worn thin by the time production week begins on the Monday we return to school. My sleep schedule is down to four hours nightly, and I'm hardly keeping on top of home-work while following my whiteboard's AP reviewing plan. I've made no progress on the reunion, which is in less than two weeks, except approving the Millard Fillmore kitchen's hors d'oeuvres menu. Ethan's equally overwhelmed. I know because he didn't object when I assigned him another editor and then wasn't obstinate enough for Julie Wang to complain to me when they were done.

With the sheer number of exams upcoming, I'm surpris-ingly nervous. Everyone is—even Ethan, who's let his new vehemence in competition with me fizzle out, suffocated under the strain of six APs. In a way, it's sad. While I didn't enjoy the week of increased contention, this harsh with-drawal is sort of worse. I feel our rivalry fading. It's for the best, I remind myself. I'll be able to handle myself maturely at Harvard, no longer consumed by our petty games.

Like everything with Ethan, though, reason doesn't help. I still find myself mourning something I feel receding into the past.

On Wednesday evening, I'm ready to drop from exhaustion. It's nearly eleven, and we're only waiting on proofs of a few pages from Ms. Heyward. I'm in my office, rubbing my eyes over the printouts of the opinion pages, when Tori rushes in.

She's breathless. *Thenewscomputercrashed.*

My exhausted mind can't quite parse her words. "What?"

"The news computer crashed," Tori repeats, controlled panic in her voice.

I eye her, not exactly understanding the gravity of the problem. Tori's generally good under pressure. She'd have to be to handle Ethan in news meetings. If she's freaking out, something's really wrong. "It's a good thing we back up everything to the cloud, isn't it?" I inquire evenly.

Tori swallows. I raise my eyebrows.

"I have the SATs next weekend," Tori starts. When I say nothing, she continues, her words falling out in a rush. "Tomorrow I have this precalc test, and I'm just really exhausted. It's my fault. I uploaded one of the pages, but I guess I forgot the other two. I promise I'll fix it, even if it takes me the entire night—"

"Tori," I cut in.

I pinch the bridge of my nose beneath my glasses, hoping vainly to banish my burgeoning headache. She's not wrong to panic. If the computer lost two news pages, it'll take hours to reconstruct the designs and re-input each story. As the editor in chief, I can't leave anyway until every page is finished and off to the printer, which means there's no reason for Tori to stay here and fail her precalc exam. "I'll handle it. Go home. Get some sleep," I instruct her.

Tori chews her lip. "No," she says. "It's my fault. I have to help."

"It's not a two-person job," I say, gentler. "I don't have a test I might fail tomorrow."

My consolation finally reaches her. She nods. "Thanks, Alison," she gets out, then trudges from my office into the newsroom.

I inhale, collecting my thoughts. Two news pages. We need the pages to the printer by tomorrow morning. While the deadline's hellishly high-pressure, it's no pressure I haven't handled before. First, I'll have to open each individual story and re-edit them. The changes the editors made were done directly on the formatted pages we lost. Once I've revised everything, I'll figure out reconstructing the layout.

I open my laptop and prepare for the punishing night.

In three hours, I'm finished with the below-the-fold piece on the school board meeting, the final story I needed to read over. Ready to start designing the new layout, I exit my office, and I'm caught up short. In my sleep-deprived daze, I wonder if I'm hallucinating.

I'm not. Ethan's sitting in front of the sports computer, with what looks like a page layout open on the screen. I didn't know anyone was here—I couldn't see him from the windows in my office.

"I've finished the layout," he says.

I don't fully process his words. "You're still here."

He faces me, dark circles under his green eyes. His polo's rumpled, the cuffing of his chinos coming unraveled. My own vision is blurry, and I'm pretty sure I nodded off in my office for ten minutes while editing the city council elections coverage. He shrugs. "I didn't want you taking full credit for saving the paper," he replies. Humor fights its way out from under the weariness of his voice.

I nearly smile. For a moment, I just stand, feeling a weight lift from my chest and something warmer and welcome replacing it. My eyes water. I don't know if it's from exhaustion or from gratitude I'd never voice out loud.

I sit down next to him, examining his screen. He really did finish the layout. I find every headline and space for stories exactly where they're supposed to be. He's left unfilled frames for photos we haven't yet input. It's enough I nearly collapse in relief.

"Did you really stay here all night when I pulled my story?" he asks, his voice coyly prodding.

If it wasn't Ethan talking, I'd think he was playing this game to help keep me awake. "Yes," I reply. "Thank you for reminding me."

"No problem. I like to relive it daily."

I cut him a glance, not nearly as annoyed as I'd ordinarily be. Ethan holds my gaze in amusement, like he's won something. In the empty newsroom with him, I don't really care what. I shake my head in feigned consternation. "Okay." I get up. "Now we just have to input the fart aisles."

Ethan stares up at me, his face stony with repressed laughter.

I realize what I've said. "I mean art files," I correct.

"Fart aisles coming up," Ethan replies loudly.

I know it's partly from exhaustion when Ethan and I collapse into laughter. I laugh until water runs down my cheeks and I'm no longer making sound, my sides aching from how hard my stomach clenches. Ethan's doubled up, his hand over his face. It's ridiculous. Unbelievable. I'm laughing with the smartest guy I know over a fart joke.

Not only the smartest guy I know. My rival. It's the first moment I've shared with Ethan in weeks without insults, without undermining or distance. Remembering I miss him hits me suddenly. It's something I've been fighting to forget, hiding the feeling under studying and the newspaper and literally any refuge I could find. But here, with Ethan in front of me, his face pink from laughter, it's impossible to keep ignoring. It's lemonade in the wound, stinging yet sweet.

I start in the direction of my office, where I'll pull up the "fart aisles." While I'm walking away, Ethan catches my wrist.

It's painfully exhilarating, our first skin-on-skin contact since we ended things. I face him, finding surprising vulnerability in his eyes.

"Have dinner with me," he says, his voice rough with sleeplessness. "This Friday."

I'm caught off guard. "What?"

"A real date," he clarifies. Whether he decided it now or some time earlier, he sounds certain.

Maybe I'm delirious with exhaustion. Maybe I'm grateful he saved me hours of work tonight. Maybe it's the invitation itself, which feels defined and real. Or maybe I just miss him. Whatever it is, I reply instantly. "Yeah," I say. "Okay."

Ethan nods, releasing my wrist. I know him well enough to read excitement and relief in his eyes. Giving him a small smile, I return to my office, where I close my door and open my computer. Just minutes ago, I could hardly hold my eyes open, vision searing with every word I edited.

Now I'm wide awake.

# Fifty-Two

I KEEP EXPECTING I'LL cancel the date. I'll find him outside class where no one's listening and say I decided it's not a good idea. Ethan would understand. He'd dismiss the whole possibility with some quip about how we were tired. Neither of us were in our right minds. We'd head to our next class and return to competing the way we always have.

It doesn't happen. Thursday passes, excitement inexplicably growing in my chest. I remember what Hector told me. *Sometimes you only think you outgrew someone when really you let them go.* I don't know if a date with Ethan will give me any confirmation. But it might.

We get the paper out on Friday, in part thanks to Ethan. It's weird, having worked with Ethan instead of against him. It feels like having a fluent conversation in a foreign language for the first time. I'm picking up the nuances, the rhythms, and enjoying myself.

By six o'clock on Friday night, I still haven't canceled our date. I'm standing in my room, having changed my outfit three times. Closing my closet door, I straighten my cream-colored sweater over my light pink skirt. While I want to look nice, I don't want to look like I labored over dressing up.

It's an odd feeling, consciously evaluating whether I'm enough *myself*. The idea of this formal date with someone who a year ago I never would've expected dating has me feeling like I'm playing an older, more mature version of myself. I want it to fit instead of hanging loosely on me like I'm wearing an oversized life.

I settle on my outfit from the day with a few minor modifications. Swapping out my oxfords for yellow heels, I wonder if Ethan will notice I've eliminated our height difference. In a moment of inspiration, I put on the peach lipstick I wore to the junior awards ceremony last year. Finally, I pull my phone and purse out from under my *Princeton Review* economics guide, making a mental note to pick up the notebooks, papers, and studying detritus scattered throughout my room.

When I come downstairs, I find my parents in the living room. Mom's reading on her iPad, probably work documents, while dad watches *The Proposal*. Mom looks over, eyeing my outfit impassively over the rims of her glasses. "Hot date?"

I freeze. It's the worst move I could've possibly made.

Mom's eyes widen. My dad pauses the movie, which really speaks to how interesting I am since he's in the middle of the scene where Sandra Bullock and Ryan Reynolds are about to collide outside the shower. "Who is it?" Mom presses me. She must be great in depositions. *Isn't it true you're going out for dinner with your onetime-nemesis-then-rival-with-benefits?*

"Um," I get out.

Dad's eyes light up. "Oh my god. It's happening," he deadpans.

"Alison Sanger, are you going out with Ethan Molloy tonight?" Mom asks. She removes her glasses, like she plans to spend the entire night dissecting this with Dad instead of reading for work.

"Pay up," my dad says, holding a hand out to my mom.

I inhale deeply, hoping it calms me. "Can you guys just pretend you're normal parents?"

"Oh, would you rather us give you a safe-sex speech?" My mom's voice is heavy with sarcasm. "Is that what normal parents would do when their daughter's going out with a good-looking young man?"

*"Never mind—"*

"You really ought to have Ethan send you a note from his care provider on his sexually transmitted disease record," my dad counsels. I honestly have no idea if he's being facetious. Either way, I feel like screaming.

My mom opens her mouth, and I shove my hands over my ears. "We're just teasing," she says, and I reluctantly release them. "We're happy for you."

"How did you know?" I ask, hearing the vulnerability in my voice. "I mean about me and Ethan. How did you know we'd get together?"

My parents exchange a wry look. "You're obsessed with

each other," Mom says. It's what she'd tell me if she were joking, except she's not. There's no humor in her tone. "Besides, we're your parents. We know stuff about you."

The words soften me. "But I had no idea, and I really thought I knew myself." I'm not used to voicing real fears to my parents. This one worked itself into my heart when I first recognized what I felt for Ethan. How could I be so blind to myself? If my hatred for Ethan could change without warning into what I'm feeling now, I wonder what other pieces of myself I'm wrong about. It's the way I felt when I talked to Jamie and heard her side of her story, like the entire vision I have of my future might end up a mirage.

"No one knows everything about themselves," Dad says.

"Sometimes the unexpected stuff is the best," Mom continues, her hand finding Dad's on the couch cushions. "Like getting pregnant with you."

I roll my eyes, not ignoring the comfort in Mom's reassurance. "Instead of giving me the sex talk, now you're encouraging me to get knocked up."

Dad cuts Mom a warning glance. "No, we're not. We're just saying you shouldn't shut the door on new experiences or shaking up your own self-image. You might surprise yourself."

I nod. It's strangely meaningful, hearing good advice from my parents, and not what I expected from this conversation. I assumed they were pretty much over parenting—but maybe that's one more thing I got wrong. "Thanks," I reply, not knowing exactly what to say.

I walk to the front door. With my hand on the handle, I hear my dad call out from the living room. "Remember the STD check, Alison."

"Okay, *bye*," I say pointedly.

"Have fun, baby girl," my mom replies.

I'm smiling as I shut the door. I guess the nickname isn't the worst.

# Fifty-Three

ETHAN'S OUTSIDE MY HOUSE, standing by his car. He's looking down the block, seemingly lost in thought, and he doesn't see me at first. I allow myself a moment to admire him. He's wearing the black-and-green-checkered button-down he had on today at school, but he's added a dark gray blazer and shiny black shoes. His blond hair is the perfect amount of unruly I'm convinced Ethan's worked to achieve.

He's cute. More than cute.

He's also . . . nervous? While I watch, he rubs the back of his neck. The gesture sends a rush of endearment straight to my heart. I could stand here staring for an embarrassing amount of the night, but I clear my throat, wanting whatever's going to come next. He looks up sharply, his eyes landing on me.

He smiles. It's one of his genuine smiles, the exceedingly uncommon kind. The kind where I'm reminded, despite our years of conflict, I'm only just meeting this side of him.

"Hi," he says. The way he says it holds other things he's not saying. It's a *hi you look nice*, a *hi I'm happy to see you*. Or I hope it is.

"Hey," I say. "Where are we going?"

"Somewhere fancy." He shrugs modestly.

While intrigued, I'm suddenly nervous. "Should I change? Maybe I'm not dressed up enough."

In reply, Ethan opens his passenger door, his smile looking more like a grin now. "Sanger. You're literally always dressed up enough."

I flush, enjoying the familiar irritation of Ethan's chiding. Getting into his car, I wait for him to drop into the drivers' seat. "I like looking professional," I reply defensively when he does.

"Oh, I know."

"You do?" I glance over, not expecting to find him eyeing me approvingly.

He starts the car, the engine humming and the dashboard blinking to life. "You don't want anyone underestimating you," he says. "It's particularly annoying to someone trying to convince himself he's capable of beating you."

I let out a laugh, pleased inside to hear him pinpoint my reasoning exactly. "Fair. What's your reason? Why do you dress like a president's kid?"

"Because you like it," he says like he's telling me what day of the week it is.

"I do not."

Ethan's headlights glare into the night, illuminating

lawns and hedges. We're the only car on the street. He glides up to the stop sign with the measured control I remember from when he drove me home. "You're usually a better liar," he comments. "Aside from enjoying your admiring glances, I dress this way to keep up with you. I changed my whole wardrobe freshman year when I realized teachers respected you more because you looked put-together."

It's not what I expected, which was more overconfidence. Ethan's kept himself a closed door for years, and I'm not yet used to him giving me occasional glimpses of what's inside. His explanation reminds me of the first time he did, when he confessed our competition was the only thing driving him. Changing his wardrobe for me is no different. I find myself wishing his choices sprung from some fundamental Ethan-ness—watching *Dead Poets Society* and falling in love with the humanities and the entire world of education, or modeling himself on his dad's Hugo Boss work wear—instead of just mirroring me.

It makes me a little sad. I change the subject. "I hope where we're going has food."

Ethan smiles. If I were to rate his smiles from one to ten, genuine to goading, this would be a six. "It's a restaurant, so odds are good," he replies.

"A fancy restaurant," I elaborate.

"Nothing gets past you, Sanger." Up to eight.

"Ethan," I say softly, "what is this?"

He looks over when we reach a red light, his expression sobering with the shift in the conversation. "You said our relationship was immature," he starts carefully. I meet his gaze, fidgeting the corner of my phone case while I wait for him to continue. "I'm going to show you it doesn't have to be."

I face forward, warmth spreading in my chest. It's like the entire night has fallen into place. We're not being driven by parents. We're not talking about Mr. Pham's class or school bonfires. We're headed into the city, into a night of our own, being who we're becoming. I imagine remembering this night in ten years. I know I will.

The light changes. Ethan drives forward, and I can almost see it—what's to come.

# Fifty-Four

THE RESTAURANT IS IN a neighborhood I've never visited, situated on the corner of a wide street near vibrant Victorian multistories and small coffee shops. The ocean is close enough it's visible when I get out of Ethan's car. I wonder how Ethan found this place until I remember his dad writes restaurant reviews for a respected website.

He holds the door while I walk past the industrial facade into the softly lamplit space. Ethan talks to the hostess, and I take in the room. It *is* fancy, if unpretentious. Walls of white-painted brick contrast with the black wood of the bar and tables. Climbing vines provide dashes of striking green, and the exposed ducts and metal light fixtures complete the upscale-warehouse image. I follow Ethan and the hostess to our table.

The place is packed. There's music playing, but the collective volume of conversation drowns out everything except the bassline. I don't notice the time passing while we sip sparkling water, inspect the menus, and order, the waiter committing our choices to memory instead of writing them down.

Conversation flows easily with Ethan. We have endless topics in common, and we make each other laugh over stories of our worst meetings with Principal Williams, whether he enjoyed his momentary stint as the Fairview puma mascot—he did—and when Simon Long submitted wonderful, engaging *Chronicle* sports coverage we later found out was completely made up. Ethan's smile seems effortless, his laughter unrestrained. Over his cacio e pepe and my scal-lops, I catch myself enjoying the little details. How his blazer hugs his shoulders, the earnest interest in his eyes when I talk about my sister.

I can think of no reason why this couldn't work in the future. Why we couldn't have this exact date in Cambridge, Massachusetts, amid finals and *Crimson* deadlines and flights home.

While we vow not to discuss reunion planning, want-ing the night off together, I can't help making one comment about how he must concede the Millard Fillmore was an excellent choice on my part. I wait for his sarcastic comeback. I'm even preparing my comeback to his comeback.

But he only nods. He changes the subject, and while I fol-low him into discussing how we pretend not to enjoy ASG, I don't realize until moments later I'm a little disappointed.

I hadn't known until he deflected my comment how much I wasn't just expecting he'd parry and strike—I was *hoping* he would. It steals some of the luster from the lighting, the color from the room. I remember this feeling. The week I decided I wouldn't compete with Ethan, I found myself frustrated after each unfulfilling docile exchange we had. Since then, I've rationalized the feeling to have been some warped form of missing Ethan in my life. I thought it was keeping my distance from him I couldn't stand.

If I'm feeling it now, with Ethan smiling in front of me across two feet of table, then this disappointment isn't about missing *him*. It's about missing the fire our relationship has never lacked in the years we've known each other. Until now.

We eat our entrees, and I keep trying to provoke him. It feels like swimming farther and farther out to sea, waiting for the scary thrill when my feet no longer touch the ground. It never comes. Ethan evades each pointed remark like he's been practicing.

Which is when it hits me. "I had no idea," I say to him.

"No idea what?" he asks.

"You liked me this much. You're really working hard." I reach across the table and take the last bite of his pasta.

Ethan's lips curl as he watches me chew. "First of all, being this charming"—he gestures to himself—"is not me working hard." My heart does a little flip when I see the momentary glint of competitiveness in his eyes. "Second," he continues, the edge in his voice softening, "you already knew I liked you."

I did know. I guess it's still surprising, hearing someone's feelings have changed so fully, so fast. It's hard to accept. "Do you think this is why we've always been . . . the way we were?"

"Are you asking if we competed with each other because we were secretly in love?" I don't comment on the word he dropped, despite it stilling my breath. Ethan gazes off into a corner of the restaurant. "I don't know. I *do* know I haven't been pining for you this whole time. I'm not the kind of guy who's awful to a girl because his feelings are unrequited. And I don't think you're the kind of girl who'd fall for a guy who treats her poorly."

I nod. Our waiter drops off the dessert menu, which we don't pick up. I project the version of Ethan I knew before onto the one in front of me. He's not wrong. If he did now a few of the things he's done to me in the past, I wouldn't be here with him on a date.

"Whether I felt this unconsciously . . . I won't write it off entirely," he continues. "I can say, I wouldn't sabotage your newspaper today."

"And I wouldn't give the math textbook you left in the journalism room to someone who thought it was theirs," I offer in return.

Ethan furrows his brow. "You—wait, *what*? I missed two assignments because of that. You know, on second thought"— he waves his hand decisively—"we don't have to retread all the terrible things we've done to each other. We're different now."

I have no objection to what he's said, which definitely is

different. I'm glad for it. Nevertheless, I can't ignore the fact that when he exchanged our disruptive warfare for our new relationship, he traded in a few qualities of his I liked. His sharp wit. His smug sense of humor. The way he pushed me to be smarter, faster, better. He's half himself. While it's a half I'm enjoying meeting, I miss his other side.

I want the irritating and competitive Ethan back, and our messy relationship—I mean, without the sabotage. It might make me immature, and might not even be worth pursuing at this point in my life. But I'm starting to wonder if none of that mattered as much as I thought.

Ethan picks up the menu. "Shall we order dessert?"

I reach across and push the menu down. "I have a better idea."

# Fifty-Five

ETHAN ORDERS THE BROWNIE Dough. I get the Royal New York Cheesecake.

We eat our Blizzards on the metal tables outside, near the parking lot, Ethan's blazer folded on the bench next to him. He's seated. I'm perched on the edge of the table, watching the drive-thru, my thigh brushing his elbow. Inside the Dairy Queen, I can see other groups of people our age through the window, hanging out, waiting in line. It's a very different clientele from the restaurant we were just in. I savor a spoonful of ice cream, noting how the sticky oversweetness doesn't complement my scallops. None of it matters. It's a perfect ending to our evening.

I face Ethan, enjoying the chill of the night on my cheeks. "You better watch your back on AP French," I say. "I've already memorized one hundred of the extra vocabulary words."

The hint of a grin flits over Ethan's lips. "Oh, is that how it's going to be?" Familiar competitiveness dances in his eyes. It's like we're years from the purposeful pretense of the first half of the date, and here, I can feel Ethan returning to himself—his perfectly frustrating, fractious self.

I slide down next to him, our eyes locked. "Just because I'm your girlfriend doesn't mean I'm going to go easy on you."

Surprise lifts Ethan's eyebrows. "Girlfriend," he says softly, like he's enjoying the sound. I don't mind it, either. His stare narrows on me, and his eyes ignite, like he's incapable of holding himself close to warmth for long without catching fire. I have a feeling I know what's coming. "I guess the word doesn't gross you out now," he remarks.

I shrug.

Satisfied, he eyes his half-finished sundae nonchalantly. "Don't worry. We could make it a blitz if you're game?"

Leaning forward in reply, I lay my lips on his, the ice cream on our tongues sweetening the kiss.

I don't care how unexpected it feels, kissing a guy I used to hate in the parking lot of the local Dairy Queen. Our relationship *is* immature, contentious and chaotic, and yet undeniably right. It's who I am right now, not who I thought I needed to be.

Which means my story isn't written just yet. I'm still finding new facts, making new discoveries. Like Ethan. Like realizing I wanted to compete with him even when it caused me sleeplessness and stress. Like feeling our fireworks fizzle when we weren't pushing and one-upping each other.

If embracing this relationship, blitzes and bickering and all, means embracing a little immaturity, then it's an immaturity I'm ready to love. In us, and in myself.

Ethan withdraws, his face close to mine. "I've been waiting all night for you to kiss me. Should I be worried it took challenging you to a competition?"

I ignore what his rogue voice does to me. "Only if you don't think you can keep up," I say with a smirk.

He grins, all cheek and confidence. It sends my stomach somersaulting. "Oh, I'll keep up." He kisses my neck, and I blame my shivers on the ice cream in my hands, not his mouth gliding down my skin. "Harvard just got much more interesting," he says when he's done.

"Ethan . . ." I pull back, the mention of Harvard leading my thoughts elsewhere. I remember the only other time we really discussed college, how Ethan only joked he wanted to study what I did. While I don't know exactly how I want my future to look, when I choose, I'm confident it'll be what *I* want. I didn't point it out to Ethan when we were in the midst of our uncertain string of hookups, but if we're going to have a real relationship, I feel like I need to. It's not because I'm curious what drives him, not because I'm worried he sees me as a game. It's because I care about him.

He watches me questioningly, no doubt not following the change in my demeanor.

I take his hand. "You can't keep making your decisions based on me. You're so smart, and really funny, and the best high school writer I've ever read," I say. It's weird—complimenting Ethan feels kind of wonderful. "You should be finding what *you* like, not just competing with me."

"I know," he says thoughtfully. Then his eyes, rebelliously playful, find mine. "I am all those things."

I raise one eyebrow flatly. "I mean it. If we're dating and at the same school and still competing, I'm worried you'll just match me, and I don't want that."

Ethan's humor fades. "You're not wrong," he says. "Competing with you has driven me to achieve things I might not have otherwise. I'm grateful for it. I mean, without you I never would have joined the *Chronicle*, and I think I really do like journalism."

"You're great at it," I say quickly, liking how the compliment sounds in my voice. Even when I hated Ethan, I respected him. Knowing he might actually care about journalism, his frustration over the NSPCA fits into place. It wasn't just losing out on the award he resented, it was losing out on recognition in something he's started to like. "But Ethan, we let our competition get in the way. You would have won the NSPC reporting award had we not . . ."

"I know. And I know I can't just follow your choices. I have to figure it out on my own instead of hoping I stumble into myself through you." His face serious, he stares past me into the parking lot and doesn't speak for a few seconds. "Honestly, though, I don't know how anyone really learns what they want."

It's the most real he's ever been with me. I squeeze his

hand. "They try new things," I say. "Maybe you need space from me to make your own choices."

He glances up, real worry peering past the wryness in his eyes. "Are you breaking up with me already?" He's straining to sound joking. "I have to admit, I thought I'd get more than three minutes."

"I'm not breaking up with you," I reply gently. "*I'm* ready for this relationship to carry into my future. I just want to make sure you are."

Ethan's expression turns faraway. I recognize the look from my own mirror. He's envisioning, projecting us into the years ahead, imaging first classes in crowded lecture halls, walks in Harvard Yard when the ground is white and the trees have lost their green, conversations with roommates, choices of extracurriculars. "What if we put us on pause for a few months when we get to campus?" he says finally. "Just long enough to establish independent lives, make independent decisions. Then . . ." He rubs my hand with his thumb.

It's hard to want what he's saying. We'd only have months together before separating. Against all my expectations, I don't want to leave our relationship behind with high school. Even if we promise to get back together, the whole point of this pause is to give Ethan room to discover who he is. When he does, he might decide he doesn't want us anymore.

But while it's hard, it's right. "I think that might be for the best," I say. Nothing with Ethan feels the way I would expect. When my previous relationships ended, I wasn't desperate or despondent. I was fine. With Ethan, the very idea of the fledgling thing we have unraveling isn't unbearable, but it is enough to hurt. I stand, wanting space from the subject. What's left of my ice cream is melted, and I throw it in the trash.

When I turn from the blue metal bin, Ethan's behind me. My breath catches in a good way. He places one caressing hand on my elbow, and it eases my heartache. "This means we don't have long to catch up on everything we didn't do while we were busy fighting." He draws me close, his eyes flirtatious.

I permit myself to forget how I'll feel if we don't work out. Tilting my head, I meet his gaze. "You're saying we're behind on the material?"

His lips move closer. "Very, very behind," he answers, smiling into my cheek.

I reach up, holding him right here, my fingers in his hair. I know we don't have long. What time we do have left, I'm determined to savor, turning my calendar from a countdown into a compendium of banter, dates, and everything else we could be. "Well," I say seriously, putting on a studious pout, "I've always enjoyed doing extra credit."

He's laughing as I tug him down to meet my lips.

# Fifty-Six

ON MONDAY, I'M DETERMINED to make a grand gesture. Instead of going to ASG when I get out of French, I cross the quad in the other direction, heading for the yearbook room. Dylan is worth my first and only tardy.

It's disorienting deviating from my regular route. I see different people, each carrying out routines of his or her own. In the late morning light, I pass the railing on the edge of the quad, where Ryan Maldonaldo and Lindsay Costello lean, holding hands. They part, presumably to head to their classes. I fight the urge to quicken my steps and double back to ASG.

The final bell hasn't yet rung when I walk into yearbook, but everyone's already working. Their deadline to get the yearbook to the printer must be upcoming. In the back of the room, I find Dylan at her regular computer, the title text of the "Seniors Reflect" page on her screen.

"Hey," I say hesitantly, "do you have a minute?" Nobody's

noticed me walk in, everyone chatting or occupied in the pre-class minutes.

Dylan turns around. It's not hard resentment I find on her face, which I guess is good. It's surprise. "Alison," she starts, her eyes wide. "What are you doing here? You're going to be late to fourth period."

"I don't care," I reply. "I wanted to talk to you, and I don't know where you've been going during lunch."

Dylan doesn't appear to process my words. "You're going to get a tardy," she tells me.

"I'm aware. Dylan, I was wrong when I told you not to hold on to your relationship with Olivia. It wasn't my place. I think people really can change," I say, reflecting on the ways Ethan and I have changed toward each other. "Maybe I just haven't spent enough time with her more recently. You two probably have a much better relationship—"

"We broke up," Dylan interrupts me.

I stop, my speech hanging unfinished. "Oh."

"Thank you for finally apologizing, though." Her eyes shift off of me, which makes me nervous. "God, you were such a hypocrite," she goes on.

My mind jumps to Ethan, my nerves winding into panic. I wonder how she could have possibly found out. "Um . . ." I swallow. "How?"

"You've always been adamant about what you wanted, and you didn't allow anyone to question you," Dylan explains. "Which I love, by the way. It's why I think you're awesome. But it was less awesome when you doubted what I said *I* wanted."

My relief she's not referring to Ethan fades quickly to the corner of my mind. I understand exactly how I wronged her, and it's hard to hear out loud. "That's fair," I say. "I'm sorry."

Dylan stares me down, then she sighs heavily. "*I'm* sorry I said our friendship wasn't right anymore and that I wanted to leave it behind with high school. I don't want that."

"Good," I reply unhesitatingly. "I don't, either."

The bell rings for the beginning of class. Dylan watches me, one eyebrow up. "You feeling okay? You're officially tardy. Take deep breaths," she says, her voice a combination of mocking and completely serious. I grin, unable to help myself. It feels like everything's returning to normal, and I'm inexpressibly grateful Dylan's teasing me the way she ordinarily would.

"You know I wouldn't risk a tardy for anyone else, right?" I ask.

"I do," Dylan replies. Class is starting, and while no one quiets down, there's a rhythm of productivity in the room. Several yearbook staffers give me glances, noticing I'm not supposed to be here. Pham passes me without comment on his way to the front of the room, where he confers with a couple editors. Either everyone figures I'm here for some very important, legitimate school purpose, or they're used to people cutting class as a symptom of senioritis.

I look past Dylan, seeing yearbook spreads on everyone's screens. "From Freshman to Senior," "Senior Superlatives," "Pumas Give Back." They're pages designed to be mementos, commemorating years and friendships far behind us. It's impossible to imagine opening this book and realizing I've forgotten much of what's in it. "I hope we stay friends after we've graduated," I say to Dylan.

"Me too." Her voice is soft.

There's no way of knowing for certain. Our lives will change next year, and we'll change with them. It's possible the places we fit together now will warp out of shape, matching our new worlds instead, their old contours existing only in yearbook pages. We might not be friends forever. But we're friends right now.

I sit down next to her. "Do you want to talk about what happened with Olivia?"

Dylan's eyes dim. "She was totally weird when I talked about visiting campus. I think I finally realized she only wants me around when she doesn't have any better options."

"She's an idiot," I say.

Dylan looks unconvinced. "Yeah."

I don't want college to be just bad memories and dashed hopes for Dylan. She deserves more. "You and I can visit Berkeley. Anytime you want," I suggest. Hoping high school relationships won't change isn't realistic. But maintaining them while giving them room to grow could be. I want to be there, or even help, while Dylan finds her own way in college.

"There's an art department open house in a couple weeks," Dylan replies. "I was thinking of going and introducing myself to the photography professors." There's a pleased flush in her cheeks.

It fills me with pride. "We'll do it." I stand, ready to return to ASG and face my tardy.

"Hey, before you go"—Dylan smiles winningly—"care to contribute a quote?" She gestures to the yearbook page open on her screen.

I reread the title. "Seniors Reflect." Had she asked a week ago, I would have scoffed and declined. Now I don't find the yearbook quite so ridiculous. I guess graduation nostalgia is getting to even me. "Sure," I say."

I examine the page of quotes where seniors have recounted their favorite Fairview memories. With each entry I read, I find reminiscences I wouldn't have chosen. Homecoming dances, bonfires, football games. It's like seeing myself in the backgrounds of everyone else's photos. I was *there* for the events they've described. They're just not my high school experience.

I could've molded those moments into memories I'd cherish. But I didn't. I don't regret it. I had my own high school experience. I wrote the life I wanted from what I knew was important to me—all-nighters, working on the newspaper, competing with Ethan. Without *my* cherished moments in the midst of a ridiculous rivalry, I wouldn't have found my relentless ambition or proved I could accomplish anything I put my mind to. They let me discover myself, and they changed me in ways I never expected. Ways like realizing I'm in love with my favorite enemy. And it was fun. I can admit that now. I had an absolute blast.

In ten years, I'll want to open this book, I think. I'll want to run into the people inside, to remember the ways they taught me who I am.

"Handing out issues of the *Chronicle*," I say, remembering one delivery in particular. An empty locker hall. Lips, heat, surprise, and inevitability. Dylan nods, putting my entry onto the page. I glance at the clock. "I should really head to class now."

"I'll walk you," Dylan offers immediately. "I have to pee anyway."

We head for the door, Dylan grabbing the hall pass on her way out. She catches the eye of Mr. Pham, who waves us off without interest. It's quiet on campus except for the voices of teachers from their classrooms as we walk. The sun glares off the concrete walls and walkways, the leaves overhead unmoving in the windless April afternoon. We say nothing, and it's the comfortable silence of studying dates and pre-slumber sleepovers.

Across the quad, we see Ethan leaving the ASG room, his emerald eyes wandering the campus. He spots us, and his expression shifts from surprise into relief.

"Ugh." Dylan shakes her head. "Of *course* he's in the way. I hope I don't see him when I visit you at Harvard next year."

Her words sting. I want to include Ethan in the visits from Dylan I'm envisioning, all of us having dinner in Cambridge or walking amid our respective dorms. I know I can't, not while our relationship is set for hiatus come September. It hurts to remember, and I wish Dylan understood instead of hating the person I'm falling for.

"Would it really be so terrible?" My voice is soft. Defenseless.

"Well, not the visiting you part—" Dylan cuts herself off short. Her eyes fly to my face, then to Ethan, who's waiting near the ASG door. "Wait."

"I wasn't lying when I said people can change," I say quietly. Dylan watches me with wide eyes. "I—we both have, and . . ." I fumble the end of my explanation, hoping Dylan understands and afraid of how she'll react when she does.

She looks at me hard. "What're you saying?"

I have a feeling I don't need to respond, what with the grin I know is forming on my face while I look at Ethan and he looks at me.

"Alison Sanger, you have some serious explaining to do." Dylan's voice sounds like shock has overwhelmed any accusation in her. I laugh. We've reached Ethan, who's idly spinning the ASG hall pass on his finger.

"I was heading to check the nurse's office for you," he says to me. "You were in third period, then gone."

I let playfulness into my voice. "Worried?" I guess Ethan notices my coyness, because his eyes dart questioningly to Dylan. I nod.

He catches my cue, pulling me to him and planting a quick kiss on my temple. "Hardly," he says with derision I know he's faking. "It was purely political. If you were going to be out, I was going to push through my Grad Night budget."

I put a hand on my hip. "Tough luck. I hope you're ready

to justify your profit margin, because I did the math and—"

"I'm sorry. What is this?" Dylan interrupts us. She gapes, looking between us.

"We're dating. Isn't it obvious?" Ethan replies, and I have to applaud him for his directness.

"*This*"—Dylan's eyes widen—"is dating?"

Before Ethan or I have a chance to respond, an angry voice I instantly recognize calls out behind us. "You three! Class. Now." I turn to find Principal Williams walking quickly down the hall, formidable in a steel-gray pantsuit. I have to take wardrobe notes from this woman. "Last I'd checked, none of you have a high school diploma yet. Don't think I won't flunk you."

"Sorry, Principal Williams," I say.

Williams neither stops nor responds. When she passes us, Ethan's hand finds my waist.

I give Dylan an apologetic glance. "I'll explain later, Dylan, I promise." Wordlessly, my friend nods. I follow Ethan into ASG, leaving her in the hallway. When I look over my shoulder, she's still staring from the doorway, her expression stunned, yet not entirely unhappy for me, either.

# Fifty-Seven

**THE WEEK FLIES PAST** in a flurry of exams and final reunion prep. Ethan wins the AP French blitz, and in penance, he has me call Adam for final budget approval. It turns out Ethan's no fan of him, either.

Dylan helps occasionally, joining me while I make the centerpieces, finish the slideshow, and pick up the fairy lights to hang in the hotel ballroom. Every event needs fairy lights, Dylan advises me. I have a feeling she only participates in my errands in order to interrogate me on the details of how Ethan and I happened. While she says she's working on "liking Ethan more," I suspect they enjoy bickering with each other too much to fully give it up. I understand the feeling.

The day of the reunion, everything's finally ready. The menu is set. The Millard Fillmore is prepared. Ethan's delivering the last pieces of décor, and with only hours until doors open, I'm in my room about to leave. I have to run to the electronics store in the mall to grab the adapter to play the photo slideshow. The Millard Fillmore's AV system is so out-rageously outdated it doesn't work with any of the numerous adapters I've accumulated over four years of ASG proposals and in-class presentations.

I have my dress in a garment bag, ready to change into when I get to the hotel, and I'm picking up my heels on my way out the door when my phone rings. Ethan's name flashes on the screen. I hit answer. "Did you hang the streamers on the northern and western walls?" I ask unhesitatingly.

"Yeah, I did." Ethan's voice is impatient. "Sanger, we have an emergency."

"Don't tell me Clint is still insisting on the signature lem-onade." I pause in my doorway, dress in one hand and phone in the other. Ethan and I eventually sampled the lemonade. It's saccharine sweet and dark yellow, a hue disturbingly rem-iniscent of urine.

"It's not the lemonade," Ethan assures me. "I'm a hero—nay, a god—and convinced him to put it out for the hotel guests instead. The DJ's sick, though."

"Avery? How sick?" I ask. We've only hired her for a couple hours. If she naps now and comes armed with cough medicine or ibuprofen, she could get through it. We'll double her tip.

"I didn't exactly ask for details. She mentioned food poi-soning," Ethan replies.

"Surely by tonight—"

"I say this with no judgment for choices you might have

made in the past," he cuts me off, "but reasonable people don't enjoy leaving the house while vomiting."

"So we have . . . no music." The realization settles into the pit of my stomach. It makes *me* want to vomit. While it's not my reunion, I feel responsible for the event. For Hector, for his friend AJ. For people in whose shoes I'm starting to imagine myself standing a decade from now.

What's more, I still want to win valedictorian over Ethan.

"Correct," Ethan says. "I did get the deposit back, and Avery asked a few of her friends if they were free. The only one available is . . . well, I watched his videos on YouTube, and he's honestly atrocious, but I don't know if we have a choice." Ethan's voice is measured, and I find myself grateful he's good under pressure the way I am. Even so, I hear a hint of stress in his explanation.

"Maybe . . ." I start, my own nerves mounting and my head spiraling. I straighten myself out with practiced focus. "Maybe everyone's going to be drunk enough it won't matter." Checking the clock on my desk, I notice I'm running late. I'll need forty-five minutes to reach downtown San Francisco from the electronics store. "I'm on my way now," I say, rushing into the hall.

"Okay," Ethan says in my ear. "I'll figure out pricing with Avery's friend."

Heading for the stairs, I pass Jamie's door. "Ethan, hold on." I pause, feeling inklings of inspiration, like remembering the right formula for a complicated physics question. "I have another idea. I'll call you back."

I hang up and walk into Jamie's room. It's a little less messy, the books she's been reading stacked neatly on her nightstand and her Columbia sweatshirt folded on her dresser.

"Hey, Jamie?" I say. She's on her computer, and I see the Fairview website open on her screen. It distracts me from why I'm here. When Jamie spins in her desk chair, looking up, I nod in the direction of her computer. "What're you doing?"

"Oh, nothing. Just an application." While Jamie's ebullient as ever, there's a waver of self-consciousness in her voice.

I come closer. It's a job application. "You want to work at Fairview?"

Jamie shrugs stiffly, playing it off as casual. I know carelessness on her, though, and this isn't it. "Well, I heard from Nurse Sharp they're hiring a new college and career center coordinator. I think it might be something I'd like."

I blink. It's not what I envisioned for Jamie, yet it doesn't feel out of place. I remember how insightful she was about my goals and my ideas for the future, and how she helped Mara with her grad school application essays. "I think you'd be fantastic," I say earnestly.

Jamie's unable to hide her excitement. "Thanks. I'll be really leaning into the whole regressing-to-high-school thing, huh?" There's gentle sarcasm in her question.

"I wouldn't call it regressing," I say. Still smiling, Jamie shifts her eyes to her room's open window, where the sunset is streaming in. This job is a new direction, which is okay. Jamie's writing new narratives instead of the pages she'd planned.

"Was there something you came in here for?" Jamie asks suddenly, facing me again.

"Yes," I say, remembering. "I need a huge favor."

# Fifty-Eight

**THE GUESTS ARE ARRIVING** when I finally pull up to the reunion. The sidewalk in front of the Millard Fillmore is packed with people in cocktail dresses and dinner jackets, exchanging handshakes and hugging old friends while they walk in. Even the outside of the hotel looks somehow done up for the occasion, the crumbling Victorian facade strangely romantic under the streetlights in the night.

I'm annoyingly late. When I got to the electronics store, despite my having called ahead and confirmed they had the adapter I needed, the clerk informed me he couldn't find it. After fifteen minutes of furious online searching, I found one other store in the area with the adapter and had to coerce them to stay open while I crossed the city. I got here frantic and half an hour past when I'd planned. Nevertheless, it was nice not having to depend on Ubers or my parents during my adapter odyssey.

Slipping past the guests, I find my way quickly to the staff room we've been using to store decorations. I shut the door and pray no one comes in while I change out of my sweaty cardigan and jeans amid the cleaning supplies and extra candles. Just when I've zipped up my dress, the door swings open and Ethan enters.

"Finally," he says. "Took you long enough. You have the adapter?"

He's reading on his phone and hasn't looked up. My gaze catches on his reunion formalwear, the light gray dress shirt he's wearing cuffed halfway up his forearms, with fitted black pants and a thin black tie. I can't help admiring him, even while I know I need my concentration in other places. Though I don't condone him changing his wardrobe in freshman year because of me, I can't dispute the results. "Of course," I say. "You? Everything set up for—"

He preempts me. "Of course. And I just got word from Adam's assistant that the vendors have been paid—" He puts his phone away and glances up, and I see the very moment he loses focus. "You look nice." It's a simple statement, in stark contrast with the volumes his expression speaks.

I straighten my dress, running my hands over the form-fitting black fabric. *"Finally,"* I say pointedly, "you noticed."

"There's no finally about it." He pulls me in for a kiss, and I'm just sinking into his lips when the door flies open again.

"And you tried to tell me you weren't a couple," Clint says from the doorway, smiling like he's caught us up to no good.

"We're not getting married, are we?" I reply dryly from Ethan's arms.

Clint eyes us. "Remains to be seen," he grumbles. "Someone out there wants to talk to you."

"Much appreciated, Clint," Ethan says, his voice conveying exactly how much he appreciated the interruption. Clint closes the door, and Ethan faces me. He looks down at his hands on my waist, reluctance to leave this room written on his features. "Well."

"We'll pick this up later," I promise him. "Right where we left off."

He grins, and we walk into the hotel ballroom.

I'm struck for a moment, seeing the reunion in full swing. The room is packed and noisy with the clinking of glasses, the laughter of friends, and the chatter of guests wearing the name tags I printed. The lights strung from the ceiling cast an elegant glow on the cocktail tables decorated with small flower arrangements and the centerpieces Dylan and I made, each incorporating photos from this class's yearbook. Dylan helped me copy and cut up the pages she found in the yearbook room closet.

The crowd spills from the center of the room onto the dance floor, where there's no DJ booth set up, and to the hors d'oeuvres station of crab cakes, ceviche cones, and chicken skewers in neat rows on trays. On the far wall is the backdrop I constructed using ten-year-old issues of the *Chronicle*, or rather, *The Paw Print*, as it was titled then. It's not the photo booth Ethan wanted. It's better. Even Ethan admitted as much. I watch guests walk up, inspecting the headlines and taking photos in front of the newsprint wall, and feel a swell of pride in my chest.

Ethan and I did this. First while feuding, then while everything else. When we got the reunion planning project, I couldn't have been less interested or more eager for the event to be over. Standing in the Millard Fillmore ballroom now, I want the night to be perfect.

Williams emerges from the crowd. Her suit is ivory and immaculate as ever. Yet improbably, she's wearing a pair of the cheap CELEBRATE glasses I ordered for people to ornament their photos with.

"Job well done, both of you," she says. Her eyes drop to Ethan's hand resting on the small of my back. She raises a superior eyebrow.

"I'm sorry," I say with light incredulity. "Did you just compliment us?"

Our principal's expression is unmoved. "Don't push it." She nods in our direction with clear insinuation. "I see you've found a way to get along at least."

"Sometimes," Ethan replies. I hear the smirk in his voice. It's a tone I'm well accustomed to.

Williams frowns deeply. "I may have preferred the fighting." She walks off, picking up a drink from one of the servers.

Glancing into the crowd, I spot Hector. He's freshly shaven, which is new. His blazer noticeably exceeds his narrow shoulders, and I wonder if it's borrowed. He looks excited and nervous, walking into the room like a seventh-grader would into a school dance. I watch him put down his drink and head for a guy in an expensive-looking suit.

Ethan follows my eyeline when I nudge him. "Ah, the

long-awaited AJ reunion," Ethan says while Hector taps his friend on the shoulder.

The guy in the suit faces him, and in a flash I recognize Adam Elliot. It's the face I found on LinkedIn and his company's website. I remember the name on the profile—Adam *Joseph* Elliot. Adam, mid-conversation with the woman next to him, looks surprised and wary until he recognizes Hector, and his expression softens. Immediately, they hug. I can't hear what they're saying, but I see Adam smile and ask Hector something, nodding when Hector replies.

"Huh," Ethan says, watching the scene play out. "Maybe Adam doesn't suck so much."

He heads in the direction of the hors d'oeuvres, presumably hungry. It's half past seven, and neither of us has eaten. Nevertheless, I don't follow. I can't. Rooted in place, I can't take my eyes off AJ—Adam—and Hector.

While they're plainly happy to have found each other, there's a stiffness to them, the out-of-practice asynchrony of playing old parts. They don't have the ready rapport Dylan and I do, but the eagerness in their eyes says they want to.

It makes me sad. They've undeniably diverged in the years since high school. Their relationship died out, and yet here they are, getting along. Which means maybe they could've stayed friends if they'd wanted, if they'd worked to maintain the friendship. What I should consider just a happy reunion for them instead feels like a decade lost. It winds a knot into my chest. Wanting to find Ethan, I pull my gaze from the pair.

The shrill of a familiar electrical screech interrupts me. When I look in the direction of the sound, I find Jamie walking onto the small stage Ethan rushed to rig in the corner of the room. She catches my eye and sends me a huge smile, which I return. In her room hours ago, my explanation of our music predicament had hardly left my lips when she said she and her friends would play the reunion. At stops on my adapter odyssey, I approved her setlist suggestions over text, mentally retracting every time I complained about or was annoyed by her band.

Ted walks up to the front of the stage. Placing his hands on the mic, he addresses the crowd. "Hello, Fairview alumni. We're the Stragglers," he shouts before Mara counts them off into their first song. It's a Fall Out Boy song I vaguely recognize.

The alumni around me, though, chant the intro lyrics immediately, jumping onto the dance floor. Instead of conversation and cocktails, the Millard Fillmore suddenly echoes with the energy of a house show for a student band. The reaction makes sense—Jamie's about the alums' age and would've listened to the same hits in high school.

When the song ends, Jamie, on one side of the stage, starts picking the opening notes of the next on her guitar. It's Green Day's "Good Riddance." The song is slower, and couples pair up, swaying on the dance floor.

I turn and find Ethan behind me, his hand outstretched. "Dance with me," he says.

Smiling, I take his hand and step close to him. In the

middle of the dance floor, the music sweeps over us, lyrics of turning points and unpredictable rightness. The lighting is soft, and my cheek fits perfectly against Ethan's shoulder, his head lowered so our mouths are close.

With alums ten years older surrounding us and a song about change and remembrance playing, something comes over me. I feel like we've stolen into the future. I'm twenty-seven, home for my own reunion. Ethan and I broke up, went to Harvard, and—what? Maybe we found each other again, or maybe we didn't. Maybe our rivalry and romance faded, and it was for the best. Or maybe it wasn't. We're in a venue not far from where we grew up, on a night like this one, celebrating a decade since we graduated from high school. If we even dance together. It might feel half familiar, like Hector and AJ's reunion, heavy with the weight of everything we wish we hadn't given up.

Worry works into me. I don't want to forget how this feels. High school *was* meaningful for me. I've built toward a future I know will come without knowing what it looks like quite yet, only to realize I've fallen hard for a few of the bricks I used. I don't want to leave these pieces of my present behind, turning my back while they gather dust and eventually crumble into it.

Especially the one in my arms right now. Holding Ethan closer, I make a decision and voice it without giving myself room for doubt. "Let's not break up," I say.

Playful light enters his eyes. "Ever?"

"Before college," I clarify. "We'll see about ever." I'll do whatever he needs to help him make his own choices in college. We'll try everything we can before breaking up.

His smile softens. "I hope you're willing to have a long-distance relationship."

I withdraw a little, studying his expression, waiting for some joke about the long distance from his Harvard GPA to mine. "What?" I ask when none comes.

"I've decided to take a gap year before Harvard," he says, "To find out what I want to do there." His voice is gentle, his expression honest.

Searching his eyes, I see what I hoped I would. He wants this for himself. It's his own decision, and it's real. I'm proud of him for it. "I could do long distance," I say, pausing for a moment and slipping into a different future. One where I'm picking him up from the airport while he visits me in my freshman year. He's working for the *San Mateo Daily Journal*, or interning for Adam Elliot's company, or volunteering for a homeless outreach charity. He comes to my graduation, and I return to Harvard a year later for his.

I'm smiling as I put my head on his shoulder, and it feels like turning a page. It's odd to me now, how I'd considered every paragraph of high school only prologue while I wrote chapter upon chapter of newspaper productions and driving lessons, fights and fantasies and food poisoning. Under the lights, I feel grateful for the exhilaration of an unfinished story and the necessity of every page before this one.

# One Month Later

I WIN VALEDICTORIAN.

Seated on the stage, I look out onto the football field, at my classmates sitting in sections of red and white, and past them, the friends and family gathered in the stands. Sweat dampens my forehead in the June sun. I reach up, adjusting my cap while Principal Williams speaks. I wondered if it would feel anticlimactic, like every other afternoon. It doesn't. It feels like the end of high school.

As valedictorian, I have the honor of graduating first. Ethan, seated next to me, is second. He's salutatorian, a fact of which I've never missed an opportunity to remind him. Including in my valedictory graduation speech. Where I referenced speaking instead of him. It earned me actual laughter from our classmates, which was good, given the serious subject matter of the rest of my speech. I said I wasn't sorry I only went to one party, never skipped class, and knew a sizable portion of the audience had never met me. I only hoped they'd done high school their way.

Williams calls my name, and I walk to the podium, receive my diploma, and shake her hand.

"Congratulations, Alison," she says. "I look forward to having a much freer calendar next year without you to contend with."

I grin, remembering months full of meetings, rigorous email chains, *Chronicle* interviews, and ASG initiatives. "I'll miss you too, Principal Williams," I reply, and Williams's features flicker the closest to a smile I've ever seen them.

I walk across the stage, flipping my tassel to the other side of my cap to the enthusiastic cheering of my parents and Jamie, who's wearing her new Fairview staff shirt. Returning to my seat onstage, I wait while Ethan walks up and receives his diploma.

For the next half hour, we hold hands, watching the rest of our class graduate. I stand and whoop when Dylan walks on stage. We went to Berkeley together a couple weeks ago, and any heartache she had over Olivia seemed erased by the cute people on whom she kept commenting. She's even been texting one girl she met in the art department. *Texting* might in fact be too insignificant a term for the constant conversation they've kept up, punctuated by Dylan's smiles or laughter every time she looks down to read her phone. I can't help smiling whenever I notice, either. I'm excited to help Dylan move in before I fly out to Boston.

When Isabel crosses the stage, Ethan whispers in my ear, "What are the odds she follows through on her class president responsibility to plan our reunion in ten years?"

"She'd better," I reply immediately. "I'm *not* planning another one of those."

"Certainly not with your co-vice president," Ethan says.

I picture planning our own reunion with him a decade from now. Poetry might require choosing the Millard Fillmore for our venue. Ethan would want a fancy hotel, and I'd fight for nostalgia. While we cooperate well now, I can't imagine the process without a little contention. "Certainly not," I say, smiling.

Once everyone's graduated and we've thrown our hats into the cloudless sky, Ethan draws me by the hand in the direction of the teachers' section.

"Ethan," I say, laughing, "I kind of have plans to see my parents."

"In a minute," he replies. He walks up to Pham, and I realize what he's doing.

The only outstanding grade of our final semester is our final English essay. While Pham reported our overall class grades—A's, of course—he never released our essay grades. Nobody else cares. Except for us. It's our very last grade of high school.

"Mr. Pham," Ethan starts with forceful casualness, "could you just tell us which of us submitted the stronger paper? We don't even need the point totals."

Pham exhales sharply. "It's your graduation day, Mr. Molloy. Can't you just celebrate?"

"You did read our essays, right?" I narrow my eyes on

him. "I wouldn't want to have to inform Principal Williams you didn't grade our finals."

"I read them," Pham gets out, clearly disgruntled by our undimmed competitiveness.

"Tell us and you'll never have to talk to us again," Ethan's voice is simultaneously sweet and sharp.

Pham considers us. "Mr. Molloy scored a point and a half higher." Then, taking Ethan up on his offer, Pham walks off immediately.

Ethan faces me. "There. I win the final, most important contest."

I tap my valedictorian sash. "Agree to disagree."

He ignores me. "You owe me one final task."

I say nothing, a little scared. Despite our new relationship, our tasks have remained as undesirable as ever. When I won valedictorian, I made Ethan man the prom ticket booth for three days straight.

"Don't find a new rival next year." He's earnest, even nervous. It dissolves my apprehension. Our relationship might not last. We might grow out of it as we grow into ourselves. I won't force it to end because high school has, though. I'm holding on to this piece of now proudly, loving it for what it could become and for the confusing, inimitable place it began.

I entwine my hand with his. "Obviously."

# Acknowledgments

On our fourth novel, it only grows more obvious how indebted we are to the many people who every day make our publishing dreams a reality. Honestly, while we do have Alison and Ethan's overachieving spirit, we never knew if we'd get here. We certainly never expected we would with these characters, who originated in our very first co-written manuscript, which was not very good. We thank our parents and our friends Gabrielle Gold, Catherine Ku, and Yani Lu for diligently reading it regardless.

This, though, brings us to the people who have made this book what it is today. Katie Shea Boutillier, our agent, helped us find the new shape of this story and continues never finding our unlikable heroines unlikable. We remain ridiculously thankful you pulled us out of the slush pile. Dana Leydig, you're the best editor we could ever wish for. Thank you not only for patiently developing Alison and Ethan's second life with us, but for being the tiebreaker when your married cowriters have differing opinions. It's a gift to have worked with you and learned from you for four books now.

We're immeasurably grateful to the behind-the-scenes queens of #Wibbroka. Tessa Meischeid, your nonstop hard work and genuine love for YA does not go unnoticed. You're everything we could hope for in a publicist. Felicity Vallence, you give the words "hype machine" new meaning. There are thousands of reasons we Penguin Teen authors love you—foremost, your round-the-clock effort to share our books far and wide and how truly fun it is to work with you.

Really, it's the people who make Penguin Random House and Viking Children's a wonderful home for our work. Kristie Radwilowicz, you continue to knock it out of the park with your stunning covers. We know what a compliment it is when readers say the inside of our books measures up to the outside. The Penguin marketing team—James Akinaka, Kara Brammer, Alex Garber, and Shannon Spann—we absolutely adore working with you. We look forward to every Sunday Shoutout, every Rec-a-Reads, and everything else. For copyediting and proofreading—Abigail Powers, Marinda Valenti, Delia Davis, and Kat Keating, we're continually grateful for your diligence and sharp eyes. We know what a hard job you all have, and you do it surpassingly.

Our friends in the writing community—not even Alison and Dylan's friendship matches how much we love you, gang. Bridget Morrissey and Aminah Mae Safi, we started this book with you two at Sparrarrow Lodge. We will never forget it. Curse Vibes Only, may we simply know peace and know joy. Maura Milan, sometimes writers just need to vent about video games. Thank you for that, and for being a true friend.

Gretchen Schreiber and Alexa DeGennaro, your industry insight is invaluable, and your friendship over years of publishing ups and downs even more so. Bree Barton, Farrah Penn, Britta Lundin, Diya Mishra, and Robyn Schneider, we feel fortunate to know such kind, talented, thoughtful human beings. Rebekah Faubion, you're the best agent sister ever and a light in our lives. Derek Milman and Brian Murray Williams, Kayla Olson, and Tara Tsai, we remain grateful for your friendship from far-flung parts of the country.

Without our family and friends, we would be nowhere. You fill our lives with everything we try to bring to our writing—joy, humor, love, and compassion—and it means so much to us how much you've learned about YA and publishing out of nothing except supportiveness and care.

Finally and most importantly, we would not be writing this fourth "finally" without the readers and booksellers who have sent us messages, posted online, shared a kind word or detailed review, and opened our pages. We write for you, now and ever.

## REAL ROMANCE FROM A REAL COUPLE!